Robinson

MW01062014

Paul Whitfield White argues that, contrary to received wisdom, Protestant authorities in Reformation England patronized the stage, along with other cultural activities, as a means of disseminating their political and religious policies. White shows that from Thomas Cromwell and John Bale in the 1530s to William Cecil and William Wager in early Elizabethan England, Protestant politicians and educators were drawn to the theatre by its proven capacity (under Catholic authority) to internalize religious belief and practice, but newly devised it for iconoclastic purposes: Reformation drama exposes the image-centeredness and theatricality of Catholicism by presenting sumptuously dressed priests and their elaborate rituals on the stage, where (according to Protestants) such pageantry belonged in the first place.

Professor White is particularly interested in the institutional aspects of Reformation theatre: the relations among patrons, playwrights, playing companies, local proprietors and audiences, as well as in the modes of presentation and conditions of performance. He concludes that such drama contributed significantly towards the formation of Protestant culture in Tudor England.

THEATRE AND REFORMATION

THEATRE AND REFORMATION

Protestantism, Patronage, and Playing in Tudor England

PAUL WHITFIELD WHITE

Assistant Professor of English, Baylor University, Waco, Texas

CAMBRIDGE
UNIVERSITY PRESS

Published by the Press Syndicate of the University of Cambridge
The Pitt Building, Trumpington Street, Cambridge CB2 1RP
40 West 20th Street, New York, NY 10011–4211, USA
10 Stamford Road, Oakleigh, Victoria 3166, Australia

First published 1993

Printed in Great Britain at the University Press, Cambridge

A catalogue record for this book is available from the British Library

Library of Congress cataloguing in publication data
White, Paul Whitfield.
Theatre and reformation: Protestantism, patronage, and playing in
Tudor, England / by Paul Whitfield White.
p. cm.
Includes bibliographical references.
ISBN 0 521 41817 8 (hardback)
1. Theater – England – History – 16th century.   2. Theater – Religious
aspects – Church of England.   3. Religious drama, English – History
and criticism.   4. English drama – Early modern and Elizabethan,
1500–1600 – History and criticism.   5. Reformation – England.
I. Title.
PN2590.R35W45   1992
792′.0942′09031 – dc20   92–979   CIP

ISBN 0 521 41817 8 hardback

To Wes
John Wesley White, Jr.
(1954–1991)

He viewes the cloudes, the Planets, and the Starres,
The Tropick, Zones, and quarters of the skye,
From the bright circle of the horned Moone,
Euen to the height of *Primum Mobile.*

Christopher Marlowe

Contents

Illustrations

Preface

This book proposes that England's earliest Protestants participated in theatre as patrons, playwrights, performers and spectators. Extending rather than ending the traditional union of religion with dramatic representation, Protestant leaders in the civil government and church recognized drama as a morally sound and profitable pastime, and used it as a means of legitimating and winning popular consent for religious reform. This Protestant consensus in favor of the theatre broke up around the midpoint of Elizabeth's reign when the establishment of the commercial stage in London and the development of pronounced ethical tendencies among certain reformers brought into dispute the use of drama for religious purposes and even the propriety of drama as an acceptable form of recreation.

In examining Reformation theatrical practice within its concrete historical setting, this book has benefited from the work of revisionist historians of the English Reformation who have stressed the roles of patronage and propaganda in shaping Protestant belief and culture, as well as from the archival and critical studies of theatre historians during the past decade or so who have given us a fascinating glimpse of a largely forgotten theatrical culture in Tudor England, particularly in the provinces. Because of their efforts, we are better able to reconstruct the interaction between patrons, playwrights, and players, the touring routes of itinerant acting troupes, and the conditions under which the players performed. Their achievements and contributions to this study are discussed in more specific terms in the introduction which follows.

This study is the result of over a decade researching, teaching, and staging Tudor drama, and examining its social, political, and religious contexts. During those years I have accumulated many debts of gratitude, and at this time I would like to acknowledge a few of the people whose criticisms and support brought this work to fruition. I owe a very large debt to Glynne Wickham, my former Ph.D. supervisor in the Drama Department at the University of Bristol. The manuscript has drawn heavily on his vast knowledge of the early English theatre, and has benefited greatly from his guidance since its beginning as a doctoral thesis and at every stage of development since. I am also grateful to Charles Leland and R. K. Harrison of the University of Toronto, and especially George Hibbard of the University of Waterloo, all former teachers who inspired my interest in Renaissance literature, drama, and history, and who have offered many insights and valuable assistance concerning one aspect of the text or another, but particularly concerning the drama. For vigorous assessments and many insights relating to Reformation history and thought, I am indebted to Alan Robb, J. I. Packard, and Basil Hall. Several other scholars have generously given of their time to read and send me written critiques of the manuscript in whole or in part, and to them I extend my wholehearted thanks: Peter Happé and John Wasson for chapter 1, Suzanne R. Westfall for chapter 2, George Hibbard for the entire manuscript in its early stage and for chapters 2 and 3, and Ida Sinkevič for various matters relating to church and hall architecture discussed in chapter 5. My graduate students here at Baylor University, especially those who took the Tudor Theatre Seminar in the summer of 1990, have influenced my understanding of Reformation/theatre relations far more than they realize. I am grateful to three in particular, Douglas Platt, Rodney Newton, and Sara Marisol Madrazo, for assisting me with the final preparation of this work for publication. Special thanks is due to Baylor University for financial assistance in the forms of a University Research Grant and a Summer Sabbatical in 1988, and to Carl Bell in the Computer Science Department at Baylor for a splendid job of computerizing the maps of England and London (figures 3 and 15) and the ground plan of St. Stephen's (figure 19). Also deserving of my sincere appreciation are the staffs of the British Library, Cambridge University Library, the Bodleian Library, the London Guildhall Library, the University of Bristol Theatre Collection, and Robarts Library at the University of Toronto. This manuscript has undergone considerable revision since sending it to Cambridge University Press, much of that revision inspired by my editor, Sarah Stanton, whose encouragement to rethink and reassess many of my original conclusions immeasurably changed the work for the better. I now take great pleasure in thanking her and all the others working with her at the Press for preparing the book for publication.

In the course of completing this book, most of chapter 5 (since revised) and appendices B and C, along with the latter half of chapter 2, appeared in articles. The articles are "Patronage, Protestantism, and Early Elizabethan Stage Propaganda," *The Yearbook of English Studies* 21 (1991): 39–52; "Lewis Wager's *Life and Repentaunce of Mary Magdalene* and John Calvin," *Notes and Queries* 226 (1981): 508–12; "Predestinarian Theology in the Mid-Tudor Play *Jacob and Esau*," *Renaissance and Reformation* (Nov. 1988): 197–207; and "Drama 'in the church': Churchplaying in Tudor England," *Medieval and Renaissance Drama in English Volume VI* (1993). In addition to drawing material from these papers, I have included excerpts from my Introduction to the old-spelling editions of *Mary Magdalene* and *Jacob and Esau* in *Reformation Biblical Drama in England* (New York: Garland, 1992). I am grateful to the editors of the above publications for permission to include the material from these other works.

Abbreviations

Chambers, *ES*	E. K. Chambers, *The Elizabethan Stage*, 4 vols. (Oxford: Clarendon, 1923).
Chambers, *MS*	E. K. Chambers, *The Medieval Stage*, 2 vols. (Oxford: Clarendon, 1903).
Feuillerat, *DRR (E&M)*	Albert Feuillerat, *Documents Relating to the Revels at Court in the Time of King Edward VI and Queen Mary* (Louvain: A. Uystpruyst, 1914).
Happé, *Bale*	Peter Happé, ed. *The Complete Plays of John Bale*, 2 vols. (Cambridge: Brewer, 1985–86).
Lancashire, *DTR*	Ian Lancashire, *Dramatic Texts and Records of Britain: A Chronological Topography to 1558.* (University of Toronto Press, 1984).
LP: Henry 8	*Letters and Papers, Foreign and Domestic, of the Reign of Henry VIII*, eds. J. S. Brewer, J. Gaidner, and R. H. Brodie, 21 vols. (London: Longman, Green, and Roberts, 1862–1932).
MSC	Malone Society Collections
MSR	Malone Society Reprints (Oxford University Press, 1907–)
PS	Parker Society
REED	Records of Early English Drama
Revels II	*The Revels History of Drama in English (1500–1576): Volume II*, ed. Norman Sanders, *et al.* (London: Methuen, 1980).
SP: Simancas	*State Papers Relating to English Affairs, Preserved Principally in the Archives of*

	Simancas, ed. M. A. S. Hume, 4 vols. (London, 1892–99).
SP: Venice	*State Papers and Manuscripts Relating to English Affairs, Existing in the Archives of Venice*, ed. Rawdon Brown and G. Cavendish-Bentinck, 7 vols. (London, 1864–90).
TFT	Tudor Facsimile Texts, ed. J. S. Farmer (London: Jack, 1907–14).
Wickham, *EES*	Glynne Wickham, *Early English Stages*, 3 vols. (London: Routledge & Kegan Paul, 1958–80).

Introduction

In the second act of John Bale's Reformation interlude *Three Laws* (*c.*
1535), the Vice Infidelity and the Catholic Bishop Ambition resolve
to suppress "the Byble readers" who threaten the Pope's authority in
England. In the course of explaining how this should be accom-
plished, Infidelity points to Ambition's mitre, the tall, divided
headpiece worn by Roman prelates in liturgical service.

Infidelitas	Yea, never spare them [the Byble readers],
	but evermore playe the bytar,
	Expressynge alwayes the tropes and types of thy mytar.
Ambitio	Why, what dost thu thynke my mytar to signify?
Infidelitas	The mouth of a wolfe, and that shall I prove by and by –
	If thu stoupe downewarde,
	Loo, se how the wolfe doth gape?
	Redye to devoure the lambes, least any escape?[1]

Here, the Vice prompts the prelate to bend forward so that the
pointed horns of his mitre give the appearance of a wolf's gaping
mouth (see figure 8). This stunning visual pun must have amused
even Bale's Catholic spectators. But its purpose is much more than to
evoke laughter. The incident satirizes the tropological significance
which Catholicism ascribes to visual images, in this case clerical dress.
And by applying an entirely different "trope" to Ambition's
elaborate headwear, one that identifies the bishop with the ravenous
wolves of Matthew 7:15 and John 10:12 who deceive and devour the
innocent sheep (i.e. "the Byble readers" of the Reformation), he
attacks the cruelty of Catholic authorities in persecuting Protestants.

This scene in *Three Laws* is a particularly apt place to begin a
discussion of Reformation theatrical practice for two reasons. First, it
is one among many striking examples in English Reformation drama
where pictorial language is used cleverly and memorably to shape
popular religious beliefs and perceptions (or in this instance to

1

subvert old ones). And this in turn should help to dispel the notion that the Reformation from the beginning looked disfavorably upon *spectacula*; indeed, the early reformers found the presentation of images in public performance and in print an acceptable and useful means of propagating their views. As the Prologue of John Foxe's *Christus Triumphans* remarks with reference to the netting ("trans-ennam") of images through which the play's message is communi-cated, "why is it less fitting for the eyes than for the ears to be trained on sacred objects?"[2] The reformers were keenly aware of the potential dangers of images to corrupt the senses, to mislead the intellect, to incite idolatry, but this should not preclude their use altogether. Moreover, why not exploit the visual resources of the stage to illustrate these very dangers? The particular wit of Bale's example cited above is that it uses an image to make a point about the *abuse* of images.

The scene from *Three Laws* reveals something no less significant about Reformation theatrical practice. Bale assigned himself a role in the play, as "Baleus Prolocutor," and if he followed his own printed casting chart, he doubled this part with that of Infidelity, who commands the stage for most of the action. In fact, he may have acted these roles when his playing troupe, "Bale and his felowes," performed before their patron, Lord Thomas Cromwell, in 1538 and 1539, or ten years later when Bale was rehearsing *Three Laws* in his parish at Bishopstoke, Hampshire. As playwright and player, Bale reflects the commitment of Protestant leaders to use drama as a means of effecting religious change. There is indeed a considerable body of evidence which shows that players (some of whom like Bale were Protestant preachers and pamphleteers) joined other publicists in disseminating Protestant propaganda. "Players, Printers, Preachers," Foxe exclaimed, "be set up of God as a triple bulwark against the triple crown of the Pope, to bring him down."[3]

It is the purpose of this book to explore the relationship between the theatre and Protestantism during what Patrick Collinson has recently called the first phase of the Reformation's relations with the arts.[4] It encompassed a period of some fifty years up to around 1580 when English Protestants extended the medieval tradition of pro-moting drama, along with other cultural activities, as a means of legitimating and celebrating religious teaching and practice, only now the authority which sanctioned that teaching and practice was no longer the Papacy and its emissaries but the English Crown and the ecclesiastical and civic officials under its central control. From the 1530s, playwrights and players, both amateur and professional, contributed to the formation of an emerging Protestant culture; moreover, they were patronized by reform-oriented leaders from the royal court to provincial grammar schools in an effort to win popular support for the religious and ecclesiastical policies of the Protestant Tudor administrations.

That Tudor Protestant leaders favored drama for a time is well known. The prevailing scholarly view of theatre/Reformation relations may be traced back to late nineteenth- and early twentieth-century drama studies, perhaps best represented by the work of E. K. Chambers. First addressing the subject in *The Medieval Stage* (1903), and then expanding his analysis in its sequel *The Elizabeth Stage* (1923), Chambers showed that early English reformers, encouraged and at times commissioned by the state, engaged drama as a potent weapon of religious propaganda.[5] This close alliance between the pulpit and the stage, he maintained, continued into the opening years of Queen Elizabeth's reign but ceased shortly thereafter. Its demise was due largely to state-imposed censorship, namely the enforcement of the Proclamation of May 16, 1559 which prohibited religious and political issues from being treated in plays, and to the rise of "Puritanism," itself explainable by "the substitution of a Calvinist for a Lutheran bias in the conduct of the Reformation."[6] For Chambers, Protestant religious support of the stage was something of an aberration from the traditional hostility of serious churchmen towards mimesis and only briefly interrupted the gradual evolution of drama towards secularism, a process underway for several hundred years and culminating in the works of Shakespeare.[7] The old antagonism was taken up by the "Puritans" who increasingly perceived scenic spectacle as an affront to their religious and ethical convictions in the course of forcing its suppression altogether in 1642.

Chambers' major contribution was to bring to scholars' attention a large body of source materials relevant to theatre/Reformation relations and to show that drama was compatible with early Protestantism under carefully controlled conditions. However, his analysis, and that of other theatre historians of his generation, rely on questionable historiographical assumptions about the Reformation, many of which persist in more recent scholarship. For example, it is now impossible to sustain the view of a Lutheran-oriented English

Protestantism generally supportive of the stage up to the 1560s and a Calvinist-oriented Protestantism generally antagonistic towards it afterwards. Such generalizations tend to ascribe too much significance to specifically "Lutheran" and "Calvinist" ideas and not enough to particular historical conditions in shaping religious views of drama. Moreover, whatever sense of doctrinal unity English Protestantism had prior to Elizabeth's reign, it was only marginally influenced by Lutheran teachings, with several leading reformers adopting an anti-Lutheran stance on some points of doctrine.[8] In fact, one already discerns Swiss Reformed theology in Bale's plays of the 1530s, and during Edward VI's reign Calvinism itself leaves a heavy imprint on the Protestant drama. Chambers acknowledges that Genevan Protestants tolerated playing under strict regulation, but he believed that "Puritanism," the main conduit for Calvinist habits of thinking and lifestyle in Elizabethan England, was the chief ideological force behind the Elizabethan anti-stage movement. This last contention, too, is now open to serious question. It rests on the notion of a monolithic "Puritanism" integrated ethically, theologically, and politically in opposition to "official churchmanship" across the entire Elizabethan era. Chambers' division of attitudes towards drama into "Humanist" and "Puritan" shows affinities with the dichotomy of "Anglican" and "Puritan" popular in Reformation studies of his own day and many since.[9] Such fixed categories generally obscure shared experiences and beliefs among Elizabethan Protestants on the right and the left and do not allow for "certain dynamic, fluid and even paradoxical features of the religious situation which obtained in Elizabethan and Jacobean England."[10] More significantly for our purposes, those Elizabethan Protestants whose religion and lifestyle earned them the name puritan were not united in opposition to playing.[11] Well into the 1570s, we find Protestant religious drama calling for further religious reform within the Church of England, and as recent theatrical criticism has demonstrated, the more activist Protestants of later years employed the London playhouses to advance their own ideological interests.[12]

One other aspect of early twentieth-century analysis which persists in more recent scholarship is the notion that officially imposed censorship brought down the religious stage almost immediately after Elizabeth came to the throne.[13] It is indeed true that the civic-sponsored biblical cycles in the north of England, some of which retained popish elements, were condemned by early Elizabethan ecclesiastical officials, but even these were not censored out of existence by Protestant authorities as was once thought. Many conformed to Reformation teaching, and it now appears clear that financial problems and declining public interest had as much to do with their demise.[14] More significantly, as I have already mentioned, Protestant religious interludes continued to provide much of the dramatic fare well into the 1570s. If these plays deal with social and economic issues, they do not, as some scholars contend, cease to treat the most pressing religious problems of the day.

Since Chambers' time, the most productive scholarship in the field of theatre/Reformation relations has resulted from the analysis of extant play texts. Scholars such as Peter Happé, Glynne Wickham, Lois Potter, Murray Roston, Bernard Spivack, and David Bevington have commented extensively on the topical, rhetorical and drama-turgical features of Protestant moral interludes and biblical plays from Bale's works in the 1530s through the interludes of the 1570s. Their efforts, along with those of T. W. Craik, Richard Southern, and Alan Dessen, who confine themselves mainly to the technical and performance aspects of the drama, have done much to illuminate our understanding of Reformation interludes, as will be borne out by this investigation.[15] However, the limitation of many play text-centered studies of the period is that in their preoccupation with formal features and the development of dramatic structure, and in relying mainly on printed plays, they tend to isolate theatrical practice from the concrete historical conditions which produced it and within which it acquired significance for contemporaries.[16]

If the analysis of individual play texts is an important function of Reformation theatrical history and criticism, it remains only one function or aspect of a broader more complex inquiry. My approach attempts to integrate this concern with a detailed investigation of the personnel, institutions, and activities involved in their production. What companies performed Reformation plays, under what patron-age, and for what reasons? In what ways did patrons, playwrights, and players interact with one another? What more can we learn about the issues treated in the plays, their methods of presentation, the conditions under which they were performed, the audiences to whom they were directed? And to what extent did Reformation theatre not merely convey but shape Protestant beliefs, attitudes, and modes of behavior in Tudor England?

In answering these questions, we must first recognize the important

connection between drama and political authority, and more
particularly the system of patronage developed in Reformation
England to facilitate the dissemination of Protestant ideology.
Revisionist studies of the Reformation by J.J. Scarisbrick, Christopher Haigh, and Maria Dowling, among others, have shown that the
growth of Protestantism in mid-sixteenth-century England was only
in a limited sense "from below," that is say, due to the more or less
spontaneous acceptance of its teachings by people disenchanted with
or dissenting from the old religion and its officials, and had more to
do with the official sanctioning of Protestantism by royal authority
and the proselytizing activities of Protestant peers, magnates, and
bishops, and their appointees and supporters in lower level civic and
ecclesiastical offices, with whom they shared a common goal of
religious reform.[17] Although more conservative in their theoretical
approaches, these Reformation revisionists share a number of ideas in
common with materialist-oriented literary scholars of the past decade
such as Jonathon Dollimore, Alan Sinfield and Leonard Tennenhouse, most notably the assumption that widespread religious and
social change in Tudor England is directly linked to shifts in political
power, and was generated largely "from above" by means of
patronage and other channels of power.[18] At the same time they
recognize the potent and persisting influence of conservative and
reactionary voices (indeed, Haigh and Scarisbrick insist that popular
consent to religious reform remained unrealized well into Elizabeth's
reign), as well as the existence of ideological tensions and divisiveness
within the Protestant movement itself. Of special interest to the
present investigation is the work of those historians and literary
scholars who have examined the relationship between aristocratic
patrons and writers engaged in the spread of a Protestant world-view
and the denunciation of Catholic dogma and practice. Eleanor
Rosenberg, John N. King, and other scholars have discovered that
writers sought support from, or were recruited by, patrons with
similar ideological interests and that what they expected in exchange
for their efforts was protection from hostile opposition, promotion of
their views, and career appointments in positions where they could
continue to carry out their own and their patron's ideological views.[19]
How much license these writers and performers were given to
criticize their superiors or to express radical or subversive opinions
remains unclear but perhaps varied from patron to patron (Bale, for
example, seems to overstep the bounds of Henrician Protestant policy

in several instances),[20] but clearly the above conclusions firmly put to
rest the notion that literary patronage was a moribund practice in
Tudor England and that poets and writers generally worked
independent of political constraints and interests.

The logical question now arises whether playwrights and players of
the Reformation era operated under comparable conditions to
writers, preachers, and other Protestant publicists who participated
in the patronage system. This question has not been adequately
investigated. However, very recent research by theatre scholars has
prepared the way for an answer. For example, Suzanne R. Westfall
has studied the expense accounts, ordinance books, and other related
records of early Tudor noblemen to show that they were directly
involved in their household revels performed by the minstrels,
choirboys, and adult actors under their patronage. She builds a
strong case for the argument that many of the surviving interludes of
the time were written by chaplains and choirmasters associated with
noble families and that they appeal for the most part to the domestic,
social and political interests of those noble households.[21] The findings
of Westfall and other scholars working in the field point to the
conclusion that noble patrons exercised considerably greater control
over the activities of Tudor playwrights and playing troupes than is
traditionally supposed.

It is the basic contention of this study that playwrights of the
English Reformation *did* operate under conditions and for purposes
comparable to those of other Protestant publicists, and that the
players they wrote for, and in many instances organized and
participated with, were similarly involved in the dissemination of
Protestantism. The players most active in performing Reformation
drama appear to have been the touring adult troupes sponsored by
prominent Protestant lords and the amateur student players in the
nation's academic institutions. For both types of playing companies,
we have a large corpus of surviving play texts and other evidence.
These players, therefore, will be considered at some length, although
attention will be given to local church and civic organizations who
patronized and participated in the production of Protestant drama.

The first three chapters of this study examine the activities and the
drama of adult companies of noble and royal patronage. Chapter 1
is concerned with a troupe active in the 1530s led by the playwright
John Bale. I begin with "Bale and his felowes" because this is the
only known professional troupe of the period for which we can

confidently attribute extant plays for performance, Bale's own. Thus, an examination of the sponsorship, personnel, travelling itinerary, and repertory of this troupe leads naturally into a discussion of the plays themselves. The dramaturgy, topical concerns, and audience reception of Bale's interludes performed on tour are seen within the context of Thomas Cromwell's politico-religious agenda during the later 1530s. Chapter 2 considers other adult troupes engaged in Protestant stage propaganda during the subsequent reigns of Edward, Mary, and Elizabeth. Particular attention is given to the King's Men under Edward VI and their anti-papal repertory, but we will also reach some tentative conclusions about the Earl of Leicester's Men and other troupes sponsored by leading Protestant lords which toured extensively during the 1560s. The Reformation interludes written for such troupes, and the playwrights who supplied them, are the subjects of chapter 3. It will be shown that playwrights worked closely with the acting troupes and with stage patrons, and that the plays exhibit considerable diversity in terms of themes and drama- turgy. One troupe interlude, Lewis Wager's *Mary Magdalene*, will be examined in detail. Chapter 4, which deals with the relationship between Reformation drama and education, continues the concern with playwrights and plays, but shifts the attention from those of professional auspices to those of amateur production in the nation's academic institutions. The discussion begins by looking at the promotion of Reformation ideology among students and their audiences by reference to plays in the grammar and choir schools, the two universities and the Inns of Court. It then engages in a detailed examination of some plays. I reserve discussion of Reformation playing places for chapter 5. Wickham, Southern, and other scholars have examined the evidence for Tudor performances in hall, taverns, and various outdoor facilities. However, the church as a location for staged drama has been largely ignored by theatrical scholarship. Consequently, the main focus in chapter 5 is on performances in churches and includes an analysis of Bale's *God's Promises* within the ecclesiastical setting. The study closes with consideration of the factors that radically altered theatre/Reformation relations during Elizabeth's reign and led to the rise of anti-stage sentiment at its midpoint.

   At this time it will be useful to discuss the kinds of source materials used in this study and some of the more vexing problems they pose. Play texts constitute the largest single body of evidence of Reformation theatrical practice. Of some seventy or so plays texts and fragments surviving from the period 1530 to 1580, about forty may be classified as homiletic or propagandist in purpose (see appendix A). Although admittedly a small representation of what originally existed, the play texts are an impressive testimony to the popularity of Protestant-oriented drama of the time. These are most useful in the analysis of Reformation themes (many of which directly correspond to those found in print propaganda of known noble patronage) and of the dramaturgy by which those themes are presented in performance. Scholars have long recognized that they also supply significant clues to the type of acting company involved and its general auspices. Nevertheless, we must be aware of their limitations as evidence. They are, needless to say, no substitute for performances. As Robert Weimann has observed, "the oral and mimetic heritage of the popular culture has sunk beneath the surface of literary history."[22] Moreover, those which survive only in printed form (which are the majority) may have undergone revision or cutting between the time of performance and the time they reached the printer, and because improvisation was common and so much taken for granted by the actors in terms of staging and so on,[23] we can never know as much as we would like about performances and their effects on a projected audience within a given place and time. Therefore my reconstruction of scenes and settings for such plays as Lewis Wager's *Mary Magdalene* (chapter 3) and John Bale's *God's Promises* (chapter 5) take into account that so much concerning their visual and mimetic aspects has been lost and that such reconstructions are in many respects conjectural.

Alongside play texts, our most solid evidence about theatrical practice is found in financial accounts recorded in court, civic, and ecclesiastical documents. Records of Early English Drama and The Malone Society Collections are currently increasing the size of this important body of factual data and correcting errors of earlier archivists such as Murray, Feuillerat, and Chambers. Expense accounts are an invaluable source of information about acting troupes. From these accounts, we have the names of some one-hundred different adult companies noted for performance between 1530 and 1580. The chief value of the thousands of troupe-related entries in chamberlains', churchwardens', and other records all over the realm, is that they supply important evidence about their travelling itineraries and finances.[24] I make use of this information in my discussion of the touring practices of Bale's troupe in chapter 1. Some accounts also provide inventories of costumes and properties which cast some light on the staging of plays. The most detailed collection of financial accounts and other related documentation for the activities of a troupe is the Revels accounts for Edward VI's reign. These provide the basis for my discussion of the King's players in chapter 2.

Because the nature of so much of the evidence is fragmentary, a picture of Reformation dramatic culture can only emerge by piecing together information from many different sources. Besides dramatic texts and financial accounts, two other kinds of sources should be noted and used in conjunction with the first two. The first one may be grouped under the label of contemporary comment. This diverse body of material includes eyewitness accounts of performances, as well as other descriptions, references, and opinions by contemporaries relating to dramatic practice. These can be found in treatises, letters, poems, and various legal documents. In some instances, contemporary comment can provide a crucial piece of evidence that illuminates information found in other sources. Further mention here may be given to eyewitness testimonies. They are, as with the entire Renaissance period, few in number and fairly limited in what they tell us. R. Willis' report of *The Cradle of Security* seen in his boyhood at Gloucester is the best known, but two others are of particular significance to the present study: the remarks by two individuals who attended *King Johan* at Cranmer's house in 1539, useful for discussing the early Reformation audience in chapter 1; and a series of reports in verse and prose occasioned by Elizabeth's attendance at performances within King's College Chapel, Cambridge. These cast valuable light on the staging of drama within the church setting treated in chapter 5. Because so much contemporary comment is polemically or at least ideologically motivated (for example the testimony of the Venetian ambassadors at Elizabeth's court), we need to assess the remarks judiciously and check them against other related evidence.

From contemporary comment, we move to materials that have a less direct connection to theatre but which are in many respects no less significant to our investigation. They include moral and theological treatises that are sources of rhetoric and actual passages in plays. For two interludes, *Mary Magdalene* and *Jacob and Esau*, we find theological sources in contemporary Calvinist writings, as evidenced in appendices B and C. They also include visual materials, such as maps, which are useful in determining touring routes, and pictorial art, which helps to illuminate such matters as costume and staging. A whole range of other works in printed and manuscript form provide valuable evidence concerning areas of Reformation politics, religion, and culture that interact with, or cast light on, dramatic enterprise. As I have already indicated, we can learn a great deal about Reformation dramatic patronage by observing the uses to which patronage was put for the printing industry or the ministry.

One final note on play texts. Despite the efforts of Marie Axton and Richard Axton (eds.) at D. S. Brewer and Stephen Orgel at Garland to improve the situation, there continues to be a shortage of soundly edited modern texts of the late moral interludes. Too frequently, the student is driven back to such unreliable modern editions as those in the Early English Drama Series and similar compilations of Tudor plays published in the nineteenth and early twentieth centuries. Faced with this problem and with the fact that no modern series (including the Malone Society Reprints) contains all of the interludes discussed in this study, I have consistently used facsimiles of the original editions. In most instances, references are to the texts in J. S. Farmer's Tudor Facsimile Texts. Exceptions include Bale's plays recently edited in original spelling by Peter Happé, and *Enough is as Good as a Feast*, published in Huntington Facsimile Reprints.

1

"Bale and his felowes"

Between 1530 and 1580 there were remarkably over fifty noblemen's troupes on record for performances in England, some no doubt playing only on an occasional basis, many others consisting of touring professionals.[1] In medieval times, these players were employed chiefly to entertain and enhance the magnificence of the courts which retained them, but scholars now believe that increasingly during the Tudor period they carried out a propagandist function of advancing their patrons' ideological interests.[2] One of these professional troupes was "Bale and his felowes," patronized by Thomas Cromwell, Henry VIII's chief minister during the 1530s, and led by the Protestant playwright and preacher John Bale. Bale's company is of special interest for two reasons. First, it remains, so far as I know, the only professional playing troupe prior to Shakespeare's stage career for which we can assign a patron, a playwright, and a small repertory of extant plays. Second, it may well be representative of many itinerant troupes operating between the 1530s and the midpoint of Queen Elizabeth's reign engaged in Reformation stage propaganda.

John Bale, or "bilious Bale" as he was reproachfully termed by Thomas Fuller and has been by critics ever since, is a fascinating topic of interest in his own right. Bale was one of those early English reformers whose zeal for the gospel and hatred of Rome was made all the more impassioned by bad memories of a previous career as a Carmelite friar. His animosity towards Catholicism is everywhere apparent in his drama, most notably in *King Johan*, a forerunner of Shakespeare's chronicle play and perhaps the only work for which he is known by most Renaissance theatre scholars today. During the past two decades, however, there has been a resurgence of interest in his works, with Leslie Fairfield and Paul Christianson hailing him as the father of apocalyptic theology in pre-revolutionary England, and

with Peter Happé, Ritchie Kendall, and John N. King, praising his
originality, expertise, and influence, as a playwright.[3] Despite this
recent critical acclaim, his role as the leader (possibly even *the leading
actor*) of a Reformation playing troupe has received scant consideration, partly because critics (Fairfield, for example) find it
difficult to imagine a puritan zealot of Bale's temperament directly
and extensively engaged in the theatre; but primarily because it has
only been very recently that theatre historians have begun to examine
the evidence of touring practices and itineraries of professional
companies. In *The Revels History of Drama in English: 1500–1576*
(1980), T. W. Craik comments briefly on Bale's troupe, but the topic
merits more extensive treatment. In what immediately follows, I
structure my discussion around several questions. First, how did
Bale's drama and his company of players fit into the programme of
propaganda which Cromwell implemented in the 1530s? Secondly,
who were the personnel of Bale's troupe – where did they come from
and what were their talents, how many of them were there? Thirdly,
what was the repertory of this company? And finally, what
constituted the company's touring itinerary? In the second half of the
chapter I examine the repertory in detail, focussing on the methods
of Bale's stage propaganda, particularly its iconoclastic dimension,
and speculating about its impact on the early Reformation audience.

Cromwell's regime and Reformation stage propaganda

Like other playwrights such as John Rastel, Nicholas Udall, and even
John Heywood for a time, Bale was caught up in the vortex of the
public relations campaign masterminded by Thomas Cromwell
during the 1530s and designed to popularize the royal supremacy
and especially to discredit papal authority and practice in England.[4]
As Secretary of State and subsequently Lord Privy Seal, Cromwell
advanced beyond his able predecessors in these posts, Bishops Foxe
and Wolsey, in organizing state-sanctioned propaganda for the
stage.[5] Some significant insights into the nature of and rationale
behind Cromwell's programme may be found in "A Discourse
touching the Reformation of the Lawes of England," written by
Cromwell's secretary and most energetic publicist, Richard Morison,
about 1535.[6] Morison maintains that the chief threat to the well-
being of the English state is the Papacy, which he views as a rival
political organization that competes with the Crown for the people's

allegiance by presenting its own humanly devised decrees and
ceremonies as embodying timeless spiritual values ordained by God
and therefore above civil authority. Like Machiavelli, whose writings
he and Cromwell probably read during their time of study in Italy,
and like other Protestant spokesmen, Morison perceives religion
under papal authority as a powerful instrument of social control and
a means of perpetuating its own institutions.[7] In commenting on the
methods of indoctrination by which Rome maintained its control
over people's lives before the Reformation, Morison states that its
superstitious beliefs and practices "were daily by all meanes opened
inculked and dryven into the peoples heddes, tought in scoles to
children, plaied in playes before the ignoraunt people, songe in
mynstrelles songes, and bokes in englisshe purposely to be dyvysed to
declare the same at large."[8] To deliver the people from the bondage
of Popery, it will not be enough to enforce the laws of the new
Reformation Parliament and to shape public opinion through
preaching and print propaganda. Morison proposes that the Crown
implement some of the very same methods that Rome itself had
shown to be successful. In place of processions, feasts, bonfires, and
prayers offered to the Pope there should be ones celebrating his defeat
in England; and in place of the pagan and superstitious theatre now
practiced there should be plays denigrating the Pope and advancing
the Reformation cause: "Howmoche better is it that those plaies
shulde be forbodden and deleted and others dyvysed to set forthe and
declare lyvely before the peoples eies the abhomynation and
wickednes of the bisshop of Rome, monkes, ffreers, nonnes, and suche
like, and to declare and open to them thobedience that your subiectes
by goddes and mans lawes owe unto your magestie. Into the commen
people thynges sooner enter by the eies, then by the eares:
remembryng more better that they see then that they heere."[9] The
fact that Morison's proposals were implemented across the realm
indicates the extent to which the Cromwellian regime recognized
drama, processions, ceremonies and other religious or quasi-religious
practices as means of legitimating and internalizing its vision of a
politically and religiously reformed England.[10]

Morison's statement that "into the commen people thynges
sooner enter by the eies, then by the eares: remembryng more better
that they see then that they heere" explains drama's particular
appeal to Cromwell. He shrewdly perceived that in a nation that
remained to a large extent illiterate and religiously conservative,

especially in those outlying regions where Catholicism was most firmly entrenched, stage-plays communicated ideology effectively and entertainingly to the general public in concrete visual terms. As Morison observes, the Catholic Church itself had proven this through centuries of popular theatre. Moreover, what better method was there to discredit Catholicism's superstitious reliance on visual images than to parody sumptuously dressed priests and their elaborate rituals on the stage, where, according to the reformers, such pageantry belonged in the first place? This is a form of iconoclasm, and like other organized forms of iconoclasm during the Reformation such as the smashing of religious statues in public exhibitions (which Cromwell also promoted) and the lampooning of the triple-crowned Pope in woodcuts and paintings, the images need to be presented in order to be literally or ritualistically destroyed.[11] As I shall explain more fully below, Bale's iconoclastic drama uses these methods to undermine papal influence during the late 1530s when Cromwell feared another Catholic insurrection at home like the 1535 Pilgrimage of Grace and a rumored invasion by papal forces from abroad, especially following the Franco-Imperial Alliance of 1538.[12]

"Bale and his felowes": patronage, personnel and touring

Precisely when Bale as a Reformation propagandist received the official recognition of Cromwell is difficult to say. Bale claims that on two occasions when he was in trouble with the authorities for his preaching, first with Archbishop Lee at York in 1534, and with Bishop Stokesley of London two years later, he was saved from prosecution by "the pious Cromwell" on account of the comedies he had written.[13] It is possible that through his mentor, Lord Thomas Wentworth of Suffolk, or through his other patron at court, the Earl of Oxford (more on him below), Bale came under Cromwell's patronage as early as July 1534, when he left his appointment as prior of the Carmelite House in Ipswich to head the priory at Doncaster in the North, where he was given license to preach throughout the diocese of York, probably in support of the official propaganda campaign then underway to support the royal supremacy.[14] However, the fact that the troubles at York were followed by his demotion to a curacy in the small parish of Thorndon, Suffolk, suggests that he was still too controversial for Cromwell to put him on the Crown's payroll. At Thorndon, his preaching against saint worship, pur-

1   John Bale with Bible in hand, a seventeenth-century engraving by Wilhelm and Magdalena van de Posse based on a sixteenth-century portrait. In the account of his scriptural plays performed at Kilkenny, Bale states, "I toke Christes testament in my hande and went into the market crosse ... " (*Vocacyon*, 24^{r-v}). The plays indicate that, as Baleus Prolocutor, he carried a Bible into the acting space during performances. Courtesy of the Guildhall Library, City of London.

gatory, and unbiblical ceremonies led to imprisonment at Greenwich at the orders of Bishop Stokesley in January 1537. Perhaps due in part to the Lutheran-influenced Ten Articles passed by Convocation in July 1536 which shifted the official theological position further to the left, Cromwell, now Lord Privy Seal, was in a stronger position officially to recognize and use Bale's proven skills as a spokesman for the Reformation and against the Papacy. At any rate, a letter to Cromwell by Bale's friend and fellow reformer, John Leland, along with his own "Answer of John Bale, priest," to Stokesley's charges, resulted in his release from jail.

We may safely assume that from early 1537 to early 1540, Bale was under Cromwell's direct patronage. Leland, the King's antiquary and one of Cromwell's print propagandists, put him to work on the bibliographical study, *Anglorum Heliades*, completed by 1540. However, more significantly for our purposes, Bale was writing and revising plays promoting the Crown's religious policy and performing

2 Lord Thomas Cromwell, 1st Earl of Essex, a sixteenth-century portrait. Cromwell was appointed Secretary of State in 1534, Vicar-General in 1535, and Lord Privy Seal in 1536; this swift ascendancy within Henry VIII's Reformation regime made him, next to the king, the nation's most powerful patron. Courtesy of the National Portrait Gallery, London.

them with his own troupe.[15] "Balle and his felowes" are recorded for two performances paid for and attended by Cromwell himself: in September 1538 in St. Stephen's Church, near Canterbury, a rectory under Cromwell's direct charge since 1535, and again in January 1539 at an unspecified location, perhaps at Cromwell House by Old Broad Street in London (see figure 15, pp. 132–133).[16] A third performance is indicated in a deposition of one John Alforde, who witnessed *King Johan* at the Canterbury residence of Archbishop Cranmer in December 1538.[17] Following J. H. P. Pafford's lead, students of Bale have identified this company under Bale's leadership with the troupe described as "Lord Cromwell's Players" and "the Lord Privy Seal's Men" in municipal, monastic, and collegiate records through the realm between 1536/37 and 1540.[18] The evidence supporting this is persuasive. Bale had already established himself as a playwright at court by 1534 when he wrote fourteen plays for the troupe of Cromwell's fellow privy counsellor and proponent of Protestant reform, the Earl of Oxford,[19] and not only was Bale's own troupe paid on at least two occasions by Lord Cromwell to perform in his presence, his extant plays promote the very reform principles that the minister espoused and propagated through other channels. *King Johan*, for example, treats the issues Cromwell championed during the late 1530s: the royal supremacy, Bible reading on a national scale, the dangers of Catholic doctrine and ceremonies. One can say without hesitation that if not for Cromwell's protection, *King Johan*'s debunking of Auricular Confession – a rite that Henry VIII would not outlaw in the liberal Ten Articles Act of 1536 – would have resulted in Bale's imprisonment, if not execution on grounds of heresy. Moreover, Bale is not known to have held a church benefice during the late thirties, and considering his passionate defense of the acting profession, his assigning himself a part in all but one of his extant plays written in the mid-to-late 1530s (a matter I will return to shortly), and his subsequent involvement with actors right up to the end of his career, it seems reasonable that leading a dramatic company would have been one means by which he earned a living during these years.[20] When not receiving direct payment from Cromwell, as was the case at Cranmer's house and St. Stephen's Church, Bale's troupe would have probably carried on tour a seal or letter from their patron as a means of identification and entrée to local civic and ecclesiastical authorities from whom they needed permission to perform in local venues. A company called "Bale and his felowes" would not have carried much weight with a mayor, town chamberlain, college master, or bishop, especially in an age when such troupes were suspected as roaming bands of masterless men; however, "Lord Cromwell's Players" or "the Lord Privy Seal's Players" would give them instant credibility among officials perhaps hostile to the virulent anti-Catholicism of Bale's plays and perhaps a higher remuneration for their services in the many provincial communities where the Lord Privy Seal had strong connections. Bale himself had connections in three of the towns where they performed; in Cambridge he trained as a Carmelite friar, in Maldon he had served as the prior of the local Carmelite monastic house, and at York he had preached during his tenure as the Carmelite prior at Doncaster. We will return to the itinerary of Lord Cromwell's Players below.

In turning now to the personnel and activities of this troupe, we may begin by considering where the players came from. Were they an already existing company, perhaps the same players earlier patronized by the Earl of Oxford? I would say that the latter is unlikely; a nobleman as distinguished as Oxford would have almost certainly retained his players until his death in 1540, and in 1547 we learn from Bishop Gardiner that, under Oxford's heir, they were performing in Southwark at the very hour of the dirge for Henry VIII.[21] Yet it was not unusual for troupes to change patrons during the course of their career, nor to remain under the auspices of an administrative post when a successor was appointed. So, for example, it is possible that the previous Lord Privy Seal, Thomas Boleyn, sponsored a troupe of players – indeed the farce depicting Wolsey's descent into hell at Boleyn's house in 1531 might suggest this[22] – and that this troupe passed into Cromwell's hands when Boleyn was forced to resign in disgrace in 1536. Another possibility is that Bale's players were previously sponsored by Boleyn's son, Lord Rochford, who supported players for at least the two years prior to his execution in 1536,[23] when he was implicated in his sister's conviction of treason. At that time Rochford, along with Henry Courtenay, Marquis of Exeter, headed the gentlemen of the Privy Chamber, which in the late thirties came under Cromwell's direct authority.[24] Either one of these noblemen's troupes, therefore, or any other in similar circumstances, would have become available to Cromwell for patronage. However, it seems to me more probable that the troupe was assembled by Bale himself than formed from a previously existing nobleman's troupe. Perhaps among them were some of the many tradesmen/players of the period whom Bale may have met during his various clerical appointments throughout East Anglia during the 1530s. One such example is Peter Moone, the Ipswich artisan who wrote polemical verse pamphlets during Edward's reign under Bale's old patron, Thomas Lord Wentworth, and who shows up in Ipswich in 1561/62 leading a band of players in performance at the city guildhall when *King Johan* was reportedly among the City Council's papers.[25] Yet I would guess that Bale would have at his disposal a rich source of playing talent in the monasteries where, as Glynne Wickham points out, scores of gifted clergymen became unemployed and ready to enter the Crown's service as scholars, musicians, players, as well as secular priests at the time of the dissolution.[26] In discussing dramatic entertainments at Thetford Priory, for example, Richard Beadle cites references in the surviving records to indicate that the monks took an active part in the staging or acting of plays there, perhaps in collaboration with visiting players.[27] It may not be insignificant that William Cornish, Jr.,

Henry VIII's brilliant master of the chapel children who devised so many of the King's entertainments during the first half of his reign, was granted a corrody at Thetford in 1523.[28] We should keep in mind that Bale himself was one such product of the monastic system (the order of Carmelites), as were other known makers of interludes. W. A. Mepham and Alan H. Nelson have discussed the connection between the civic drama and the Carmelite Houses at Maldon and Ipswich, where Bale was appointed prior in 1530 and 1533 respectively.[29] At Maldon, plays were performed in the Carmelite Friary, and in Ipswich, three surviving dramatic documents, two from the fifteenth and one tentatively dated early sixteenth century, show the Carmelites participating in the city's procession of pageants, and since this procession was conducted in conjunction with a sequence of religious plays under the supervision of a local magistrate, it seems probable that the Carmelites also contributed to the drama. It is therefore entirely possible that Bale himself was involved in such productions at both monastic houses, perhaps staging his own plays, and that he recruited apostate monks like himself to perform in those plays as early as 1530 and as late as 1537. He may have also found some disgruntled priests already out of the cloister who were willing to pursue their preaching ministry on the stage. We have one such case noted in Foxe's *Acts and Monuments*, a Salisbury priest named Richard Spencer in 1541 "who leavynge his Papistry, had maryed a wife, and become a player in interludes, with one Ramsey and Hewet, which iii. were all condemned and burned: Against whom, and specially agaynst Spenser, was layde matter concernyng the Sacrament of the altar."[30]

Now we come to the question of the number and background of the players in Bale's troupe. Happé assigns five actors to *King Johan* and *Three Laws*, and five actors could also be assigned to *Johan Baptystes Preachynge* and *The Temptation of Our Lord*, including Bale himself who (as "Baleus Prolocutor") delivers prologues and epilogues.[31] There are few feminine parts in the plays, so it is possible that the troupe consisted of five adults, not the four men and a boy that make up the Lord Cardinal's Players in *The Book of Sir Thomas More*, nor the more usual troupe number of four players in early- to mid-Tudor England.[32] The players probably had some musical training, since music figures significantly in most of the extant plays. Happé suggests that Bale's actors may have been associated with the contemporary choir schools. Since choir schools produced drama (e.g. the choir schools of St. Paul's and Westminster), Bale may have also recruited from them, or possibly from one of the choir troupes on tour; we know that the Duke of Suffolk sponsored an itinerant choir troupe in the early 1530s.[33] Of course, every monk who had to participate in the divine office would have had some experience with plainsong and perhaps even with the polyphony fashionable in Tudor anthems and antiphons. I have mentioned that Bale himself may have been the leading actor in this troupe. This is suggested in the casting charts and projected doubling patterns in his plays. In four of his five surviving interludes, "Baleus Prolocutor" delivers the prologue and the epilogue. The division of the parts for *Three Laws*, explicitly stated in colophon at the play's conclusion, require that Baleus Prolocutor double with the Vice Infidelity, the play's dominant and most theatrically taxing role.[34] In a troupe known as "Bale and his felowes," it is not unreasonable to suppose that Bale combined the responsibilities of manager and chief player. It has been argued that in mid-Tudor companies the leading actor played the part of the Vice and assumed the responsibilities of stage management.[35]

The Lord Cardinal's Players depicted in *The Book of Sir Thomas More*, along with other evidence, indicates that a professional troupe on the road in the early sixteenth century worked with a repertoire of as many as seven plays.[36] But in moving from town to town where they might appear only once, they could obviously do with far fewer. We have strong evidence of only one play by "Bale and his felowes," *King Johan*, but it is likely that *Three Laws* and possibly the other surviving plays suited for five acting parts and advancing Cromwell's Protestant Injunctions of 1536 were also taken on the road. These other plays were later performed – probably by amateurs – in Kilkenny, Ireland when Bale served as the Edwardian Bishop of Ossory. Bale had a large pool of scripts to draw from (he lists twenty-four), and with the exception of the play about the King's two marriages, any one of the fourteen already composed for troupe performance which Bale supplied to Oxford's Men in 1534 (given that they had been returned from De Vere for rehearsal by early-to mid-1537) might have been suitable.

The recent collections of dramatic records completed by the Malone Society and Records of Early English Drama have provided us with more information about the itinerary of the Lord Privy Seal's Players in particular and the touring patterns of professional playing companies of Tudor England in general. If, as most scholars agree,

Cromwell's troupe was led by Bale and was responsible for the three above-mentioned performances, then we can link ten different locations and thirteen separate performances with this troupe. They are as follows: Cambridge, Shrewsbury (1537), Leicester, Oxford and Thetford (1537/38), Cambridge, St. Stephen's by Canterbury, Cranmer's house Canterbury (1538), Cromwell's house London (1539), Thetford, Cambridge, Maldon and York (1539/40).[37]

From this list and other evidence we can speculate about the company's touring patterns. However, as Suzanne R. Westfall has observed in her tentative reconstruction of the touring of the Duke of Suffolk's troupe,[38] there are a number of vexing problems facing the theatre historian attempting to draw conclusions about the touring of professional companies in Tudor England. Records of payments to patronized troupes, still our primary evidence, are currently incomplete and in need of systematic analysis. More records of performances by Cromwell's Men may be yet discovered. Also, the records that *have* been collected identify only the company and payment in the majority of instances and are difficult to date with any precision. Few indicate the day or month of the company's appearance, and because the year ends in the spring, it is difficult to know whether those dated 1537/38, for example, occurred in 1537 or 1538. Another problem is that records may never have existed of troupe visits to many parts of the country, since payment often was made by collection or charging admission, or, as in the case of the game house at Great Yarmouth from about 1538, no payment was made at all.[39] In his collection of records for Kent, Giles E. Dawson points out an additional complication: some city chamberlains only contributed to payment when the spectators did not sufficiently recompense the troupe with personal donations.[40] As Westfall concludes, in the records of towns where no payment to players is shown, "the omission of rewards to players does not prove that players were never there, only that municipal funds were not expended for them."[41] One might add that geographers are still not sure of all the major roads and tracks linking towns and cities during the Tudor era, although we do know of the major Roman and Goth roads such as Watling Street, Ermine Street, and Fosse Way.[42] Nevertheless, the available evidence does enable us to engage in a plausible, if conjectural, reconstruction of the touring practices and itinerary of Cromwell's troupe.

Lord Cromwell's Players would have set out perhaps in the noble livery of their patron as a mark of their privileged status and means of entrée before municipal authorities. The players may have walked on foot with a pack horse, but in addition to the actors' usual belongings, a sizeable load of costumes and properties for Bale's plays, perhaps larger than average, may have required a wagon.[43] We may assume for the moment that the costumes and properties for *King Johan* and *Three Laws*, the two surviving plays of Bale designed clearly for professional use, are representative of what was taken on tour.[44] Most of the apparel required for *King John* is clerical, a large supply of which would have been readily available to Bale and his troupe by way of Cromwell's seizure of monastic property and valuables from February 1536.[45] Among the garments required are those for a pope, cardinal, bishop, a friar and monk, and a priest (including a stole for confession). Player's outfits for a king, nobleman, magistrate, and a common widow, would also be needed. Some of these costumes could be used in *Three Laws* as well, e.g. those for the monk, priest, and bishop. Since the troupe appears to have performed at religious houses, perhaps at Shrewsbury and Maldon, as well as at Thetford, several of the clerical garments could have been borrowed while on tour, and the same may be said about properties. The latter are numerous but portable, so would not have been too much of a burden to transport. They include a testament, scroll, sword, king's crown, "a candle, bell, and book," and assorted "relics." Again, some of these would have been used in different plays (e.g. the testament, relics).

Considering Cromwell's vast network of correspondents and loyal officials throughout the realm, it seems probable that at least for the major cities, a travelling itinerary would have been set up in advance.[46] Local magistrates and noblemen based in the shires were eager to receive companies sponsored by powerful and influential Lords like Cromwell, and even more so provincial authorities who shared his ideological views (in Kent and Suffolk his connections were particularly strong).[47] The players, however, may have been required to follow the customary procedure of performing at the guildhall at the mayor's request or command before permission was granted to use venues elsewhere in the community. The approval of an ecclesiastical official, e.g. the presiding bishop, may have been required for use of a church as a playing venue.

The locations on record for paid performances by Lord Cromwell's players in 1537 and 1537/38 suggest a tour through the Midlands. In

——— Midlands Tour 1537–38

– – – Canterbury Tour 1538

·········· East Anglia Tour 1538/39

- - - - North Country Tour 1540

3   Conjectured touring routes of Lord Cromwell's players, 1537/38, 1538/39, and 1540.

1537 there are records for performances at Shrewsbury, and in 1537/38 at Leicester and Oxford. There were well-travelled roads connecting these major cities. It is conceivable that Bale's troupe set out in a northwesterly direction to Shrewsbury, along Watling

Street, and during the course of the 130 mile trip, they stopped at Leicester, which would have required them to turn northeast at the junction of Watling Street and Fosse Way (the major artery linking Bristol with the Midland cities of Leicester and Nottingham) for a distance of 20 miles. Since the performance here is recorded in the municipal accounts, it may have taken place in the guildhall or across the street in St. Martin's Church, where we know from other records plays staged there were paid by the town council.[48] At Shrewsbury, Tudor performances are recorded in the Benedictine Abbey (the nave of which was used as a parish church before and possibly after the dissolution), St. Chad's churchyard, and a quarry just outside the city walls made famous in Elizabeth's reign by the local schoolmaster, Thomas Ashton, whose Protestant *Passion of Christ* and *Julian the Apostate* were staged before some 10,000 people.[49] If Bale's troupe were commissioned to stage plays before monastic audiences – as seems to have been the case at Thetford and Maldon – then the Abbey would have been the likely choice for playing in, but of course it is impossible to know this on the available evidence. Supposing that Oxford was visited on the return leg of the journey, the best road would have taken them through Coventry (about 60 miles from Shrewsbury), where they might have performed and spent the night. The following day, they would have set out towards Oxford, some 45 miles, where they performed at New College (perhaps in the college hall or chapel). Here, Bale's savage attacks on monastic life in *King Johan* and *Three Laws* would have gone down particularly well with Dr. John London, the College Warden and the most notorious of Cromwell's agents in charge of suppressing the greater monasteries.[50] These plays also may have been seen at this time by Lewis Wager, an Oxford Franciscan-turned-Protestant preacher, whose play *Mary Magdalene* is so strongly influenced by Bale's drama (see pp. 80–87 below). The final portion of the journey to London would have taken them another 56 miles. The records indicate a range of possible audiences, a popular one at Leicester and Shrewsbury, perhaps clerical as well as popular at Shrewsbury if they played in the Abbey, and an academic audience at Oxford, although we know that even at the universities the townspeople were invited to attend (and spend their money).[51]

It is of course highly unlikely that the troupe would have limited its playing to these major cities during a Midlands tour. I have already mentioned Coventry as a probable stop along the way. Moreover, despite the absence of evidence (at least to date), it seems also very probable that the troupe would have entertained at country estates and noblemen's homes in the provinces as well. John M. Wasson has discovered in the course of researching Derbyshire and Yorkshire for REED that the travelling players performed most of the time not in the towns but at noble households where they could be assured of several good meals, safe lodging, and a sizeable remuneration for playing.[52] As to how many stops would have been made is difficult to estimate, but if a typical troupe travelling by foot moved at a pace of several miles per day (Westfall suggests five), then the journey would have involved a month or more and many performances. Perhaps the tour did not take in every town, but for the company to defray expenses and make a basic living from playing, it would have required far more bookings than the surviving records indicate for the 1537 and 1537/38 tours, involving visits to other population centers, monastic houses, and private estates between London and Shrewsbury.

During 1538 and 1539, Lord Cromwell's Players may have confined their touring to Kent and to East Anglia where Bale grew up and spent a good portion of his early career. In 1537/38, they are recorded at Thetford Priory and Cambridge (town and university)[53] and Canterbury, and in 1539 again at Canterbury and again at Thetford. There is good reason to believe that Cambridge and Thetford were visited on the same tour and that Norwich might also have been included, since we know of other companies such as the King's Players under Edward VI and the Duke of Norfolk's Players who visited Cambridge and Thetford and also travelled up to Norwich in the same year.[54] From Norwich, the company may have journeyed eastward to Great Yarmouth, where, as mentioned earlier, the "game house" was used for performances of interludes and plays. No companies are recorded for visiting the game house because the manager, Robert Copping, was instructed not to take profits for the entertainments. The company may have also stopped at other small communities, such as Archbishop Cranmer's own small parish at Hadleigh, which had its own dramatic tradition; or even Ipswich, a strong Protestant center where a copy of *King Johan* was evidently among the Corporation's documents dated about 1560.[55] The old main road from London to Ipswich was lined with large trade centers such as West Ham, Chelmsford, and Colchester, with other communities known to have staged plays fairly regularly, including

Maldon and Heybridge not far away, all of which may have been visited by Bale's players.

The last three locations recorded for performance by the company in 1540, Maldon, Cambridge, and York (at the common hall), suggest another major tour, although the precise dates of the visits are not known. Bale previously had connections with all three of these places, as I mentioned earlier. The tour may have begun at Maldon, followed a direct road leading from there up to Cambridge (town accounts may suggest the town hall), and then along Ermine Street through Stamford and Lincoln, then slightly westward to Doncaster, where Bale was prior of the Carmelite house based there in 1534, and finally to York, where during his Doncaster years he had been licensed to preach by Archbishop Lee.

Bale's repertory and the early Reformation audience

Having now considered the patronage, make-up, and itinerary of Bale's troupe, it will be useful to examine in more detail the plays Bale evidently wrote for them, particularly in the context of their early Reformation audience and the methods Bale used to shape public opinion in support of Cromwell's Protestant policies during the mid-to-late 1530s.

All Bale's surviving plays vigorously champion Cromwell's reform objectives. *King Johan* treats the Papacy as a foreign political institution which surreptitiously uses its clerical agents and ceremonies to gain dominion over the English state and overthrow divinely sanctioned monarchical authority. The play reflects Crown fears that while the doctrine of papal supremacy had been legally dead since 1534, the religious and cultural fabric on which it rested was not, and with the ever-present threat of invasion by Catholic powers on the Continent, made more real by the solidifying of the Franco-Imperial Alliance of 1538, propaganda against the Papacy would need to be stepped up to sway public opinion against Rome and reduce the risk of further seditious uprisings such as the Pilgrimage of Grace in 1535. *Three Laws*, which deals with more specific matters of religious doctrine, depicts the Catholic clergy as the contemporary manifestation of a timeless spiritual evil corrupting God's laws through the ages; in calling for obedience to those divine laws it also implied obedience to the newly instituted legislation of the Reformation Parliament which was an extension of them. Bale's less controversial biblical interludes, *God's Promises*, *Johan Baptystes Preachyng*, and *The Temptation of Our Lord*, were no doubt intended as a more scripturally accurate and gospel-centered alternative to the Catholic mysteries and miracle plays and were designed to compliment the Crown's policy of distributing Bibles to every parish church in 1538.[56] The titles of Bale's eighteen nonextant works indicate that several would have been eminently suitable for the anti-papal offensive of 1537–40, including *Against Corruptors of the Word of God*, and *Concerning the Deceptions of the Papists*. *On the Papist Sects*, which is clearly an attack on the religious houses, might have been performed on tour in support of the programme of their dissolution, and *The Knaveries of Thomas Becket* undoubtedly supported the systematic attack on images and shrines devoted to saints. It would not have been out of character for Bale to have staged the Becket play on the eve of the Translation of St. Thomas on July 6 at Canterbury after the suppression of the pageant honoring the saint in 1538. Henry VIII himself proposed that a play depicting him decapitating papal clerics should be performed on the Eve of St. Peter's, which suggests that the government may have planned anti-papal productions on popular Catholic feast days to celebrate the demise of the Pope and his clergy.[57] It was during the summer of 1538 that the Saint's shrine was torn down and its treasures carted off to Westminster.[58] Saint worship, in Bale's view, was among the most notorious of popish superstitions which served as one more means by which the Papacy secured its devilish influence and prevented the true worship of God prescribed by Scripture. Becket was an especially reviled figure by the King and the early reformers because his glorification brought shame to the English Crown and perpetuated the myth of Henry II as an apostate.[59] Moreover, the shrine at Canterbury, among the most famous in all of Europe and destination to thousands of pilgrims annually, was an additional grievance to the Crown because it amassed a huge revenue from the English people that went straight to Rome.[60]

The five extant plays indicate that Bale was writing drama not primarily for an elitist audience, as were, for example, his contemporaries Heywood and Udall, but for the socially diverse audience that the Lord Privy Seal's Players would have been expected to address while on tour. This was in line with Cromwell's propagandist objective of disseminating Crown policy through print, preaching, and playing to all sectors of society.[61] The "plain style" of the dialogue and speeches, though usually in clumsy five-stress couplets, was sufficiently close to the language of the contemporary parish pulpit for both learned and illiterate to understand, and the frequent use of familiar proverbs is a clear sign of the plays' popular interests.[62] For special appeal to the intellectual elite, Bale provides passages of learned debate over theological issues and the teachings of the Church fathers and depicts characters such as Nobility, Clergy, and Civil Order (in *King Johan*) with whom members of the ruling class could identify. For the illiterate, he communicates his anti-Catholic message through visual symbolism, accompanied by verbal exposition in simple direct language; and they too view characters who mirror their self-image.

The most important piece of external evidence concerning Bale's audience during the late 1530s is found in a deposition by John Alforde, age eighteen, who witnessed "an enterlude concernyng King John, aboute 8 or 9 of the clocke at night" at the Canterbury home of Archbishop Cranmer during Christmas 1538. Alforde and Thomas Brown, a man of fifty who also attended, praised the play's treatment of King John as a noble prince and the Pope as England's adversary, with Alforde stating "that it ys petie that the Bisshop of Rome should reigne any lenger, for if he should, the said Bisshop wold do with our King as he did with King John."[63] It seems likely that in attendance at the Archbishop's residence were members of the higher clergy and nobility, but neither Brown nor Alforde (who may have been Brown's servant) are identified with either class. A clue to their social status, as well as a less favorable view of the play's content, is suggested in a conversation sometime after the performance in Brown's home where a shipman, Henry Totehill, objected to the mistreatment of the Pope and St. Thomas Becket, stating "that the Bisshope of Rome was made Pope by the clergie and by the consent of all the Kinges Christen," and "That it was petie and nawghtely don, to put down the Pope and Saincte Thomas; for the Pope was a good man, and Saincte Thomas."[64]

The deposition is revealing therefore in not only suggesting a demographically diverse audience for Bale's drama but also in illustrating the controversy and division of opinion occasioned by its performance. Indeed, religious strife and angry opposition are linked with every known production of Bale's plays. During Edward VI's reign, an irate priest in Bale's parish of Bishopstoke, Hampshire, accused a servant of heresy apparently for rehearsing a role in *Three*

Laws; Bale also met opposition in heavily Catholic Kilkenny, Ireland, where his biblical trilogy was performed on the eve of Mary Tudor's coronation, and in Canterbury in 1561, priest-bating in an unidentified play by Bale provoked the wrath of some local magistrates.[65] It is of course quite possible that it was because these performances were controversial that they drew attention (many others might have been favorably received). Nevertheless, as Christopher Haigh observes, Protestant proselytizing often encountered hostility and resentment, especially in the provinces, well into Elizabeth's reign.[66]

During the Cromwellian years, the opposition was likely to have been even greater. The popular Reformation in England lagged far behind the legislative and political one of the early thirties. Protestantism had made significant inroads in London and in prominent ports such as Ipswich, Dover and Bristol, where trade with Reformed cities on the Continent was strong, as well as in textile towns of Essex and Kent where Lollardy prepared the way. Its authority and influence were further strengthened by the efforts of Cromwell and Cranmer to place advanced Protestants in positions of civic and ecclesiastical leadership in the provinces. And yet, as revisionist historians have argued, the general populace evidently were either resistant or indifferent to change.[67] Catholic values were too deeply rooted in the people's consciousness for the government to sweep them away in a very short period of time. Keith Thomas reminds us that for the typical medieval Catholic, religion was not so much a matter of belief as of practice. The penitential system, the sacraments of Baptism, Marriage, Extreme Unction, etc., the whole calendar of Saint's days and their accompanying rituals, feasts, and pastimes, testify to Catholicism as "a ritual method of living," not merely a formalized code of religious doctrine.[68] Consequently, it was one thing for the Crown to impose new legislation and to proclaim salvation by faith; it was another to expect the people to abandon habits of mind and rituals that were entrenched for centuries of papal control of religious ideology and practice.

As a highly learned scholar acquainted with the Humanist-oriented drama of his contemporaries at home and abroad, Bale could have experimented in his own plays with classical models, but other than the rather awkward subtitles of "tragedie" and "comedie" (terms he possibly derived from Chaucer and Lydgate), the use of a "Chorus" in *God's Promises*, and the division of *Three Laws* into five acts, there is little trace of the new methods in his plays.

Always conscious of his popular and largely Catholic audience, he relies on the indigenous conventions of form and presentation familiar to that audience and by which he could most effectively impose his views on them. These conventions derived not only from medieval religious drama but from the folk plays as well. Thus when Infidelity appears before the audience in *Three Laws* sweeping the acting space with his broom, singing, "Brom, brom, brom, brom, brom. By brom, bye, bye," and promising to return momentarily with his candle, he would have been immediately recognizable to the audience as Robin Goodfellow.[69] He is of course also the play's chief Vice figure familiar to audiences of *Mankind* and *Youth*. Moreover, like earlier medieval audiences, the spectators attending Bale's plays brought with them to the playing area the notion of drama as "game" imparting "earnest," with the players functioning (often simultaneously) as direct expositors of truth through direct address and as representative of historical types and allegorical ideas whose actions and dialogue advance a dramatized argument or a sequence of thematically related scenes.[70] Bale could also count on their previous play experience to recognize visual significations of meaning transmitted through costumes, gesture, movement, and properties, as well as the conventions of disguise, parody, and inversion, that were staple features of English drama for centuries.

Yet to repeat Chambers' observation of many years ago,[71] Bale is a largely original playwright who combines traditional stagecraft with innovative techniques to carry out his homiletic or polemical purpose. His biblical interludes are the closest of his plays to medieval tradition in their reenacting scenes from the Old and New Testament, but as Peter Happé points out, the mysteries which Bale perhaps saw in his youth in East Anglia (e.g. the Norwich cycle) serve less as models than as "points of departure towards a Protestant goal."[72] His plays follow scriptural incidents much more closely, and they exhibit a polemical dimension that is wholly absent in their medieval counterparts. More problematic is identifying his other surviving plays, *Three Laws* and *King Johan*, as "moralities," particularly if we regard the *Humanum Genus* hero as a staple feature of that dramatic kind. While both the latter dramatize the opposition between personified "Vices" and "Virtues," neither one exhibits a central "mankind" figure who is alternately tempted and admonished by wicked and wise advisors during the course of a spiritual journey from this world into the next. It has been argued that Nobility, Clergy, and

4   Robin Goodfellow, with horns, goat-feet and a phallus, a sixteenth-century
woodcut. Like Robin Goodfellow, Infidelity in *Three Laws* carries a broom and will
soon return with a candle ("...ye shall have a candle, / Whan I come hyther
agayne"). Reproduced by M. Murray in *The God of the Witches* (London: Faber and
Faber, 1931); cited in Richard Axton, "Folk Play in Tudor Interludes," pp. 22, 227.

Civil Order in *King Johan* are vacillating everyman figures,[73] but it
seems highly unlikely that Bale was following any set dramatic
formula. In neither play does Bale begin with the preconceived
pattern of morality structure in mind. In *Three Laws*, he desires to
illustrate in dramatic fashion the nature and corruption of the laws of
Nature, Moses, and Christ, and thus devises a structure which best
suits that purpose.[74] On the other hand, in *King Johan*, the sequence
of scenes is dictated by certain events of great significance to Bale in
the life of the English King and by Bale's overall purpose of depicting
the King as martyr-saint who was both a victim to the tyranny of
Rome and a forerunner of Henry VIII's Reformation.
    Bale was England's first Reformation historiographer, and there-
fore it is not surprising to discover that the view of history he was to
develop systematically in *The Image of Both Churches* during his exile in
the 1540s informs his approach to dramatic narrative and character.[75]
The notion that history repeats itself in a series of cycles was a

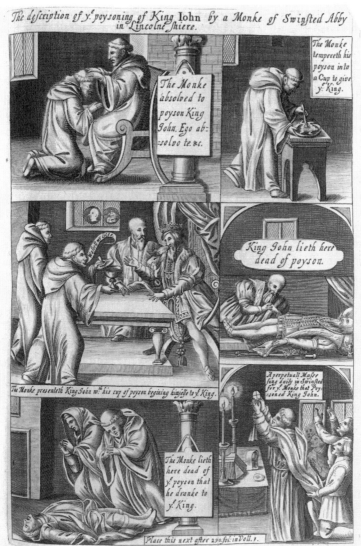

5   "The description of yᵉ poysoning of King Iohn by a Monke of Swinsted Abby in Lincoln Shiere," a woodcut from John Foxe's *Acts and Monuments* (1584). Alfred Pollard observes: "The preliminary absolution, the offer to the King of the poisoned wassail-bowl, the death of the monk and the promised mass being sung for his soul are all here shown in accordance with Bale's dialogue and it is perhaps not wholly fanciful to connect the appearance of this large picture in the *Book of Martyrs* with the revival of the play in the reign of Elizabeth." *English Miracle Plays, Moralities, and Interludes* (Oxford: Clarendon, 1927), p. lxxi. Courtesy of Robarts Library, University of Toronto.

medieval commonplace, but Bale gave it a new twist: the cycles themselves are all variations on the one true biblical chronicle envisaged by St. John in Revelation where the forces of Christ are engaged in spiritual warfare against those of Anti-Christ and are indeed for a time defeated before the gospel truth is finally restored. With these ideas in mind, the dramatic world of his plays interrelates and depicts biblical and historical past with historical present. Thus, the events dramatized in *King John* are foreshadowed by biblical chronicle and anticipate the history of the Reformation. His characters are sharply polarized into representatives of the true Church of Christ and the false Church of Anti-Christ and are typological in the sense that while they may bear the names of biblical or historical personages, they may be perceived as contemporaries as well. The polemical dimension of his plays derives in part from his identifying all the exponents of Anti-Christ with contemporary Roman Catholicism, and all those of Christ with the Reformation. It was therefore possible for him in *The Temptation of Our Lord* to depict Satan not merely as a hermit but as a Catholic priest and Christ as the prototype of the Protestant evangelist who suffers at the hands of a corrupt church, and in *Three Laws* to show the Old Testament Laws of Moses corrupted by a popish doctor and cardinal. Bale's stage typology (popish priests as villains, Protestant preachers as godly counsellors) is a consistent feature of Reformation plays through the 1570s, not to mention much later Elizabethan and Jacobean drama (see figure 13).

Bale's iconoclastic theatre

The notion of the Papacy and Catholic religion as present-day manifestations of Anti-Christ is a persistent feature of Bale's drama, and while one of his purposes is the inculcation of Protestant values, the general thrust of his stage propaganda is directed against the Papacy and the predominantly Catholic customs and attitudes of his popular audience. Recognizing the significance of visual images to Catholic authority (e.g. clerical vestments) and worship (e.g. the sacraments, relics, icons), Bale's most effective weapon is to present those revered images before the spectators only to discredit them by depriving them of their original sacred context, and substituting a profane or diabolical one instead. And in doing this he draws on their prior experience of the Catholic theatre. For example, in medieval drama Catholic priests were commonly represented in the acting place as agents of virtue and repentance who counsel the unregenerate characters in the teachings of the church and mediate between God and man through the offering of the sacraments as the means of salvation. Mercy in *Mankind*, Confession in *Everyman*, and Charity in *Youth*, are three well-known examples of this convention. What Bale does with these traditional stage images of religious truth is to expose them for what they are – mere *images*, without an underlying reality; they are still presented, almost certainly dressed as they would have been in traditional plays, but they are now revealed to be the old "Vices" in disguise. Thus Bale's chief Vices, Infidelity (*Three Laws*) and Sedition (*King Johan*), make their initial appearances as conventional proponents of evil – as Vices – only to turn up later in the action dressed as Catholic clerics. Commenting on his work, the Elizabethan reformer Laurence Humphrey would later say that Bale "tore away the mask that Pope and Popery wore."[76] Actually, in *King Johan* Pope and Popery do not wear the mask; they *are* the mask, the fictions of true religion behind which diablerie and Anti-Christ hide and cozen the public into damnation. Thus, this dramatic inversion of the old Virtues as new Vices gives the satire a double-edge, for it not only identifies the Catholic priesthood as agents of evil, it exposes their duplicitous behavior in masquerading as proponents of religious truth. Bale wants his audience to question their conditioned responses to the external signs of religious truth in an age when competing institutions were laying exclusive claim to it.[77]

Implicit of course in this characterization of Catholic priests as disguised Vices is the notion of them as actors, as recent commentary has observed.[78] This identification of the Catholic priesthood with mimicry was apparently widespread in the Reformation (and during Elizabeth's reign supported the puritan attack on the medium of playing itself). Tyndale compares priests to players and contrasts them with Christ who "is not a hypocrite [who] playeth a part in a play and representeth a person of state which he is not."[79] In similar fashion, Bale's contemporaries Nicholas Udall, Thomas Becon, as well as Archbishop Cranmer, compare hypocritical priests to "jugglers" and medieval Vice characters who deck themselves in game-players' garments.[80] Bale skillfully and extensively exploited the player/priest analogy and the theatrical qualities of Roman Catholic worship in both his prose works and his plays. In *The*

Resurrection of the Masse and other tracts, he compares the movements of the priest celebrating mass to play-acting and juggling. With reference to the Mass-priest, he says "Ffor of all occupacions me thinke / it is the most folish. Ffor there standeth the preste disgysed / lyke one that wolde shewe some conueyaunce or iuglyng playe. He turneth his back to the people / and telleth a tale on the walle in a foren language ..."[81] The plays are equally explicit in describing priests as "dysgysed players," "Layne mummers," "dysgysed shavelynges," and in reenacting Catholic ritual on the stage as hollow scenic spectacle.

In depicting Sedition, the popish Vice of *King Johan*, as an actor who admits that "In every estate of the clergy I play a part" (the roles include monk, nun, friar, bishop, and chantry priest), Bale may have been developing an idea derived from Tyndale's *Parable of the Wicked Mammon* where he states that the nature of Anti-Christ (i.e. Catholicism) is like that of a player: "to go out of the play for a season and to disguise himself, and then to come in again with a new name and a new raiment."[82] Several scenes after his early appearance in the play as the Vice, Sedition does come into the acting place again with a new name and a new raiment, that of a monk named Good Perfection, who is called on by Nobility to hear Confession. The parody of Auricular Confession then begins, following the orthodox procedure, with Sedition donning the stole required by the Church for the Confessor, and seating himself before Nobility. The Confessional, as depicted, is very typical of the times, but of course the context in which it takes place exposes it as a sham.[83] For the Confessor here is a devil, and as we learn a few minutes later, the purpose of the Confession is not to grant forgiveness of sin, but to make Nobility a traitor to the English state and an agent of Anti-Christ. Bale's point is that Confession is not a divinely ordained rite, but an invention of the Catholic Church to gain ideological control over the people and to maintain its authority over the State.

The effects on the audience of the 1530s of displacing the sacraments by depriving them of their original sacred context must have been not entirely unlike the effects of the public exhibitions of images in the marketplace which Cromwell arranged around the time the plays were performed in 1538 and 1539. The most famous of the images was the Rood of Grace at Boxley monastery, which contained a mechanism making the eyes and lips to move simulating sight and speech. The image was the object of widespread adoration in Kent and inspired an annual pilgrimage. However, when the contrivance was discovered by the Henrician authorities during the iconoclastic campaign of 1538, the image was hauled to the marketplace in Maidstone and publicly exhibited as a fake, to the considerable anger of the local population. In a subsequent displaying of the image in London, the public exhibition of the image was followed by a sermon by the Bishop of Rochester, who condemned it before turning it over to the spectators who in turn smashed it to pieces and placed it on a bonfire.[84] Both in these public exhibitions of images and in Bale's iconoclastic treatment of Catholic ceremonies, the shock value derives from changing the physical context – in one instance taking the holy object to the marketplace, in the other reenacting it on a stage – and from the exposure of the rite or image as a meaningless sham. In both cases, an object of holiness is displaced and demystified.

In another scene of *King Johan*, the formal pronouncement of Excommunication, or the Great Curse, with "cross, book, bell, and candle," is applied to King John by Usurped Power, alias the Pope. The ritual involved here is highly theatrical and emblematic, with Usurped Power gesturing with the crucifix to signify the withdrawal of divine grace, closing the Bible to symbolize the deprivation of spiritual benefits, extinguishing the candle to close off God's guiding light, and ringing the bell, to announce impending eternal death and damnation. Again the incongruous context of the ritual holds it up for ridicule and shows it for what Bale thought it was: a piece of good theatre. Bale apparently was not the only Protestant who perceived the Anathema in theatrical terms. According to John Foxe, one Thomas Benet laughed when he saw it publicly pronounced, and then asked, "Who can forbear, seeing such conceits and interludes played by the priests?"[85] To ensure that his audience did not miss the point, the Catholic hierarchy immediately follow this solemn rite with a bit of merrymaking: the Pope suggests a song and Stephen Langton (Sedition in disguise) invites the other Catholic vices to join in. Elsewhere in the play the Litany of the Saints, Prayers for the Dead, Confession, Absolution, and other ritualistic elements, are accompanied by the obscene language and scurrilous behavior of the Catholic Vices.

Bale's parody of the Catholic clergy and of Catholic liturgy, and especially his mixing of sacred rite with vulgar songs and comic buffoonery, is indeed an original feature of his Protestant stage polemic,[86] but on closer investigation one finds a fairly well-developed medieval tradition for this practice in such festivals as the *Festum Stultorum* or *Festum Asinorum* and the *Festum Archiepiscopum Puerorum*, better known as the Feast of Fools and the Feast of the Boy Bishop.[87] In these Christmas festivals of inversion and irreverence, clerical subdeacons (the Feast of Fools) and boy choristers or pupils (the Boy Bishop) dressed up in the clerical apparel of bishops, deans, abbots, and the Pope, mimicking their authority and burlesquing the liturgy and sacraments of the Church.[88] They jangled bells, sang "dissonantly," repeated meaningless words in mockery of the spoken liturgy, ate sausage and played dice at the altar, and presided over mass and censing with smoke from burning old shoes.[89] Anticipating Bale's visual parody of the Pope in *King Johan* by several hundred years, the *dominus festi* in the Feast of Fools was vested in full pontificals, possessed the Pope's seal, and joined in a religious procession. Although the Feast of Fools took place in England only sporadically after the fourteenth century due largely to ecclesiastical censorship,[90] the Boy Bishop festivities remained sufficiently popular during the second quarter of the sixteenth century for its celebration and all ceremonies associated with it to be banned by a Royal Proclamation in 1541 on the grounds of blasphemy and idle superstition.[91] Some indication of how the people reacted to these festivities (and possibly to Bale's irreverent parodies) is found in the diocesan prohibition by Bishop John De Grandisson of Exeter who on December 10, 1360 denounced the Boy Bishop's "detestable parodies of divine worship within the church itself." He states that the people are "drawn away from due devotion by [the participant's] jeering gestures and derisory laughter," and the spectators themselves "are dissolved into disorderly laughter and illicit mirth... the divine worship is mocked and the office is basely hindered (by those things)."[92]

Bale's parody, of course, is used as a subversive weapon to discredit the Church hierarchy and liturgy, and not as a form of innocent merriment or "festive release" from "sacred and tedious ceremonies with which [the performers] were only too painfully familiar,"[93] and which might have been perceived by papal officials (despite their charges of blasphemy) as a means of reaffirming their authority. To be kept in mind is that the relatively unstructured ceremonies and processions of the Feast of Fools are in the mode of "spectacle" rather than stage-play, and therefore lack the moral framework of a typical medieval drama, and certainly lack the deliberate propagandist dimension of Bale's Reformation play. Therefore, the "disorderly laughter and illicit mirth" may have derived more from the incongruity of children and commoners impersonating high church officials than from deliberate ridicule of those officials and orthodox religious practice. And yet, as Wickham and Weimann observe, in addition to its allegedly sacrilegious nature the pageantry of the Feast of Fools and the Boy Bishop often did contain an element of criticism directed against the abuses of institutional authority and against the church hierarchy itself.[94] One of the ideas associated with the Feast of Fools was that of a "primitive Christian state of equality," based on Luke 1:52: "He hath put down the mighty from their seats, and exalted them of low degree," a verse in the *Magnificat* that the subdeacons "shouted at the top of their lungs before they overthrew church office and travestied divine service in what was called *festum subdiaconorum.*"[95] The implication therefore is that bishops, abbots and other highly appointed clergy are really no different from anyone else, a basic premise of the Lollard and later Protestant doctrine of the priesthood of all believers. In *King Johan,* Bale's "impersonated" papist officials might have evoked the same kind of response. The effect of mere rogues and vices impersonating them shows that the only difference between them and members of the audience is the apparel which up to Henry VIII's time entitled them to preferential treatment and separation from the laity as a special privileged class. The disparity between person and high office signified in dress is shown in the Vatican scene in *King Johan* where the Pope is exposed as a buffoon in an unseemly garment (l. 864). Bale's deliberate intention here and elsewhere in the play is to shock his spectators, to force them to reconsider their built-in responses to papal practices, to persuade them to perceive such ceremonies as hollow spectacle, as "game" without "earnest."

Bale's satire of Catholicism's reliance on visual display reflects his typically Protestant distrust of images in religious worship. He would have shared Calvin's view that "Figures are illusory without an explanation" and that whenever "God offered any signe to the holy fathers, there was added an vnseparable knot of doctrine, without which our senses should be made amazed with bare beholding"[96] (see figure 7 and caption). This helps to explain why every scene in every play Bale wrote is accompanied by verbal commentary pointing to the scene's homiletic significance. In contrast to Scripture

through which God directly reveals his will to the elect, truth
mediated through visual means is much more susceptible to abuse
and misunderstanding. For Bale, the nonscriptural visual signs of
Catholic images are purely arbitrary, without eternally fixed
referents, as the papists claimed. As we have already observed, in
Three Laws Bale debunks the tropological significance which the
papists ascribe to visual icons by having Infidelity liken Bishop
Ambition's mitre to the gaping mouth of a wolf (ll. 1181–85).

Notwithstanding Bale's criticism of images, he did not exhibit the
iconophobia of some later Protestant divines under Elizabeth I who
objected to the stage on the grounds that its powerful visual appeal
led to idolatry. Indeed, stage pictures could be a very useful teaching
tool. Like his fellow propagandist under Cromwell's patronage,
Richard Morison, he recognized that "Into the commen people
thynges sooner enter by the eies, then by the eares: remembryng
more better than they see then that they heere," even if this was a
sorry reflection on the state of illiteracy in the country.[97] In all of his
plays, as in all subsequent Reformation drama following his lead,
 visual symbolism is an integral aspect of stagecraft. Perhaps the most
extended example of his use of visual symbolism to convey his
message occurs early in *King Johan* where Sedition and the other
Catholic Vices devise a comic pageant which shows in allegorical
fashion England's corruption by sedition. As director of the pageant,
Sedition orders Dissimulation to enter the acting space first, and to be
followed by Private Wealth, who in turn brings in Usurped Power
(alias the Pope). These three then carry in Sedition. The visual
allegory is explained by Sedition:

> ...fyrst Dyssymulacyon
> Browght in Privat Welth to every Cristen nacyon,
> And that Privat Welth browght in Usurped Powre,
> And he Sedycyon in cytye, towne and tower.
>
> (ll. 793–96)

There may have been an element of parody in the carrying in of
Sedition, who later appears as Bishop Stephen Langton, for bishops
were often carried to the church altar in a formal procession.[98]

Whether Bale's plays did have a major impact on their early
Reformation audience is impossible to substantiate, since hard
evidence is scarce, limited to a few scraps of reported information
such as that found in the Alforde deposition. Yet the plays themselves,

as well as what we know about Bale's connections with Oxford and Cromwell and what we can reasonably assume about his leadership of a professional touring company that apparently toured extensively during the late 1530s, all point to the significance of drama as an agent of Reformation propaganda in Cromwell's administration.

2

The King's Men and other troupes

The Reformation troupe of Bale and his fellows raises the question of what other professional companies were supporting the Protestant cause during the Cromwellian era and the following thirty-five years when overtly religious drama was written and staged. The answer to this question depends in part on the kind of relationship such companies had with their patrons. Following Chambers, theatre historians have tended to see this relationship, at least as it applied to the major noblemen's companies of the Tudor age, as mainly a nominal one.[1] They have observed that a nobleman usually only required the services of his players a few times a year to provide entertainment at Christmas, Shrovetide and Easter, and on important diplomatic occasions, and that for the rest of the year the actors had to fend for themselves by means of performing before popular audiences in London and on tour in the provinces. This led to the troupes' financial independence, the theory goes, which in turn gave them virtual autonomy from their Lord, on whom they relied only for some measure of prestige and for protection when they got into trouble with local authorities.

This argument, at the very least, needs qualification. A large measure of financial independence was certainly possible from the midpoint of Elizabeth's reign onwards when daily performances in the newly established commercial playhouses in London offered noblemen's troupes continuous employment throughout the year and even shareholding in the theatre as a business venture. Yet even then, as a number of scholars have recently shown, major companies had sufficiently close ties with patrons to propagate their political and religious views.[2] Prior to 1576 or so, however, it is questionable whether more than a few highly privileged players in noblemen's troupes could enjoy financial independence by means of playing alone, or anything approaching complete freedom to choose their

42

play texts and touring routes. The fact that many known professional actors in early- and mid-Tudor England, including some of the King's players, also worked as tailors, glaziers, and household servants during their tenures as troupe members, suggests that few could live on and support families as professional entertainers all-year round, and that as retainers of a royal or noble household, they carried out other duties for their Lords when not on tour.[3] It is therefore only in a qualified sense that we may call them "professional." Moreover, recent investigations contend that the repertories and itineraries of at least some major companies were monitored to a great extent by their patrons who recognized drama as a useful public relations vehicle and as a potent means of disseminating their ideological interests to both elite and popular audiences in regions of the country over which they exercised some influence.[4] The conclusions drawn above about both Oxford and Cromwell support this. This is not to say that all stage patrons exercised tight control over their troupes' activities. Surely it varied from one patron to the next. However, when we consider the large number of noblemen's troupes on the road and the fact that after Henry VIII's break with Rome many of those noblemen espoused advanced Protestant views, it seems only reasonable to question whether some of these troupes in addition to Oxford's and Cromwell's were promoting or at least reflecting Protestant religious opinions.

The present chapter will begin by observing what contemporaries had to say about the link between players and the dissemination of Protestant teaching. Their opinions, I will proceed to show, find substance in the activities of the King's Men at the court of Edward VI. The remainder of the discussion will investigate other professional troupes engaged in Protestant stage propaganda in Edwardian, Marian, and early Elizabethan England.

Playing companies and the Protestant ministry

That playing companies did contribute in a significant way to advance the Reformation cause is indicated in contemporary comment by both Protestant supporters and their adversaries. Bale was surely thinking of troupes in addition to his own when in exile in 1544 he attacked Henry VIII's reactionary administration for tolerating the Catholic stage but suppressing players of interludes who persuaded "the people to worship theyr Lorde God aryght,

accordyng to hys holie lawes and not your own, and to acknoledge
Jesus Chryst for their onely redeemer and saviour, without your
lowsie legerdemains."[5] John Foxe, commenting on Bishop Stephen
Gardiner's written protest to Protector Somerset against Protestant
propaganda on the stage and in the pulpit, considered players
important enough in effecting religious change to group them with
preachers and printers as the divinely-appointed "triple Bulwark
against the triple crown of the Pope, to bring him down."[6] Even
under Queen Mary, players of interludes were singled out for
propagating Protestant doctrine in the Proclamation of August 18,
1553 and in a Catholic propagandist tract of the following year by
John Christopherson, Marian Bishop of Chichester, who regarded
players as adept "as false preachers ... in the pulpet" in furthering
heresy and in "defacing of all rites, ceremonies, and all the whole
order, used in the administration of the Sacraments."[7] Christopherson would have been in a good position to assess the threat they
represented to Mary's government; he himself was a highly
skilled writer of religious drama. Proof of his claims is found in a Privy
Council letter of 1556 to the President of the North, the Earl of
Shrewsbury, instructing him to suppress "the servaunts unto Sr
Frauncis Leek" who "wandered abowt the North partes, and
represented certaine playes and enterludes, conteyning very naughty
and seditious matter touching the King and Quene's Ma[jesty] and
the state of the realme, and to the sla[n]uder of Christe's true and
Catholik religion, contrary to all good ordre, and to the manifest
contempt of Allmighty God, and daungerous example to others."[8]
Catholic writers continued to protest against what Abbot John de
Feckenham called "the preachers and scaffold players of this new
religion" after Elizabeth came to the throne.[9] Thomas Dorman's *A
Provfe of Certeyne Articles*, published in 1564, attacks the work of the
reformers and identifies playing companies as an important means of
propagating the gospel: "I passe ouer here insilence the infamouse
companie of common minstrelles and entrelude plaiers, who be all
brothers of your fraternitie, membres of youre corporation, and in so
good credite emongest youw, that they haue their charge of
dispensing the worde as well as yow."[10] What is of particular
significance is that these commentators do not (as we tend to do
today) set playing apart from other modes of discourse commonly
used for propaganda purposes such as preaching and print. It may
have been a love for mimetic entertainment and for drama as a

traditional holiday pastime that attracted popular audiences to performances by professional players, but it is clear from the statements of Bale, Wylley, Foxe, Christopherson, and Dorman that in these politically charged times they were perceived, as were travelling musicians, as disseminators of Protestant doctrine working in conjunction with the ministries of preaching and publishing to advance the Reformation. A marginal note accompanying the above passage by Dorman makes this point explicitly: "Minstrelles and players [are] chief ministres in publishing the nevve ghospell."

Unfortunately, specific information about these troupes is difficult to come by. All we know about the majority of them is the name of their noble or city patron (for town corporations also sponsored troupes), and some of the venues where they performed. In most instances, very little or nothing can be substantiated concerning their repertories. If the extant Protestant interludes designed for professional troupes are in any way representative of scripts in those repertories, they are only in a few instances helpful in linking plays to particular troupes, since (unlike so many prose works) the surviving texts do not contain dedications or prayers to patrons, with the exception of the Queen and "her council," who are conventionally addressed at the conclusion of several works.

During the Henrician Reformation, we know that boy choristers and other students were performing Protestant drama (see chapter 4) but little evidence for specific professional troupes other than Bale's own has survived. One troupe possibly was the Lord Warden's Players, performing in the service of Arthur Plantagenet, Viscount Lisle, and Warden of the Cinque Ports from 1536 to 1542. This troupe was among the best-travelled companies of Henry VIII's reign, touring the South of England from Dover to Bristol. Lord and Lady Lisle were associated with pietistic circles, perhaps from the early 1530s when Lady Lisle developed ties with Anne Boleyn.[11] Lady Lisle's interest in ecclesiastical matters becomes evident in her correspondence with John Husee, her agent in London, in the autumn of 1538, the same year the Lord Warden's players acted at court before Cromwell for 20 shillings. At that time she dispatched Husee to purchase "an interlude which is called Rex Diabole," among the "new Scripture matter," along with costumes suitable for the piece, apparently for staging at the Staple Inn, the Plantagenet residence in Calais, where Lord Lisle was governer.[12] Since the Lord Warden's Players were performing along the coast of southeast

England in 1538/39, with stops at Lydd, Sandwich, and New Romney, they would not have had to travel far from their usual touring route to make the trip from Dover across the Channel to Calais, and it seems reasonable to assume that they included *Rex Diabole* in their repertory for subsequent performances in Faversham, Dover, Folkestone, among other towns in Kent during the early 1540s.[13]

The King's Men and anti-papal revels at Edward VI's court

Besides Bale's troupe, however, the only other professional company for which we can draw some confident conclusions about personnel, itinerary, and at least a partial repertory of Reformation-oriented plays is the King's Men during their career under Edward VI. A close look at this troupe, made possible by the rich source of information supplied by the Loseley manuscripts and related court documents, has the added benefit of providing a glimpse into the staunchly Protestant – and more specifically anti-papal – revels at the court of Edward VI and the agencies involved in regulating and producing those revels. The King's Men or "Kynges maiesties pleyers," who had been on the Crown payroll and had toured extensively since the reign of Henry VII, received under Edward VI a fixed annual reward from the royal chamber, usually on New Year's day, of £6.13s.4d, plus an additional wage of £3.6s.8d. per year for each member, and the regular livery assigned to yeomen officers of the royal household.[14] The troupe is specifically identified in the Revels accounts for four performances before the court at Westminster and Greenwich during King Edward's reign. They nevertheless certainly performed far more frequently than these documents indicate, especially since few detailed accounts of the Privy Purse, which funded royal entertainments, have survived.[15] They were able to supplement their annual income by touring the provinces, probably with their court repertory, and are on record for over twenty appearances during Edward's reign, mostly in the eastern and southeastern counties.[16] The size of the troupe seems to have fluctuated during the course of the reign. A list of September 30, 1552 gives us the names of six members: George Birch, Richard Coke, John Birch, Henry Harriot, Richard Skinner, Thomas Southey. A seventh member, John Browne, received a warrant on June 9, 1552, and apparently replaced Robert Hinstock, the former leading player whose acting career at court began under Henry VIII.[17] This suggests a seven-member troupe, which is consistent with the casting requirements of a play about a seven-headed dragon performed by the King's Men at Shrovetide 1549. However, as few as five members are listed in a warrant of 1548, while eight are numbered in the annual fee-lists, which, as Chambers observes, are unreliable in determining the troupe's size.[18]

While at court, like the other players on the Crown payroll, the Gentlemen and Children of the Chapel Royal, the King's Men worked closely with the Privy Chamber, on the one hand, and the Revels Office on the other, in choosing and producing plays. There is little doubt that the young King, who wrote one play and performed a role in at least one other, had, like his father, a direct hand in determining the kinds of entertainments performed at court, and that the preponderance of anti-papal plays evidenced in the Revels accounts complied with his wishes. The Revels documents indicate that final decisions and plans for court revels were made in the Privy Chamber, with a warrant signed by several of the privy counsellors dispatched by the Lord Chamberlain or one of his deputies to the Revels Office giving instructions. Thus, on Christmas day 1551, Thomas Cawarden, the Master of the Revels, received the following warrant:

After our hartie comendacions. Theis be to require you to delyver to the bringer hereof one of the Kinges maiesties pleyers out of the store in your charge, soche apparrell and other fornyture as theye shall have nede of, for their playeing before the kinges maiestie this Christmas taking order with them for the save garde therof as you shall thinke conveniente. So fare you well ffrom Grenewiche on christmas Daye A 1551.

                                        your loving frendes
            [endorsed]   winchester, Northumberland, I bedford
                                        Penbroke, T. darcy
                                        w Cecyll[19]

Cawarden, appointed the first Master of the Revels on March 11, 1544 by royal patent, exercised more control over court pastimes than this warrant might suggest. In addition to reorganizing the Revels Office and functioning as its efficient chief administrator until 1559 (he died shortly after arranging the new Queen's coronation festivities), he is praised by contemporaries as artistically inclined and a skillful deviser of entertainments, who hired, advised, and coordinated the large army of persons involved in writing scripts,

6   The Dragon with seven heads and ten horns, a woodcut by Lucas Cranach for
Luther's September Bible, Revelation 12. This woodcut presents a popular image of
the Pope as Anti-Christ. Courtesy of the British Library.

making costumes, designing and constructing sets, transporting these materials from the Revels Office to the court and back again, and performing in the productions.[20] No less significantly, he was a committed Protestant who was accused of heresy in 1544 for protecting Protestant dissidents (during Henry VIII's reactionary period), suspected of complicity in Wyatt's rebellion in 1554, and imprisoned on two occasions for suspected treason during Mary's reign before being restored to favor by Queen Elizabeth whom he had earlier supported and befriended.[21] Along with the King and the Privy Council, therefore, he may help account for the pro-Protestant and virulently anti-Catholic character of so many productions staged at the Edwardian court, several of which involved the King's Men.

Until the last year of Henry VIII's reign, only one play, a "Moralite" at the Scottish court in 1503, can be identified in the repertory of the King's Men. In 1546, however, they performed a moral interlude, *The Market of Mischief*, at Norwich, and from 1547 to 1553, they are recorded in the Revels accounts and mentioned in other documents for rehearsing or performing several works: a play requiring an oven and weapons of wood at Shrovetide 1548, an interlude requiring a seven-headed dragon at Shrovetide 1549, *The play of Aesop's Crow* in 1551, and *The play of Self-love* around the same time.[22] Two of these works indicate anti-Catholic themes. The dragon with the seven heads in the 1549 Shrovetide play performed at Westminster undoubtedly refers to the seven-headed dragon described in Revelation 12 and 17, which during the Reformation was a widely disseminated image of the Pope in the role of Anti-Christ (see figure 6).[23] For this work, Cawarden's tailors made costumes for a king, six priests (wearing albs and surplices) and seven hermits, as well as a dragon of seven heads "with all necessaries."[24] Since doubling was a widespread practice among professional troupes of four to eight players of the time, it is reasonable to infer that six of the King's Men doubled the parts of priests and hermits (probably as alternating virtue and vice figures),[25] with a seventh actor (perhaps the leading player) taking the part of the king and also doubling as a hermit.

The play of Aesop's Crow, which William Baldwin observes was under rehearsal by the King's Men during the 1552/53 Christmas season with disputing animal characters, also appears to have been polemical.[26] This is arguably the anti-papal play "Of crows in the habits of Cardinals, of asses habited as Bishops, and of

7 The Whore of Babylon (with triple-crown) and the Beast with seven heads, a woodcut by Lucas Cranach for Luther's September Bible, Revelation 17. Note the assembly of people, including a king, a cleric, and several commoners, who gaze worshipfully at the dazzling figures of the beast and its gorgeously attired rider: clearly an instance of Protestant art as iconoclasm. Courtesy of the British Library.

wolves representing Abbots,'' that was subsequently staged before
Queen Elizabeth on January 6, 1559, and evidently also performed
by the King's Men and produced by the Revels Office during
Cawarden's final year as Master.[27] Be that as it may, there is other
evidence that points to its controversial nature. Citing a passage in
The Acts and Monuments where Foxe compares the Roman rite to the
crow in Aesop and Horace whose plumage was a counterfeit
assortment of artificial feathers pieced together from various sources,
Lily B. Campbell has contended that *Aesop's Crow* depicts a
staged debate between talking animals to satirize the Eucharist at a
time when the revisions of the second Book of Common Prayer were
under debate in Parliament.[28] Campbell's theory becomes all the
more plausible when we observe that such rough animal imagery is
associated with religious quarrels throughout Tudor drama, the most
notorious instance being the scurrilous "mock mass" witnessed by
Queen Elizabeth at Hinchenbrook in 1564 in which a Marian bishop
is depicted as a dog with the Host in his mouth.[29] Moreover, such
titles as William Turner's *The Huntyng of the Romishe Fox* (1543) and
Bale's *Yet a Course at the Romyshe Foxe* (1543) demonstrate further that
the beast fable itself, either staged or written, was a popular mid-
century means of satirizing the Papacy. These works derive from the
Roman de Renard tradition in which the fox, the ape, and various birds,
are shown in religious guise or pose to satirize the hypocrisy, guile,
vanity and greed, of the Roman clergy (see figure 8).[30]

Needless to say, the King's Men hardly earned their annual wages
by performing only four plays at court over the course of Edward VI's
five year reign. It is probable that they performed on their own or
participated with the Chapel players in many of the productions
recorded in the Revels accounts for Christmastide, Shrovetide, and
other occasions during this period. It was mentioned earlier that the
interlude of "the Dragon with Seven heades" performed by the
King's Men at Shrovetide 1548 called for seven actors. This same
number of actors is evidently required for an undated Protestant
interlude on the seven deadly sins described in a Revels Office
document. In a series of horizontal columns, the document shows the
following: (1) "A kinge ... honour with wisdome ... A woman with to
faces and in eache hand a glas ... pride, A pope; (2) A knighte in
harnes ... knightehoode with Loialtie ... A woman with a payre of
ballance ... wrath, A bisshopp; (3) A Iudge ... Iustice with Mersie ...
envie, A fryer; (4) A precher ... Religeon with Goddes worde ... A

woman with a bible in her armes ... couetus, A fryer; (5) A Scholler ... Science with Reason ... glotonye, A Sole preste; (6) A seruinge man ... Servise with affexion ... lecherye; (7) Labour with diligence ... labour a woman with many handes ... Slothe. Below these seven columns is another series which seems to be a revision of the dramatis personae:

honour	wisdome	pride	A pope
Knightehoode	loialltie	wrath	A bisshoppe
Iustice	mercye	enuie	A ffryer
Religeon	Scripture	couetous	A person
Science	Reason	glotonye	A Sole preste
Seruys	affexion	letcherye	A Muncke
labour	diligence	Slothe	An hermett[31]

It would seem that *The Seven Deadly Sins* is best suited for seven actors each doubling two or three parts each. It would also seem that it uses the technique, first evident in Bale's *King Johan*, of having an actor represent a particular vice (e.g. pride) in the costume of a Catholic cleric (e.g. the Pope).[32] The play may indeed be Bale's own *On the Seven Sins* (*De Septem Peccatis*), one of the fourteen plays he composed for the Earl of Oxford in the early- to mid-thirties,[33] which may have been performed at court during this earlier period and retained among the Revels documents under Edward VI. If *The Seven Deadly Sins* implemented the doubling pattern observed above, then it would have been unsuited to the players of the Chapel Royal, whose large casts of twelve and more actors made doubling an infrequent practice. During King Edward's reign, three other companies of professional players were paid from the Privy Purse for performances, the troupes of the Duke of Somerset, the Duke of Suffolk, and the Marquis of Northampton,[34] but none of these are mentioned in the surviving Revels Office papers. It is a reasonable speculation, therefore, that this play designed for a professional troupe was meant for the King's Men.

Among the other court spectacles they may have participated in

---

8   Mitred Fox Bishop preaching to birds and rabbits, displaying cowl, chasuble, and crosier, a carved bench end, Brent Knoll. The rather squat mitre, with its distinct appearance of a gaping mouth, reminds the viewer of what the hypocritical fox's true intentions are in assembling this congregation. Photograph by J. C. D. Smith. Courtesy of Leicester University Press.

was an anti-papal interlude performed at Westminster on Shrovetide Tuesday February 22, 1547, shortly after Edward VI's coronation. The Revels Office supplied costumes for the "bishop of Rome," cardinals, priests, friars, and a prophet or king.[35] Some of the garments (including one for a priest) evidently were made for young King Edward himself and for the young Duke of Suffolk and Lord Strange. Streitberger has recently suggested that some of the other costumes were assigned to the King's Men, although it is equally plausible that the Children and Gentlemen of the Chapel performed in the production.[36] This Shrovetide play was possibly an adaptation of *The Bishop of Rome*, a prose drama by the Italian reformer Bernardino Ochino, who came to England in 1547, and translated by Bishop John Ponet in 1549. The following Christmas, another piece of anti-papal propaganda was shown requiring an elaborate "Tower of Babylon," constructed in the Revels Office at Blackfriars and shipped upstream to Hampton Court for the occasion.[37] Carwarden had the tower designed by architectural artist Robert Trunkey, under the direction of Nicholas of Modena, the celebrated international architect.[38] Whether this interlude was King Edward's own *De meretrice Babylonica* (*The Whore of Babylon*) is not clear,[39] but the title points to a familiar Reformation theme (see figure 7). From Luther to Heinrich Bullinger, the Zurichian Reformer who was so influential in Edwardian England, Babylon signified Rome, and the infamous Tower of Babel or Babylon (as it was also known), which presumptuously rose to the heavens and housed pagan images and ceremonial objects for worship, was a powerful prophetic image of the Roman Catholic Church in full decadence and likewise destined for destruction.[40] Unfortunately, we know next to nothing about the dramatis personae or the costuming of *The Tower of Babylon*, only that the King's interluders, along with the players of the Chapel Royal, received their annual reward around the time it was performed. It is also not certain whether the royal players participated in the spectacular festivities surrounding the Lord of Misrule (played by George Ferrers, future co-author of the *Mirror for Magistrates*) during the Christmas seasons of 1551/52 and 1552/53, in which costumes for friars and a "serpente with sevin heddes called hidra" appear once again in the records, although it seems likely that they did.[41] We may recall that it was during the 1552/53 Christmastide that *Aesop's Crow* was under rehearsal, and Ferrers may have had a hand in its composition, since Baldwin reports that he and Ferrers were together at court at that time "setting forth of certain interludes, which for the King's recreation we had devised and were in learning."[42]

Among the Revels papers, scraps of information have survived regarding two other plays apparently intended for performance at court. "Parte of a play," or so-called in a note in Cawarden's own handwriting, is a 118 line fragment expounding Calvinist theological ideas relating to grace and charity (and in this respect is reminiscent of Lewis Wager's contemporary *Mary Magdalene*). Since no speech prefixes are noted, it is difficult to determine whether the piece is from a dramatic dialogue or a play. Its untheatrical nature suggests that it belongs to a dialogue, perhaps one among several recorded for performance before the King and his court. A memorandum in one of the Revels Office books indicates another court play with the following dramatis personae:

scoler	vertue zele
gent.	Insolens diligens
preste	old blynd Custom
prentes of London	Hunger of Knowledge
Colyer	Thomas of Croyden

This play, presumably intended for five actors, has been identified as *Old Custome*, a copy of which is listed in an "inventory of effects" for 1545–50 belonging to the Earl of Warwick, later the Duke of Northumberland.[43] This would suggest that the piece was performed at court by Warwick's own players who are on record for several provincial performances during Edward VI's reign,[44] but for none at court. Of course the King's Men might have staged *Old Custom*, since the Office of the Revels seems only to have prepared costumes and scenery for the Crown companies, the King's Men and the Chapel Royal Players, and since court records suggest that the number of actors in the King's troupe may have varied from year to year. At one point, for example, a warrant from Thomas Darcy, the Lord Chamberlain, commands Cawarden to give John Birch and John Browne, and three other of the "kinges entrelude players," garments for a play on the eve of Twelfth Night 1551.[45]

The King's Men, then, contributed to Protestant stage propaganda in the court of Edward VI, and it seems probable that the repertory of plays taken on tour included *Aesop's Crow*, *The Dragon with the Seven Heads*, as well as *The Seven Deadly Sins* which we may confidently ascribe to them on the basis of doubling for seven actors.

All of these plays seem to have disseminated the continuing anti-papal policy of Edward's Protestant administration. The simulated dragon, perhaps made with masks, hoops and canvas,[46] would have posed little difficulty transporting, and for the other plays an elaborate set of costumes appears to have been the major demand for staging, but no more problematic than what Bale and his fellows faced in putting on *King Johan* or *Three Laws*. All these materials would have been manageable with a small wagon, if not by horseback. While they continued to tour during Queen Mary's reign and to draw fees and livery allowances from the Crown, the King's players are not rewarded again for a court appearance until the outset of Elizabeth's reign, probably for the anti-papal farce of January 1559 mentioned above. This, apparently, was their last performance at Westminster, although they toured extensively during the sixties and early seventies when, as Chambers speculates, they were permitted to dwindle away as members retired or died.[47] What new plays they took on is not known, but the unattached interludes surviving from the 1560s and early 1570s are probably representative of their repertory.

Patronage, regulation, and other troupes

At the outset of Edward VI's reign, the King's Men were probably one among many professional troupes encouraged by the government to perform plays advancing the Reformation. With its upper and lower houses controlled by radical Protestants in 1547, Parliament repealed not only Henry VIII's reactionary Six Articles Act of 1539 but the autocratic measures of the 1543 "Act for the Advauncement of true Religion" prohibiting interludes and printed matter meddling with "interpretacions of scripture, contrary to the doctryne set forth or to be set forth by the kynges maiestie."[48] It was this statute which Bale so bitterly opposed in his outburst against Henry's administration quoted earlier. The numerous Protestant and virulently anti-papal plays that either survive or are known to have been written and staged in Edwardian England, along with reports of their popularity, demonstrate that the effect was immediate and far-reaching.[49] Two years later in 1549, the Act of Uniformity's prohibition of plays dissenting from the Prayer Book would have protected Reformation drama in line with official policy while forbidding Catholic plays (in conjunction with the banning of Corpus Christi day and related festivities in the previous year) and the more radical seditious drama, such as the one which occasioned Kett's rebellion in the summer of 1549 and led to a prohibition of all interludes throughout the realm for two months.[50]

By 1550 one may discern the administration's recognition that some kind of centralized system needed to be devised and implemented to regulate troupe playing. Scripts and performances now had to be approved by the Privy Council itself, according to the Proclamation of April 28, 1551, with Secretaries William Cecil, William Petre and Thomas Smith, in charge of licensing play texts, as part of the Crown's policy of licensing printed works in general introduced in 1549.[51] It may have been merely coincidental, but three months prior to the April 1551 Proclamation, King Edward had received a copy of Martin Bucer's *De Regno Christi* in which the influential Strasbourg reformer sketched in broad outline a plan for regulating drama, whereby officials knowledgeable in theatrical matters and possessing "a constant zeal for Christ's kingdom" should be appointed to determine the suitability of plays for performance in a Christian commonwealth.[52] John King has shown that Cecil was the chief licensing official and patron of print propaganda during Edward's reign,[53] and the fact that the case of a forged license of a playing company was assigned to him for judgment in 1552 suggests that in addition to approving play texts he might have handled theatrical affairs nationwide for the court.[54] Certainly he was involved in coordinating stage propaganda at the outset of Elizabeth's reign, possibly even writing "arguments" for plays, as we shall see shortly.

In a nation without a standing army or an effective method of monitoring or policing cultural events, a system of regulation in which all play texts were to be perused, censored, and approved by the Crown before performances would be permitted could not possibly have been enforced throughout the realm. Yet this policy seems to have revived Cromwell's attempt to bring the popular stage fully under centralized control as a means of suppressing seditious plays and gatherings, and for the purpose of using it to its own advantage in shaping public opinion. By licensing play texts and performances from the court, the administration could determine to at least some degree not only what would be performed but who would do the performing. Naturally, at a time when professional companies were fast replacing civic drama in London and the

provinces, troupes patronized by noblemen loyal to the Crown would
be best suited to staging approved plays. It stands to reason that in
addition to the King's Men, Protestant stage propaganda was carried
out by such companies as the Duke of Somerset's Men,[55] the Lord
Admiral's Men (they may have performed *Old Custom*, as noted
above), and the Marquis of Dorset's Men, who are recorded for
playing *Zacheus* at the Norwich guildhall in 1551 and who may
have performed plays by Richard Radcliffe, one-time tutor to
Dorset's children and prolific writer of Protestant polemical plays.[56]
It was noted earlier that several of these troupes performed at King
Edward's court.

Despite reports that some Protestant-oriented players managed to
perform controversial religious drama well into Queen Mary's reign,
by the mid-fifties a policy of active suppression was underway, as the
case of Sir Francis Leek's troupe demonstrates (see p. 44, above).
With Elizabeth I's coming to the throne in late 1558, however, the
Revels accounts at court, state papers, and various other documents,
indicate that pro-Protestant and anti-papist entertainments were
once again popular from the court to the streets, taverns, and hostels
of London and other cities. We have already noted that during the
Christmas revels of 1559/60 at Westminster the Queen witnessed an
elaborate spectacle debunking Catholic prelates as crows, asses, and
wolves. Foreign ambassadors reported that in London itself the Mass
was mocked, priests derided, and Catholic heads of state satirized in
plays and processions in the streets.[57] The practice spread to other
cities, such as Canterbury, Ipswich, and Shrewsbury, where city
corporations, churches and schools staged plays denouncing every-
thing Catholic and reviving the advanced Protestantism of Edward
VI's reign.[58]

As spontaneous as many of these events might have been, there is
also clear evidence that they were encouraged, and in some instances
organized, by officials at the highest level of government as part of a
nationwide programme of propaganda, headed by Thomas Cromwell's most able successor as Secretary of State, William Cecil. That
Cecil was actively involved in patronizing stage polemic in the early
years is indicated in a letter from the Duke of Feria to King Philip of
Spain dated April 29, 1559. After reporting his protest to the Queen
of plays containing religious attacks against Spain, Feria states, "I
knew that a member of her Council had given the arguments to
construct these comedies, which is true, for Cecil gave them, as

indeed she partly admitted to me."[59] Previously as Secretary and Licenser of the Press under Edward VI, Cecil would have had plenty of experience reading Protestant playscripts which were submitted to his desk along with books for licensing and censorship. A sharp memory would have had little difficulty recalling the contents of such works when they might prove suitable under new circumstances such as those celebrating the restoration of a Protestant monarch to the English throne. As the leading official in the Privy Council, which gave its signed permission of all royal entertainments, he likely approved the anti-papal beast fable at Christmas in 1559 (possibly having seen it as *Aesop's Crow* in 1551), as well as other works espousing strong Protestant principles shown before the Queen, from *Gorboduc* in 1562 to *Ezechias* and the Hinchenbrook farce attacking Transubstantiation in 1564, the latter two performed by the students of Cambridge where Cecil served as Lord Chancellor.[60]

If we are to assess the continuing role of professional playing troupes in disseminating Protestant doctrine during the 1560s and early 1570s, we must first discuss the legislative apparatus regulating drama during this period. Additionally, some consideration must be given to the surviving play texts which constitute the most explicit evidence of the patronage and practice of stage propaganda by professional troupes, although detailed attention to troupe repertories will be reserved for discussion in the next chapter. Interestingly enough, both early Elizabethan stage legislation and play texts have been cited as evidence that state-sponsored stage propaganda of a Protestant bias rapidly declined or ceased to exist altogether at the popular level after the opening years of the reign. An often cited piece of legislation is the Proclamation of April 7, 1559 prescribing that licenses not be granted to plays dealing with matters of religion or the governance of the state. This was apparently drafted by the Queen herself, under pressure from foreign dignitaries offended by plays attacking the Papacy and Catholic monarchs.[61] That this prohibition was not seriously enforced, however, is clear from a letter by the Spanish ambassador as late as 1562 who reported that he was tired of complaining to the Queen of the continuing output of insulting books, farces and songs, despite her promise to put a stop to them.[62] As Harold Gardiner observes, " the establishment of the law [of 1559] was an easy method by which authority could apparently disown an activity which it was in reality favoring."[63] Ironically, the Proclamation of 1559, in its later form of May 16 may have helped to protect Protestant drama promoting the national religious policy. For the very officials it appointed to license and monitor plays for performance, noblemen sponsoring touring troupes, and Mayors and Justices of the Peace in the provincial towns and municipalities, were, in many instances, progressive Protestants themselves interested in advancing the cause of religious reform. This was certainly the case of the local magistracy in such cities as Ipswich, Canterbury, Chelmsford, and Leicester, and it is also true of the patrons of some of the nation's leading noblemen's troupes, as will be seen shortly.[64]

Some scholars, nevertheless, contend that the extant play texts of the sixties and early seventies demonstrate that the prohibitive measures outlined in the 1559 legislation were enforced. For example, Norman Sanders in the second volume of *The Revels History of Drama in English*, published in 1980, states that during the 1560s "there is a general shift in play content away from religious doctrine and towards problems arising from the economic and social changes of the first twelve years of Elizabeth's reign."[65] The evidence, however, does not bear this out. Plays dealing explicitly with theological and ecclesiastical issues were printed or written for performance by professional troupes throughout the sixties and well into the seventies. They include Lewis Wager's *Mary Magdalene*, printed in 1564, a play that draws entire passages on religious doctrine from Calvin's *Institutes* (see appendix B); *The Tide Tarrieth No Man*, printed in 1576 and one of the few plays supporting Presbyterian reforms; and *New Custom* (printed 1573), an interlude dealing with the controversial issue of church vestments.[66] Furthermore, while it is true that some plays such as *Enough is as Good as a Feast* and *All for Money* deal with social and economic issues, like countless contemporary sermons and other religious works by such Calvinist preachers as Crowley, Pilkington, and Gilby (which, by the way, were also subject to censorship for controversial content), they are more concerned with the spiritual implications of wealth and social conduct than they are with temporary, this-worldly solutions to such problems. Another reason given for the rapid decline of Protestant drama during the early sixties is a changed attitude towards drama *per se* by returning Marian exiles of a Calvinist persuasion.[67] Yet the same year that Edmund Grindal made his famous rebuke of popular drama to William Cecil (1564) was also the year that *Mary Magdalene* appeared in print, a Calvinist interlude which in its Prologue offers the first known defense of the stage in a play by an English dramatist. As I have argued elsewhere, there were Calvinists who defended the stage ✓ and Calvinists who opposed it in Elizabethan England.[68] It is of course possible, as Chambers maintained, that while these plays were written and found their way into print, they probably were not actually performed.[69] This view has now been fully discounted by such stage historians as T. W. Craik, David Bevington, Glynne Wickham, Richard Southern and Alan Dessen, who have praised their theatricality. As we shall see in the next chapter, it is a serious misjudgment to dismiss them as "anachronisms of a disappearing tradition, lacking a vital audience and written largely by well-wishing clergymen who were out of touch with the times."[70]

Of the fourteen early Elizabethan plays (1558–76) which Bevington has characterized as "popular" in the sense of being intended for professional touring troupes playing before popular audiences, ten are overtly Protestant religious interludes.[71] Some of these plays probably were staged by small bands of players often licensed and patronized by city corporations and other civic institutions. Civic and ecclesiastical records show that there were many such troupes in early Elizabethan England, either bearing the name of the chief player or the name of the city from which they originated. Reference has already been made to one of these troupes: "the plaiers Peter moone and his co[m]panie" performing before the Ipswich Corporation in 1561, possibly Bale's *King Johan*. Since Moone, an artisan by trade, had written Edwardian verse pamphlets promoting the Reformation and attacking the "olde customes" of the Papacy, it is reasonable to suppose that he wrote plays for the company he managed. Other artisan troupes and players associated with civic companies appear to have been popular in London, notably during the early 1540s.[72]

Yet, most of the extant popular or "troupe" interludes of the Tudor period, religious and nonreligious alike, appear to be of noble auspices and performed by noblemen's troupes. In her recent investigation of Tudor household revels and playing companies, Suzanne R. Westfall argues that the surviving interludes of early- and mid-Tudor England were written by chaplains and choirmasters associated with noble families and that they appeal for the most part to the domestic, social and political interests of those noble households. It was then at the bidding or with the support of the noble patron, who retained the troupe's playscripts within his possession, that such interludes subsequently found their way into print.[73] One might add, in the light of "Bale and his felowes," that with the advent of the Reformation and Cromwell's propaganda policy of reaching a broad public audience through all channels of communication, noblemen's troupes gave increased emphasis to appealing to both nobles and commoners, and that the many printed Protestant interludes "offered for acting" indicate an "effort to place topical plays in the hands of itinerant troupes for performance before popular audiences."[74]

There is both internal and external evidence to support the notion that noblemen's troupes appealed to mixed audiences of nobles and commoners. We have already observed this to be true of Bale's plays and it is also typical of professional Reformation drama of the early Elizabethan period. Consider Lewis Wager's *Mary Magdalene*, which portrays its heroine as a child of noble upbringing – early on in the play we hear of her childhood in the castle of Magdalene. Like many other youth plays of the time, Wager's interlude offers a lesson to noble audiences on how to raise a child in a godly way. At the same time, the play is a dramatized sermon on the nature of religious conversion from a distinctly Calvinist perspective, which applies to any spectator, regardless of his/her social class. External evidence for this mixed audience is found in a eyewitness account of a Protestant moral interlude performed by a travelling nobleman's company and seen before a popular audience in the guildhall at Gloucester about 1570. R. Willis reports that in the play he saw there as a child, *The Cradle of Security*, a prince represented the wicked of the world, three lady acquaintances impersonated the vices of pride, covetousness and luxury, who drew him away from hearing godly sermons and good counsel, and two old men who revealed his spiritual damnation signified the end of the world and the last judgment. Like these other interludes, *The Cradle of Security*'s characters are drawn from an aristocratic household, and yet the play has a universal religious message applicable to spectators of all classes in the Gloucester guildhall.[75]

Elizabethan Protestant patronage of the stage: the Earl of Leicester

We have now reached the point where we may consider *which* early Elizabethan noblemen's companies would have been most likely to have performed these plays. Although I am confident that many noblemen's companies, like the one Willis witnessed at Gloucester, were engaged in performing similar Protestant interludes, naming specific troupes is mostly guesswork since little hard evidence exists. As mentioned earlier, all we know about the majority of noblemen's troupes, over forty of which can be identified between 1558 and 1580, is the name of their noble patron and some of the venues they performed in.

Having said that, it is interesting to note that three of the leading patrons of touring companies during the 1560s and early 70's were also at the forefront of Protestant propaganda during these years: the Duchess of Suffolk, the Earl of Warwick and the Earl of Leicester. All three protected and supported advanced Protestant preachers, pamphleteers and printers, engaged in producing works treating the same ecclesiastical and theological issues as those found in the moral interludes.[76] Is it not reasonable to suppose, therefore, that when the company of one of these nobles appeared before him or her at the household revels held at Christmas and Easter a moral interlude reflecting the patron's religious interests would be presented, and that subsequently it would have been included in the troupe's touring repertory for performances in provincial towns across the realm?[77]

This, I believe, to have been almost certainly the case with the Earl of Leicester's Men. Leicester himself was a keen advocate of drama, directly involved in producing it on several occasions. At the Inns of Court for Christmas, 1561, and in the royal court in the summer of 1572, he was put in charge of organizing plays, masques, and other entertainments, and of course his festivities in honor of the Queen at Kenilworth in the summer of 1575 formed the most celebrated royal visit of the entire reign.[78] We may also be assured that he was responsible for securing an exclusive license for his company to perform in London in 1574, an example of his protection and support which dated back to 1559 when he requested permission from the Earl of Shrewsbury for his players to tour in the North of England. That Leicester was not beyond using the stage to advance his own interests was demonstrated in a performance by the players of Gray's Inn which he arranged at Whitehall before the Queen in March 1565. The play centered on a debate between Juno and Diana on the question of marriage, with Jupiter's verdict in favor of matrimony. According to De Silva, the Spanish ambassador, the Queen turned to him and said, "This is all against me."[79] In the light of this, and in the light of his probable role in bringing *Gorboduc* to the royal court in

1562 to lecture the Queen on politics, it is reasonable to suppose that Leicester either commissioned or encouraged his professional company to promote his ideological views in their plays, for performance not only before him on festive and diplomatic occasions in his residences at Leicester House in London's Strand, Wanstead, and Kenilworth, but also while touring the Midlands and eastern counties, where the Earl had extensive connections among local magistrates who approved performances in their guildhalls.

Regrettably, not a single play can be certainly ascribed to Leicester's Men prior to 1573.[80] Between that year and 1584 the Revels accounts record some eight plays on classical and romantic themes for performance before the Queen who by this point found religious polemics tiresome and distasteful, and when Leicester may have been maneuvering for the prized office of the Lord Chamberlain.[81] These apparently noncontroversial plays are not necessarily typical of the troupe's entire repertory for both popular and elite audiences during their previous thirteen or fourteen years of touring, especially since the company did not appear at the royal court for almost a decade before 1573. It is impossible to say precisely how many, but Leicester's professional troupe must have performed dozens of plays during the sixties and early seventies. Even if it changed its repertory only every other year, a company working with, say, five plays, would have performed thirty or more works between 1559 and 1573.[82] Although classical and romantic interludes were probably included, some idea of the type of plays performed by Leicester's company during the early years may be gained by noting the moral plays of Robert Wilson, a member of Leicester's Men during the 1570s and early 80s who, along with James Burbage, was to enjoy a successful career in the Elizabethan theatre. Wilson's *Three Ladies of London* and its sequel, *A Pleasant and Stately Moral*, reflect the puritan religious values as well as the aggressive foreign policy that Leicester himself was known to defend, and as Bevington has observed, these plays are composed in the spirit and form of many surviving Protestant interludes of the sixties, though somewhat displaced by the commercial conditions of the stage during the 1580s.[83]

There is good reason to believe that these early Elizabethan interludes are representative of at least some of the plays performed by Leicester's Men in the sixties, since so many of them champion the same Calvinist reforms promoted in polemical works which the Earl sponsored. Eleanor Rosenberg and Patrick Collinson have both scrupulously documented Leicester's extensive patronage of the more advanced reformers from the first year of the reign when he was instrumental in the appointment of Marian exiles returning from Geneva, Zurich and Strasbourg to the leading posts in the Church and the Universities.[84] Some indication of his personal interest in Calvinist views is found in the religious writings dedicated to him during the 1560s. The list reads like a catalogue of Calvinist works. In 1561, *A most necessary treatise of free will*, by Jean Veron, a French Huegonot; in 1562, *The Lawes and Statutes of Geneva*, by Robert Fill, another Calvinist; 1563, *A Goodly Gallerye ... of naturall contemplation*, by the distinguished Cambridge Puritan, William Fulke; 1564, *The Commentaries of Peter Martyr*, a noted Continental Calvinist; 1565, *A Handbook of Christian Instruction*, by Pierre Viret, close friend of Calvin; and 1565, *The pedegrewe of Heretiques*, by John Barthlet, a militant London preacher. Leicester probably also had a hand in the printing of Robert Crowley's *Brief Discourse against the outwarde apparell* (*c.* 1566) the earliest puritan manifesto. In 1569, Dudley's protégé Thomas Wilson dedicated to him *A Discourse vppon Usurye*, one of several early Elizabethan works of a Calvinist persuasion contributing to a campaign to impose severe restrictions on money-lending. One writer exclaimed that "the noble and famous Erle of Leicester hath been already a fauourer of this cause, and no doubte will further it to the vttermoste of his power ... ."[85] These and other works by Protestant activists supported by Leicester discuss the doctrines of predestination and irresistible grace, the importance of the preaching ministry, opposition to pseudo-Catholic vestments and ceremonies in church worship, and the need for social, economic, and educational reform according to biblical principles in the godly state. As we shall see in chapter 3, these are the very issues treated in such popular interludes as *The Life and Repentaunce of Mary Magdalene*, *The Tide Tarrieth No Man*, *Enough is as Good as a Feast*, *The Trial of Treasure*, *The Longer Thou Livest the More Fool Thou Art*, and *New Custom*.

The correspondence in religious subject-matter and polemical purpose between print propaganda and the extant troupe interludes does not, of course, prove that any of these plays were either known to Leicester or performed by his professional troupe; yet when this evidence is pieced together with Leicester's known use of drama to advance his interests, with contemporary comment about playing companies disseminating Protestant doctrine, and with the examples of such troupes as Bale and his fellows and the King's Men, one can reasonably infer that interludes of this kind were probably a significant part of the repertory of Leicester's Men in the 1560s and the early 1570s. My own conjecture is that at least one of these named interludes, *New Custom*, reflects Leicester's own shifting views on the contentious issue of church vestments, and that its author, along with another Reformation playwright of the 1560s, William Wager, may have supplied his troupe with playscripts, but these matters will be taken up in the next chapter which will give more detailed attention to the troupe plays themselves.

3

Reformation playwrights and plays

While attention has been given to John Bale's career in chapter 1, we have yet to consider in more general terms the vocation of the Reformation playwright, his relations with patrons and players, and the printing of his plays. This is the first concern of the present chapter, especially as these matters relate to dramatists writing for the professional acting troupes. My second concern, and the one that will occupy most of our attention, is with the troupe plays themselves. I mentioned earlier that very few extant play texts of our period (those few would include Bale's works) can be confidently ascribed to a known professional acting company. What can be said with some confidence, however, is that among the sizeable corpus of scripts that *do* survive are many that are representative of the repertories of the touring troupes considered in the last chapter. By examining these surviving "unattached" troupe plays,[1] including a fairly detailed look at one of them, Lewis Wager's *Life and Repentaunce of Mary Magdalene*, we can learn about the issues and ideas propagated by the professional companies following the time Bale's were performing in the 1530s, and we can get at least some sense of how they were constructed for performance before popular audiences.

Playwright relations with patrons and players

The first point to be made about Reformation play authorship is that there was no such thing as a "professional" dramatist during our period. It would not be until the opening of the commercial theatres in London in the last quarter of the century that a market was created for playwrighting as a full-time occupation.[2] Most dramatists of the Reformation era were ordained ministers or schoolmasters (or both), a few were courtiers or lawyers, for which playwrighting was one

among several responsibilities.[3] We know that the playwrighting
schoolmasters wrote for their own students; the authors of the troupe
plays also appear to have composed with particular actors in mind.
The fact that so many of their works include complex doubling
schemes for a specified number of players is one indication of this.
Other evidence points to playwrighting affiliated with noble or royal
patrons. Theatre historians of the early Tudor period, for example,
have linked plays by Skelton and Medwell to the households of the
Earl of Northumberland and Cardinal Morton respectively. The
anonymous *Wisdom* has been attributed to the Bishop of Ely's court,
The World and the Child to the Earl of Kent's, and *Hickscorner* to the
Duke of Suffolk's.[4] That this arrangement continued after the
Reformation has already been demonstrated in chapter 1 where we
observed Bale's connections with Oxford and Cromwell, and it is
likely that the anti-papal interludes of Edward VI's court were
written by Thomas Chaloner, George Ferrers, and William Baldwin
(possibly also Bale and Thomas Becon), who reportedly devised
interludes for the Revels office and were (at least in the case of Ferrers
and Baldwin) residing at the royal court.

As one would expect with such arrangements, dramatists were in
some instances directly commissioned by patrons to write plays; in
other instances they offered finished works to them. The former was
the case with John Heywood during the Henrician Reformation,
according to his former student, Thomas Whythorne, who recalled
about 1570: "At the request of doctor Thomas Cranmer, late
archbishop of Canterbury, he [i.e. Heywood] made a certain
interlude or play, the which was devised upon the parts of Man, at
the end whereof he likeneth and applieth the circumstances thereof to
the universal estate of Christ's church all the which aforesaid [plays],
before they were published, I did write out for him, or had the use of
them to read them."[5] This also was the case with Ferrers (appointed
the Lord of Misrule in 1551) and Baldwin, although in a letter to
Cawarden in 1556 Baldwin implies that he offered already finished
compositions to the Revels Office.[6] Heywood, Ferrers and Baldwin
had been established court favorites before being invited to write
plays, but how did the aspiring Reformation dramatist of little
renown get the attention of a powerful patron and his works
performed by the patron's players? One way perhaps was through
the influence of a local official with connections at court. Bale, for
example, may have received help from Lord Thomas Wentworth of

Suffolk in arranging for his plays to be staged by the Earl of Oxford's Men in the early 1530s. A more familiar course of action would have been to address a letter directly to the patron and therein dedicate one's work to him. While we have plenty of examples of such letters by nondramatic writers (almost all of which appear at the outset of the printed work), there is only one that I know of by a Reformation dramatist, and since it casts light on the patron/playwright relationship, it is worth quoting in full. The letter is by Thomas Wylley, Vicar of Yoxford, addressed to Thomas Cromwell in 1536:

> The Lorde make you the instrument of my helpe, Lorde
> Cromwell, that I may have fre lyberty to preache the trewthe.
>   I dedycat and offer to your Lordeshype A Reverent Receyving of
> the Sacrament, as a Lenton matter, declaryd by vj chyldren,
> representyng Chryst, the worde of God, Paule, Austyn, a Chylde, a
> Nonne callyd Ignorancy; as a secret thyng that shall have hys ende ons
> rehersyd afore your eye by the sayd chyldren.
>   The most part of the prystes of Suff. wyll not reseyve me ynto ther
> chyrchys to preche, but have dysdaynyd me ever synns I made a play
> agaynst the popys Conselerrs, Error, Colle Clogger of Conscyens, and
> Incredulyte. That, and the Act of Parlyament had not folowyd after, I
> had be countyd a gret lyar.
>   I have made a playe caulyd A Rude Commynawlte. I am a
> makyng of a nother caulyd The Woman on the Rokke, yn the fyer of
> faythe a fynyng, and a purgyng in the trewe purgatory; never to be seen
> but of your Lordshyp's eye.
>   Ayde me for Chrystys sake that I may preche chryst.
>   Thomas Wylley
>   of Yoxforthe Vykar
>   fatherlesse and forsaken.[7]

Wylley offers four Protestant interludes to Cromwell, one of which is yet to be written. The letter reveals that he seeks patronage for the same reasons that nondramatic writers seek patronage: to avail him the opportunity to propagate religious and political ideas that he shares with his prospective patron, and to receive protection and approval of his works in the face of hostile opposition. It is not absolutely clear, but it seems that Wylley's plays are offered not only for approval for performance by his own choirboys which, presumably, he desires to bring to court, but perhaps also for production by other troupes supporting the Reformation cause. It is just this kind of letter that Bale might have written to the Earl of Oxford to get his plays performed by the Earl's company.

There is no indication in the letter that Wylley expected any monetary reward for supplying his scripts to Cromwell, despite the fact that in unpublished form they were often an expensive commodity, as will be seen shortly. However, many writers did hope for career advancement in exchange for their labors. Bale, as much as any suitor to patronage of his generation, took advantage of such opportunities. It was likely as a result of his comedies, as well as his scholarly achievements and service to the church, that he eventually was promoted to the Bishopric of Ossory under Edward VI, a monarch who, as we have seen, was fond of the type of drama Bale wrote and produced.[8] Further evidence of dramatists writing plays, at least in part, to advance their careers is provided by Nicholas Grimald, who dedicated his play on John the Baptist, *Archipropheta*, to Richard Cox, Dean of Christ Church, Oxford in 1546/47, expressly for the purpose of procuring a teaching appointment at the university;[9] and the young John Foxe sent a copy of his play *Titus et Gesippus* to one Dr. Hensey in 1545 also to gain work as a teacher or tutor.[10] In the next chapter, we will see that schoolmasters used playwrighting as a means of advancing their careers.

A Reformation troupe dramatist of the early Elizabethan period who may have gained preferment on account of his playwrighting for a prominent patron is William Wager, author of *Enough is as Good as a Feast* among other homiletic interludes (and not to be confused with Lewis Wager, his father). Wager was presented by Dean Alexander Nowell to the rectory of St. Benet, Gracechurch in 1567; collated to St. Michael at Queenhithe in 1575/76, and awarded a third rectory in 1571 at the parish church of Cradley, Herefordshire, all of which he served until his death in 1591.[11] Much in demand as a preacher, he was appointed to lectureships (salaried preaching appointments free from the restraints of the Prayer Book) at St. Mary Woolnoth and other London parishes. He served as governor of Barnet grammar school beginning in 1573, participated in a Crown-appointed commission with the preacher, Robert Crowley, to hear the petitions of poor prisoners in Ludgate and other London prisons in 1575, and was appointed licenser for the press in 1589. Wager's several benefices, lectureships, and state appointments, suggest strongly that he had connections in high places, and one is tempted to speculate that like his puritan associates Thomas Wilcox, Crowley, and Nowell, he benefited from the patronage of a Protestant nobleman such as Leicester, Warwick, or Bedford.[12] Certainly Wager's plays propagate the same Calvinist reforms, the same conservative economic policy, including opposition to usury,[13] which these nobles openly favored and supported through the channels of printing and preaching. As we noted in chapter 2, Wager's plays have much in common with those of Robert Wilson, who was a member of Leicester's company in the 1570s.

Some Reformation playwrights evidently directed or acted in the productions of their own plays. This was surely true in the case of the playwrighting schoolmasters, some of whom probably followed Bale's example of delivering the opening and concluding speeches. Thus in the school play *Jacob and Esau*, "The Poet" (probably William Hunnis) enters the playing area to offer final reflections on the action and to offer a prayer to the Queen.[14] Perhaps the most famous actor/playwright of King Edward's reign was George Ferrers, who combined the tasks of devising plays and acting as the Lord of Misrule at Christmastide 1551/52 and 1552/53. Bale of course provides an example of a preacher/playwright who headed a professional troupe. He was not the first and he would not be the last English churchman to combine playing with preaching. As subdean of the Chapel Royal, John Kite acted at court in 1511 and, as Chambers says, "stepped almost straight from the boards to the bishopric of Armagh."[15] We noted in chapter 1 that the Salisbury priest, Richard Spencer, became a player of Protestant interludes. Considering the number of parish-sponsored plays which continued well into Elizabeth's reign, there were probably many others. One was Mr. Philips, minister at Carleton and Claxton, Norfolk, who reportedly acted in interludes during the 1570s.[16] This evidence makes it all the more plausible that such clerical playwrights of the 1560s as Ulpian Fulwell, Lewis Wager, and William Wager had first-hand experience of the stage and that they might have been, like Bale, affiliated with a specific professional troupe at one time or another. The plentiful stage directions in their plays are written for actors rather than readers, and as Bevington observes with regard to William Wager's interludes, "the directions for doubling are flawless; and in several cases, as in *The Longer Thou Livest*, it is nearly impossible to contrive any other arrangement of the parts that would work."[17]

Comparatively few Protestant playscripts made it into print, especially prior to Elizabeth's reign, and when they did so it was apparently after they had served some time on the stage. Only four of Bale's twenty-three original compositions were published, and the earliest of them as much as a decade after Bale's troupe is on record for performances in 1538/39. There is no indication that any of the Edwardian court interludes discussed in the last chapter were submitted for publication. One reason few were printed is obvious. Like musical scores, plays were first and foremost scripts written for performers and rarely intended for a reading audience. They also appear to have been eagerly sought for and, at least in the 1530s, could be very expensive to purchase by a patron without the luxury of having a playwright in his service. In 1538, John Husee discovered in searching for "the new scripture matter" for Lady Lisle that such material was difficult to come by and that one of them, *Rex Diabole*, was selling for the exorbitant fee of forty shillings.[18] Perhaps this involved the scribe's fee of writing out parts for the players. Understandably, having paid this amount, a patron or his company might have been reluctant to make such plays available to other troupes (or to printers), particularly during their period of greatest popularity. It is interesting to note, however, that during the 1560s and early 1570s, most of the Protestant interludes that *were* printed advertised on their title pages casting or doubling charts for the benefit of interested acting troupes, to whom (along with readers) they were being marketed.[19] It may have been that by Elizabeth's reign, reformist playwrights and patrons recognized that a play's propagandist value could be maximized by making Protestant play texts available to as many playing troupes as were willing to perform them. Publication of the scripts made this possible. My guess is that most of these plays were written originally for performance by noblemen's players, and perhaps also by the more prominent artisan troupes of London and elsewhere, and that after running their course on the stage they were turned over to printers for general distribution.

It is highly doubtful that printers could profit much from selling interludes at this time, especially if they were sold mostly to groups such as the wardens of Bungay Holy Trinity who, in 1558, evidently purchased one printed playbook for fourpence, and then turned it over to a scribe for copying out individual acting parts.[20] Printers, therefore, may have been motivated to publish such plays not only by the prospect of courting the favor of noble patrons whose companies performed them, as Ian Lancashire suggests,[21] but also by a commitment to advancing the Protestant cause which they shared with playwrights and patrons. One such printer was William Copland (died 1568) who published *Lusty Juventus* and *Jack Juggler* during the early 1560s. Copland was responsible for several Protestant pamphlets during Edward VI's reign, including works by Peter Moone, the Ipswich artisan/writer who headed a playing troupe in 1560/61, and in March 1556 he was interrogated by Queen Mary's Privy Council for printing Cranmer's *Recantation*.[22] Copland was one among the many activist members of the newly formed Stationers' Company in 1557 who specialized in printing Protestant propagandist works during Elizabeth's reign. Others who printed Protestant interludes were John Alde (*Enough is as Good as a Feast*; *Like Will to Like*; *Cambises*), Richard Jones (*The Longer Thou Livest*), John Charlewood (*Mary Magdalene*), Thomas Purfoote (*The Trial of Treasure*), Henry Bynneman (*Jacob and Esau*), and John Day (*The Dialog betwene thangell & the Shepherdes*; *Gorboduc*). There is persuasive evidence that at least three of these, Purfoote, Bynneman, and Day, were patronized by the Earl of Leicester, yet what role Dudley had in arranging for plays performed by his professional troupe to be published remains unclear.[23]

Reformation troupe play dramaturgy

Like the majority of Tudor plays written for indoor performance, the typical Reformation troupe play is described as an "interlude" on its printed title page. The term interlude normally refers to a relatively short play that is ethical or homiletic in purpose and at least partly allegorical in method, but since it is used interchangeably with "stage-play" and "moral play" by contemporaries, I shall do the same here.[24] However, troupe plays usually differ from other interludes written exclusively for the court or for academic institutions, as well as from the provincially sponsored civic drama, in several important respects. Unlike these other plays that may employ as many as thirty amateur actors, the troupe plays are designed for between three and eight experienced and often highly skilled players belonging to a professional company who would have performed them repeatedly on tour. They therefore usually required extensive doubling to present many parts. In *From Mankind to Marlowe*, David Bevington has shown the extent to which the troupe play design is affected by the doubling patterns. For example, characters are suppressed or "written out" of the script early on so that the actor could impersonate other figures as the action progresses. Secondly, because they were taken on tour, the staging of the plays requires very little in terms of scenery and properties. Typically, they could be performed in a bare acting area with a few portable properties and a modest wardrobe of costumes. And finally, while most were composed with a demographically diverse national audience in mind, some do seem to be addressed to certain sectors of society. For example, the "money" plays of the early Elizabethan period (about which more will be said shortly) appeal to the large mercantile audiences of London and other urban centers.[25] A play such as *New Custom*, with its treatment of clerical dress and other ecclesiastical issues, seems to have a message for the large numbers of puritan congregations in the south of England, a point I will bring up again later.

Much of what I have said here about the typical troupe play of the Reformation we have already observed in Bale's works, although *King Johan* is rather long for an interlude. If Bale was perhaps the first playwright of the era to apply medieval stagecraft for Protestant purposes, he was also the most influential. A number of features may be traced back to his extant plays: the presentation of sober and earnest-speaking godly figures as Protestant evangelists, of game-loving villains as Catholic clerics; the typology of these opposing dramatis personae as universal representatives of Christ or Anti-Christ; the persistently derisive treatment of Catholic doctrine and customs; the practice of taking ideas and rhetorical patterns from homiletic works – sermons, catechisms, dialogues, treatises – and incorporating them verbally and visually into the action.

The debt to Bale notwithstanding, the later interludes show greater diversity in stagecraft than they are usually credited for. In terms of overall structure, some playwrights rely on a dramatic model well established before Bale's time to propagate their message. For instance, interludes which anatomize the internalized spiritual struggle of the individual soul (a feature but not the central theme of Bale's extant plays) make use of the so-called psychomachia plot of the medieval moral play. The basic pattern of *Humanum Genus* degeneration into sin at the hands of personified vices followed by a sequence of repentance and forgiveness at the hands of personified virtues is used in many Reformation plays. It probably supplied the model for Heywood's earlier noted non-extant interlude "devised upon the parts of Man" (see p. 68, above). It is also discernible in surviving texts such as *Mary Magdalene* (combined with certain saint play features) and *Lusty Juventus*, only now the theological frame of reference is clearly Calvinist rather than Catholic. However, the

Calvinist emphasis on predestination, on divine justice rather than mercy, and on the homiletic notion that fear of divine judgment is an effective inducement to repentance (the "fire and brimstone" approach to homiletics), contributed to modifications of this pattern. Thus, in a number of other plays – *Enough is as Good as a Feast*, *The Longer Thou Livest the More Fool Thou Art*, and *The Conflict of Conscience* – the final "comic" phase of repentance and forgiveness is supplanted by a tragic one of persisting impenitence and retribution. It is widely recognized that these incipient tragedies, some of which give psychologically penetrating depictions of the experience of spiritual reprobation, prepare the way for *Doctor Faustus* and *Macbeth*.

There has been a distinct tendency in Tudor drama studies to see most popular interludes and moral plays of sixteenth-century England as offering variations on, or evolving out of, this single dramatic formula with its central Mankind hero.[26] This view has been questioned in recent years, if only because it imposes a misleading pattern of evolutionary development on popular drama leading up to Shakespeare.[27] But two additional observations should be made concerning this matter. The first is that it is difficult to trace the development of Tudor play construction with any precision when so much of the drama has perished, including almost all saint plays and folk drama. Yet what has survived suggests that the Vice and other conventions are at least as much a product of secular folk drama as they are of the medieval morality play, and that the technique of mingling allegorical figures and more "realistic" historical personages, commonly thought to have "emerged" in mid-Tudor England with "hybrid" plays such as *Cambises* and *Horestes*, can be traced back as least as far as the Digby *Mary Magdalene* of the late fifteenth century.[28] Thus, the emphasis given to the Mankind-centered morality obscures the contributions of other medieval dramatic traditions. My second point is that we should recognize that for the Reformation dramatist, the thesis or argument conveyed to the audience takes precedence over "story" and "character." When Laurence Humphrey introduces Foxe's *Christus Triumphans*, he writes, "if you would like to see this idea [Christ's message of redemption], behold, Foxe's stage presents it to your eyes." Similarly, the purpose of Beza's *Abraham's Sacrifice* is not simply to reenact the story of Abraham and Isaac but, that with God's help, "each of us may fare the better by / The liuely faith set foorth before our eye."[29] In some instances, the dramatic formula centering around a *Humanum Genus*

figure suits the playwright's purposes. In other instances, however, it
does not. As Alan Dessen has recently observed, there are many other
troupe plays of mid-sixteenth-century England that lack this medieval morality "gene" and indeed bear little more than a superficial
resemblance to *The Castle of Perseverance* and *Everyman*.[30] Plays such as
Like Will to Like and *The Tide Tarrieth No Man* are less concerned with
individual religious experience and its theological components than
they are with the spiritual condition of the society as a whole. They
therefore resort to a different structure demanded by this subject-
matter, one presenting a series of episodes in which a central Vice
figure, signifying the omnipresence of evil in society, propels various
social types into acts of treachery and deceit, and usually concluding
with the punishment of that Vice in the final scene. The interlude *All
for Money* illustrates yet another construction that has little to do with
the *Humanum Genus* formula. This play does not present a continuous
sequence of scenes, but rather six independent episodes, each with its
own distinct set of characters and logic of presentation, which are
interrelated by their thematic concern with money, its power and its
corrupting influence in a society devoid of spiritual values.[31]

   Once the Reformation playwright had his argument and a cast-list
of "characters" to act out and give verbal expression to the
components of the argument in a series of scenes, he could then
enhance and elaborate the play's meaning by exploiting the visual
resources available to him in the acting space.[32] This was the chief
advantage the stage had over the press and the pulpit as an
instrument of propaganda. To make a point about hypocrisy, for
example, an actor's speech could be contrasted with his physical
appearance. A character who introduces himself as Perverse Doctrine
(*New Custom*) or Malicious Judgment (*Mary Magdalene*), and
proceeds to illustrate these abstract concepts through action and
speech, appears before the audience in an outward cloak of apparent
holiness, i.e. dressed as a Roman Catholic priest. This device, along
with the related one of characters disguising themselves as other
characters (e.g. of Vices as Virtues), was already commonplace in
medieval moral drama, but it was ubiquitous in the Reformation
interludes from Bale's time onwards, and *was* so because of the
dilemma experienced by English audiences of discerning between
true and false representations of truth in times of tumultuous religious
change.[33]

   Another visual device, used more frequently for expository than polemical purposes, was to convey an argument or concept through a series of stage pictures. One remarkable instance of this is found in scene 2 of *All For Money* in which the playwright's purpose is to show how love of money can lead eventually to damnation. To achieve this, he gives dramatic expression to a familiar literary trope: the genealogy of evil. The action centers around a chair and begins with the seated Money "giving birth" to Pleasure, who in turn sits down to deliver Sin into the world; Sin then engages in the same stage business to bring forth Damnation. The stage directions make clear that in each incident the "newborn" is to appear from beneath the chair by means of "some fine conveyaunce." As Southern speculates, this does not call for a trap door, but probably only required the seated actor to be dressed in a long skirted gown, with the "child" emerging from between his legs and through the skirt.[34] A variation of this same device is to introduce a series of figures, one after another in pageant-like fashion, to dramatize a spiritual process, as in the concluding scene of *New Custom* where the repentant Catholic priest, Perverse Doctrine (now renamed Sincere Doctrine), welcomes and embraces in succession, Light of the Gospel, Edification, Assurance of Salvation, and Godly Felicity. In some plays the spiritual process, whether it be a conversion to grace or a backsliding into unregeneracy, is dramatized by having figures represent the conflicting impulses, desires, beliefs, in the acting space, usually with them standing behind or on one side or another of the central character as he undergoes change. These last two strategies are used with considerable effect in *Mary Magdalene*, as will be seen later.

The impression one may receive at this point is that the dramatis personae in these plays function little more than as visual emblems and verbal expositors of moral and religious ideas in a dramatized argument.[35] This impression is especially strong when reading the play texts themselves where the allegorical names of the characters in the speech-prefixes tend to emphasize their abstractness. What is more, one wonders whether the term "character" should be applied at all to so many of these figures who introduce themselves as abstractions and explain their significance directly to the audience.

> I am Gods promise whiche is a thing etern,
> And nothing more surer then his promise may be:
> A sure foundation to such as will learn
> Gods precepts to observe.
>
> *(Like Will to Like)*

Forsothe, I am called Natural inclination
Whiche bred in old Adams fostred bones;
So that I am proper to his generation
I will not awaye with casting of stones,
I make the stoutest to bowe and bende:
Againe when I luste I make men stande vprighte.[36]

(The Trial of Treasure)

Because I am a man endewed with treasure,
Therefore a worldly man men doo me call.

(Enough is as Good as a Feast)[37]

What is conveyed through these self-presentations is the *idea* of God's promises, natural inclination, and worldly man. Only in the last example, with Worldly Man, is there any sense of the lines being spoken "in character," but even here the function is to define his moral significance so that the audience can more easily grasp the argument conveyed in the play. Some interlude figures (God's Promises is a good example) do not advance beyond this simple emblematic function, and it is therefore hard to imagine them as impersonated characters. But we need to keep in mind that such figures become at least in some sense lifelike by the very fact that they are represented by human actors performing before an audience, a fact easily overlooked when reading the text. Moreover, many other figures who are named after abstractions clearly exhibit naturalistic behavior and dialogue and often emerge as engaging stage personalities. As such, they function mimetically as well as emblematically. To a modern audience raised on naturalistic theatre, the disjuncture between actor as expositor commenting on and critically detached from the action and actor as the impersonator of a "character" (whether social type or distinct individual) may be unsettling, although it is not an uncommon feature of modern stagecraft, Brecht's for example.[38] To Tudor spectators, however, rooted in the notion of drama as "game" imparting "earnest," the shifting modes of presentation are accepted as a convention. The disjuncture, however, is perhaps not as pronounced as might be thought initially, for frequently a character will demonstrate through his actions the quality he represents. On the level of psychological allegory, for example, the Vice Covetous in *Enough is as Good as a Feast* is an outward projection of Worldly Man's acquisitive nature, but as the steward of his estate who at times engages in realistic conversation with him, he also stands for the type of companion who both practices

9 "Let the Vice weep & houl & make great lame[n]tatio[n]" to the Worldly Man. The recorrupting of Worldly Man by Covetous the Vice in the author's and Bryan Humphrey's production of *Enough is as Good as a Feast*, by William Wager. Baylor University Theatre Department, April 1987. Courtesy of the Theatre Department and Photography Office, Baylor University.

covetousness and encourages such behavior in an individual who struggles with his good and evil impulses. This brings up one last point about characters in the Reformation troupe drama that might already be obvious but may also be obscured by the allegorical names given to many of them. In most instances, the audiences would have clearly recognized themselves and other familiar persons represented in the acting space. Popish priests, Genevan evangelists, courtiers, merchants, landlords, lawyers, city apprentices, prostitutes, common laborers, servants, fill the dramatis personae of these plays and enable the playwright to add an additional layer of topical meaning. This topical dimension is also helpful in locating the play's action within particular time and place.

The Life and Repentaunce of Mary Magdalene

In turning now to specific examples of Reformation troupe plays, I wish to begin with *The Life and Repentaunce of Mary Magdalene*, since its Prologue adds to our knowledge of a typical Reformation troupe on tour and because the play illustrates many general features of the troupe interludes in the wake of Bale's accomplishments during the 1530s. The fairly detailed analysis of this one play will lead into a discussion of the the main thematic interests of the other Protestant interludes in the remainder of the chapter.

Mary Magdalene was not printed until 1566 but the statement in the Prologue that it teaches "true obedience to the kyng" (rather than the Queen),[39] as well as the play's extensive indebtedness to Calvin's *Institutes* which was widely circulating among university students towards the end of Edward VI's reign (see appendix B), points to an Edwardian date. Its author Lewis Wager, like Bale, was a former friar-turned-Protestant preacher. A Franciscan of the Oxford convent, Wager was ordained subdeacon by the Bishop of Sarum on September 21, 1521, and studied at Oxford sometime prior to 1540. The next we hear of him is in April 1560 when he became rector of St. James, Garlickhithe, London; he was buried in his own parish two years later in July 1562, the administration granted to his widow Elinore.[40] In the same year in the parish church of St. James, William Wager was married, his four children subsequently christened there as well. From this and the fact that William was born about 1537, we can reasonably infer that William was Lewis' son and that Lewis

Wager himself married and converted to Protestantism in the mid 1530s.[41] On the title page of *Mary Magdalene* Lewis is described as "a learned clarke," and given the topical satire of young ladies of wealth and noble descent in the earlier scenes, he may have served in a major household as an almoner, chaplain, or tutor, like other playwrighting scholars of the Reformation (e.g. Thomas Becon, Ralph Radcliffe, John Foxe, and Stephen Gosson).[42] Historians have noted that the relations between the aristocracy and the monastic orders had always been close and that the more privileged and talented among the ex-religious were well cared for following the dissolution.[43]

In all likelihood, *Mary Magdalene* was written for a nobleman's troupe of "four men and a boy," the adults doubling thirteen parts among them, and the child-actor portraying Mary, as the casting chart on the printed title page indicates. Like Bale and his fellows, the players appear to have been experienced singers, with treble, base, and "meane" parts assigned for the song which concludes the first phase of the action (D3^v). The troupe faced criticism from those who questioned the propriety of playing, according to the play's Prologue (see chapter 6 below). In offering a moral lesson to youth of aristocratic descent, a performance of the play would have been appropriate for the great hall of a noble household (a reference to "without the door" [sig. F4^r] suggests an indoor setting), perhaps one where wards and other privileged adolescents were educated, but the play's homely language and lively dialogue and action, as well as its more general evangelical theme of justification by faith through imputed grace, made it (like *The Cradle of Security*) also suitable to the diverse audiences on tour. That it was taken on tour is evident from the Prologue who tells us that he and his colleagues "haue ridden and gone many sundry waies; / Yea, we haue vsed this feate at the vniversitie" (A2^r).[44] It also reveals how a professional troupe earned its keep on the road: spectators are invited to give money for the performance: "Truely, I say, whether you geue halfpence or pence. / Your gayne shalbe double, before you depart hence" (A2^v). Perhaps a hat or plate was passed around, as was evidently the case in performances of the medieval *Mankind*.

Mary Magdalene is a saint play, or perhaps more properly a Protestant adaptation of a saint play.[45] Wager's choice of subject-matter is readily understandable when we consider that the Franciscans and other monastic organizations were believed responsible for the many dramatized saints' lives which were presumed destroyed

along with the great monastic libraries.[46] Although their playbooks
do not survive, we know of a Mary Magdalene play performed in the
parish church at Taunton, Somerset, in 1504, an outdoor production
at Chelmsford in 1561 (this may have been the Digby version),
and quite possibly another at Magdalen College, Oxford in
1506–7.[47] Whether Wager was familiar with any of these works or
with the surviving East Anglian Digby *Mary Magdalene* is unknown,
but his play does share some features in common with the latter play.
Following the Digby author, Wager identifies the profligate woman
who washes Christ's feet in Luke 7 with Mary Magdalene in Luke 8
out of whom Jesus expelled seven demons (and in both plays the
exorcism is highly theatricalized), he makes references to Mary's
upbringing in the castle of Magdalene, and he depicts at some length
the dinner at Simon's house where Mary washes Christ's feet and
listens to the parable of the two debtors. In terms of dramaturgy,
both plays mingle biblical figures with characters signifying moral
abstractions. Nevertheless, the similarities basically end here. As a
troupe dramatist, Wager could not remotely accommodate the
elaborate staging and casting requirements of the Digby spectacle. As
a Protestant, he had no place for the post-biblical miracles and other
legendary aspects of the saint so dear to the medieval cult of Mary
Magdalene such as her conversion of the king and queen of Marcylle,
her being fed by the angels from heaven, and so on. Moreover, while
he is no less committed to combining edification with entertainment
in treating the saint, his play is infused with an entirely different
religious outlook, one which is positively hostile to the medieval cult
of saints and other Catholic dogma and iconography that underpin
the Digby *Magdalene*. Wager's Protestant hagiography recalls the
writings of Tyndale and Bale in which such martyrs as William
Tracie, Sir John Oldcastle, Anne Askew, and King John offered
models of biblical piety, evangelical zeal, and extraordinary faith in
the face of Catholic persecution. This type of saint was, to quote Bale,
"not canonized of the Pope but in the precious blood of his Lord Jesus
Christ."[48] As Mary explains to the audience, "To all the worlde an
example I may be, / In whom the mercy of Christ is declared" (H1ᵛ).
    As much as Wager may have been familiar with the saint play
tradition, his dramatic technique owes more to moral play dramaturgy, as we noted earlier. He has in fact interweaved a few biblical
episodes into a standard psychomachia plot used to dramatize the
process of religious conversion in pre-Reformation moral plays and

interludes such as *Mankind* and *Youth*. As in these plays, the acting space becomes, at least on one level, a kind of spiritual landscape in which the protagonist's allegorized companions represent the motives, impulses, and thoughts of his own heart that mark individual religious experience. The chief difference of course lies in the theological basis of that religious experience, which is explicitly Calvinist. In the Catholic *Mankind*, for example, the hero begins in innocence (he is purged of original sin by Baptism), and while his fall into sin is inevitable, it is an act of his free and efficacious will. His salvation likewise is based on his voluntary acceptance of the offering of redemption. In *Mary Magdalene*, as in other Protestant interludes, unregenerate man is no longer a mutable being in the sense of being free to initiate the process leading to salvation. The action begins with Mary, the representative of universal man, depraved and already rampant in sin, and it is only when she is wrenched from sin to a state of regeneration by means of irresistible grace that salvation is awarded.

This rejection of free will in favor of predestination and irresistible grace is already evident in Bale's plays, which Wager may have had the opportunity to see in 1537/38 when Lord Cromwell's players visited Oxford (see chapter 1 above). *Mary Magdalene* does seem to have benefited from Bale's stagecraft. As in *Three Laws*, Wager introduces a Vice named Infidelity who is associated with Catholic corruption and heads a gang of his own offspring, and personifies the Old Law as a type of Moses who appears bearing the tables of the law. Moreover, *Mary Magdalene* inherits the Protestant typology of *King Johan* and Bale's scriptural plays in which biblical and historical narrative foreshadow the present (and universal) conflict between the forces of Christ and Anti-Christ. As with Bale, Christ's struggle with the pharisees is treated as the struggle of the Protestant preacher against Roman Catholic persecution and the doctrine of justification by works.

Wager's main homiletic argument is made transparent through a sequence of interactions between Mary and her allegorical companions. Through Infidelity, Mary is led to Pride, Cupidity, and Carnal Concupiscence. With her degeneracy complete, the process leading to salvation begins. By the declaration of the Law of God, she is brought to Knowledge of Sin, who prepares the way for Christ's preaching. Through Christ, Infidelity is expelled along with the other sins, and Faith and Repentance are received. Mary washes

Christ's feet in Simon's house to show her heart-felt love in contrast to the malice and outward sanctity of the accusing Pharisee. In the end, Justification and Love are explained as the fruits, not the causes, of Faith.

The degeneracy phase of the action, which occupies more than half the play, is worth careful consideration, for Wager overlays the familiar pattern of vice intrigue and spiritual corruption with a topical satire on the youth of the privileged classes. From the standpoint of the play's central argument, the purpose of the degeneracy phase is to dramatize the working and final dominance of sin in the heart of Mary. Mary is a willing participant in wrongdoing long before she formally meets the personifications of her sins in the play. Infidelity, who is the "head of all iniquitie" and has replaced Pride (in the Digby play) as Mary's besetting sin, recalls cradling her in his arms when she was just a babe of three years of age (B1^v), and his fellow henchmen, Pride, Cupidity, and Carnal Concupiscence, all admit to knowing and having their way with Mary from a very tender age (B3^v). Together, the four vices represent the whole gamut of human sin ("In us foure. . . be contained / As many vices as euer in this world raigned," [sig. B4^r]), and have their origins in (are in fact, a condensed version of) the Seven Deadly Sins of medieval drama and art. Their homiletic function is not so much to tempt Mary as to augment the sins which she is already naturally disposed to due to her depraved condition. The scheme which they devise is a familiar one. They will appear to Mary under the assumed names and identities of virtuous counsellors. Like Bale, Wager finds the theatrical metaphor useful to convey the duplicitous and specious nature of the Vices. "In our tragedie" (C1^r), as one Vice describes the plot, Infidelity will play Prudence, Pride will appear to her as Honour, Concupiscence as Pleasure, and Cupidity as Utility.

Following medieval practice, the degeneracy phase is depicted in lively, comic realism, and to enhance the play's appeal to youth, particularly to those of noble birth for whom it may have been originally written, Mary is presented as a beautiful, but no less spoiled and coquettish, gentlewoman who has just come into the inheritance of a wealthy estate. Her recently deceased parents, she tells us, brought her up "In vertuous qualities and godly literature," and "nourtred [her] in noble ornature," but they also gave her much liberty and granted her every request (B2^v). When she first appears before the audience, she is berating her tailors for failing to keep her fitted out in the latest fashions and chiding her maids for insubordination. Expressing her need for assistance to help her run her estate and keep her in good cheer, Infidelity promptly offers his services, along with those of "persons of great honor and nobilitie, / Felowes that loue neither to dally nor scoffe, / But at once will tell you the veritie" (B2ᵛ). The Vices now take on a more human (and topical) dimension with Infidelity as Mary's chamberlain and the others as her newly appointed attendants. The action which ensues gives us an engaging glimpse into sixteenth-century women's fashions and beauty-care, recalling the Lisle letters describing the dressing of Lady Lisle's daughters at the royal court.[49] The Vices proceed to instruct the fashion-conscious young profligate to dress provocatively in the latest style, dye her hair blonde with the help of a goldsmith and curl it with a hot needle, wearing some of it piled on her forehead, and heighten her looks with cosmetics, all in the interests of alluring rich young suitors. The scene is spiced up with mimicking of courtly manners, a "song of .iv. parts, " sexually explicit punning, and much sensuous kissing and embracing between Mary and her upstart companions. The transvestism of Mary (remember, she is played by a male actor, likely a boy) must have added considerably to the humor of the scene, although this may have provoked the criticism alluded to by the play's opening Prologue.

One may ask how a contemporary audience, either noble or popular, responded to this scene and how the scurrilous behavior of Mary and the Vices could be reconciled with Wager's homiletic intentions. There is little doubt that the burlesquing of contemporary gentlewomen's fashions and coquettish behavior would have delighted Tudor audiences, amply supplying the "mirth" promised by the Prologue. However, before we too hastily conclude that the comedy of Mary's corruption in this scene is intended primarily to amuse the audience, we should recognize with Robert C. Jones and other critics that laughter evoked by the Vices in Tudor homiletic drama is a means of implicating and involving the audience in the very experience of temptation and corruption the protagonist undergoes. This is not to say that the comedy is always associated with evil and exclusively didactic in function (as Bernard Spivack suggests), yet it was often used to disarm audiences and seduce them along with their representative in the playing area.[50]

The audience's warm, sympathetic response to the charming Vices is brought into serious question in the conversion phase of the action

that follows where their worldly counsel and behavior is shown to
have damnable consequences. Infidelity's trio of assistants exit from
the acting place (never to return), leaving Mary and Infidelity alone
before the audience. The floor is about to be occupied by a procession
of godly figures who externalize the inward changes Mary is
experiencing as she is transformed from abject sinner to regenerate
saint. Where the Vices' inspired merriment had primarily appealed
to the audience's sense of play, the serious, homiletic speeches of the
Virtues now encourage critical detachment.[51] Moreover, as Alan
Dessen has observed in a perceptive analysis of the scene, their
physical appearance, groupings, properties, entrances and exits are
all coordinated to objectify what is happening within Mary on the
spiritual plane.[52] The acting space becomes the mirror image of the
psyche not only of Mary but of every spectator who is elected by
divine grace. Entering first is the Law of God carrying tables of stone,
and compelling Mary and Infidelity to retreat to the side of the acting
area ("Come asyde a little, and geue hym roume" [E3ᵛ]). Now
holding the floor and speaking perhaps in a deep voice (for this actor
doubles with Cupidity who is assigned the base part in the song), he
delivers his self-introduction in formal, dignified verse, stating that
"to a glasse compared I may be, / Wherin clerely as in the sunne
lyght, / The weakenesse and sinne of him self he may se; / Yea, and
his owne damnation, as it is ryght" (E4ʳ). Although restrained by
Infidelity, Mary's conscience is sorely afflicted as she gazes upon the
Law of God. Shortly thereafter, a second figure enters who states,
"By the Law commeth the knowledge of synne, / Whiche knowledge
truely here I represent" (E5ᵛ). His apparent physical ugliness (if we
are to believe Infidelity) also must have made a striking impression
on the audience and accentuates his allegorical significance. Wager
continually reminds the audience that the action is operating on the
spiritual level, as when the Law points over at Infidelity who is
presumably still standing by Mary's side, exhorting her: "O sinner,
from thy heart put that Infidelity, / Which hath drowned thee
already in the pit of hell" (F1ᵛ). And again, when Knowledge of Sin
says just before he departs from the place:

> Though I appere not to hir carnal syght,
> Yet by the meanes that she knoweth the lawe,
> I shall trouble hir always both day and night,
> And vpon hir conscience continually gnawr.

(F2ᵛ)

With the declaration of the Law and Knowledge of Sin showing Mary that she cannot save herself by any human means, Christ now enters to award her salvation. This is unquestionably the pivotal and most highly theatrical moment in the play. At this point, Mary seems to be flanked on one side by Infidelity and on the other side by Christ to create a kind of "Good Angel/Bad Angel" configuration as in *The Castle of Perseverance* and later in *Doctor Faustus*, for she finds herself alternately tempted and admonished by the two figures. Finally, Christ exclaims:

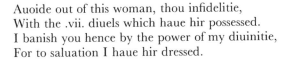

> Auoide out of this woman, thou infidelitie,
> With the .vii. diuels which haue hir possessed.
> I banish you hence by the power of my diuinitie,
> For to saluation I haue hir dressed.

> (F3ᵛ)

The stage direction then reads: "Infidelitie runneth away. Mary falleth flat downe. Cry all thus without the doore, and roare terribly." Following this flurry of stage activity, Mary rises to her feet to signify her spiritual rebirth, and is then introduced by Christ to Faith and Repentaunce who give self-introductions similar to those of the Law and Knowledge of Sin. Faith's many references to "the Word" suggest that he may be holding a Bible like similar figures in other Reformation interludes. In typically Calvinist fashion, they stress that they are "gifts" of God and that salvation is not due in any way to human merit. And again to emphasize their objectifying Mary's interior experience, they inform Mary before exiting with her from the place that "though in person we shall no more appeare, / Yet inuisibly in your heart we will remayne" (G2ʳ).[53] What the spectator witnesses in this theatrically engaging and memorable sequence of actions, therefore, is a dramatization of the process of religious conversion in specifically Calvinist terms. Indeed, the general pattern of salvation, as well as whole passages of dialogue, are taken straight from Calvin's *Institutes* (for this, see appendix B). The pageantlike figures who follow one another into the acting space symbolize the steps in that process, clarifying their significance in expository speeches; their distinctive physical appearances, properties, and movements, are all utilized to give highly memorable expression to Wager's evangelical message.

Ecclesiastical reform in the troupe plays

Mary Magdalene reflects the shift in emphasis within Reformation teaching during Edward VI's reign. We observed in chapter 1 that while Bale concerned himself with disseminating Protestant ideas, the general thrust of his stage propaganda was directed against the Roman Catholic Church, its political structure centered in the Papacy and its principles of doctrine and worship as practiced pervasively in England during the 1530s when Catholicism posed the most serious threat to the new political and religious order established by Henry VIII. However, as the Reformation progressed under Edward VI and then after Mary's short Catholic revival under Elizabeth, Protestant leaders at court and in the Church, along with lower-level officials and publicists who shared, disseminated, and enforced their views, recognized that a doctrinal consensus needed to be reached and a wide range of pressing issues addressed before a truly Protestant state could be realized and secured for future generations. Under Edward VI, a general consensus on matters of doctrine, worship, and church polity was achieved, as evidenced in the Prayer Book of 1552. By this time the most influential English Protestants identified themselves with the international movement of Reformed Protestantism originating in the Swiss and Rhineland cities of Geneva, Zurich, and Strasbourg.[54] *Mary Magdalene* illustrates the impact of Calvin's own theology even at this early stage in the history of English Protestantism. Calvinism gave English Protestants a coherent theological outlook, one emphasizing the primacy of Scripture, God's sovereignty and man's depravity, predestination, and the transforming power of God's irresistible grace. It showed a no less pronounced aversion to the Papacy and Roman Catholicism than that exhibited by the Henrician reformers of the 1530s, and through its notions of stewardship and calling ascribed religious significance to the individual's conduct in social and economic affairs.

This Calvinist theological outlook is a basic feature of the extant Protestant interludes after Bale, and explains this drama's call for a more thorough reformation of the Church's approach to worship, its government, and its ministry. This is especially the case after Elizabeth's accession when the Marian exiles returning from the Reformed communities on the Continent desired to remodel the Church along more apostolic lines, an effort that branded its more

10   Interior of a Huguenot Temple at Lyons, France, a late sixteenth-century painting, showing the broad hats and plain black frocks popular among Calvinist clerics and laity. In *New Custom*, the Genevan preacher appears "With a gathered frocke, a powlde head, and a broade hatte, / An vnshaued bearde, a pale face ... " (A3ʳ). Courtesy of the Public and University Library, Geneva.

activist proponents as puritans. Sympathy with the puritan proposals for ecclesiastical reform is evident in most of the Reformation troupe plays of the time, but especially in two, *New Custom* (printed in 1573) and *The Tide Tarrieth No Man* (printed in 1576).

    New Custom warns against the dangers of a Catholic restoration by reminding its audience of the cruelty, avarice, and superstition of the Marian regime, but it is of particular interest for its treatment of the controversy over church vestments and ceremonies during the 1560s and early 1570s. The play juxtaposes two pairs of clergymen. On the one hand, we see two aged popish priests "aboue sixtie," Perverse Doctrine and Hypocrisy, decked out in elaborate Catholic clerical attire; they are pitted against two dynamic preachers "not fully thirtie" and fresh from Geneva named New Custom and Light of the Gospel, who carry Bibles and wear plain frocks and broad hats,

Matth. 15.13. *Every plant which mine heavenly Father hath not planted should be rooted up.*

11   "Of God, of Man, of the Divell," a late sixteenth-century woodcut.
The accompanying caption reads:

Loe, here are three men, standing in degree,
The leaste of these, the greatest ought to be.
The other two, of men and of the Devill,
Ought to be rooted out for ere as evill.

The two conforming clerics "Of Man" and "Of the Divell" are dressed identically
in square cap, ruff, rochet and chimere (the prescribed attire of the Elizabethan Act
of Uniformity). The Bible-carrying cleric, "Of God," displaying puritan preferences
in dress, discards the square cap, rochet and chimere in favor of a simple skull cap,
cassock and gown. See Janet Mayo, *A History of Ecclesiastical Dress* (New York:
Holmes and Meier, 1984), p. 74. Courtesy of the Mansell Collection, London.

popular attire for Calvinist clerics of the time (see figures 10 and 11).
The contrasting physical appearances of the two sets of clergy makes
a clever visual statement associating the Reformation with the
vitality of the younger generation and identifying Catholicism as the
moribund religion of the elderly. But it also gives the author the
opportunity to attack the image-centered character of Roman
Catholic practice and its continued presence in the Anglican
communion. The distaste for the popish ornaments and vestments

becomes obvious near the beginning of the play, when Perverse Doctrine informs us that New Custom and his colleagues "disaloweth our ceremonies, and rites." Among the offensive items listed by New Custom are several which continued to be authorized by the Elizabethan Prayer Book:

> ... hee wyll haue priestes no corner cappes to wear.
> Surplices, are superstition, beades, paxes, and such geare,
> Crosses, belles, candells, oyle, bran, salt, spettle, and incence,
> With sensing, and singing hee accomptes not worth iii halfpense,
> And cries out on them all.[55]

Further attacks upon the prescribed Anglican vestments occur in Hypocrisy's advice to Perverse Doctrine to wear "Square cappes, longe gowns, with tippettes of silke, / Braue copes in the churche, surplices as white as milke" (C1^v). Behind this criticism is the vestarian controversy of the 1560s, beginning with the Convocation of 1563 when the proposal to substitute the Genevan academic gown for the surplice, among other reforms, was narrowly defeated, continuing with Archbishop Parker's "Advertisements" of 1564, a set of articles requiring strict conformity to clerical attire prescribed in the Act of Uniformity, and culminating in 1566 with the suspension of thirty-seven London ministers for rejecting the official dress.[56] Nevertheless, the play concludes on a moderate note, with New Custom acknowledging his preference for the simpler dress but admitting these are matters indifferent, adding that the Queen's ecclesiastical laws ought to be observed. My guess is that *New Custom*, like so many moral interludes which underwent considerable revision, was originally written without the moderate conclusion for the vestarian controversy of 1565/66, but by 1573 when the piece was published, the author or the company in possession of it, in conjunction with its printer Abraham Veale, adopted a more tolerant position on the matter, perhaps in line with the playing troupe's patron.

This patron may well have been Leicester or a like-minded Protestant lord sponsoring a professional troupe. Dudley himself had been directly embroiled in the vestarian dispute. In 1565, he took the side of the puritans, at that time known by their opponents as "the Genevans," who refused to wear the surplice during communion, the square cap in out-of-service attire, or any other "livery of Babylon" prescribed by Parker's "Advertisements," preferring instead the simple attire of a Calvinist minister. We know this from Parker's complaints to Cecil of Leicester's protection of the puritans and from the puritans themselves who stated that Leicester was their chief patron.[57] In 1573, however, when the issue arose again in the context of the Admonition crisis, Leicester took a more conciliatory role between the disputing parties. This is evident in his arranging for a letter to the leading reformers on the Continent requesting their opinion on the issue, as well as in a statement he made blaming both sides for the problem.[58] The fact that *New Custom*, with its counsel of moderation on the vestment issue, was printed in the same year that Leicester was trying to reconcile the bishops and the puritans over this matter may be only coincidental, but the hypothesis recently forwarded by Madeleine Robinson that his company was responsible for the piece is not implausible. As Robinson has shown, the play's eleven parts could easily have been accommodated by the troupe's six actors in the early seventies.[59] I would add that *New Custom* would have had enormous topical appeal to both civic corporations and audiences in such staunch Protestant centers as Ipswich and Canterbury, where Leicester's Men made the most frequent visits while on tour.[60]

That such matters of ecclesiastical reform seriously concerned large segments of the populace (as opposed to being the exclusive preoccupation of a few militant clergy as was once thought) has been convincingly shown by Patrick Collinson and other revisionist historians of Elizabethan Protestantism. In a letter to the Privy Council at the height of the Admonition controversy in 1573, Edwin Sandys, Bishop of London, reported that the puritan leaders Wilcox and Field were "esteemed as God's" by the London populace,[61] and as Collinson has discovered, congregations across the southeast of England vehemently protested the donning of the surplice and the square cap by their preachers and the administration of pseudo-Catholic ceremonies, since they (as opposed to the ministers) were the ones who had to view the offensive garments and rituals during the service of worship. The fact that successive "Acts of Apparel" were passed by English monarchs and that numerous pamphlets devoted detailed attention to the subject indicates just how seriously dress was taken at the time, and it is therefore not surprising that churchgoers were concerned about what their pastors wore when they mounted the pulpit or passed them in the street. "The pope's attire" elicited an emotionally charged reaction from early Elizabethan churchgoers, many of whom lived through Queen Mary's reign and associated it with Catholic tyranny and oppression.[62]

George Wapull's *The Tide Tarrieth No Man* is another troupe interlude printed in the 1570s that undermines the persisting notion that the Elizabethan puritans were unanimously opposed to the stage and its use as a vehicle of religious instruction.[63] During the second half of the play Wapull introduces two figures, Christianity and Faithful Few, through whom he makes a carefully guarded but no less controversial point about the wayward and decaying state of the national Church. The stage directions prescribe that Christianity "must enter with a sword, with a title of pollicy, but on the other syde of the tytle, must be written gods word, also a shield, wheron must be written riches, but on the other syde of the Shield must be Fayth."[64] Thus, Christianity enters with the worldly labels visible: the sword of "pollicy" and the shield of "riches." In his opening speech to the audience, he says:

> ... I beare this deformed sword and shield
> Which I may be ashamed to hold in my hand,
> But the Lord deliuer me from their thraldome and band,
> For if the enemy assayle me, then am I in thrall:
> Because I lack such Armoure, as is taught by S. Paule,
> For in steade of Gods word, and the shield of fayth,
> I am deformed with pollicy, and riches vayne.
>
> (F2ᵛ)

The rhetoric here is unmistakably puritan. Around the same time *The Tide* was printed (1576), Anthony Gilby, a co-editor of the Genevan Bible and active in the puritan movement of the seventies, charged that the teaching and practice of God's Word in the Church was being challenged by the "policye" of the Anglican hierarchy. "The haltinge in Religion for policye," wrote Gilby to his Presbyterian colleague Thomas Cartwright, "dryvesth awaye the true feare of God forth of mens hartes."[65] He goes on to say, "So in the steade of the olde beaste popery that is wounded to death by Gods worde, we rayse up this seconde beaste policye to do all that the other beaste dyde before." The result is that "religion shall wax cold and become an outward hypocritical show, only for custom and policy." Likewise, Wapull's point is that the Church has lost its true aims of preaching God's Word and engendering faith, because the clergy have been diverted from the founding truths by their preoccupation with political or secular interests, and by their pursuit of riches. William

Wager, whom we know to have been involved with the puritans, makes the same point in *Enough is as Good as a Feast*.[66] One cannot help but conclude that Faithful Few, who turns the titles to signify the Church's return to teaching the fundamentals of faith and God's Word, refers to Cartwright and his followers, who pushed for church reform along the lines of a scripturally based church, stripped of its wealth and its dependence upon the Crown. *The Tide Tarrieth No Man* was published at a time when the puritan party was rapidly growing in strength, although still opposed by the Crown and the rich and powerful bishops, "the greedy great ones" who persecute Faithful Few (F3^{rv}). Christianity hopes that his reformation will not be long in coming (G1^{r}), but in addition to the efforts of the Faithful Few, support and cooperation will be needed from men of authority in the civil government (G4^{r}).

Reformation money plays

If Wapull's proverbial title "the tide tarrieth no man" applies to the state of the Church (it echoes contemporary puritan jargon of not "tarrying for the magistrate" indefinitely in exercising ecclesiastical reform), it is also used in the very different sense of referring to the reprobate majority in society who, faced with a short and fleeting existence in this world, restlessly strive to experience as much pleasure and acquire as much wealth as possible while time lasts. The play's critique of greed and acquisitiveness reflects the reaction of many Elizabethan preachers and religious playwrights to the rapid expansion of commercial activity which England witnessed during the latter half of the sixteenth century, and especially to the continuing problems of inflation, unemployment, and poverty which the Protestant Tudor governments inherited from pre-Reformation times but had failed to solve. *The Tide* suggests that few Christians pursue their divinely-appointed callings in accordance with God's will, and that the growth of materialism in England at the expense of sound biblical values has not only caused corruption and error within the established Church, but increased wrongdoing and social upheaval in the secular realm as well. Wapull assumes that commercial abuses and disorders have their origins in the base drives and desires of corrupt human nature, signified by the play's Vice, Courage. Courage's assistants, named Hurtful Help, Feigned Fur-

therance, and Painted Profit, are financial brokers and middlemen
who illustrate the dangers of a cash-nexus economy in which
individuals are increasingly defined in monetary terms.[67] Among the
predatory rogues deceived by Courage and his henchmen are
Greediness, a usurious money-lender and double-dealing merchant,
and No-Good-Neighborhood, a wealthy immigrant and landlord
who is equally unscrupulous. Those most victimized by such
economic conditions are the virtuous and the poor, exemplified in the
persons of the Tenant and the Debtor, who get caught up in the
network of intrigue engineered by Courage.

Social and economic reform is the chief concern of several other
Reformation troupe plays of the 1560s and early 70s. These
include three plays attributed to William Wager, *Enough is as Good as
a Feast*, *The Trial of Treasure*, and *The Cruel Debtor*, as well as Thomas
Lupton's *All for Money* and Ulpian Fulwell's *Like Will to Like*. Like
The Tide, these "money" plays decry the evils of excessive commercialism: the restless pursuit of wealth, oppression of the poor, usury,
rent-racking, etc. For the London mercantile class to whom these
criticisms appear to have been addressed,[68] the early years of
Elizabeth's reign promised great prosperity and economic growth.
The recoinage of 1562 restored confidence in English currency on the
international market following the successive (and economically
disastrous) debasements of the Henrician and Edwardian governments, the Statute of Articifers the following year provided a labor
code and settled disputes over wage-earning, and in 1567 and 1571
respectively Sir Thomas Gresham opened the Royal Exchange and
convinced the Crown to pass new legislation permitting interest up to
ten percent (the Usury Act of 1571). Despite the growth of wealth
and the strengthening of the economy, the central government
remained conservative in its views of economic practice and
suspicious of the more adventurous proposals of the rich merchants,
with some administrators, namely Leicester and possibly also Sir
Christopher Hatton, supporting the anti-usury campaign led by
Thomas Wilson, Thomas Rogers, Crowley and others.[69] The money
plays voice the opinion of these moralists and their patrons that the
advancement of commerce has done little to alleviate the suffering of
the poor and dispossessed and only compounded social and economic
problems by promoting greed and exploitation in the areas of trade
and housing. Commercial success was in part responsible for the
thousands of provincial laborers and foreign emigrants (the latter

welcomed by the Crown in the early 1560s) who flooded into London looking for work, which in turn contributed to overcrowding and squalid living conditions. Between 1530 and 1563, the population of the built-up area reportedly grew from an estimated 50,000 to 93,000.[70] In his *Survey of London* (1598), John Stow recalls that "filthy cottages" and row upon row of tenements "letten out to strangers, and other meane people" now occupied the dissolved monastic lands which were seized and sold off to laymen.[71] When the demand outstripped supply, rents for housing to let rose to unaffordable rates for poor commoners, many of whom were evicted to make room for the much-resented foreign tradesmen from France and the Low Countries. Food prices similarly rose as grain production failed to keep up with the population growth, so that it was widely believed that merchants, like landlords, used the price-rising trends to profiteer even further.

The authors of the money plays, like most commentators of the time, seem to have had little grasp of the complex interplay of forces causing price inflation, high unemployment, and other economic realities of the time. The playwrights *do* take the government to task for contributing to the current situation, openly challenging its legalization of interest in the Usury Act of 1571, its lax immigration policy which encouraged foreign laborers to work in England, and the 1559 parliamentary bill authorizing the Crown's seizure of Bishop's lands which impoverished many parish clergy. Yet they are generally skeptical that "policy" can change social conditions. Like the so-called Commonwealth Men of Edward VI's reign, they perceive covetousness, ambition, and oppression ultimately as "spiritual" evils, the responsibility of which resides with individual sinners, not with the "system." This strong sense of individual responsibility derived in part from the Calvinist doctrine of the calling which taught that the manner by which a man pursues his divinely appointed vocation in the social order is a direct reflection of his spiritual condition.[72]

Elizabethan Calvinist notions about calling and stewardship in the money plays do not challenge but reinforce traditional political opinion about social order and relations. One must live within the bounds of one's vocation by observing social rank and degree.[73] Thus, in *Enough is as Good as a Feast* and *The Trial and Treasure* the ruling class are exhorted to fulfill God's will in the important vocations to which they have been called, the "poor men &

commons" to "walke well in your vocation," banishing greed and ambition in the pursuit of heavenly treasure.[74] *All for Money* likewise teaches that the poor laboring class should accept its lowly station, even if it means a life of poverty, and that the wealthy and privileged have an obligation to practice charity towards the poor and sick (C3^r). Within this scheme of things, the rapid social advancement of ambitious merchants and middle-class landlords are perceived as a threat to social stability. In *The Tide Tarrieth No Man*, the courtier, Willing-To-Win-Worship, becomes a victim of the acquisitive rogues, Hurtful Help and Feigned Furtherance, who lend him money at an exorbitant rate of interest and seize his property when he is unable to pay it. Only in a society where wealth is valued above principles of morality and order can an upstart merchant advance to the level of a gentleman while the gentleman, landless and broke, descends to the lowly station of a pauper.

The chief vice which leads men to abuse their callings and jeopardize their own souls is covetousness, "the Londoners sinne," as one Calvinist preacher describes it.[75] This is the main theme of Wager's *Enough is as Good as a Feast*.[76] Thinking only in terms of his welfare in this lifetime, the greed-driven landlord, Worldly Man, justifies his accumulation of wealth on the ground that misfortune may strike at any time and therefore one must prepare for old age by storing up riches now (A3^v). This leads him to embrace the most presumptuous argument of all: he ought to be in the business of making money because it is his divinely appointed vocation (D3^r). The suffering and oppression caused by his covetous practices are dramatized by three tableaux figures who recall Wapull's lowly victims noted earlier. Tenant complains that his rent has been doubled due to Worldly Man's greed and to the influx of foreigners who cause prices to rise. He is joined by Servant, who complains that he is treated more like a slave than a servant, being deprived of basic needs. A third victim, Hireling, claims that Worldly Man has cheated him out of a half year's wages. When the three request to have their grievances redressed, they are callously turned away by the landlord and his steward. Through this behavior, Worldly Man manifests his spiritual reprobation. Failing to respond to the sermon of the Prophet, he is visited by God's Plague and dies impenitent and damned. If Worldly Man's restless and acquisitive drive for wealth brought him to damnation, Wager implies that the government must be in some measure responsible for encouraging such behavior through its condoning of usury. Wager's alignment with the anti-usury campaign of Wilson and others is voiced through a speech by Satan who enters to carry off the reprobate's corpse to hell:

> How cunningly put he his mony to usury:
> Yea, and that without offense of any law.
> ...
> All you worldly men, that in your riches doo trust,
> Be merry and iocund, build Palaces and make lust cheer:
> Put your money to usury, let it not lye and rust,
> Occupye your selues in my lawes while ye be heer.
>
>   (G1^{r-v})

Like Wapull, William Wager and Thomas Lupton comment upon the ruinous effects of covetousness when practiced by authorities in the nation's leading institutions. Wager joins Wapull in condemning the wealth and ambition of the bishops and their indifference towards the widespread poverty and illiteracy of the parish clergy. In *All for Money*, the corrupt judge, appropriately named All-for-Money, demonstrates how the power of money can cause injustice at all levels of society. While one of his suitors, a rich franklin named Nichol-never-out-of-law, is able to use All-for-Money's services in evicting a poor neighboring tenant from his land, Moneyless-and-Friendless is sentenced to hanging for petty theft. The law, Lupton implies, is on the side of the rich when covetous officials control the courts (D1^{r-v}).

As a remedy for the restless drive for gain and status, the money plays urge every man in his calling to restrain his affection from the world, to trust in divine providence, and to practice contentation.[77] William Wager conveys this alternative lifestyle through the example of Worldly Man's elect counterpart, Heavenly Man. Heavenly Man accepts his social station with providential resignation, and regards the temptations and adversities of this world as means of strengthening his faith. In contrast to Worldly Man's deserved damnation, he is visited with Rest, who brings him joys "prepared for the heauenly from the beginning: / And giuen unto them for a rewarde of their godly liuing" (G2^v).

This last quotation, implying that Heavenly Man's salvation is foreordained, draws attention to the most anomalous feature of Reformation religious drama as a whole. At the same time as it attempts to evangelize, to press for changes within the Church and within society, it also insists on an Augustinian view of predestination.

If Heavenly Man's salvation is predestined, "the worldly man will needs be a worldly man still," we are told, since "it will not out of the flesh that is bred in the bone verily" (D3ᵛ). The sense of determinism is no less pronounced in *The Trial of Treasure*, *The Tide Tarrieth No Man*, *All for Money*, and *Like Will to Like*. In these interludes, the majority in society are perceived to be hopelessly depraved and fixed in their evil ways. Their reprobation is depicted largely in economic terms. On the other hand, only the Faithful Few practice virtue and attain salvation. The authors apparently did not see any inconsistency between the notion of predestination and their proselytizing aims. In their study of Elizabethan religious literature, Charles George and Katherine George have observed a similar incongruity between the ministerial enthusiasm of English Protestantism and its adherence to predestination. They write:

However emphatically the concept is presented – that God and not man is the only effective agent in man's salvation – the very activities of an intensely proselytizing and evangelical church, as early Protestantism was, are directly contradictory, in terms of simple logic, to strict predestinarian doctrine. Indeed, the whole literature of English Protestantism is a product of a ministerial enthusiasm which seems constantly to be overstepping the limits which logically it has set for itself – bringing to the listeners a mere awareness of their eternal destiny, whatever that might be. It certainly does not merely inform of salvation: it exhorts to it.[78]

Thus, the assumption taken for granted in the Reformation drama, as in many contemporary sermons, is that those who respond to the message are imbued with the necessary grace to do so (this is Mary's experience in *Mary Magdalene*), and therefore must have been elect in the first place. As Godly Admonition states at the conclusion of *All for Money*:

Here haue you had [seen] inordinate loue
Which man hath to money although it worke his wo:
But *such as haue any grace, this will them stirre and moue*
To cast their loue from money and other pleasures also
For feare they dwell with the deuill, their cruell and mortal foe.
(G3ʳ; my italics)

Nevertheless, a sense of fatalism remains strong in many of these plays. As we shall see in the next chapter, adherence to the notion of predestination becomes a particularly thorny problem to the Calvinist playwright who maintains at the same time the reformative power of education.

4

Reformation drama and education

Several of the troupe plays discussed in the last chapter present adolescents or young adults in central roles, and if not dealing specifically with youth-education they offer some message to wayward youths or their negligent parents. *Mary Magdalene*, we may recall, depicts Mary as the young gentlewoman of the court who is heir to a large estate, and holds her Catholic, negligent parents at least partly responsible for her profligate lifestyle. In *Like Will to Like*, the two delinquent youths, Cutbert Cutpurse and Pierce Pickpurse, openly admit that their parents similarly spoiled them and failed to educate them in virtue. Not all young people, however, are depicted as ill-bred or incorrigible. In *New Custom* the old popish priest Perverse Doctrine rails against the preachers of the gospel "not past twenty years old" and New Custom himself is "a young upstart lad" in his twenties. All this attention devoted to youth in the Reformation drama becomes more understandable when we consider that as much as half of England's population of about three million in the mid-sixteenth century was under the age of twenty,[1] and that young adults made up a large segment of the playgoing public, so much so that legislation was proposed and passed to curb the large throngs of youths attending performances in Edwardian and early Elizabethan London.[2]

If the popularity of drama among youths occasionally posed problems for local magistrates, the Crown did not squander the opportunity of using this popularity to its own advantage. As I will try to show in the present chapter, schoolmasters and other Protestant playwrights, backed and in some instances directly patronized by the central government, used the amateur drama of the nation's academic institutions as an instrument of promoting the state's educational aims and policies. They, as well as foreign and native reformers who influenced public opinion on domestic and social issues, had the foresight to see that England's future as a Protestant nation largely depended on a sound Christian education for its young people. They recognized that Roman Catholic religion could not be effectively challenged and uprooted without it; for education, at the very least, would equip people with the ability to read the Scriptures for themselves and thereby come face to face with the true gospel without corrupt priests, idolatrous images, and superstitious ceremonies getting in the way. However, more than the nation's spiritual well-being was at stake. Many young people were needed to take leadership roles in the reformed church and the expanding state bureaucracy. With the dissolution of the monasteries and the transfer of power and property from church to state, there was a great demand for men with legal training and other skills to work within the households of prominent statesmen and provide service within the government.[3] Moreover, the result of the dissolutions was the loss of the major agency for recruiting clergy for service within the church. Something had to replace it. "When a system of recruiting the clergy was eventually built up it was on the foundation of a school and university education."[4]

Protestant educators regarded stage-playing as a useful adjunct to formal study. In mixing profit with pleasure, it could reinforce the moral and religious values taught through textbook and schoolroom instruction and, in the case of those who acted, provide the verbal and oratorical skills, as well as the "good behaviour and audacitye," needed for leadership within the reformed Christian state.[5] These views, which originated with such Humanists as Erasmus and Vives, were embraced and put into practice in the Protestant centers of Wittenberg, Geneva, and Strasbourg, and received their most eloquent expression in England by Martin Bucer, the continental reformer who served as Regius Professor of Divinity at Cambridge from 1549 to 1551.[6] Coming to England from Strasbourg where the noted educator John Sturm used drama extensively for pedagogical purposes, Bucer devotes a part of his treatise on social and educational reform, *De Regno Christi*, to the production and regulation of drama performed by schoolboys and others engaged in academic pursuits. Dedicated to Edward VI as a new year's gift in 1551, the treatise was offered as a kind of blueprint for the governing of a Christian commonwealth. In the chapter entitled "De Honestis Ludis," Bucer considers drama a useful form of entertainment for youth, and when properly staged, a means of promoting piety and moral character in society at large. But whether they be comedies or tragedies, plays must be composed by religious men, "schooled in the knowledge of Christ's kingdom and also endowed with discrimination."[7] The moral and spiritual lesson of course is all important. The plays should imitate Bible stories in aiming to "strengthen faith in God, to arouse love and desire of God and to create and increase not only admiration of piety and justice, but also the horror of impiety and of the sowing and fostering of every kind of evil." Bucer is very concerned that the depiction of evil on the stage be handled with tact and discretion; the activities and sins of men must at all times be presented within a moral context:

these qualities must be handled in either kind of poetry, comic or tragic, in such a way that when the faults and sins of men are being described and shown in action as though before our eyes, even the crimes of the most abandoned of men, yet some dread of divine judgement and of a horror of sin should appear in them: no exultant delight in crime or shameless insolence should be displayed.[8]

Bucer adds that it may be necessary to sacrifice some of the eloquence and charm that characterizes the great classics in order to give first priority to the Christian message.[9]

Schoolmasters and Reformation drama

That views similar to Bucer's on drama and education were circulating among Protestant administrators and playwrights in Reformation England is indicated in the records of theatrical activity in the academic institutions, particularly in the song and grammar schools. At this level, the period produced an unusually large and energetic group of Protestant educators, among them Ralph Radcliffe, Nicholas Udall, Thomas Ashton, and William Hunnis, who were directly engaged in writing and producing plays for their own students. The first known schoolmaster to stage religious plays promoting the Reformation was Thomas Wylley, the vicar of Yoxford, Suffolk, who (as noted in the last chapter) wrote to Cromwell in 1536 seeking patronage for his boy choristers, and he may well have been "Master Hopton's priest" who brought a boys' troupe to perform before Cromwell the following year.[10] Like so many other provincial clerics in Tudor England, Wylley evidently combined the roles of pastor and schoolmaster and presided over the

12 Martin Bucer, Regius Professor of Divinity, Cambridge University, 1549–51, an eighteenth-century mezzotint by R. Houston of a portrait by an unknown artist. Reproduced from C. Hopf, *Martin Bucer and the English Reformation* (Oxford University Press, 1945).

local song school.[11] The titles of his plays, *A Reverent Receyving of the Sacrament*, *A Rude Comynawlte*, and *The Woman on the Rokke*, as well as the persecution he apparently experienced on account of them, suggest that Wylley intended the instruction they offered to extend far beyond the schoolroom. Another early reformist schoolmaster to write Protestant religious drama for his students was Ralph Radcliffe, former Jesus College Cambridge MA and tutor to the Marquis of Dorset's children, at Hitchin Grammar School, founded in 1546. There, according to Bale who visited the school about 1552, he converted the lower quarters of the dissolved Carmelite house into a "theatrum."[12] Like Wylley, Radcliffe seems to have had connections with Henry VIII's Reformation government,[13] and this too may explain the reformist, and in some instances controversial, nature of his plays, among them *The Burning of Sodom*, *The Condemnation of John Hus*, *The Disobedience of Jonah*, *The Afflictions of Job*, *The Deliverance of Susanna*. Bale lists the titles in Latin, but as Craik observes this does not imply that they were Latin plays: Bale's own vernacular plays are listed by him in Latin.[14] Moreover, the plays were performed before the townspeople as well as the students. It has been said that Radcliffe turned Hitchin into a highly profitable enterprise for himself as well as for the successful school before his death in 1559.[15] It is possible therefore that the plays were staged not only to improve the student-actors' public speaking and to disseminate Protestant teaching, but perhaps also to raise money for the school in the same way that parish productions helped to finance repairs and new furnishings in churches (see chapter 5 below).

Whether or not Bucer's rules of dramatic composition and regulation in schools influenced educational policy in the court of Edward VI, it should be noted that Bucer was tutoring the future schoolmasters of England at Cambridge, among them the Calvinist Thomas Ashton.[16] In 1561 Ashton became the headmaster of Shrewsbury Grammar School, founded during Edward's reign. During the 1560s, he staged several lavish productions of his own plays for the general public, including *The Passion of Christ* (performed in 1561 and 1569) and *Julian the Apostate* (1565). Since the Statutes of the school required acting as a student exercise,[17] we may safely assume that the schoolmaster's own students were among the principal performers (they may have included Philip Sidney and Fulke Greville who entered in 1564), and certainly the anti-Christian Emperor Julian (361–63 A.D.), whom Roger Ascham in *The Scholemaster* condemns for prohibiting "knowledge of God's doctrine" in schools, would have been a suitable subject for students.[18] The plays were acted in a quarry near the city in which a huge semi-circular amphitheatre was constructed, attracting between 10,000 and 20,000 people for the town's major theatrical event of the year at Whitsuntide.[19] The Queen herself had reportedly planned to see Ashton's *Passion of Christ*. In 1569, the passion play "lasted all the holly daies," and in doing so provides another example besides Bale's mysteries of a Protestant attempt to supplant the Catholic cycle plays with similar entertainment espousing Reformation teaching. Described by his contemporary Thomas Churchyard as a "good and godly preacher,"[20] Ashton, like Wylley and probably Radcliffe, sought favor from Protestant leaders at court. He had ties with Lord Cecil and other members of the Privy Council, including the Earls of Leicester, Bedford, and Essex, and followed his resignation as headmaster in 1571 by undertaking such political tasks as reporting on the extent of papist influence in the western counties.[21] He further demonstrates that schoolmasters, like other ecclesiastical and civic leaders in the provinces, worked in conjunction with the central government to disseminate Protestant ideology.

By Edward VI's reign there were over 250 petty, song, and grammar schools in England, as many as 350 by 1577 when William Harrison remarked in his description of England that nearly every corporate town had at least one grammar school.[22] It is impossible to know whether more than a very few of these offered dramatic productions on any regular or seasonal basis, since the surviving records are so sparse; indeed, without Bale's writings we would know nothing about Radcliffe's productions at Hitchin. A school's programme of drama would naturally depend on the interests of the choir or grammar master, on the facilities and funds available, and on whether a tradition of drama existed. Schools for which we have statutes, financial records, or other evidence of dramatic performances include King's at Canterbury, Ipswich, Norwich, Wells, Louth, Ludlow, Beverley, Kettering, Winchester, Eton, Merchant Taylors', Westminster and St. Paul's.[23] In the grammar schools, where Latin dominated the curriculum, the plays of Terence and Plautus were taught as early as the third form and were evidently performed in the original tongue with some frequency.[24] Other secular and noncontroversial works such as *Wit and Science, The Marriage of Wit and Wisdom,* and *Ralph Roister Doister,* have been ascribed to the children's companies of the Chapel Royal, St. Paul's, Merchant Taylors', Westminster, and Eton, especially for performance at the royal court during the 1560s and 1570s when Queen Elizabeth showed a preference for entertainment on classical and romantic themes.[25] Yet other evidence, including the many surviving youth plays of a Protestant bias, indicate that such works were also performed with some frequency at the famous song and grammar schools near or in London. Nicholas Udall's *Ezechias* and *De Papatu* were probably written for his schoolboys at Eton College, and perhaps performed before Thomas Cromwell when they were summoned to court in 1538.[26] Another schoolmaster, William Hunnis, presumed author of the Calvinist *Jacob and Esau,* is known to have written many plays for the Children of the Chapel,[27] and may have participated in the polemical court drama of Edward VI. St. Paul's Choir School is also linked to polemical religious drama early in the sixteenth century (they acted an anti-Lutheran play before Henry VIII in November 1527), although with the inception of Sebastion Westcott, a Catholic recusant, as choirmaster under Elizabeth, Protestant religious drama presumably declined.

Reformation drama at the universities and Inns of Court

As the nation's leading centers of Reformation learning, the two universities staged Protestant religious plays, yet their tradition of academic drama developed much later than the schools' and it would not be until William Gager's career at Oxford in the 1580s and 1590s that one finds a figure comparable to Ashton, Radcliffe and Hunnis who was engaged over an extended period in both the writing and production of plays. Moreover, surprisingly few university play texts survive; those that do are mostly in Latin and Greek and would seem to support college injunctions, statutes and contemporary reports that the study of such works should enhance students' knowledge and pronunciation in the classical languages.[28] Nevertheless, at such colleges as St. John's at Cambridge, a Christmas lord was appointed and paid to arrange dramatic performances, drama was encouraged as a suitable pastime for students between terms, and occasionally visiting itinerant troupes acted before the scholars, as the Prologue to *Mary Magdalene* and accounts at various colleges indicate.[29] Oxford's most acclaimed biblical playwright was Bale's friend Nicholas Grimald, whose Latin resurrection play, *Christus Redivivus*, was performed at Brasenose in 1541, and according to a dedicatory letter, before the townspeople as well as the scholars. Seven years later, his *Archipropheta*, on the life of John the Baptist, was seen at Christ Church. The dramatic records at Oxford, however, reveal mostly plays by classical authors – Aristophanes, Euripides, Terence, and Plautus. While the same is basically true for Cambridge, the religious drama acted there lived up to the university's contemporary reputation for Protestant controversy, beginning in 1545 with Kirchmayer's anti-papal *Pammachius* at Christ's, which provoked an angry response from reactionary Bishop Stephen Gardiner, who described it as "so pestiferous as were intolerable."[30] In 1562, John Foxe's *Christus Triumphans*, the purpose of which was "to transfer as far as possible from the sacred writings into the theater those things which pertain primarily to ecclesiastical affairs," was staged at Trinity College Cambridge.[31] Following Kirchmayer and Bale, Foxe's characters are polarized into the proponents of the true gospel and the emissaries of the popish Anti-Christ (see figure 13). However, it was during Queen Elizabeth's visit to Cambridge in August 1564, that the polemical religious drama received a royal audience. A few days before the Queen's arrival, Secretary William Cecil, who was also Chancellor of Cambridge, went up to the University to discuss with a committee of administrators what sermons, debates, and plays, would be suitable for the Queen's pleasure.[32] One of the plays approved was Udall's *Ezekias*, performed by the students before the Queen in King's College Chapel on the evening of Tuesday, August 8. *Ezechias* is an openly iconoclastic work which places the new Protestant Queen in the role of a latter day Ezekias sweeping aside superstition and idolatry to make way for genuine religious worship. However, if this elaborate production was to receive an appreciative royal audience (see pp. 142–46, below), an impromptu performance a few days later at Hinchenbrook where some overly enthusiastic students had followed the Queen to her overnight lodging there deeply offended her. Guzman de Silva, the Spanish Ambassador reported:

The actors came in dressed as some of the imprisoned [Catholic] bishops. First came the bishop of London carrying a lamb in his hands as if he were eating it as he walked along, and then others with [other] devices, one being in the figure of a dog with the Host in his mouth. They write that the Queen was so angry that she at once entered her chamber using strong language and the men who held the torches, it being night, left them in the dark, and so ended the thoughtless and scandalous representations.[33]

The obvious targets of this burlesque were Edmund Bonner, Bishop of London under Queen Mary and now in prison, and the doctrine of transubstantiation. From that time forward, polemical religious drama seems not to have been tolerated at the universities, at least not at such highly publicized events, as the Queen's subsequent visit to Oxford two years later clearly demonstrated.

Current knowledge of the legal dramatics of the Inns of Court, staged annually during the Christmas season and on various feast days, reveals more about the early influence of Italian comedy in England with Gascoigne's *Supposes*, Jeffere's *Bugbears*, and *The Two Italian Gentlemen*, than it does about the performance of Reformation drama, yet if the Inns' revels were "largely untouched by public

13 "The word of God vs popish superstition," a woodcut from the 1576 edition of John Foxe's *Acts and Monuments*. The juxtaposition of serious and plainly dressed Protestant saints with comical-looking and luxuriously attired popish clerics is a staple feature of English Reformation drama. Courtesy of Bridwell Library, Southern Methodist University, Dallas.

events, "[34] there were two notable exceptions. The first is of particular interest because the play in question illustrates the incipient English Protestantism of the 1520s with none other than Simon Fish, author of the anti-Catholic *Supplication of Beggars* (1528), in the leading role. At Christmas 1526, the students of Gray's Inn staged a play by one John Roo which reportedly contained a veiled attack on Cardinal Wolsey's character and conduct in national affairs. Wolsey immediately seized on the play's seditious contents, despite the denial of the actors when several of them were sought out by Wolsey's henchmen.[35] Among them was Fish, whom John Foxe says took the chief actor's part "after all others had refused it," and on "the same nyght that this Tragedy was playd, was compelled of force to voyde his owne house, & so fled over the sea unto Tyndale."[36] The second play was *Gorboduc*, staged by the Inner Temple in 1562 when the Earl of Leicester served as Constable-Marshal of the Christmas revels at the Inns of Court. This no doubt also had a politico-religious message for the central administration. Co-written by Thomas Norton, the translator of Calvin's *Institutes*, and subsequently acted before the Queen at court, the play offers advice not only on the succession but also on how to rule a Christian commonwealth, espousing Calvin's own political notion of a Christian monarchy strongly guided by and indeed ruling in conjunction with Parliament.

Extant youth plays and their auspices

While scholars generally agree on which surviving Protestant religious plays were written for students, the specific auspices for most of them remains uncertain since they are not mentioned in school or college records. If we set aside the Latin drama at the universities, most extant plays thought to be of academic auspices present young central characters, deal with educational or youth-related issues, include Latin quotations and other learned features, and show at least some familiarity with classical dramatic style. They also require a sizeable cast of actors with few or no doubling of parts and in some instances call for large props and scenery. Reformation play texts fitting this description include *Nice Wanton*, *The Disobedient Child*, *The Glass of Government*, *Jack Juggler*, *Jacob and Esau*, and *Misogonus*. With some of these plays, the name of the author is helpful in identifying auspices. *The Disobedient Child*, for example, was written by Thomas Ingeland who is described on the play's printed title page as a "late

Student in Cambridge," and therefore as Boas conjectures, *The Disobedient Child* might have been acted there. *Misogonus* may also be a Cambridge play. Scholars have attributed it on strong evidence to Anthony Rudd of Trinity College.[37] Both these plays with their adolescent characters, however, were equally suitable for school children. In *The Disobedient Child*, the young auditors are addressed as "children," and the fact that *Misogonus* was revised in 1577 by Laurence Johnson, schoolmaster of Kettering, Northamptonshire, suggests that he was adapting it for performance by his own students.

From other evidence within the plays themselves we can draw some useful, though admittedly tentative, conclusions about the sponsoring institutions and the audiences attending performances. The full title of *Jack Juggler*, as it appeared in printed form, is *A New Enterlued for chyldren to playe named Jacke Jugeler: both wytte, very playsent, and merye*, indicating that it was intended for schoolboys rather than college students. Since it contains no singing, it seems more suitable for a grammar school than for a choir school. For *Jacob and Esau* with its several songs assigned to boy actors, the opposite is almost certainly true (more on this play shortly). The youths portrayed in *Nice Wanton* are quite obviously of citizen rather than noble descent, and the play's urban setting points to a city grammar school such as St. Paul's. The sponsoring school may well have been one of many which permitted female students, since through the negative example of the heroine, Dalilah, the play stresses the importance of girls, as well as boys, attending school paid for by their parents.[38] On the other hand, *The Disobedient Child*, in which the main character is a "young gentleman," seems more directed at young men of birth who marry out of their class (the wife is a penniless maid) and choose "vain pleasure, pastime and vanity" over academic pursuit and careers worthy of their privileged position, recurring criticisms in Tudor treatises on the education of a gentleman.[39]

Play texts also support external evidence that in addition to students and faculty, parents and the general public were invited to performances. *Misogonus*, *Nice Wanton* and *The Disobedient Child* directly address moralizing speeches to parents in the audience, as do the youth interludes *Lusty Juventus* and *The Longer Thou Livest*. Moreover, one cannot help but believe that the religious polemics of *Jacob and Esau* and *Jack Juggler*, no less than those in the plays of Wylley and Radcliffe, were intended more for the enlightenment of parents and other adult spectators than for the children's.

I mentioned earlier that large casting requirements are a typical feature of the academic drama. Yet we should not categorically exclude plays with troupe-style casting and doubling conventions. Take, for instance, William Wager's *The Longer Thou Livest the More Fool Thou Art* which requires only four actors doubling several parts apiece but appears in most respects to be a children's play. As Craik observes, "with its abundant Latin quotations and the humour of beating the intractable young fool Moros at the beginning of the play, [*The Longer Thou Livest*] seems particularly apt to schoolboy performance."[40] We may recall, moreover, that Wager was a grammar school governor, and since he also lectured at the hospital of St. Mary Woolnoth, he may have had some contact with the foundation's singing children who in 1557 were led by John Taylor, subsequently choirmaster of the playing choristers at Westminster School (beginning in 1562).[41] Be that as it may, it should also be kept in mind that noble households often were centers of instruction, and so a nobleman would naturally find it appropriate to have his own or a visiting professional company perform plays on youth themes that would be relevant to his children and other minors under his guardianship. We know, for example, that the households of William Cecil and William Petre, following the pattern set by Sir Thomas More, provided facilities for teaching wards and other noblemen's children. Indeed the lost comedies which More himself is reputed to have written might have been for the students in his household.[42] There seem to have been many other similar household schools, since Ascham's *The Scholemaster* was "specially purposed for the private bringing up of youth in gentlemen and noblemen's houses."[43] I have already conjectured that *Mary Magdalene* (*c.* 1550) was written for the children of the ruling elite, and this may well have been the case of *The Longer Thou Livest* (*c.* 1565) which deals with the education of a reprobate gentleman's son who later becomes a tyrannical ruler.[44]

One other Reformation play which is clearly addressed to youth but is neither a "school" play nor one composed for the privileged classes is the Edwardian interlude *Lusty Juventus*. The play's Vice, Hypocrisy, is a butcher "simple and rude of fashion," Abominable Living is a serving maid (and part-time prostitute), whereas Lusty Juventus himself, while a generic character representing all youth, has much in common with the restless young apprentices of Edwardian London who rejected the Catholicism of their parents, attended sermons and at least outwardly professed to be of the new faith, but who were frequently chastised in official prohibitions and moral treatises for lechery, idleness, rowdiness and general public mischief.[45] The catechism-oriented exchanges between Juventus and his spiritual advisors, the treatment of abstract theological issues, combined with the play's urban setting, suggest that the author, Richard Wever, was one of the several preacher/playwrights who wrote for a local professional playing troupe catering to the large audiences of apprentices and other youth flocking to plays during the early part of Edward VI's reign.[46]

Extant youth plays: education vs. predestination

As I suggested earlier, most extant academic plays relate to the experiences of young people, and in particular to the problems of raising and educating them. In treating these issues, the schoolmaster playwrights experiment with classical methods of structure and play presentation already exhibited in student textbooks of classical dramatists, particularly those of Plautus and Terence. The influence of Latin comedy is most explicitly evident in *Jack Juggler*, where the Prologue promptly announces that the play is modeled on Plautus' *Amphitruo*, with its story of mistaken identity. It is also evident in *Misogonus* and *Jacob and Esau*, both of which follow classical precedent by dividing the action into acts and scenes and by presenting saucy, quick-witted servants and their gullible masters. Humanist educators on the Continent had long been working with classical dramaturgy, and as scholars have frequently observed, Tudor schoolmasters were undoubtedly familiar with their works which were made available through publication.[47] The latter interludes, along with *Nice Wanton*, *The Disobedient Child* and *The Glass of Government*, are clearly influenced by the "prodigal son" plays of Ravisius Textor (1470–1524) and other continental Humanists who dramatized contemporary versions of the biblical parable in the spirit and style of Roman comedy. Nevertheless, many of the same dramaturgical features we observed in the troupe plays in the last chapter appear in the academic interludes. As in them, stage presentation, story-line and character are devised to support a homiletic argument.

The views on childrearing and education expressed in the Reformation youth plays are typically those found in royal injunctions, school statutes, and the homiletic writings of such reformers as Bucer, Calvin, Thomas Becon and James Pilkington. While they encourage responsible Protestant elders to spurn idleness in youth and exhort them to pursue vocations profitable to the common-wealth,[48] they share the basic assumption that education is above all else a religious undertaking, that its primary purpose is to engender piety and lead the way to salvation.[49] Their perception of childhood is basically Calvinistic, and it is chiefly in this respect that they differ from Humanist-oriented youth plays such as *Wit and Science, The Marriage of Wit and Wisdom, Thersites,* and *Gammer Gurton's Needle.* Rejecting the early Humanist notion of a new-born child as a *tabula rasa,* they see the infant soul blackened by original sin to such an extent that the will is naturally and impulsively drawn towards evil. The statement made by the Prologue in *Lusty Juventus* is echoed in many of the plays:

> Forasmuch as man is naturally prone,
> To euil from his youth as scripture doth recite,
> It is necessary that he be spedely withdrawen
> From concupiscence of syn, his naturall appetite.　(A1ᵛ).[50]

This inborn propensity for wicked behavior can be checked, but it is important for parents and guardians to begin correction and teaching in infancy, since it would be next to impossible to reform an individual's character later on.[51] The playwrights and contemporary moralists were fond of likening a child to a young plant which in its tender years is flexible but becomes increasingly more difficult to shape or bow as it grows older.[52] Instruction involves above all else teaching the Scriptures, not only because it provides a moral code by which to live but also because it is only through God's Word that unregenerate man comes to a knowledge of his depraved self, totally reliant on God's mercy for salvation.[53]

If youngsters fail to respond to godly instruction, they are to be disciplined with the rod of correction. Spoiling or "cockering" children was considered an unwholesome and even dangerous way of raising them. *Nice Wanton, Misogonus, Lusty Juventus,* and *The Longer Thou Livest* all depict dissolute youths whose elders spoiled them in infancy. In the latter play, the schoolmaster Discipline says "Two things destroy youth at this day":

> *Indulgentia parentum,* the fondness of parents
> Which will not correct their naughty way,
> But rather embolden them in their intents;
> Idleness, alas idleness, is another.　(D3ʳ)

As the inevitable consequence of parental negligence and indiscipline, idleness is particularly reprehensible in youngsters because it was believed to give birth to a host of other harmful diversions and sins and to lead the more impressionable ones into the company of wanton and dishonest persons.[54]

The most detailed portrayal of a doting, negligent parent is the mother Xantippe in *Nice Wanton*. She pampers her children, excusing rather than chastising their faults, resents and dismisses the wise counsel of her neighbors, and complains about the strict discipline which her youngsters are expected to comply with at school. Later, learning that her daughter Dalilah has died of the pox and that her son Ismael has been hanged for robbery and murder, she is driven into despair by the recognition that this was due to her own negligence and indiscipline.

Parents are blamed for their children's unregeneracy in these plays not only because they fail to exercise discipline but also because they raise them in Roman Catholic superstition. The counsel of the older generation, steeped as it is in popish religion, is specious and unreliable, and in some interludes youths are encouraged to reject parental authority. As the Devil exclaims in *Lusty Juventus*, Youth "telleth his parentes that ... they of long time haue deceiued be" (C1^r).[55] In *Nice Wanton*, it is Xantippe's only godly child, Barnabus, a recipient of "special grace," who is instrumental in the religious conversion of his mother and his pox-stricken sister before her death. Barnabas illustrates the eagerness with which some Protestant children in Reformation England sought to win their parents and other family members to the gospel.[56]

In all the Reformation plays dealing with raising children one discerns an ideological tension between a basically Humanist-derived belief that a Christian education can ensure moral and spiritual regeneracy and the prevailing Calvinist conviction that salvation is a predestined consequence of irresistible grace. In the Prologue to *The Longer Thou Livest*, William Wager recognizes this problem and arrives at the conclusion that parental influence and education are subordinate to the absolute will of God in forming human character:

> Bringing up is a great thing, so is diligence,
> But nothing, God except, is so strong as Nature;
> For neither councell, learninge nor sapience,
> Can an euill nature to honest manners allure.   (A2^v)

Nevertheless, the question remains that if divine grace is irresistible, and man in his natural depravity lacks the power to obey godly instruction, then what role, if any at all, can a religious education have in bringing about moral and spiritual regeneration? The answer to this, as explained in contemporary religious writings and as illustrated in the plays themselves, is that while godly instruction is not in itself efficacious, it is the most common vehicle through which God outwardly dispenses saving grace. Of relevance here is Calvin's reply to the advocates of free-will who argued that teaching and exhortation are pointless if the individual lacks the power within himself to learn or obey. To this Calvin responded: "O man, what arte thou to appoint a lawe for God? If it be his pleasure, that wee be prepared by exhortation to receiue the self same grace, whereby is wrought that the exhortation is obeied, what hast thou in this order to bite or carpe at?" He goes on to say, "If any man require a plainer answere, let him take this":

God worketh after two sortes in his elect, inwardly by his spirite, outwardly by his worde: By his spirit, by enlightning their mindes, by framing their heartes to the loue and keeping of iustice, he maketh them a new creature: By his word, he stirreth them to desire, to seeke & atteine the same renuing ... So though Christ pronounce that no man commeth to him, but whome the father draweth, and that the elect doe come when they haue heard and learned of the Father: yet doth not he neglect the office of a teacher, but with his voice diligently calleth them, whome it necessarily behoueth to bee inwardly taught by the holy Ghost, that they may any thing profite.[57]

According to Calvin, then, God's Word, embodied in the Scriptures, is the external means by which God moves men to righteousness, and as we have seen, to English Protestants education was primarily concerned with the inculcation of biblical principles and values. The educator/reformer Thomas Becon speaks for most of his contemporaries when he states that "the office of a godly father is to see that his children be virtuously brought up and in the knowledge of God's most holy word."[58] This is not to say that a godly education ensured salvation any more than reading the Bible did, for it must be conjoined with the inward workings of the Holy Spirit, as Calvin points out.

There were, moreover, some exceptional instances in which God's "special grace" directly intervenes to save the most incorrigible of youths and those who have been raised by negligent parents. *Nice Wanton*'s Barnabus himself provides a good example. In spite of the

fact that he was raised in the same unwholesome environment as his
delinquent brother and sister, he remains an unfailingly righteous
and responsible son. The explanation for his virtuous behavior is
given towards the end of the play, when he reproaches his mother:

> In that god preserued me, small thanks to you.
> If god had not giuen me speciall grace,
> To auoid euil, and do good, this is true,
> I had liued and dyed in a wretched case
> As they did, for I had both suffraunce and space.   (C1ᵛ)

"Special grace" also accounts for the salvation of those who seem
beyond redemption. Youths such as Lusty Juventus and Dalilah (and
here we may include Lewis Wager's Mary Magdalene as well) are
saved in spite of their ungodly upbringing. However, practical
experience proves that a regime of inculcating biblical principles and
values usually produces a strong faith and sound Christian character,
while those deprived of such an education rarely experienced
religious conversion.[59]

I say "usually" produces faith, for if God is sometimes merciful to
a child of ungodly parents, he also on occasion excludes grace from
the offspring of God-fearing parents, without, however, relieving
them of responsibility for their actions. This is the case in *The
Disobedient Child*, in which the rich man's son defies his godly father's
counsel to continue his schooling, and instead leaves home to marry
a poor maid who turns out to be a shrew. When he returns home
years later, penniless, disinherited and abandoned by his wife, the
father informs him that it is now too late to make amends and that he
must suffer the consequences of his folly. This is also true of *Glass of
Government* (1575), by George Gascoigne, and *Jacob and Esau*, both of
which (like *The Disobedient Child*) present the reverse family situation
to that of *Nice Wanton* and *Lusty Juventus*. In juxtaposing older and
younger brothers, these plays explore the question of how it is that
youths, given the identical Christian upbringing and education, can
turn out so differently. In Gascoigne's play, two younger brothers
grow up to be of exemplary moral character, one of them becoming
a successful preacher in Geneva, the center of Christian culture in the
eyes of the Elizabethan puritans. The two elder black sheep, on the
other hand, defiantly reject the good counsel given to them, fall in
with bad company, and live out their lives in vice and crime before
being brought to justice: one of them hanged for robbery, the other

whipped almost to the point of death for fornication. How, then, can one explain the wickedness of these boys who have been instructed in the godly precepts since early childhood and tutored by one of the finest schoolmasters in the city of Antwerp? The answer is given by the Fourth Chorus who declares that "the grace of God it is, wheron good gyftes must growe, / And lacke of God his grace it is, which makes them lye full lowe."[60] Even more emphatically, *Jacob and Esau* illustrates the notion that since all persons are deserving of damnation by reason of original sin and deliberate disobedience, God is not bound to save any child, even if he is born into a righteous family. Esau has been nurtured in the ideal family environment, yet he still grows up to be an inveterate sinner. A key scene in the play is the one in which Isaac's two neighbors, Hanan and Zethar, discuss whether predestination or education determine human character, a sort of sixteenth-century version of the nature vs. nurture debate. Zethar claims that Esau's degenerate condition is due to a lack of parental discipline and instruction on Isaac's part. If children were trained under the rod, he argues, they would eschew lewdness and other vices, and embrace virtue. Hanan replies that in the case of Esau, the quality of his upbringing has not been a decisive factor, since Isaac and Rebecca have been good, conscientious parents (A4^r). Esau's reprobation is apparent in his "yll inclination," a natural taste for wrongdoing and a stubborn refusal to receive godly instruction:

> Esau hath ben nought euer since he was borne.
> And wherof commeth this, of Education:
> Nay it is of his owne yll inclination.
> They were brought yp bothe under one tuition,
> But they be not bothe of one disposition.
> Esau is gyuen to looce and leude liuying. (A4^r)

As a reprobate, Esau is denied the necessary grace to be a righteous and obedient son. In Calvinist terms, his mind has been exposed to the Word, but his heart has not been illuminated by the Spirit. There is perhaps no better gloss to the above passage than the remarks of James Pilkington, the Edwardian and Elizabethan Bishop of Durham who established two grammar schools in his diocese: "This is the secret judgement of God, that of one good father, Isaac, came two so contrary children; the one so wicked, the other so good ... But this is to teach us the free grace of God, without any deserts on our part, whensoever he calls any to the true knowledge and fear of him; and

that it is neither the goodness or evilness of the father that makes a
good or evil child; for many good fathers have had evil children, and
evil fathers good children."[61]

Jacob and Esau

In *Jacob and Esau*, the subject of predestination is not limited to
questions of raising and educating children; it is the central topic of
the play which the author also applies to contemporary political
circumstances. As scholars have argued, the play identifies Jacob and
Rebecca with the Protestant elect and Esau with reprobate Catholic
authority against which rebellion is justified under certain conditions.
That a play written by a schoolmaster and performed by children
would adopt such a radical politico-religious stance should not be
surprising. The polemical titles of the plays by Wylley and Radcliffe
demonstrate that the playwrighting schoolmasters of the Reformation were no less concerned with the most pressing religious and
political issues of their day than they were with the practical matters
of educating youth.[62] For the remainder of this chapter, I would like
to focus on *Jacob and Esau* and one other school play that merits
particular attention for its treatment of controversial religious and
political issues of grave concern to English Protestants at mid-
century. That play is *Jack Juggler*, apparently the only surviving play
to attack the Roman Catholic doctrine of transubstantiation. Both
plays are representative of much Reformation school drama in their
use of neoclassical principles of dramaturgy, and both comment on
Roman Catholic oppression.

Jacob and Esau was entered in the Stationers' Register in 1557/58.
Despite this fact, most discussion of the play assumes an Edwardian
rather than a Marian date, assigning its composition sometime
between 1547 and 1553, primarily on the basis of its staunchly
Protestant (specifically predestinarian) theology. However, we
should not rule out the possibility that the play was written or at least
revived for performance during Queen Mary's reign. Under the new
regime numerous pro-Protestant and anti-Catholic interludes continued to be staged in defiance of official prohibitions; moreover,
political tracts espousing resistance to ungodly (i.e., Roman Catholic)
authority – an issue in *Jacob and Esau* – were published by Protestant
Marian exiles abroad and circulating in England. The author may
well have been William Hunnis, a playwrighting gentleman of the

Chapel Royal under Edward and Mary who was jailed for insurrection by the Marian authorities in 1557/58 but later pardoned and promoted to chapelmaster by Queen Elizabeth.[63] This would logically place the play within the repertory of the children of the Chapel Royal. The hymns in the interlude resemble those performed at the Chapel Royal, with the solo singing assigned to little Abra clearly intended for a specially gifted boy chorister. The parts of both Abra and Mido require skillful coordination of speech, song, and movement, as when, for example, Abra sweeps the floor as she sings the play's second song or when Mido mimics the gesturing and speech of his elders. This high calibre of acting was demanded at the Chapel Royal where the Master was given free license by the Crown to choose his choristers from any of the choir schools throughout the realm. The play's ten listed acting parts (excluding "the Poet") seem suitable for the eight children residing at the Chapel in 1553, assuming that Isaac's neighbors Hanan and Zethar (who briefly appear in the second scene never to return) involved doubling, as David Bevington suggests.[64]

Like Lewis Wager's *Mary Magdalene*, *Jacob and Esau* draws on a well-known biblical story to propagate Calvinist doctrine in rather explicit terms. Yet in spite of this shared religious outlook and homiletic intention, the two plays offer an interesting contrast in dramatic style, stage presentation, and treatment of biblical subject-matter. Indeed, the main differences are really those between a troupe play following traditional English dramaturgy and an academic play drawing on (though by no means exclusively) classical dramatic principles. We may recall that in Wager's play, a few well-known biblical scenes are interwoven into a psychomachia plot dramatizing the progress of the individual soul from unregeneracy to salvation. Mary, while not losing her biblical identity, is portrayed anachronistically as a contemporary social type (a young gentle-woman) and emblematically as representative of all mankind. Other "characters" also move freely amongst the worlds of biblical story, spiritual allegory, and topical satire, and are often self-presentational in that they explain their significance to the audience in direct-address speeches. Settings, which include Magdalene Castle, the "road to Jerusalem," a Jerusalem street, and the home of Simon the Pharisee, are only vaguely identified and unrepresented by scenery. In *Jacob and Esau*, on the other hand, the action focuses on biblical events throughout (although it gives fictional names to the Hebrew servants: Mido, Ragan, Abra), and the author takes further measures to give the work a sense of historical reality.[65] According to the title page, the players are "to be consydered to be Hebrews, and so should be apparailed with attire," which indicates the first professed attempt in an English play at "period costume."[66] The characters are as naturalistically portrayed as any in the drama of the time, with no breaking out of their roles to summarize the action or comment upon its significance as one finds commonly in the troupe plays, and they are unaccompanied by personified abstractions. To enhance the sense of verisimilitude, three greyhounds, "or one as may be gotten," are led in by Esau's servant Ragau for a hunting expedition as the play begins, and later in the action two kids are carried into the acting space.[67] All the action takes place in a single localized setting, in the Hebrew settlement in front of Isaac's tent, which is represented in some concrete fashion, perhaps by a *domus* similar to those prescribed for court productions in the Revels Accounts, although a curtained traverse might have sufficed.[68] The play holds up to the description in the title as a "mery and wittie Comedie," consistently comic throughout (apart from Esau's angry outburst in act 5), and exhibiting little of the coarseness and profanity, on the one hand, and few of the long serious sermonlike speeches on the other, that characterize the dialogue of Vices and Virtues in Wager's biblical interlude.

We should not be misled into thinking, however, that the play is any less homiletic in purpose. The doctrinal argument is announced in the prologue, applied to the audience in the concluding epilogue, illustrated through the contrasting characters of Jacob and Esau, and further elaborated in the dialogue and speeches of the other characters (particularly in the prayers of Rebecca and Isaac), although these are delivered "in character." The play's several delightful songs add direct moral commentary on the action. But no less important in conveying the message is the biblical narrative itself. The technique of using scriptural analogy to teach a lesson was a common practice among Protestant preachers and playwrights alike, and in this respect, the author of *Jacob and Esau* is at one with Lewis Wager and Bale before him. All three dramatists regard the Bible as a storehouse of archetypal stories and characters which not only prefigured the temporal world but were a key to understanding and resolving its religious and political crises. And in identifying with the chosen people of the Old Testament, Protestants believed that they were in a sense reliving the experiences of the Israelites.[69] Therefore, while *Jacob and Esau* lacks the explicit personification-allegory of Wager's play, the Old Testament story would have been subject to a topical reading by its contemporary audience, with explosive political implications, as we shall see shortly.

Jacob and Esau treats two issues, the theological problem of predestination, and the related political question of active resistance against reprobate (i.e. Catholic) authority. The former is explicitly addressed at the outset by "the Prologue, a Poet," perhaps the choirmaster or playwright, with considerable care taken to ground the notion of predestination in biblical verses from the books of Malachi and Romans, as well as Genesis:

> But before Jacob and Esau yet borne were,
> Or had eyther done good, or yll perpetrate;
> As the prophete Malachie and Paule witnesse beare,
> Jacob was chosen, and Esau reprobate:
> Jacob I loue (sayde God) and Esau I hate.
> For it is not (sayth Paule) in mans renuing or will,
> But in Gods mercy who choseth whome he will.

> But now for our comming we shal exhibite here
> Of Jacob and Esau howe the story was,
> Wherby Gods adoption may plainly appeare:
> And also, that what euer Gods ordinance was,
> Nothing might defeate, but that it must come to passe.

The dramatic action which follows illustrates the validity of predestination chiefly through the contrasting characters of the elect Jacob and his reprobate brother Esau. In the twin brothers we encounter two different and irreconcilable types of mankind: the one God's elect who is destined to inherit worldly prosperity as well as salvation in the next life; the other an unregenerate without conscience who is deterministically bent on a course leading to eternal damnation. Jacob, as one would expect, is a faithful, obedient son, his mother's favorite, and beloved by all in the community for his piety and quiet disposition. Above all, he is portrayed as a humble servant of God, subordinating his own will to what he believes to be God's providential will. As he reveals to Rebecca early on in the play: "what soeuer he hath pointed me vnto, / I am his owne vessell his will with me to do" (B1^r). Jacob may strike the modern reader as somewhat self-righteous and a crafty opportunist, but clearly this is not the author's intention. His motives to acquire Esau's birthright and blessing are not selfish or in the interests of self-advancement, but based on his conviction that he is acting in accordance with God's will. "Forasmuche as my said mother, / Worketh upon thy worde O Lorde," he prays before going through with the plot, "It shall become me to shewe mine obedience" (E4^r).

Esau, on the other hand, is as wicked as Jacob is unswervingly righteous. Deprived of the necessary grace to seek goodness, he is portrayed as a profligate youth who shows no signs of redemption. Esau is selfish and inconsiderate by nature, and so preoccupied with his favorite pursuit, hunting, that he can devote no time or attention to his parents or his responsibilities as the heir apparent.[70] In our first glimpse of him, he awakens the neighbors by his incessant hornblowing at an unearthly hour of the night, and then proceeds to drag his servant, Ragan, off to the forest, without sufficient food or sleep. An unregenerate fool, he does not value or grasp the spiritual significance of the birthright, which he sells impetuously for a morsel of food and momentary gratification. When he discovers his undoing, he explodes like a tyrant, swearing to take vengeance on all who were involved in the plot (F4^v).

The treatment accorded predestination in the play follows neither the specific ideas of Calvin, as George Scheurweghs argued in 1933, nor those of Erasmus, as Helen Thomas more recently contended, but rather the mainstream Protestant teaching of the English ecclesiastical leadership at mid-century: Cranmer, Ridley, Latimer, and Bradford. According to their "moderate Calvinist" position, God predestined the elect to salvation from the beginning of time but only foreknew (rather than foreordained) the reprobate to damnation. The dispute over the play's theology is addressed in appendix C. What is extraordinary about *Jacob and Esau*, however, is its departure from the orthodox Christian view that the deceptive plotting of Jacob and Rebecca to procure Esau's inheritance was both immoral and totally unnecessary.[71] Instead of showing that they were self-seeking and presumptuously intervening in the divine plan (the standard view of Tudor biblical commentaries), the author attempts to demonstrate that the seizure of the birthright was in fact sanctioned by God as the means of unseating corrupt authority and fulfilling his promise to Jacob. This has led several scholars to recognize a political dimension to *Jacob and Esau*. As David Bevington concludes: "*Jacob and Esau*'s chief ideological purpose is to justify seizure of power, and to insist that the seizure is reluctantly undertaken," and adds that the dramatist's "theory dangerously sanctions any rebellion when divine command may be taken to oversway established order."[72] *Jacob and Esau*, in fact, appears to anticipate the political views of such Marian exiles as Bishop John Ponet, the former high-ranking official of the Edwardian Church, who settled for a time in Strasbourg, and John Knox and Christopher Goodman, who came under Calvin's influence in Geneva. After witnessing and hearing reports of the Protestant executions under Queen Mary, these exiles abandoned the early Protestant doctrine of nonresistance, hitherto unchallenged in England since Tyndale enunciated it in *The Obedience of a Christian Man*, and adopted the view that the usurpation of corrupt authority is justified on scriptural grounds.[73] While *Jacob and Esau* lacks the strident tone and the anti-Catholic virulence of Bale's plays, the dramatist obviously sees in the analogy of the Old Testament story a two-edged sword against contemporary Catholicism. He uses the analogy of Jacob's supremacy over the elder Esau, first of all, to demonstrate the validity of the doctrine of predestination as opposed to the Roman doctrine of free-will and justification by works. And secondly, if Esau does not represent Queen Mary, he may be seen as the older generation of English Catholics who have no place in England's future; Jacob, on the other hand, stands for Protestant elect who are predestined to live in prosperity as the new Israel: "The one shal be a mightier people elect: / And the elder to the yonger shall be subiect" (B1ʳ).[74]

Jack Juggler

Jacob and Esau may have been one among many Protestant and anti-Catholic plays which challenged the Marian administration and its restoration of papal authority and religion. So serious was the problem by 1557 that the Crown turned over the whole process of licensing plays and players to the Church in the form of certain "Commissioners for Religion."[75] In chapter 2 we noted John Christopherson's observations about Protestant drama continuing under the new regime and the suppression of Sir Francis Leek's troupe in the North in 1556 for plays "to the slau[n]der of Christes true and Catholik religion" (see p. 44). The most popular target of these plays was the Roman Mass. In "tavernes and innes, at commen tables, and in open streets," Christopherson charges, "players of

enterludes...set forth openly before mens eyes the wicked bla-
sphemye, that they had co[n]trived for the defacing of all rites,
ceremonies, and all the whole order, used in the administration of the
b[le]ssed Sacramentes." State papers and other legal documents
from the period demonstrate that these subversive works were
quickly suppressed and their perpetrators severely punished when
discovered, which may explain why there appears to be only one play
that has survived from the period which deals with the Mass, *Jack
Juggler*.[76]

Like *Jacob and Esau*, *Jack Juggler* is a boisterous witty comedy in the
neoclassical style. The setting is a London street, with much of the
animated dialogue and action taking place in front of the "house" of
a London gentleman, Master Boungrace, and his shrewish wife,
Dame Coy.[77] The Prologue informs that the interlude follows
Plautus' "first comedie," *Amphitruo*, although only two scenes
heavily rely on Plautus' story of mistaken identity in which Jupiter
arranges an adulterous affair with Alcumena by disguising himself as
her husband Amphitryon and having Mercury impersonate his
servant Sosia.[78] Moreover, the Plautine theme of adultery is only
vaguely hinted, with the chief correspondence being the case of a
servant confronting his disguised double who has usurped his identity.
In the play, Jack Juggler, the Vice,[79] impersonates Boungrace's page,
Jenkin Caraway, donning the boy's attire and familiarizing himself
with Jenkin's daily activities, which include dicing, stealing, and
other adolescent vices that keep him from carrying out an errand for
his master. Jack then proceeds to bully the exasperated boy into
believing that he is not himself but that he (Jack Juggler) is Jenkin
Caraway. The boy's bewilderment leads to a series of beatings at the
hands of his superiors and finally to a comical encounter with
Boungrace who is insulted by being asked to believe the absurdity
that one person can have two bodies and be in two places
simultaneously (D3^r). The story seems innocuous enough, and this is
insisted upon by the Prologue, so much so, in fact, that one may
wonder whether "mirth and game" is the only purpose and whether
he is serious in warning "That no man looke to heare of mattiers
substancyall / Nor mattiers of any gravitee either great or small,"
especially in the light of an earlier remark that "the tyme is so
queasie, / That he that speakith best is lest thanke worthie" (A2^v). If
one suspects early on that the play may contain some hidden
meaning, this is confirmed by the Epilogue who informs the audience

that "this trifling enterlud th[a]t before you hath bine rehersed, / May sygnifye some further meaning, if it be well serched" (E3ᵛ). This is followed by some startlingly grave remarks apparently intended to make that search a little easier:

> Such is the fashyon of the worlde now a dayes,
> That the symple innosaintes are deluded,
> And a hundred thousand divers wayes
> By suttle and craftye meanes shamefullie abused,
> And by strenth, force, and vyolence oft tymes compelled
> To belive and saye the moune is made of agrene chese
> Or ells have great harme, and percace their life lese.   (E3ʳ)

Moreover, through cunning sophistry and "the exersise and practise of their scoles" the stronger compel simple folk to confess as they command them, and if the people resist they will resort to "playne terani" (E3ᵛ). Who "they" are is not revealed, "for I will name no man in particular."

On the basis of the controversial references in the text and especially by the Epilogue, early twentieth-century scholars have located the play in Queen Mary's reign and argued that it is a shrewdly executed satire on Marian Catholicism.[80] More recently, Bevington has followed previous scholarship in giving a Marian date to the play and in acknowledging the subtle allusions in the Epilogue to the Catholic doctrine of transubstantiation and to Catholic abuses, but he maintains that the Epilogue is the work of an Elizabethan publisher who has foisted a retrospective interpretation on to an original text entirely lacking in political motive.[81] This is certainly possible: printers who gained control of play texts once placed in their hands were notorious for meddling with their contents; but one may ask why an Elizabethan revisor would feel compelled in the Epilogue to be so circumspect in attacking Catholic oppression and so oblique in referring to transubstantiation, a doctrine that was far from sacrosanct in the newly restored Protestant state where other interlude writers (working with the same printers William Copland and John Alde) openly and vociferously denounced the Catholic tyranny and practices of Mary's reign in no uncertain terms. My guess is that if the Epilogue is an interpolation, it was added by a Marian rather than an Elizabethan Protestant revisor for a pro-duction before an audience of Protestant sympathizers (although the carefully guarded language would have protected him from charges of heresy), perhaps in a grammar school like Hitchin, where Radcliffe appears to have run his school and produced his plays undisturbed by the Marian authorities until his death in 1559.

Yet the name Jack Juggler that gives the interlude its title and most intriguing character, and more generally the terms "juggler" and "juggling," had strong anti-Catholic overtones in Reformation England, and suggest compellingly that the play was intended to be polemical from the start. We have already observed in chapter 1 (p. 36 above) Bale's comparison of Mass-priests to jugglers and the Catholic Mass itself as an act of juggling. Here we ought to be reminded that in addition to its more narrow modern meaning of tossing and catching pins or other objects, juggling was used interchangeably with "gaming," "playing," and especially "conjuring."[82] It is in this latter sense that Wycliffe uses it when calling priests "the divels iugglers." The same sense is picked up in *The Ressurreccion of the Masse* (*c.* 1540), which states:

> To the good playne people ye turn your backes
> And playe many a pratye iugling caste
> Brandon the iuglare had neuer goodlyer knackes
> Than ye haue at your masse bothe fyrste and laste.[83]

In her 1982 introduction to *Jack Juggler*, Marie Axton has discovered several other, mid-century comparisons of jugglers to priests in contemporary writings. The most significant appear in *A Discourse ... concernynge the Sacrament of the Lordes Supper*, originally composed by Peter Martyr and translated about 1550 by the individual many believe wrote *Jack Juggler*, Nicholas Udall. Here the writer inveighs against "the iuglyng sleyghtes of the Romish Babylon" and adds that "Christ is no iugler neither doth he mocke or daly with our senses ... such iugling castes as the adversaries would have here in this matier of the sacrament" (D1–D2).[84] It is also interesting to note and perhaps not merely coincidental that in addition to equating transubstantiation with "juggling," Archbishop Cranmer uses *Jack Juggler*'s source, Plautus' *Amphitruo*, to illustrate the illusion of reality created by the Roman Catholic Mass: "When Jupiter and Mercury, as the comedy telleth, appeared to Alcumena in the similitude of Amphitrio and Sozia, was not Alcumena deceived thereby? ... Whye then is not in the ministration of the holy communion an illusion of our senses, if our senses take for bread and wine that whiche is not so indeed?"[85]

Central to the Protestant argument against transubstantiation is the contention that the *body* of Christ (as opposed to his spirit) ascended to heaven at the resurrection and will not return to this world until the Second Coming, and consequently, it defies both Scripture and reason to "conceive of a Christ with two bodies, so that he who sits visible in heaven may lie hidden in secret under the bread."[86] An audience familiar with the theological dispute could hardly miss the additional significance of Master Boungrace's outburst in response to Caraway's absurd claim that there is a second Caraway posing as his servant:

> ... darest thou affirme to me
> That which was never syne nor hereafter shalbe
> That on man may have too bodies & two faces
> And that one man at on[e] time may be in two placys[?]   (D3ʳ)

It is of course through the "iuggling caste" of Jack that Caraway has been deluded into thinking so. However, "I woll playe a jugling cast" has additional applications within the context of early Reformation drama. Like other stage Vices such as Bale's Sedition and Wever's Hypocrisy, Jack is an "actor" who pretends to be someone other than himself to delude innocent people; and also like Sedition he may be dressed in the likeness of a Catholic priest at his first entrance before changing into Caraway's servant's attire, if the woodcut on the title page of the play's first edition is any indication (see figure 14). On this level, the contemporary identification of "juggling" with "playing" or "gaming" is illustrated. If *Jack Juggler* attacks transubstantiation as an absurdity and the Catholic priesthood as gamesters, the story of young Jenkin Caraway's identity crisis is a more general indictment of the Marian administration which resorted to coercion and violence to impose its religious ideology on the people, many of whom (including Protestant members of the nobility) sided with Mary's claim to the throne over that of Lady Jane Grey's in the summer of 1553.[87]

Who wrote *Jack Juggler* is a question that has not been satisfactorily answered, yet Nicholas Udall has the best claim. The interlude's comic vitality, perceptive characterization, and reliance on Plautine comedy are highly reminiscent of *Ralph Roister Doister*. Moreover, it is also not difficult to believe that the author of *Jack Juggler* is the same man who was suspected of heresy at Oxford along with the Lutheran Robert Frith in 1528, and who contributed to the Protestant cause

14 "Jak iugler, M.bou[n]grace, and Dame coye," the title page woodcut from the first known editon of *Jack Juggler* (Q1), printed by Wyllyam Copland (*c.* 1562). Marie Axton describes the figures' dress: "Jugeler has a clerical look, is heavily

two anti-papal plays, *Ezechias* and *De Papatu*. Moreover, his signed prefaces to Erasmus' *Paraphrase of Luke* and *The Discourse of Peter Martyr Concernynge the Sacrament of the Lordes Supper*, make his Protestant convictions (at least up to 1553) unmistakably clear.[88] Yet if Udall enjoyed the patronage of such committed Protestants as Anne Boleyn, Catherine Parr and the Duke of Somerset, and if he lost his clerical appointments with the restoration of Catholicism in 1553, he continued to enjoy preferment in the new reign (as a tutor in Bishop Stephen Gardiner's employment), and was so favored by Queen Mary (for whom he had earlier translated the gospel of John) that a royal warrant of December 13, 1554 placed him in charge of dramatic productions at court for the Christmas season. Too much significance, however, should not be ascribed to this latter appointment as an indication of a conversion to Catholicism. Several known Protestants were active in the Marian court revels up to at least 1556. They included William Baldwin, whose play *A Discourse of the Whole World* was offered to the royal court for Christmas 1555; Sir Thomas Cawarden, Master of the Revels; his assistant and later Master under Elizabeth, Sir Thomas Benger; and William Hunnis, mentioned earlier as the most likely author of *Jacob and Esau*. In 1556 and 1557, Cawarden, Benger and Hunnis were all suspected of conspiring against the throne and briefly jailed. In December 1556, Udall died, having been appointed master of Westminster Grammar School the previous year. Therefore, if we accept him as author of *Jack Juggler*, then the play may well have been performed by the boys of Westminster in 1555.

---

robed, with a shoulder cape and high collar at the back, a hat with a rolled brim. Mayster Boungrace is fashionably dressed in a lapelled knee-length coat and hose, with windowed shoes, necklace, and pill-box hat ... Dame Coye wears a long dress with skirt and sleeves fully pleated, a wimple and cross-stitched cap." The three figures are printed from separate movable blocks, with the print of Boungrace used previously to represent Everyman and Youth in editions of those plays; see Marie Axton, *Three Tudor Classical Interludes*, p. 181. Courtesy of the Rosenbach Museum and Library, Philadelphia.

5

Churches and other playing places

The settings of play performances in Reformation England

In previous chapters reference has been made to the particular venues and settings of Reformation drama, but at this time it will be appropriate to discuss the subject at greater length. Theatre historians have shown that a favored location for dramatic performances in Tudor England was the multi-purpose hall: the guildhall in cities and towns where players often were required to give their first showing before the local mayor and magistracy, and the great hall or refectory in a private household, academic institution, and monastery.[1] Although used for administrative, dining and various other social functions, the typical Tudor hall was ideally suited for occasional and regular dramatic performances, with its screen at one end serving as a convenient facade for the action, the two screen doors allowing for entrances and exits, and the gallery above (if one existed) supplementing the broad expanse of the hall floor for actors to perform. That many of the extant plays discussed in this study were written with hall conditions in mind has been argued on the basis of a sizeable body of external and internal evidence by several scholars, most extensively by Richard Southern in *The Staging of Plays before Shakespeare*.

There were of course other public meeting places available for playing, among the most frequently investigated being inns and taverns. Performances could take place inside these establishments, although the cramped, dimly lit and low-ceiling quarters of most inns must have seemed far from satisfactory to actors and audiences alike. Much more suitable for playing were the open-aired galleried court yards typical of Tudor coaching-inns where, on occasion, a booth stage might have been constructed.[2] Inn-playing seems not to have occurred with much regularity, at least not in London, until the third quarter of the sixteenth century. During Queen Mary's reign, the Boar's Head, Aldgate, and the Saracen's Head, Islington, are linked with subversive drama in Crown records.[3] By the time Elizabeth came to the throne, the practice had become more popular, with what appears to have been a theatre district developing in the vicinity of Gracechurch Street where two of the most popular play-producing inns, the Cross Keys and the Bell were located, with a third, the Bull in Bishopsgate, just a few streets away.[4] These inns, as well as several nearby halls, the Merchant Taylors' Hall, Leadenhall (also on Gracechurch Street), and the Drapers' Hall, were connected with dramatic performances during the early decades of Elizabeth's reign or before.[5] All were within easy-walking distance of William Wager's parish church of St. Benet's Gracechurch, the registers of which, incidentally, yield the first known Elizabethan reference to a named professional actor, "Robert Burger, a common player" (April 14, 1559).[6] It seems to me entirely plausible that interludes such as Wager's own *Enough is as Good as a Feast* and *The Cruel Debtor* would have been the popular fare at both the public halls and the inns in London during these years.

It was mentioned above that inn-yard performances were in the open-air. The only hard evidence I know of concerning outdoor settings for English Reformation drama relates to amateur productions, e.g. the "market crosse" in Kilkenny, Ireland, where Bale's biblical plays were performed by boys in 1553, and the amphitheatre constructed in the quarry outside Shrewsbury, famous for its productions of Ashton's school plays, *Julian the Apostate* and *The Passion of Christ*. Glynne Wickham has noted a number of affinities of the Shrewsbury setting with the use of the local terrain for the staging of Sir David Lindsay's *A Satyre of the Thrie Estaitis* in Cupar, Scotland, on Whit-Tuesday, 1552.[7] One might add to these other large-scale civic-sponsored entertainments, *Old Tobit* at Lincoln in 1564, the revived Whitsuntide plays at Norwich in 1565, and *The Destruction of Jerusalem* at Coventry in 1584; these were among several unsuccessful attempts to offer ongoing annual Protestant replacements for the suppressed Catholic cycle plays. They were unsuccessful at least partly because civic and ecclesiastical leaders could no longer cope with the vast expenditures involved in mounting such productions.[8]

However, a popular venue for Reformation dramatic performances which has not received the attention it deserves is the church.

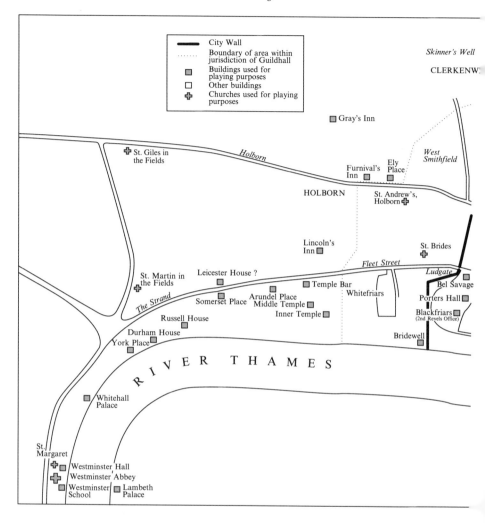

William Tydeman, building on the work of Karl Young and medieval architectural historians, has offered a general survey of church interiors and performances therein during the Middle Ages, but his discussion of the earlier period does not address many of the problems of staging (e.g. of troupe plays) from the late fifteenth century onwards.[9] On the other hand, treatment of the church as a playing place after that time has been largely ignored or at least heavily overshadowed by the attention given to halls and inns. In discussing

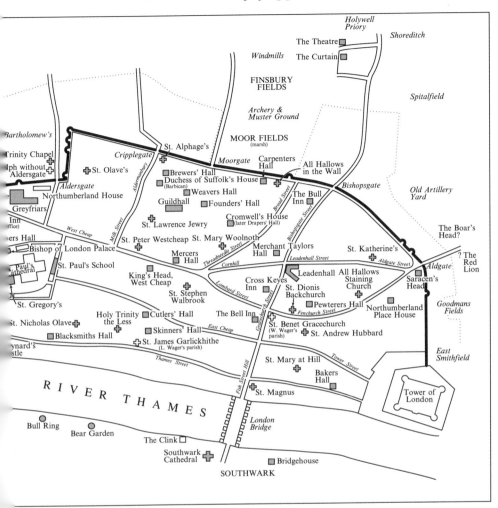

15   This map of London and surroundings before 1580 shows known halls, churches, inns, private homes, and theatres used for dramatic performances. Based on "Map of London *c.* 1600," in Wickham, *EES*, II, 50–51, "Map of London Based on an Original *c.* 1558," in Lancashire, DTR (illustration 25), and "City Churches of London at the Time of the Reformation," in Brigden, *London and the Reformation*, pp. 24–25.

the interior staging of the Tudor interludes, Craik makes no reference to drama in the church whatsoever, while Southern mentions it as a possible setting for only one of the sixty-odd plays he examines in *The Staging of Plays Before Shakespeare*.[10] A few critics, however, have given the matter more consideration. Despite his now largely dismissed theory about early English drama migrating from the church to the market place, and finally to the banqueting hall, Chambers acknowledged the church as a playing place under the Tudors, yet goes little beyond that and identifying a few known locations.[11] Until very recently, David Bevington was one of the few scholars who granted that "even the provincial churches and churchyards were not excluded as impromptu theatres," viewing the church as a second (or last) choice for accommodating plays.[12] It would take John Wasson in his 1984 article on "Professional Actors in the Middle Ages and Early Renaissance" to bring the matter more fully into the open by identifying "some sixteen villages and towns where the church seems to have been the normal playing place for professionals, and of others, such as Plymouth and Norwich, where it was sometimes used."[13] Since that article, more evidence has come to light to support Wasson's contention that church playing was a more widespread practice than is commonly believed.

In the present discussion, therefore, I would like to address the issue in some detail. My first main concern will be to consider the evidence indicating that churches were used for playing purposes in Reformation England. I will then consider the staging of plays and other conditions of performance within churches during the Reformation era, rounding out the discussion with a conjectural reconstruction of the staging of Bale's biblical interludes at St. Stephen's Church near Canterbury, where "Balle and his felowes" were paid for playing before Lord Thomas Cromwell in September 1538.

The church as a popular playing place

Perhaps what contributes to the resistance among modern scholars of accepting the church as a popular playing place is the notion that in an age when the theatre was often viewed as a kind of anti-church such entertainments as plays would have been entirely inappropriate in the official institution of religious worship. It was indeed considered intolerable by such moralists as Anthony Munday, who while writing in support of the London city council in 1580 charged that professional players "are priuiledged to roaue abroad, and permitted to publish their mametree in euerie Temple of God, and that through England, vnto the horrible contempt of praier. So that now the Sanctuarie is become a plaiers stage, and a den of theeues and adulterers," a passage in itself which (despite Munday's tendency to exaggerate) supports other evidence that churchplaying continued well into Elizabeth's reign.[14] Yet Munday's remarks help create the distorted and historically inaccurate impression that in late Medieval and Renaissance England the church was deemed unsuitable by conscientious clerics and laymen for anything other than religious worship. As M. C. Bradbrooke has observed, the great central aisle of St. Paul's Cathedral was a fashionable promenade throughout the late Middle Ages and well into the Renaissance.[15] In the provinces, moreover, parish naves were turned into makeshift banqueting halls for church ales and memorial feasts.[16] And while many Reformers condemned such unbridled commercialism and merriment within the sanctuary, they rejected outrightly the Roman rite of church consecration, grouping this ritual along with other superstitious ceremonies and emphasizing the doctrine of the "church universal," the communion of saints. As Bale's Evangelium states in *Three Laws*, the church is not "as they [the papists] call it, a temple of lyme and stone, / But a lyvyish buyldynge, grounded in fayth alone, / On the harde rocke Chirst whych is the sure foundaycyon."[17] This helps to explain why Bale and other English reformers, at least prior to the wave of anti-stage sentiment during Elizabeth's reign, could with all good conscience accept dramatic performances within church buildings, provided they promoted the gospel message and contributed to the worship service.

Throughout the Tudor era churchwardens' accounts for parishes in the capital as well as in the provinces reveal numerous payments for locally sponsored productions and visits by travelling players. Some of these remunerations no doubt were for outdoor playing, as in the churchyard at St. Chad's in Shrewsbury, and "at the Cherch gate" at the East Harling parish in Norfolk.[18] Many others, however, are explicitly stated as taking place "in the church."[19] Indeed, contrary to widespread opinion, parish drama was on the *increase*, not in decline, in various parts of the realm in the sixteenth century. At Braintree, Essex, for example, native religious drama (mostly saint plays) performed in the local parish churches of St. Andrew and St. Swithin flourished between 1523 and 1579.[20] Hadleigh, Leicester, Canterbury, Norwich, Barnstaple, Plymouth, Poole, are among other provincial communities where dramatic performances took place in the church during the second and third quarters of the sixteenth century. In London, Ian Lancashire has observed that productions of parish drama began towards the close of the fifteenth century and remained popular after the Reformation. All Hallows in the Wall (1528), St. Katherine's Christ Church (1529), St. Andrew Hubbard (1539–40), and St. Martin-in-the-Fields (1539–40), are among the London parish churches where plays were performed.[21] The first two were granted licenses to stage plays, so it appears that permission from ecclesiastical authorities was required for productions. That such church productions took place inside, and that the widespread practice was creating problems for the London authorities during the late Henrician period is indicated by the injunction of Bishop Bonner on April 17, 1542 prohibiting all "common plays games or interludes" in churches or chapels. Those who violently enforced them were to be reported to the bishop's office.[22] Bonner's injunction coincided with a number of other prohibitions against religious drama of any kind introduced by the Crown and the city in the aftermath of the Six Articles Act (1539), which reversed the advances the Reformation made during the 1530s. These prohibitions, along with reports of Protestant players being punished or even burned at the stake strongly suggests that much of the parish drama in London, as in the provinces, was in support of the Reformation or was at least anti-Catholic. Religious drama remained sufficiently popular in 1545 for Bishop Gardiner to "forbad the players of london ... to play any mo playes of Christe / but of robin hode and litle Johan / and of the Parlament of byrdes and suche other trifles," which, interestingly enough, would precisely reverse the policy recommended to the Crown by Cromwell's publicist, Richard Morison, only a few years earlier.[23]

Bonner's injunction obviously did not put an end to plays in churches in London, for during Queen Mary's reign in 1557, St. Olave's Church staged a production based on the parish's patron saint, and under Elizabeth churchplaying resumed for a number of years at "Trinitie Hall or Chapell," under the control of the parish of St. Botolph's Without Aldersgate. This building, which prior to the dissolution served as the chapel of the Fraternity of the Holy Trinity, retained its pulpit, altar area, and vestry down to 1782 when John Carter made a plan and elevation of it (see figure 16). If the auditorium continued to be used on occasion for such religious ceremonies as weddings by the St. Botolph clergy, the surviving churchwardens' accounts demonstrate that between 1557/58 and 1567/68 it was rented out for dramatic performances over one-hundred times. Unfortunately, no play titles are listed in those

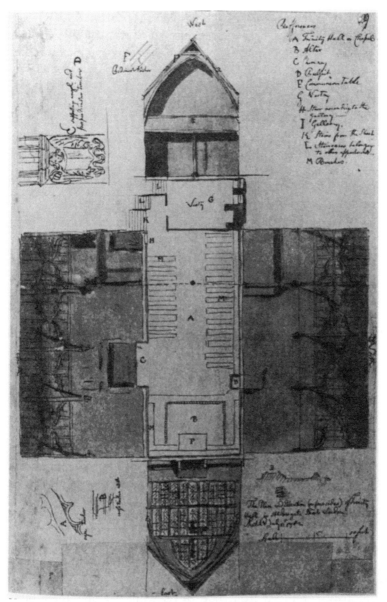

16 Trinity Chapel/Hall, St. Botolph's Parish, Without Aldersgate. This sketch of
the interior by John Carter in 1782 shows altar, pulpit, vestry, gallery and bench
seating. Courtesy of the Guildhall Library, City of London.

accounts.[24] Also under Elizabeth, it would appear that the boy actors of St. Paul's rehearsed and performed either in the Cathedral (Gosson refers to their plays "at Paul's") or in the small church built next to it, St. Gregory's, where the singing school had been housed since the twelfth century.[25] Elsewhere in the realm, playing in churches continued to be a common occurrence through most of Elizabeth's reign, including several recorded performances by such nationally renowned troupes as Leicester's Men and the Queen's Players.[26] There does appear to have been a decline in number as the century came to its close, however, at least to the extent that they were a distant memory for Samuel Harsnet in 1601 who recalled fondly the "old church-plays, when the nimble Vice would skip up nimbly like a Jack an Apes into the devil's neck, and ride the devil a course."[27] The changing times are best illustrated by reference to Syston, Leicestershire, where in the following year Lord Morden's players were paid twelve shillings so that "they should not play in the Church."[28]

Churchplaying and Reformation drama

Although the Vice was depicted in some folk plays and Humanist interludes, Harsnet's remarks suggest that he probably had in mind Protestant moral interludes similar to those discussed in chapter 3. Yet what other external evidence is there for drama of an explicitly Reformation nature sponsored by or at least performed in English churches? While we may assume that plays on Robin Hood and other secular themes found their way into churches, the existing evidence suggests that parish-sponsored or financed performances were to a great extent religious in nature, extending a common medieval practice.[29] No doubt Catholic plays espousing papal supremacy, transubstantiation, image worship, and the cult of the Virgin, continued to be performed under parish auspices well into the Reformation, perhaps more frequently in the relatively isolated communities of the north and the west than in the more heavily Protestant southeast, but if the great cycle plays are any indication, these offensive elements were either suppressed by state censorship or voluntarily expunged from play texts while leaving their biblical story-lines basically intact.[30] It seems entirely plausible to me that Protestant polemic plays and Protestant adaptations of the medieval interludes became popular as early as the 1530s in parishes, almost certainly in Kent and East Anglia. This seems to have been the case when Bale and his fellows acted at St. Stephen's Church in 1538. Another early example is provided by Thomas Wylley's anti-Catholic plays, presumably staged in his own vicarage at Yoxford, in Suffolk. Unfortunately, evidence is sparse for Reformation drama in other communities. However, we may draw some tentative conclusions by observing the religious character and commitment of the clerics and congregations of particular parishes and other significant information about the individual churches. For example, the parish of Hadleigh, in Suffolk, which was under the direct patronage of Archbishop Cranmer, was, according to John Foxe, one of the earliest towns "that received the word of God in all England ... The whole town seemed rather a university of the learned, than a town of cloth-making or labouring people."[31] From 1544 until his death at the stake in February 1555, the rector here was Rowland Taylor, a noted and popular Protestant preacher. With the church facilities under his direct control, and in a community supportive of religious reform, it is reasonable to suppose that a play similar to those sponsored by Taylor's fellow Suffolk reformers, Bale and Wylley, was the one performed upon a stage constructed in the church in 1547/48.[32]

Two other examples are worth noting. One of them comes from Poole where the local parish sponsored plays at least from the turn of the sixteenth century and where the records of 1551 state that drama was acted in the church by visiting players, and perhaps also by a local group.[33] From 1547 to shortly after Queen Mary's accession, the militantly Protestant divine, Thomas Hancock, was the parish priest at Poole. Invited to Poole by the town's ruling Protestant government, Hancock preached against transubstantiation and saints' worship, which stirred some controversy in the first year of his residence, but after receiving the backing of Protector Somerset, who knew him personally, and Cecil, who called for peace in the town, thereafter, according to Hancock, the word of God was preached without open hindrance.[34] What is significant here is that the town council, including the mayor who protected and defended Hancock against hostile Catholics, was militantly Protestant at the time the drama was performed in the church. If as was the case with other towns, the mayor and the aldermen had to approve of a play before it could be publicly performed, then we can only infer that the city council must have permitted its performance. And since Hancock was in charge of the church, the play must have met his approval as well. Like Bale in neighboring Bishopstoke, Hampshire, Hancock himself may have had a personal hand in the production; he had at least one interlude staged at his house in London during the early 1540s when subversive anti-Catholics troubled Henry VIII's reactionary administration.[35] One touring company we know to have acted at Poole in 1551, the Marquess of Dorset's players, included at least one religious play in its repertory, *Zacheus*, based on the story of the New Testament rich man, which they later performed at the guildhall in Norwich in 1551–52.[36]

A final example is provided by St. Martin's Church, Leicester, a strong Protestant congregation dating back at least to Edward's reign when the city magistrates hired "Master Turner the Preacher" to deliver regular lectures to the parishioners.[37] He and other local reformers must have had an impact, for twenty-eight people at the parish were indicted for "displaying scorn toward the sacrament of the altar" during Queen Mary's reign,[38] and the regular lecturing resumed shortly after Elizabeth's accession, under the patronage of the puritan Earl of Huntingdon. Thomas North, in his *Chronicle of the Church of St. Martin*, observes several occasions when plays, some evidently Protestant or anti-papal in character, were performed in the church during the Reformation. In 1546/47, the accounts of the churchwardens of St. Martin's refer to a property and costume for Herod: "Item pd for makynge of a sworde & payntyng of the same for harroode ... viiid."[39] A few years later, in 1551, a very curious entry appears in the city chamberlain accounts: "It[e]m pd for expences that went to the buck that my lady of Huntingdon gave to the xlviii whych was ordeyned at the hall for the Company [i.e. the magistrates], and they came not because of the play that was in the churche; whych wth bred, alle, flower, pepper, bakyng, and other charges, amountyth to the some of ... X.s." The item indicates that the city burgesses witnessed drama in the church, and that on this occasion the performance was of sufficient importance for them to miss a prearranged feast in the guildhall, which, incidentally is located right next door to St. Martin's. In 1559/60, the church-wardens paid six pence to "ye plears fo the paynes," and in the following year we read "Rec. for serten stufe lent to the players of fosson vi. d."[40] What the "stufe" was and whether this contributed to a performance in the church is unclear, but considering the Edwardian references to plays in St. Martin's and indeed its accommodating productions dating back to the Middle Ages, it seems reasonable enough that it applies to a church performance and

17 St. Martin's Church, Leicester (now Leicester Cathedral), lower nave and screen. With the very large side aisles, the church offered ample space for seating and acting either before the screen or "in the round."

that the materials lent out may well have been vestments. There are numerous instances of such clerical garments rented to players by English churches at the time,[41] since many were no longer of use in the worship service prescribed by the First Edwardian and the Elizabethan Book of Common Prayer. One wonders, moreover, whether any of the many entries in the city chamberlain's accounts for performances, especially on Epiphany, Easter, and other religious occasions, contributed towards productions in the church. We cannot assume that playing in the sanctuary was in all instances financed by clerical officials. Bale's production in St. Stephen's Church already provides us with an example of where funding came from an outside source, the office of the Lord Privy Seal, Thomas Cromwell.[42] Anyone who has been to the famous surviving guildhall at Leicester will see that its very small auditorium of 20 feet in width by 62 feet in length offered rather cramped quarters for playing. At best it could accommodate a hundred (mostly standing) spectators.[43] St. Martin's Church, on the other hand, with its exceptionally large south wing (where the original church was built), could stage an elaborate production before a much larger audience of, say, 500, more comfortably and conveniently, especially during holidays and during visits by the more famous noblemen's companies such as the Earl of Leicester's (who visited five times between 1563 and 1575); and as I have already mentioned, the church is situated within yards of the guildhall. The frequent phrasing in the chamberlain accounts of "besyde the money that was gatheryed" during the 1560s might suggest that the collection of money over and above which the Corporation paid to the visiting troupe was taken at a church performance, but this is admittedly conjectural.

The royal performance of Udall's Ezechias *in King's College Chapel*

We shall now consider the staging and conditions of performance in the churches during the Reformation. A most useful place to begin is King's College Chapel, Cambridge, where Nicholas Udall's anti-Catholic *Ezechias*, along with Plautus' *Aulularia* and Edward Halliwell's *Dido*, were performed before Queen Elizabeth during her first Progress to the University on the evenings of August 6, 7, and 8, 1564. These are among the few named plays known for certain to have been staged in a church setting during our period and, fortunately, the surviving records are fairly detailed and illuminating as regards both the arrangements leading up to these momentous dramatic events and the performances themselves. And while the occasion and the conditions were quite extraordinary and merit attention in their own right, one can make some general deductions about other contemporary performances of drama in churches as well.

Matthew Stokys, the University Registrar, reports that there "was made by her hieghnes Surveyor and at her owne cost in ye bodye of ye churche a gret stage *conteynyng* ye breadth of ye churche from thone syde vnto thother *yat* ye chapels myght serve for howses. In lengt it ranne twoe of the Loer chapels full with the pillers on a syde ..."[44] The four surviving eyewitness accounts of these performances give us a clear idea of their theatrical setting.[45] The acting area was located on a great oakwood platform raised five feet from the floor and extending across the eastern half of the nave, with the two side-chapels against the north wall providing a stage facade with mansions and houses and the opposite south wall displaying a hanging cloth of state. The Queen with her immediate entourage entered by way of a railed bridge leading from the choir door to the stage. She viewed the action from near the south wall, where she was enthroned on a raised dais in full view of all the spectators. Officers of the court and ladies and gentlemen watched from galleries in or in front of the rood loft, a "veraye fewe" were assembled at the north end of the platform, while along the east and west sides royal guards stood holding wax torches for illumination.

Although the text of Udall's biblical interlude *Ezechias* does not survive, Abraham Hartwell's eyewitness account of the performance in verse makes it possible to envisage the action in general terms and to draw further conclusions about its staging in the Chapel. Following II Kings 18–19, the play apparently opened in iconoclastic fashion with King Hezekiah's destruction of the idolatrous brazen serpent, pagan altars, and other superstitious images worshiped by the Israelites. Hezekiah's restoration of true religion, however, proved short-lived, for in the action which followed priests, elderly men and women, and others among the ignorant populace were depicted defying the true forms of worship and returning to their superstitious ways. This provoked the appearance of the Prophet (Isaiah), who warns of impending retribution, which subsequently manifested itself on the stage in the form of the heavily armored Assyrian invaders, many of coal-black complexion and led by Rabsaccus. In response to Rabsaccus' threatening speech demanding surrender in the name of

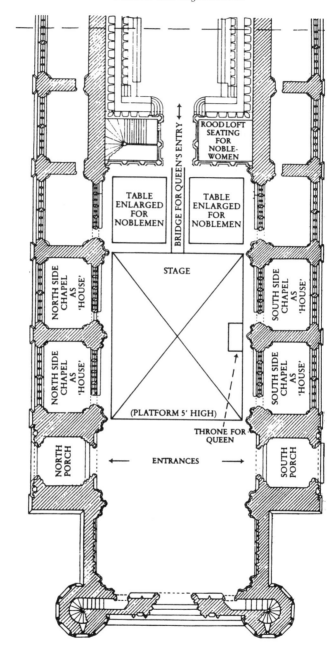

pagan religion, King Hezekiah goes to the altar and prays for God to intercede on Israel's behalf. The play concludes with the invaders mysteriously dying in their sleep the night before battle, although it is unclear whether this is shown on stage or merely reported by a chorus or messenger.

While Hartwell's account does not provide details of staging or of individual scenes, it is possible to draw some inferences about characters, costumes, properties and scenery. The generous acting area would have easily accommodated what appears to have been a sizeable cast of characters (not unusual for university productions), which in addition to the historical figures of King Hezekiah, the Prophet Isaiah, and Rabsaccus, also included various social types among the Israelites – priests, old women, old men and "the rustic crowd" (the latter quite possibly a single character like Bale's Common Crowd in *Johan Baptystes Preachynge*), and a host of soldiers among the Assyrians. The actor playing the Assyrian leader must have towered over the other performers, for Rabsaccus is described by Hartwell as "Huge in armament and of a huge body."[46] Entrances could be made from the two north chapels (possibly closed off by a traverse) and perhaps also from the choir and the nave sides of the stage as well. Hartwell's description also suggests that a large image of a serpent was shown on stage, along with pagan altars, incense boxes, "incense-burning gifts," and other objects of superstitious worship. These images must have received special significance within the church setting. The overthrowing of the pagan altars and the breaking up of the brazen serpent performed right in the Chapel would have evoked fresh memories in many of the spectators of the iconoclastic campaigns of Elizabeth's father and younger brother which officially sanctioned the smashing of statues, paintings, and stained glass windows in parish churches and cathedrals throughout the realm. King's and other Cambridge college chapels had experienced the same upheaval immediately following the intro-duction of the first Book of Common Prayer in June 1549, when the high altars, images, plates, and other splendid furnishings were systematically removed on command of the authorities, and the nave

---

18   Staging in King's College Chapel, Cambridge, in 1564, a conjectural ground plan. Reproduced from Alan H. Nelson, ed., *Cambridge*, REED, 2 vols. (University of Toronto Press, 1989). Courtesy of Alan H. Nelson and University of Toronto Press.

altars replaced by stone or wood communion tables. The rood screens and lofts, however, remained.[47] Since the term "altar" now came to be used interchangeably with "the communion table" and "the Lord's board," it is quite possible that the altar before which Hezekiah stood or knelt during his prayer to God was the communion table. The destruction of images in *Ezechias* suggests that the play may have been intended in part to justify the iconoclastic policy of the Protestant Tudor administrations.

Conditions of performance in the church setting

The performances at King's College Chapel illustrate conditions that would have been equally applicable in other churches in England at the time. They reveal that a most suitable location for playing is the eastern part of the nave or what is sometimes referred to as the crossing in churches and cathedrals with transepts. The transepts or side chapels to the north and south, as well as the choir door, provided points for entrances and exits and for costume changes. Curtained traverses could easily be erected to close off these areas to the spectators. Such structures, for example, are indicated in *Godly Queen Hester*, a play apparently written for chapel performance under the auspices of Henry VIII's court (more on this presently). While the nave floor would have sufficed for most productions, some churches, like King's College Chapel, constructed raised stages. This seems to have been the case at All Hallows in the Wall, London, where materials for scaffolding are required between Easter and Michaelmas in 1538, although we cannot say for sure that all the performances took place indoors. In other churches, however, the evidence is clear-cut. In 1543 in Sherborne, Dorset, a religious play was "acted on boards or scaffolds in the church before the two low altars."[48] And at Hadleigh, Suffolk, in 1547/48, the Collectors' Accounts show that funds were "payd ffor makyng ye stage yn the chorche & ffor nayls."[49]

At King's College, where the Queen, surrounded by her attendants, was the principal audience and faced the action from a raised dais near the south wall, the two side-chapels on the north side of the nave created the stage facade; but normally in most sanctuaries, with the spectators presumably looking on from the main body of the nave, the choir screen or rood screen could be used as a natural facade, with the rood loft above (if it supported a gallery) providing a second level for action in some sanctuaries if needed.[50] However, in some churches after the Reformation, particularly during Edward VI's reign, the rood screens were taken down or mutilated, eliminating or obscuring the boundary between the nave and chancel areas and thereby potentially expanding the playing space.[51] No doubt, with the chancel and choir no longer regarded as uniquely consecrated ground reserved only for the priesthood, some performances extended into them. Evidence of this is found in an injunction prohibiting plays in Boston, Lincolnshire, in March 1578, which reads: "there shalbe no mo playes nor interludes in the churche nor in the Chauncell nor in the hall nor Scolle howse."[52]

The church performances at Cambridge, Sherborne and Hadleigh indicate that at least in some instances the playing area was located at the east end of the nave before the rood screen or altar area. Alternatively, Charles Prouty's analysis of Trinity Chapel at St. Botolph without Aldersgate supplies an example of where it might have been preferable to set up at the west end of the nave in auditoriums where the gallery is located there. In either one of these arrangements, the audience might be seated in the nave watching the action taking place at one end of the auditorium or the other, as the extant ground plan and elevation of Trinity Chapel showing two rows of bench-seating divided by a central aisle so conveniently illustrates. However, there is no reason to doubt that the *platea* could have extended across the entire nave floor in a set-up similar to hall playing as Southern and others have reconstructed it. We ought to keep in mind that, as is still the case in cathedrals today, at the time of the Reformation many churches limited seating to stone benches along the side aisles and around pillars, and that fixed, as opposed to movable, seats in the form of pews were not the staple feature of church furnishing that they are today. At St. Martin's Church, Leicester, for instance, most of the seats were "movable benches without backs, and with low ends finialed" apparently until 1568/69 when entries in the churchwardens' financial accounts indicate that workmen anchored the benches to the stone floor. As one of the wealthier parishes in England, St. Martin's may have been the exception to the rule in having fixed seating.[53] With banquets for church ales taking place within the sanctuaries of some of the poorer parishes, the floor space would have needed to be cleared to make way for dining tables with the benches either moved to the sides or placed around the tables. Such clearing of the main area of the nave might have been done to accommodate plays as well, perhaps at the request of visiting acting companies accustomed to playing under hall conditions. There is little hard evidence to support such an arrangement, but it is worth noting that in 1577, two churchwardens of West Ham, Essex, were brought before the archdiaconal court to answer the charge of allowing two plays to be staged in their church during Lent, "and the people were suffered to stand upon the communion table, diverse of them."[54] If the "people" referred to were spectators (which seems likely), then the logical inference to be drawn is that they were facing the nave where the action was taking place. The rest of the spectators, as in a hall setting, would have surrounded the players, perhaps along the side aisles and across the west wall and entrance. Whether the Sunday performances took place in the evening (as the Sunday showing of Plautus' *Aulularia* at King's did) is not known, but that church plays did take place at night elsewhere is clear from the St. Olave's production in London in 1557 which began at 8 p.m. and ended at midnight, and from dramatic records at Norwich where in 1564/65 payment was made for "Torches to show light in the Chappell when they played."[55]

In many instances the church functioned as a playing place because other venues were either unavailable or unsuitable. The former was clearly the case in small villages without a church house or town hall. The latter was the case for the royal visit at Cambridge where the original stage was mounted in King's College Hall, "But by Cause it was judged by diuers to be to lytle, and to close for her Highnes & her Co[m]panye, and also to farre from her Lodgynge, it was taken downe."[56] However, after the Reformation the church also was for certain occasions the first and *favored* choice, as it had been for centuries when liturgical drama was intended and designed for performance there. At the royal court and in the wealthier noble households, where the lord chamberlain had his choice of venues, plays were evidently staged in the chapel and usually performed by the resident Chapel children. The most detailed evidence of this is supplied by the surviving Wressle household accounts of the Earl of Northumberland during the early Tudor period, which reveal that the Earl's boy choristers performed Christmas and Easter plays in his Nether and High chapels.[57] One play which may have been performed in the Chapel Royal of Henry VIII was *Godly Queen Hester.* The stage directions call for a "traverse" to be used exclusively for King Assuerus' entrances and exits, which might have been the same as "her Majestes Travess" in Queen Elizabeth's chapel at St. James Palace to curtain off a particular area from the rest of the sanctuary, perhaps for the monarch's private worship.[58] Moreover, the audience is addressed as "this congregation" and is dismissed with a benediction. As David Bevington concludes, "It seems likely that the play was actually produced in the chapel by the chapel choir, using for its stage the same structures employed in religious ceremony."[59] There are other works which even more strongly suggest the intention of church production. Among these are plays of a liturgical character such as *The Dialog betwene thangell & the Shepherdes* (c. 1547) by Thomas Becon. John N. King observes that the ritualistic, catechetical manner of the dialogue, the interlude-like stage directions, and the twin choruses of Angels and Shepherds, all point to a church or chapel performance, perhaps involving two half-choirs, during Christmastide.[60] As chaplain to the Duke of Somerset at the height of his power under Edward VI, Becon had strong connections at court, suggesting that his nativity play was composed either for the Chapel Royal or possibly Somerset's own chapel during the Christmas season when playing was frequent at court.

Bale's God's Promises *and St. Stephen's Church, Hackington*

Bevington and King have both mentioned that Bale's mystery plays were probably intended for production in the church, with Bevington stating that for *God's Promises* church performance is "convenient, if not mandatory, and the work may well have been intended primarily for tours of churches."[61] That it was not in fact mandatory is evident from Bale's own report that the play was staged outdoors at the "market cross" in Kilkenny, Ireland, on Queen Mary's coronation day in 1553.[62] However, Bale's working with a professional company in the 1530s suggests that these plays were probably conceived for indoor production,[63] and while we may not be quite as certain as Harbage and Schoenbaum (they are followed by Braunmuller and Hattaway) in identifying the place of performance as St. Stephen's Church in Canterbury in 1538,[64] the same year Bale wrote or revised the text of *God's Promises*, it will be worth giving this matter careful consideration.

God's Promises is a prophet play which, like earlier medieval plays in the *processus prophetarum* tradition, uses liturgical texts and music in its presentation of a series of biblical patriarchs (Adam, Noah,

Abraham, Moses, Isaiah, David, John the Baptist), each of whom appears in his own scene conversing with God in a foreshadowing of the advent of Christ. The traditional advent theme, however, has been adapted to convey the covenant theology of early Protestantism. Each act ends with the prophet alone in the *platea* singing the opening lines of an Advent antiphon (one of the seven "Great O's" prescribed for vespers during the seven days before Christmas Eve in the *Sarum Breviary*), which is followed up by a choir with organ accompaniment, as the actor playing the prophet departs from the stage area to prepare for his reappearance as another prophet in the subsequent scene. For example, after Adam finishes his speech near the end of act 1, the stage direction reads:

Tunc sonora voce, provolutis genibus Antiphonam incipit,
O Sapientia, quam prosequetur chorus cum organis, eo interim exeunte.
Vel sub eodem tono poterit sic Anglice cantari:

[translation]

Then on bended knee he begins in a loud voice the anthem,
O Wisdom, which the Chorus takes up, with an organ accompaniment,
as he goes out.
Or with the same accompaniment it could be sung in English thus:[65]

This stage direction remains basically the same for the following six scenes, although a different antiphon is prescribed. It has been suggested that Bale's chorus, or choir (an equally suitable translation from the Latin), was perhaps made up of the three or four other members of the troupe not directly involved in the action, for the play only requires two actors – one playing Pater Coelestis and the Prologue, the other portraying the prophets.[66] Arguing as we did in chapter 1 that Bale's troupe consisted of five players, the choir would have four singers, the three not performing in the action, and the fourth provided by the player taking the role of Pater Coelestis who leaves midway through each scene perhaps to join them. This is admittedly a very small choir in an era when most had no fewer than ten members.[67] However, small vocal ensembles were known to consist of four or five singers performing works of polyphony, and in the French mystères the heavenly "choirs" apparently were similarly numbered, as Jean Fouquet's well-known miniature illustrating the *Mystère de Sainte Apolline* demonstrates.[68]

    Granting that Bale might have had in mind a small singing ensemble made up of his own players, there is no reason to doubt the

possibility that a full church choir was intended, especially when one
was available. It is well known that the chorus of angels in the
medieval mystery plays were assembled from the local church choir,[69]
so for a church performance of *God's Promises* why not include the
local parish choir, or a nearby one affiliated with a grammar school
or cathedral? Moreover, considering Bale's connections in high
places, he might have had access to the touring choirs patronized by
powerful magnates, one of whom was the Duke of Suffolk.[70]

What makes the hypothesis of a standard church choir even more
plausible is the reference to organ accompaniment, since by the
sixteenth century the organ had long been used in conjunction with
choir performances, often alternating sequences with the choir in
church antiphons. By this time, choirs usually had their own
organists; the organ had become so closely associated with choral
music that as early as 1478 all the Gentlemen of the Chapel Royal
were expected to be "sufficiaunt in organez playing."[71] Commenting
on *God's Promises*, Peter Happé has suggested that the organ used in
the play was a portative organ, a small wing-shaped instrument of
few pipes that could be carried about and played in the same manner
as an accordian is played today. He states that *organis*, the Latin
plural form of organ that Bale uses in his stage directions, "usually
means the portative organ, as in the Norwich *Grocers' Book* which
records payments for 'organs' in 1534."[72] However, as musicologists
have noted, it was commonplace to refer to an organ of any kind or
size in the Latin plural form, *organis* or *organa* (or the popular phrase
"pair of organs" in English) since *organum* (the singular) was used for
any sort of machine, musical or otherwise; moreover, *organum* came to
denote a special method of singing among medieval musicians.[73] It is
certainly true that the portative would have been the most practical
instrument for the outdoor performance of *God's Promises* in Kilkenny,
although a somewhat larger instrument known as the positive organ
(of sufficient size to be "set down" or "placed in position") was
known to be supported on a moving car in processions.[74] Perhaps
Bale was intentionally vague in his use of "organis" in the stage
directions of *God's Promises* so that the available conditions of
performance determined the kind or size of instrument used. It is now
well documented that organs were in general use in churches, great
and small, all over England in the fifteenth and sixteenth centuries.
Bale's company, therefore, could count on using either the small
portative instrument they might have carried with them during their

travels or a larger organ available in the community where they performed. Rimbault notes several instances in the records of where an organ was borrowed and transported from one church to another for a special occasion. For example, the churchwardens' accounts of St. Mary at Hill, London, in 1519, paid 5d. "For bringing the organs from St. Andrew's Church, against St. Barnabas' Eve, and carrying them back again."[75] The one known instance of an organ being transported from a church for a dramatic performance occurred in 1465 when the churchwardens of Thame, Oxfordshire, report the organ being borne home from "our pley."[76] The usual location of the organ in English parish churches was on one side of the choir or chancel, although occasionally it was placed above the choir screen or over the west door.[77]

We have no proof that *God's Promises*, along with Bale's other mysteries, was actually performed in St. Stephen's Church in September 1538 when Bale's troupe was paid for playing there before Cromwell. Nevertheless, it is a reasonable conjecture to make, and at any rate this church will serve as a representative location for a reconstruction of the play within the church setting. St. Stephen's is in fact located in Hackington, a small parish about one mile from Canterbury where the archdeacons of Canterbury, beginning with Simon Langton (brother to Archbishop Stephen Langton) in the early thirteenth century, resided until the Reformation.[78] The original church was built by Archbishop Anselm about 1100, and by the time it came under Lord Thomas Cromwell's auspices in the 1530s its interior consisted of a nave (80′ × 22′), a chancel (40′ × 22′), including a large "quire," north and south transepts (18′ × 22′), and a south porch (11′ × 12′). A tower rises above the vestry at the west end of the nave. The tower's eastern wall contains a central arch which may have been decorated by a carved screen with doors leading to the vestry, like the one installed in 1626. The chancel is also set apart from the nave by what was once a very elaborate rood screen and loft. An indenture dated October 6, 1519, shows that the parish vicar at the time, John Rooe, commissioned the construction of the rood loft for the church at that time at the cost of 20s. In his description of St. Stephen's original rood loft and screen in the light of this indenture and the surviving remnants, Aymer Vallance has shown that it spanned the 15′6″ width of the chancel arch and comprised of three arched openings or bays, the middle one of which rose to a height of 4′ and was adorned by doors for entry to the

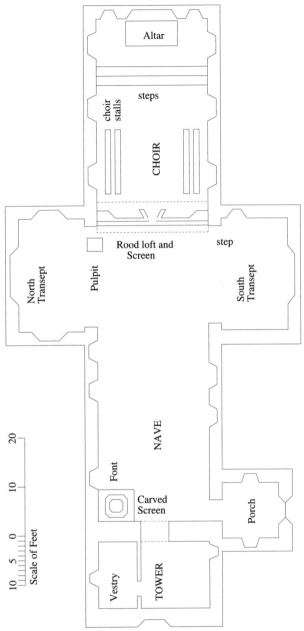

19 St. Stephen's Church, Hackington, a plan based on Canon G. M. Livett's
plan in *Archeologia Cantiana*, 44 (1932): 268.

chancel.[79] The screen overhung with vaulting that projected into the nave as well as into the chancel, perhaps concealing the struts supporting the floor of the rood loft, the parapet of which was decorated with "howses" containing images. Such lofts in English churches were generally 6' deep and often used as galleries for choirs and musicians.[80] Although at St. Stephen's the roodstairs have not survived, access to the loft, either by way of a wooden stairway or a ladder, was necessary at the very least to light candles and to veil the images and the rood itself during Lent.[81] Other significant features of the interior are choir stalls (facing each other on the north and south sides of the choir), a pulpit (the current one is early seventeenth-century), located, until recently, at the north-east corner of the nave, and a fourteenth-century font situated on the north side of the nave facing the porch. Since the churchwardens' accounts prior to 1580 have not survived, it is impossible to know whether pews existed when Bale's troupe performed there in 1538, or whether a permanent organ had been installed by that time.

Equipped now with information about church performances in general and the architectural setting of St. Stephen's in particular, it will be useful to envisage a staging of Bale's biblical drama in the church.[82] The most appropriate location in St. Stephen's for performing *God's Promises* would be at the east-end of the nave before the rood screen, with the "most Christen audyence" looking on, either standing or seated (if pews existed), from the large body of the nave. This would enable Bale as "Baleus Prolocutor" to enter from the choir behind the rood screen, or possibly from one of the side transepts, to establish the play's serious tone and announce its theme: the faithful acceptance of God's promises of salvation by the biblical patriarchs which the present congregation should emulate. Perhaps dressed in preacher's attire and carrying a testament, as he is depicted in a woodcut in the printed edition of *Three Laws* and apparently as he appeared for the performance at Kilkenny, Bale exits to make way for the actors impersonating God and Adam in scene 1, although it is possible that Bale himself returned to play God, if only two actors were used. The time between his exit and re-entrance in that event could be filled with music, the amount of time depending in part on the costume requirements for God. A contemporary German woodcut shows God dressed in imperial robes with crown, orb and scepter which, if donned by Pater Coelestis, would convey Bale's political identification of God and king.[83] As for Adam and the other prophets, they possibly appeared in a conventional "prophets sute," which apparently consisted of a long flowing garment, sometimes with a cap, in an attempt at Hebrew dress.[84] The illustration on the title page of *Three Laws* shows Adam covered in animal hide, while John the Baptist is depicted on the title page of *God's Promises* wearing a cloak, clasped at the right shoulder, billowing in the wind.[85] They might have appeared as such in the play; however, one must practice caution in applying such woodcut images on play title pages to actual costumes in performance since illustrations were often selected arbitrarily by printers.[86] The only exception to the prophets' rather simple apparel would be David's. David, whose "seat" will be succeeded by the throne of Christ (ll. 644–45), probably also appeared in imperial robes with orb and sceptre.[87]

God and Adam perhaps enter together standing side by side, with God following his self-introduction with reference to Adam and then to the other prophets.[88] As E. S. Miller observes, the pattern of this and all the acts is the following: "Dialogue develops through (1) attack on mankind by God, (2) defense of mankind by the prophet, (3) debate between God and the prophet, (4) a promise and a sign given by God to the prophet, (5) praise for the promise said by the prophet, and, finally, (6) antiphon begun by the prophet and taken up by choir and organ."[89] Act 1 affords one of the few interesting bits of theatrical business in the play. After some forty lines of diatribe in which God voices his displeasure at man's disobedience, a stage direction reads: "Here Adam falls headlong to the ground, and after the fourth line he gets up again" (l. 70; Happé's translation). The action signifies visually his humility and his hope of redemption,[90] and is followed by a speech in which he urgently pleads with God for mercy. Also probably signified visually is the promise to Adam that Eve's seed will crush Satan and clear mankind of wrongdoing. The "syne" referred to in the text was perhaps in the form of a scroll, the first of what evidently were a series of hand properties symbolizing the promises in the subsequent scenes: the rainbow (Noah), the lamb (Abraham), the temple – a model (David), the rod of Jesse (Isaiah), and the golden tongue (John the Baptist).[91] Shortly after announcing the promise to Adam, Pater Coelestis exits (l. 143), as he does at the same point in all the scenes. His departure at this point allows for the focus to be on the prophet who engages in a speech of praise and thanksgiving. It may also have had the practical function of freeing the actor playing God to join the choir. After his concluding speech in the scene, Adam then kneels to begin the antiphon "O Sapyence," the Advent anthem at Vespers for December 17, which as official church liturgy lends authority to the preceding action, places it in the context of the Christ's coming (for it is addressed to Christ), and ends the scene with a flourish. As the actor exits from the *platea*, probably through the central rood screen doorway, the choir picks up the singing of the antiphon, which would be followed by the Magnificat, if the musical sequence conformed to the normal programme of the divine office.[92] Since Bale would later show an aversion to elaborate part-music for choir and organ – "fresh descant, prickson, counter-point, and fa-burden"[93] – the setting of the music was probably in plainsong, chordal and non-melismatic in style.[94] Assuming that a full chorus were available, the singers were probably positioned in the choir stalls behind the rood screen, perhaps reading from a single large score or "choirbook," as was the custom at the time. Since organists often read from that same choirbook as the singers, the organ might also have been located in the choir. It has already been noted that even the larger organs of the period were transported from one place to another for important occasions. In the event that no large choir or organ participated, the small musical ensemble of four or five player-musicians, equipped with a portable organ, might have been visible to the audience from one of the side transepts as opposed to being located behind the choir screen, but this is guesswork. It may be surprising that such a radical Protestant as Bale left it optional for the antiphon singing to be in Latin or in English, but Bale would later in life display a conservative bent on matters of liturgy (during the Marian exile he sided with the conservative Coxians over the liberal Knoxians), and perhaps more significantly, the English liturgy during the late 1530s and 1540s was in a phase of transition, with Cranmer evidently favoring the Lutheran pro-gramme, which accepted both Latin and English in the reciting and singing of the liturgy.[95]

   Dramaturgically, acts 2 to 7 basically follow the pattern established in the play's opening section. Variety is achieved primarily through the changes in character, costume, and antiphon, and tone of singing voice. The antiphons *O sapientia, O oriens splendor, O rex gentium, O Emmanuel, O Adonai, O radix Jesse,* and *O clavis David,* are led off by their respective prophets in *sonora, magna, alta, clara, canora, concinna,* and *resona,* demanding some versatility of the singing voice of the

20   "Pater Coelestis," in the University of Bristol Drama Department production of *God's Promises* (1969). God is portrayed as a combination of *rex* and *paterfamilias* seated on a throne 8 feet in height, with steps leading up to it. The chorus was placed in choir stalls on both sides of the throne. Photograph by Roger Gilmour. Courtesy of the Theatre Collection, University of Bristol.

actor taking on the seven prophet roles. Bale changes the original
liturgical order of the seven antiphons for the week leading up to
Christmas Eve for the purpose of historical consistency.[96] Further
variation is enhanced by God's change of attitude in acts 6 and 7. In
act 6, his former anger and threats of retribution are less evident, and
in his subsequent appearance with John the Baptist he is ready to
show "wonderfull kyndnesse" and mercy to mankind. The play's
emphasis on faith in God's promises of redemption through Christ is
made explicit once again by Baleus Prolocutor at the conclusion of
the action.

Bale's other biblical plays in the church setting

Scholars have generally shared the view that *God's Promises* is the first
part of a biblical trilogy Bale devised, with *Johan Baptystes Preachynge*
and *The Temptation of Our Lord* following it chronologically and
thematically.[97] Indeed, the three plays were performed on the same
day at Kilkenny. It seems to me, however, that Bale may have
written *God's Promises* originally as a separate piece designed for
performance during the Advent season, perhaps at his Thorndon
parish in 1536 or earlier.[98] The play was printed separately from the
one-volume edition of *Johan Baptystes Preachynge* and *The Temptation*
(c. 1548), and there is no assurance that the 1538 date on the printed
title page of four of the five extant plays is the original date of their
composition; Bale was constantly revising earlier texts of his works, as
the manuscripts of *King Johan* clearly demonstrate. Having said that,
the relatively large payment of 30 shillings to Bale's troupe for
playing at St. Stephen's might indicate that several works were
performed there, and that the other "mysteries" were included along
with *God's Promises*, as Harbage and Schoenbaum indicate.[99]

Johan Baptystes Preachynge and *The Temptation* do suggest some
interesting possibilities for presentation in the church. Of the former
play, the acting area is unlocalized for the most part, as in *God's
Promises*. However, there are three aspects of staging worth special
attention: (1) the baptisms: how and where were they depicted? (2)
the stage direction for Christ's baptism calling for the Holy Spirit to
descend, with God speaking from "heaven"; (3) and the reference to
singing in John's final speech to the audience: who sang and what did
they sing? Concerning the first matter, stage directions are given for
baptizing the three representatives of society in the opening act,

Turba Vulgaris (Common Crowd) in line 120, Publicanus (Tax Collector) in line 145, and Miles Armatus (Armed Soldier) in line 170. For all three the direction is roughly the same: "He then kneels and John baptizes him." Christ's baptism takes place much later in line 421 : stage direction. "Here Jesus raises John, and submits to him in baptism." In the medieval mystery plays, the baptism of Christ by John was administered according to the official rite. As Rosemary Woolf explains, "the baptism in all of them was no doubt performed, not by immersion as in the gospels and early representations of the scene in art, but by infusion as in the familiar ceremony, and later iconography where John pours the water on Christ's head from saucer, cup or jug."[100] Commenting on Bale's handling of baptism in the light of the earlier scenes, Happé says that "Naturally he ignores the emphasis in the mystery cycles upon the ritual element in Baptism."[101] Certainly Bale would have expunged the Latin blessing with oil and cream but I would disagree with Happé if he is suggesting that no attempt was made to follow the familiar Anglican rite. The Anglican rite of baptism retained the medieval practice of infusion with water while dispensing with the more ornate aspects of the Latin ceremony; moreover, while Protestant teaching varied somewhat on the nature and significance of baptism, Bale probably shared the widespread Reformed view that it was primarily a symbolic act of remembrance, having no efficacy if the recipient was not among the elect.[102] This would seem to make it less likely for him to view a reenacting of it in a play as a blasphemous act. However, the evidence that the ritual was probably depicted in orthodox fashion in the acting place is found in the dialogue when Christ addresses John thus: "Take water therefor and baptyse me thys houre, / That thy baptyme maye take strength of hyghar poure, / The People to marke unto my kyngedome hearvenlye" (ll. 415–17). The directions for Christ and the other characters to kneel during baptism suggest that water was poured on their heads, presumably using a cup or bowl.[103] Christ's reasons for being baptized are similar to those given in the mystery plays: to be a guide and example to the people to follow (ll. 410–17).[104] If in a church performance baptism was instituted according to the official rite, one may reasonably ask whether the baptismal font might have been used for the purpose. In St. Stephen's, as noted earlier, the font is located towards the west end of the nave on the north side, across from the porch. The space between the font and the porch would have been suitable for the action of the play to take place there, with the porch and the archway leading to the vestry providing points of entry and departure. However, whether the troupe would want to go to the trouble of switching ends of the sanctuary after *God's Promises* is impossible to say. I suggest this only as a possibility.

Addressing the second matter, John's baptizing of Christ is followed shortly by a curious stage direction: "Then the Holy Spirit descends upon Christ, and from heaven the voice of the Father is heard in this way" (l. 431). As in Luke 3:22, the Holy Spirit takes the form of a dove, and there seems little doubt here that some mechanical contrivance was called for to control the descent of an articifial dove, perhaps requiring a thin line of rope suspended from the rood loft. A similar mechanism is required for at least two earlier plays, the Chester *Noah* and *The Conversion of St. Paul*, and as Sydney Anglo remarks, such devices were commonplace in medieval pageants across Europe. An instance of one's use closest to Bale's time was the descent of the white falcon in the Cornhill pageant of Anne Boleyn's coronation in May 1533.[105] The voice of Pater Coelestis "from heaven" (*caelo*) suggests that God does not appear before the audience but speaks from behind the screen. Since the next two stage directions require John to look towards and stretch out his hands towards heaven one wonders whether Pater Coelestis may have been situated in the rood loft to give his speech.

The final point of interest in *Johan Baptystes Preachynge* concerns the singing near the play's conclusion. In his final speech to the audience, John says: "Lete us synge therfor togyther, with one accorde, / Praysynge these same thre as one God and good Lorde" (ll. 452–53). Although the following stage direction only instructs John to sing, the text itself seems to suggest that the audience itself is invited to join him. The music, as Blatt notes, is probably taken from the antiphons for Trinity Sunday, and it is known that congregations often participated in the singing of such antiphons.[106]

The Temptation of Our Lord raises more difficult questions about staging than the two other biblical plays, primarily because the action throughout is localized, first with Christ being approached by Satan in the wilderness ("Here are for pastyme the wylde beastes of the desart"), then with Satan taking Christ to the pinnacle of the Temple ("Come here, on the pynnacle we wyll be by and by"), and finally with both overlooking the world from the mountaintop ("A mountayne here is whych I wolde yow to se").[107] As adaptable as the troupe interlude is for staging, *The Temptation* may have been performed with nothing more in mind than a bare acting space, leaving it to the characters to identify the location for the audience through dialogue, as I have shown in the parenthetical quotes above. We have noted, however, that raised stages were constructed for church performances, and the architectural setting of the sanctuary itself provided further possibilities for dramatizing particular scenes. Let us take, for example, the scene in the Temple. The dialogue in this part of the text suggests that a raised stage with steps leading to it might have been used, perhaps a trestle stage as Craik suggests,[108] or what seems equally possible within the church setting, the use of the floor space in the rood loft. Shortly after asking of Christ, "shall it please ye any farther with me to walke?" Satan leads him to Jerusalem: "here is the holy cytie; / The holy temple and the holy prestes here be" (ll. 183–84). Having reached the Temple, he says, "Come here, on the pynnacle we wyll be by and by" (l. 187). The "by and by" indicates that some time will lapse before they reach the pinnacle. A few lines of dialogue later, they have reached it: "if ye leape downe here in scoff / From thys hygh pynnacle ye can take no harme theroff" (ll. 197–98). In responding to this challenge, Christ replies, "Truly that nede not; here is other remedye / To the grounde to go, than to fall downe folyshlye. / *Here are gresynges made to go up and downe therby*: What nede I than leape to the earthe presumptuously?" (ll. 201–3; my italics). "Gresynges" means "steps." Although the English mystery plays indicate no steps in their versions of the scene, in the French mystères, Christ responds to Satan's invitation to throw himself off the temple tower by calmly walking down some steps to the ground.[109] One way this scene may have been played in St. Stephen's was for there to have been a raised stage with steps constructed in the nave, in front of which Christ and Satan walked to dramatize the journey to Jerusalem. They would have then proceeded to mount the steps to the stage, which would have represented the topmost part of the Temple. Christ would at this point refer to the "gresynges" from whence he came to the pinnacle, and proceed back down to the nave floor. On the other hand, Satan and Christ might have entered through the rood screen entrance to reach Jerusalem ("here is the holy cytie; / The holy temple and the holy prestes here be" [ll. 183–84]), and then climbed stairs leading to the rood loft ("Come here, on the pynnacle we wyll be by and by" [l. 187]). This of course assumes that the original stairway (if one existed at all – a ladder might have sufficed) was located behind the rood screen in the chancel. Yet considering Cromwell's sizeable payment to Bale and his troupe at St. Stephen's, it is conceivable that (had the play been acted before him in the church) a series of steps up to the rood loft would have been especially constructed for the performance. That the pinnacle of the Temple was represented by some elevated point in the acting area is suggested later on when Satan states, "As I byd ye leape downe from the pynnacle above" – "above" being unusual here considering that at this point Satan and Christ are supposedly at the top of a mountain.

As stated earlier, Bale may not have used the many options for staging available to him at St. Stephen's. Like most troupe interludes of the time, *God's Promises* and the other mysteries could be performed with a minimum of hand properties in a bare acting place without a raised stage or full supporting choir and musicians. Yet in directing a command performance before the most powerful Crown minister in the land, Thomas Cromwell, the staging in St. Stephen's – for whatever drama was chosen – might have been as elaborate as some plays presented at court. I have dwelt at length on Bale's biblical interludes because they may be representative of many such sacred plays composed and produced for parish audiences within English churches well into Elizabeth's reign. *God's Promises* was reprinted by J. Charlewood in 1577, which suggests that it might have been performed in conditions similar to those proposed for St. Stephen's at that late date. We should not assume that because few plays of this nature survive from Elizabeth's reign that many others like them were not composed or performed. We have already noted that most play texts from the period are lost, since so few got into print. Whether or not liturgical plays continued to be popular, the evidence is fairly convincing that drama in the church was quite popular throughout most of the sixteenth century and that its architectural setting could be used with considerable ingenuity in staging dramatic productions.

6

Changing Reformation attitudes towards theatre

I have tried to show that the Reformation, during its first fifty years in England, did not impose radical changes on English attitudes towards drama, nor did it suppress its traditional function as a popular pastime and as an effective means of winning popular consent for officially sanctioned religious policy and practice. To be sure, some early reformers expressed ambivalence and even hostility towards scenic spectacle, but up to the midpoint in Queen Elizabeth's reign they were no more censorious than medieval church authorities.[1] What did change, of course, was the Christian teaching which defined itself in opposition to the Roman creed, and also the degree to which drama was self-consciously and systematically used as an instrument of propaganda. This is most obviously the case with the plays of John Bale under the patronage of Thomas Cromwell in the 1530s, but it is also true of other stage patrons, playwrights, and players involved in the sponsorship, composition and performance of drama at both the professional and amateur levels. We have seen that Reformation drama was not mere preachment. *God's Promises* shows that it could be every bit as liturgical in character and celebratory in purpose as medieval religious drama. Moreover, a theatrical performance was usually a festive occasion, and was accepted as so through centuries of habit and custom. Yet popular audiences expected instruction along with the merriment. Interludes such as Bale's *King Johan* and Wager's *Mary Magdalene* offered liberal servings of both.

This alliance between drama and Protestantism continued throughout the early decades of Elizabeth's reign – and indeed beyond, as we shall see later, but already a number of historical developments were underway to complicate, if not irreversibly change, theatre/Reformation relations. By 1580 or so, the old consensus of opinion among Protestant leaders and writers in

163

supporting or at least tolerating the theatre was over. There was now a pronounced division of attitudes, apparently with most siding with the opposition during the stormy period of the 1580s. In this concluding chapter, we will consider the significant changes taking place within the English dramatic scene during the 1560s and 1570s which led to the break-up of the pro-drama consensus among Protestants and examine the relationship between the Reformation and Elizabethan anti-theatrical sentiment.

The early years of Elizabeth's reign were a time of rapid change for theatrical practice. In the provinces, depleted funds, declining interest, and state-imposed censorship combined to reduce significantly the number of civic and parish sponsored productions (many of which were religious in origin), leaving it to visiting professional troupes to provide most of the dramatic entertainment.[2] In early Elizabethan London, the story was quite different. Public playing was transformed within the span of a decade and a half from an occasional form of recreation performed intermittently in rented halls, taverns, a few churches and private rooms, to a regularly scheduled event in permanent playhouses operated by impresarios and their partners. It had become, in other words, a highly successful business enterprise. The number of people frequenting plays seems to have grown enormously with each passing year so that by 1576 several thousand spectators would pack into Burbage's Theatre to see performances on a regularly scheduled basis.[3] The increased popularity and commercialization of the London stage brought with it new opportunities for playwrights and players alike and altered the character of drama and the conditions under which it was performed. We may recall that despite differences in temperament, motivation, and viewpoint on particular issues, most Reformation playwrights were ministers or schoolmasters who were linked to a nationwide system of Protestant patronage and who saw drama's appeal as recreation working hand in glove with its usefulness as a medium of religious instruction and edification. Furthermore, they were mostly amateurs for whom playwrighting was one of several responsibilities carried out on behalf of the church or the state. In contrast, the new breed of dramatists, created essentially by the expanded market for public playing, were free from such institutional obligations to earn a living from the profits of play productions, and consequently were much more inclined than their clerical predecessors to satisfy the demands of paying audiences who came to the playhouses more to be entertained than instructed.

Actors (some of whom of course were also playwrights) likewise benefited from the new circumstances, provided they were among those "belonging to any Baron of this realme" or "other honourable Personage of greater Degree," since the 1572 Act against Vagabonds now outlawed the "lesser" troupes.[4] I mentioned in chapter 2 that during the Reformation era most of these noblemen's players were really only semi-professional in the sense that out of economic necessity they combined playing with some other trade in their patron's household. This was no longer the case for the London-based companies. According to John Stockwood, master of Ton-bridge Grammar School, by 1577 London troupes earned a combined income of £2000 per year from performing several times a week in eight "ordinarie places in the Citie" where dramatic entertainment was regularly offered.[5] What this and other evidence indicates is that while the London troupes continued to enjoy the prestige, protection and support provided by their noble patrons, they were now capable of achieving economic independence from their lords by means of regular weekday playing all year round centered in London.[6] This, in turn, must have affected their repertories not only in terms of significantly increasing the number of plays but in terms of their subject-matter as well. Whereas in earlier times the first priority might have been given to meeting their patron's demands (ideo-logical as well as aesthetic), considerably greater attention had now to be given to the interests and tastes of the large throngs of paying patrons frequenting the commercial theatres.

This is not to say, of course, that drama promoting Protestant religious interests ceased to be written and performed, nor to imply that politically powerful patrons could no longer exercise con-siderable influence on the major companies.[7] Such interludes as *New Custom* (1573) and *The Tide Tarrieth No Man* (1576), with their treatment of clerical apparel and ecclesiastical reform, may well have been typical of many no longer extant plays of the 1570s, and if they are more circumspect than earlier works in pressing for religious change, there is not, to my knowledge, a single instance of Protestant religious drama creating problems for the Elizabethan authorities during the 1570s.[8]

Nevertheless, during this same decade, the establishment of professional playing as a commercial enterprise, with its own

permanent facilities, hired playwrights, full-time actors, and regular
weekday performances, served to alienate a good many sober-
minded Protestants who could justify the existence of the popular
stage only on the ground that it promoted their ethical and religious
convictions. They may have included among their ranks earlier
homiletic playwrights such as William Wager and Ulpian Fulwell
who, while remaining active in the Anglican ministry well into the
1580s, did not continue to compose plays much after 1570. Like
Stephen Gosson, himself an ex-writer of moral interludes, they may
have been sufficiently disenchanted with the new conditions to join
the campaign to suppress the commercial stage. Considering their
arguments against playing, it is entirely appropriate to refer to these
Protestant opponents as "puritans" and their campaign to overthow
the stage as a "puritan" campaign, so long as we do not equate them
exclusively with the Elizabethan Presbyterian movement led by
Cartwright, Wilcox, and others to "purify" the Church's prescrip-
tions of worship and polity. For there were many spirited opponents
of the stage who had no known grievances with official religious
policy. As far as we know, Philip Stubbes, author of *The Anatomie of
Abuses* (1583), was a loyal and conforming member of the Church of
England, as was Anthony Munday, who is believed to be the author
of *A Second and Third Blast of Retrait from Plaies and Theatres* (1581).
Gosson was an outspoken opponent of Cartwright and the English
Presbyterians.[9] One might add that those favoring radical reforms in
the church were not unanimous in their condemnation of the stage.
George Wapull (*The Tide Tarrieth No Man*) obviously believed that
he could influence public opinion in favor of their ecclesiastical
reforms. The Earl of Leicester of course was both a strong proponent
of Presbyterian reforms within the church and the patron of the
nation's leading acting company during the 1570s. He and Walsingham found themselves in conflict with their clerical associates over
the propriety of playing. This is evident in the correspondence
between Field and the Earl of Leicester and in the intervention of
Walsingham on behalf of the Queen's players (he was involved in
their formation in 1584) when his nonconformist friends, through the
London Corporation, attempted to stop their play performances on
weekdays.[10]

Before we consider more closely Protestant opposition to playing,
we need to be reminded that a good deal of the criticism and action
taken against the stage had little to do with religion *per se*. A quick

look at the "Remembrancia" and other surviving documents of the London Corporation during Elizabeth's reign reveal that many objections were practical in nature, stemming from the risk of infection in crowded assemblies during plague time, of injury due to collapsing scaffolds and outbreaks of public disorder. Moreover, the newly built playhouses in the liberties provided ideal conditions for pick-pockets, prostitutes, and beggars to ply their trade, and for apprentices during afternoon hours to waste their employers' time and their own wages. Chambers, Wickham, and others have further observed that feelings on both sides of the debate were intensified because of the protracted and at times acrimonious dispute between the Crown and the City over rights to regulate (and prohibit) playing in the capital. By virtue of its jurisdiction over all property within the walls of the City, the London Corporation believed that it had sole authority to determine when, where, and what plays would be licensed and which companies would be permitted to perform them. This was an ancient privilege that was backed up by law as recently as the Proclamation of 1559. On the other hand, by virtue of its acting on behalf of the sovereign, the Privy Council could exercise the right to overrule City ordinances when circumstances warranted it, and in fact did so on several occasions to arrange for playing within the City for the noblemen's troupes under its patronage and protection.[11] As the players no doubt defended their views from the scaffold (as Wager had done in the Prologue to *Mary Magdalene*), the City Corporation boosted the free publicity it received from the pulpit by patronizing writers such as Gosson and Munday who wrote polemical pamplets attacking the professional stage.[12]

However, we should not doubt the sincerity of the anti-stage polemicists backed by the London Corporation, nor underestimate the extent to which religious convictions and interests fueled the efforts to suppress playing. Ideological developments within Elizabethan Protestantism were beginning to change the way many thought about the stage, and especially about the effectiveness, even propriety, of its use of visual images as a medium of religious instruction. From the very beginning when its attack on papal supremacy was based on the exclusive authority of Scripture, Protestantism was a religion of the written (and printed) word. Yet recognizing that evangelism must appeal to the illiterate masses in a way that they had been accustomed to receiving religious instruction in the past, the Reformation dramatists followed their medieval

predecessors in believing that "into the common people things sooner
enter by the eyes than by the ears."[13] Moreover, if Bale and other
Reformation dramatists were keenly aware of the dangers of visual
spectacle in appealing to the senses, they also showed how the
presentation of the hated Catholic images right on the stage could
function iconoclastically by exposing them for what they were: mere
superstition. However, as Patrick Collinson has suggested, this early
Reformation defense of the visual image as a supplement to the
written and spoken word became "old-fashioned" by the 1570s when
a kind of "iconophobia" set in.[14] Emphasis was now especially
placed on preaching of the Word, and on preaching as the only
acceptable means of proclaiming the gospel and teaching morality
and doctrine. In London and throughout the provinces, non-
incumbent preachers – or "lecturers" as they were more commonly
called – were hired by city corporations and churchwardens, and in
some instances funds that had previously been designated to pay for
plays now went to cover the wages of the town lecturer. In York, for
example, Archbishop Grindal arranged for a city preacher to take
the place of the city players, and as John Coldewey has argued, in the
puritan Essex of the 1560s "prophesyings" – conferences of the
preaching clergy "combining public participation, entertainment,
and dissemination of doctrine" – provided an alternative form of
communal expression to the civic religious drama.[15] By the 1570s, the
Word dramatized, as opposed to the Word preached, came under
serious attack. Whereas the Reformation dramatists had incorpor-
ated biblical speeches into the dialogues of expository characters
and virtue figures, the use of "actors" to impart the Word was now
considered an intolerable affront to the gospel message. As one
opponent of religious drama put it:

When I see the word of truth proceeding from the hart, and vttered by the
mouth of the reuered preachers, to be receaued of the most part into the
eare, and but of a fewe rooted in the hart: I cannot by anie means beleeue
that the wordes proceeding from a prophane plaier, and vttered in scorning
sort, interlaced with filthie, lewde, & vngodlie speeches, haue greater force
to mooue men vnto virtue, than the wordes of truth vttered by the godly.[16]

This passage is indicative of two further developments in the thinking
of many Protestants, especially of the former Marian exiles who
witnessed the theocracies of Calvin's Geneva and other centers of
reform on the Continent. One is a new ethical strain, arising from a
more legalistic interpretation of the Bible, which found offense in the

use of bawdy and scurrilous language in treating religious topics. Certainly the earthiness of Bale's Vices now would be categorized as "filthie, lewde, & vngodlie,"[17] something, incidentally, the old reformer would not contest, though he would see nothing wrong with representing it in a play. The second has to do with the growing reverence for the Bible as the literal word of God, and the concern that nothing be added or omitted in modern expositions or renditions of original biblical texts. This mainly affected plays based on biblical stories, and conflicted with the trend in late Tudor drama favoring greater complexity of plot design.[18]

Protestant ideology and rhetoric, much of which interestingly enough informed earlier Reformation drama itself, figure prominently in the arguments attacking and calling for the overthrow of the stage. To begin, the argument against professional acting includes the contention that it is a violation of the laws by which a man should choose his calling. Reformation playwrights such as William Wager and Thomas Lupton had invoked Protestant teachings on divine vocation and stewardship to condemn social ambition and acquisitiveness, as I have already shown in chapter 3. Now, within the context of theatrical commercialism, these same notions were being applied to a new end. Citing the Act against Vagabonds, the stage's opponents charged that professional actors are glorified beggars who fail to contribute anything of use to the common welfare of the state,[19] and not only do they abandon their true callings and exemplify idleness by making a living out of recreation, they promote this vice in the community at large by attracting vagabonds and other loitering types to the playhouse, and by drawing people away from honest work.[20] By extracting money from spectators who can ill-afford it, acting serves to impoverish rather than enrich the commonwealth. This charge of profiteering was not a new one. It was the same objection that in part provoked Lewis Wager's angry response to the stage's detractors during Edward VI's reign in the Prologue of *Mary Magdalene*. Many Elizabethan Protestants, following Bradford, Latimer, and the other Commonwealth Men of the Edwardian era, were strongly critical of economic abuses (see chapter 3, above), and saw stage proprietors as they saw unscrupulous merchants, engaging in economic exploitation.[21]

Some moralists were led beyond the condemnation of playing as a full-time profession to question the moral propriety of acting itself. As Stephen Gosson says: "In Stage Plays for a boy to put one the attyre, the gesture, the passions of a woman; for a meane person to take vpon him the title of a Prince with counterfeit porte, and traine, is by outwarde signes to shewe them selues otherwise then they are, and so with the compasse of a lye."[22] There was really nothing new to the thinking behind this charge, for it may be traced back at least to the early Reformation era, in plays as well as in prose writings, where mimicry – in the sense of pretending to be what one is not – is associated with hypocrisy, deceit, and self-sufficiency.[23] We may recall Tyndale's statement that "Christ is not a hypocrite [who] playeth a part in a play and representeth a person of state which he is not."[24] In the Reformation interludes, the evils of hypocrisy and role-changing are concentrated in the character of the Vice who, as we know from Bale's *Sedition* and Lewis Wager's *Infidelity*, is explicitly compared to a player.[25] The Vice's mimicry is evil on two counts: first, it is a means of deceiving others; second, it signifies an impious subversion of one's God-given identity and the biblical mandate to imitate Christ in all things. What is here applied to the Vice would soon be applied to actors *playing* the Vice and other villainous characters, and eventually to actors in general. Thus, in Geneva where, as noted earlier, many Elizabethan Protestants had spent time as Marian exiles, the Genevan minister William Farel charged that actors "who delight in assumed characters when they should conform their own to Christ in every kind of duty," do grave spiritual harm to themselves by representing the sins of others.[26] Developing this point thirty-five years later, Anthony Munday questioned whether the constant role-changing habits of actors during working hours carried over into real life to have a destabilizing effect on their sense of self. "As for those stagers, are they not commonlie such kind of men in their conversation, as they are in profession? Are they not variable in hart, as they are in their parte?"[27] As the earlier quoted remarks by Gosson indicate, the gender-changing practices of the theatre illustrate the worst dangers of the actor's profession, for God never intended boys to assume the identity of the opposite sex. Calvin was the first to mark this convention as an abomination. In his *Sermons on Deuteronomy* which appeared in England in two separate editions in 1583 and would be constantly quoted thereafter by the stage's opponents, the Genevan reformer argues that the change of sex-costume in masks and mummeries is forbidden, because it violates biblical law (explicitly stated in Deuteronomy 22:6), blurs the sexual distinction between

men and women, and encourages sexual immorality.[28] Interestingly
enough, Calvin's playwriting successor at Geneva, Theodore Beza,
found the practice of boy's playing female roles entirely acceptable,
and just as the stage's detractors in England cited Calvin, enthusiasts
cited Beza.[29] What is also very interesting is that Bale had earlier
exploited the gender-changing convention to make a polemical
statement about the sexual perversion of the Catholic clergy. In *Three
Laws*, the transvestism of the male actor playing the old witch
Idolatry is explicitly drawn to the audience's attention (Infidelitie:
"What, sumtyme thu wert an he!"; Idolatry: "Yea, but now ych am
a she") so that the subsequent fondling of "her" by the licentious
monk Sodomy would demonstrate the homosexual practices of the
monasteries.[30]

To pursue the early Reformation drama a little further in this
context, it is not by accident that the Vice-as-player is almost
invariably depicted as a member of the Roman clergy, for it is *their*
hypocrisy, deceitfulness, and self-sufficiency that Bale, the Wagers,
and the others are specifically aiming to expose. Popish priests are
compared to players who pretend to be Christ-like and virtuous when
their religion is at best mere human invention and at worst the
product of Anti-Christ; furthermore, their elaborate attire and
gesturing during Mass are as mesmerizing to unsuspecting sinners as
the appearance and actions of stage-players are to spectators in the
theatre. This early Reformation rhetoric of describing Catholicism in
terms of theatricality is quite important, for it resurfaces in the later
anti-stage literature, only the comparison of popery to playing is
reversed to become a comparison of playing to popery. Thus, stage-
plays are "the bastard of Babylon" delivered directly from the
papists to Protestant England, players the devil's own "professed
Massepriests and Choristers," the "Playhouses his Synagogues."[31]
As Edmund S. Morgan and Michael O'Connell have argued,
Protestants leaders believed that they had no sooner banished the
Mass and restored the preaching of the Word than a new institution
emerged to satisfy the idolatrous tendencies and enslave the affections
of the unregenerate majority.[32] Indeed, "theatre" had become an
institution in the most concrete sense of the term with the construction
of two public playhouses (the Theatre and Curtain) in 1576/77. Its
notoriety in the eyes of civic and religious officials was enhanced by
its flourishing in the Liberties, beyond their jurisdiction and in the
vicinity of other landmarks associated with moral degeneracy or

divine displeasure: brothels, madhouses, lazar-houses, prisons and
scaffolds of execution.[33] The popular theatre now began to be
perceived as a kind of alternative church or anti-church. Like the
real church, it had its own buildings, and like the real church it held
regularly scheduled performances on Sundays, a practice that was
loudly condemned by the preachers and magistrates alike as a
profanation of the Sabbath. Anti-stage writings give the impression
that people either went to the House of God to hear his Word
preached, or to the Synagogue of Satan to gratify their senses. The
problem was that the anti-church was more popular. "Wyll not a
fylthye playe, wyth the blast of a Trumpette, sooner call thyther a
thousande, than an houres tolling of a Bell, bring to the Sermon a
hundred?"[34]

To the Elizabethan Presbyterians in particular, the permanent
playhouses, with the many abuses and disorders accompanying their
operation, did not fit in with God's plan to transform England into a
biblical theocracy.[35] Their political mission was given a sense of
urgency by the growing conviction that England was God's chosen
nation, and that unless a course of obedience to scriptural precepts
was followed, the nation would suffer the same fate as the Israelites,
who in breaking their covenant of faith and obedience, were cast
aside by God. Thus John Field describes England as "the paradise of
the world," and states that "God hath given himselfe unto us to be
our God, and hath chosen us to be his people."[36] He warns, however,
that if England persists in wrongdoing, e.g. flocking to stage-plays
and bear-baiting exhibitions on the Sabbath when church services
are in progress, the grace of God will be withdrawn and his wrath and
judgment shown in the destruction of "the *Theatre*, the *Curtain*," and
their godless spectators.

Considering the doctrinal basis for the total suppression of stage-
plays, it is simple enough to see why the stage's opponents were
entirely sceptical of the Humanist and early Protestant views of
Bucer, Beza, and Lewis Wager, that drama can serve as a vehicle of
moral and religious instruction. During the Elizabethan age this
view was expressed in treatises and prologues to plays by Thomas
Lodge, Thomas Nashe, Sir Philip Sidney (whose defense of drama,
however, did not apply to the commercial stage), and Thomas
Heywood. In *An Apology for Actors*, Heywood was speaking for most
serious playwrights when he states that the "action" of a dramatic
performance, the gestures, motions, and passions, of men visually

represented upon the stage, "hath the power to new mold the harts of spectators and fashion them to the shape of any noble and notable attempt."[37] He justifies the depiction of vice in plays on the ground that it teaches the beholder to avoid wrongdoing. "What can sooner print modesty in the soules of the wanton," he argues, "then by discouering vnto them the monstrousnesse of their own sin?"[38] However, the stage's opponents would have none of this sophistry, and remained totally unconvinced of the validity of the arguments in favor of drama. The subject-matter of the majority of contemporary plays, in their opinion, is shamefully immoral and amply demonstrates that playwrights are more concerned with amusing and corrupting spectators than with exhorting them to virtue and righteous living.[39] Moreover, even if a play *was* written and performed with the noble intention of teaching a moral lesson, the spectator would be too engrossed in carnal pleasure to consider vice objectively within the play's moral context. For human beings are weak, vulnerable sinners, more easily enticed by the presentation of vice in the flesh than moved to virtue by the example of good characters.[40]

The foregoing discussion has taken us somewhat beyond what I have regarded as the first phase in theatre/Reformation relations, a fifty year period extending to about 1580, but if the anti-theatrical movement of the 1580s, along with the commercialization of drama, signposted a new phase in those relations, we need to resist the commonplace notion that the views of Gosson, Stubbes, and Prynne typified the mainstream, or even "the left wing" or so-called "Puritan" segment, of Protestant opinion over the next sixty years. It would appear that after an initial period of outrage and resistance, many Protestant leaders in the church and in the civil government came around to accepting playgoing as suitable recreation and recognizing once again its power as a medium of shaping public opinion. This is why it is possible for Renaissance theatre historians to speak of "Puritan" stage patrons, playwrights, and audiences in the decades immediately leading up to and following King James' accession.[41] Of course many committed Protestants did not come around, but this makes my point that there was not one, but a number of different attitudes towards the stage among them, no one of which predominated in late Elizabethan and early Stuart England.

We should also resist the persisting view that a theatre of religious polemic or instruction could not survive in the commercial environs

of the new playhouses. To be sure, commercial interests became
central after Burbage opened the Theatre, and plays thereafter were
written, performed, and enjoyed for their "entertainment" value.
Moreover, the new conditions and freedoms inspired Marlowe,
Shakespeare and the other major playwrights of the time to offer a
more complex and problematic view of the human condition than
their clerical predecessors had done. Yet this does not mean that we
should adopt the view of Stubbes, Munday, and other anti-stage
polemicists, that, for example, the biblical plays so popular during
the 1590s, or the domestic (or homiletic) tragedies and Protestant
saint plays at the turn of the century, were deeply offensive to any
Elizabethan with serious religious scruples and were staged like all
the other plays to cater to popular tastes or increase profits.[42] The
Protestant values and models of piety and ethical conduct which
earlier Reformation drama helped create and popularize continued
to find expression in these plays, and with the ongoing threat of a
Catholic insurrection or even seizure of the Crown, it was in the
interest of Protestant stage patrons such as the Earls of Leicester and
Walsingham and Lord Howard of Effingham to sponsor these plays.
And despite new censorship legislation prohibiting treatment of
church and state issues on the stage, most notably that of the
Licensing Commission formed in 1589 and of the Act of Blasphemy
in 1605, the more controversial propagandist drama occasionally
found its way on to the commercial stage. Middleton's *Game of Chess*
in 1624 comes to mind, as does *The Cardinal's Conspiracy* as late as
1639, which attacked the ceremonialism of the Laudian church in a
manner recalling the iconoclasm of Bale's *King Johan* and Udall's
Ezechias a century earlier. These matters, however, deserve more
detailed attention than can be given in this study, and indeed have
been addressed already by a number of scholars.[43] Suffice it to say in
conclusion that Reformation involvement with the theatre did not
decline but became considerably more complex in the age of
Shakespeare and his contemporaries, for Protestantism was no longer
the religion of a minority of English subjects, as it had been at least up
to Elizabeth's reign, but had become a central feature of the national
consciousness and culture.

Appendix A

A list of Reformation playwrights and plays

The following list identifies both extant and non-extant plays, along with information about auspices, players, and location of performance. Titles in italics indicate those plays which have survived either in whole or in fragmented form; titles in quotations are not extant. Asterisks indicate plays described in contemporary sources but for which the original title is uncertain. Abbreviations: C = College; S = School; U = University.

AUTHOR	TITLE	DATE	AUSPICES/PLAYERS/LOCATION
Anonymous	*"Against Priests"	1541	Shermons, keeper of the hall/civic players?/Carpenters' Hall, Christ's parish, London
—	*"Against the Cardinals"	1533	Court/King's players?/Westminster
—	*"The Bishop of Rome"	1547	Court/King's players? and/or Chapel Royal players?/Westminster
—	*"The Conversion of St. Paul"	1562	Chelmsford City Council/local amateur and "property" players/outdoor staging
—	*The Cradle of Security*	1565–75	Nobleman/professional troupe/Gloucester Guildhall
—	*Detraction, Light Judgement, Verity, and Justice*	1550	Unknown
—	*The Dragon with the Seven Heads*	1549	Court/King's players/Westminster
—	*"Herod's Killing of the Children"	1562	Chelmsford City Council/local amateur and "property" players/outdoor staging
—	"John Baptist"	1562–63	Trinity C, Cambridge/student players

AUTHOR	TITLE	DATE	AUSPICES/PLAYERS/LOCATION
—	*King Darius*	1558–65	Professional nobleman's troupe?
—	*"Love Feigned and Unfeigned"*	1540–60	Unknown
—	*"Mary Magdalene"*	1562	Chelmsford City Council/local amateur and "property" players/outdoor staging
—	*"Matter Touching Queen's Majesty and Catholic Church"*	1556	Sir Francis Leek's Servants/North of England
—	*"Mock Mass"*	1564	Cambridge U/student players/ Hinchenbrook
—	*New Custom*	1564–71	Earl of Leicester?/professional troupe
—	*Nice Wanton*	1547–53	St. Paul's Grammar S?/boy players
—	*Norwich Grocers' Play* (revised)	1565	Norwich City Council/local players/ outdoor setting?
—	*Old Custom*	1547–51	Earl of Warwick/Warwick's players/Court?
—	*Old Tobit*	1564	Lincoln City Council/local players (amateur?)/elaborate (outdoor?) staging in Broadstreet
—	*"On the Apocalypse"*	1535	Henry VIII?/town players/outside London
—	*Parte of a Play*	1545–50	Court
—	*"Papists"*	1559	Court/King's players/Westminster
—	*"The Painful Pilgrimage"*	1567–68	Court/Lord Rich's Men?/Westminster
—	*The Pedlar's Prophecy*	1559–70	Unknown/professional troupe?
—	*Processus Satanae*	1570–80	Limebrook, Herefordshire/parish play?
—	*The Resurrection of Our Lord*	1545	Unknown: parish mystery play?
—	*Rex Diabole*	1538	Lord and Lady Lisle/Lord Lisle's players/ Staple Inn (Lisle residence), Calais
—	*"A Sackfull of Newes"*	1557	London players/Boar's Head Tavern, without Aldersgate
—	*"..."*	1567	James Burbage/Red Lion Inn, Stepney

Author	Title	Date	Players/Location
—	"Self-love"	1551	Court/King's players/Westminster
—	*The Seven Deadly Sins (same as Bale's?)	1548	Court/King's players/Westminster
—	*Somebody and Others	1547–50	Unknown
—	*"Tower of Babylon"	1548	Court/King's players and/or Chapel Royal Choristers?/Hampton Court
—	"The Two Sins of King David"	1562	Unknown
—	*"Wolsey Sent Down to Hell"	1531	Lord Thomas Boleyn/Lord Privy Seal's players?/Boleyn's house
Alley, William	"Zacheus"	1547–51	Marquess of Dorset's players/Norwich
	Aegio	1560	Bishop Alley of Exeter/Bishop's players?/towns in West Country (1559–61)
Arthur, Thomas	"Microcosmos"	1522–32	Unknown
Ashton, Thomas	"Mundus Plumbeus"	1522–32	Same as above
	"Julian the Apostate"	1565–66	Shrewsbury Grammar S/student players/amphitheatre, Shrewsbury
Baldwin, William	"The Passion of Christ"	1561–69	Same as above
Bale, John	"The State of Ireland"	1553	Court/King's players/Westminster
	"About Certain Critics"	1533–36	Earl of Oxford/Oxford's players
	Against Corruptors of the Word of God	1533–36	Same as above
	"Baptism and Temptation"	1533–38	Lord Cromwell/Bale's players
	"Christ and the Twelve"	1533–36	Earl of Oxford/Oxford's players
	Concerning the Deception of the Papists	1533–36	Same as above
	God's Promises	1536–38	Lord Cromwell/Bale's players/St. Stephen's, Canterbury (1538)? Kilkenny, Ireland (1553)
—	"The Image of Love"	1536–38	Lord Cromwell/Bale's players
—	*Johan Baptystes Preachynge*	1536–38	Same as above/St. Stephen's, Canterbury (1538)? Kilkenny, Ireland (1553)
—	*King Johan*	1533–38	Lord Cromwell/Bale's players/Cranmer's house, Canterbury (1538/39); Moone's players/Ipswich Hall (1561)?

AUTHOR	TITLE	DATE	AUSPICES/PLAYERS/LOCATION
—	*The Knaveries of Thomas Becket*	1533–36	Earl of Oxford/Oxford's players/Lord Cromwell/Bale's players
—	"The Life of John the Baptist"	1533–36	Earl of Oxford/Oxford's players
—	"On the Council of Priests"	1536–38	Lord Cromwell/Bale's players
—	"On the King's Two Marriages"	1533–36	Court?/Earl of Oxford/Oxford's players
—	"On the Lord's Prayer"	1530–34	Earl of Oxford/Oxford's players
—	*On the Papist's Sects*	1533–36	Same as above
—	"On the Seven Sins"	1530–34	Same as above
—	"Simon the Leper"	1536–38	Lord Cromwell/Bale's players
—	"The Last Supper and the Washing of the Feet"	1536–38	Same as above
—	"The Passion of Christ"	1533–36	Earl of Oxford/Oxford's players
—	"The Raising of Lazarus"	1536–38	Lord Cromwell/Bale's players?
—	"The Resurrection of Christ"	1533–36	Earl of Oxford/Oxford's players
—	*The Temptation of Our Lord*	1536–38	Lord Cromwell/Bale's players/St. Stephen's, Canterbury (1538) ? Kilkenny, Ireland (1553)
—	*Three Laws*	1533–36	Earl of Oxford/Oxford's players/ Cromwell/Bale's players/Bishopstoke, Hampshire (1548) George May's house, Canterbury (1559) ?
Becon, Thomas	*Dialog betwene thangell & the Shepherdes*	1550	Duke of Somerset?/boy choristers/Somerset's chapel, Sheen?
Beza, Theodore	*Abraham's Sacrifice* (trans. by William Golding)	1575	Unknown
B[ower], R[ichard]	*Appius and Virginia*	1567	Westminster S?/boy players
Chaloner, Thomas	"Riches and Youth"	1552	Court/King's players/Westminster
Edward VI	"The Whore of Babylon" (same as Tower	1548	Court/King's players?

Author	Title	Date	Auspices
		1552–53	Court/King's players/Westminster
Foxe, John	*Christus Triumphans*	1556	Trinity C, Cambridge/student players (1562)/college hall?
Fulwell, Ulpian	*Like Will to Like*	1567–68	Protestant nobleman?/professional troupe/hall setting
Garter, Thomas	*Virtuous and Godly Susanna*	1563–69	Oxford U?/student players?/college hall
Gascoigne, George	*The Glass of Government*	1575	Unknown
Grimald, Nicholas	*Archipropheta*	1541–46	Christ Church C, Oxford/student players/college hall (Christmas 1547)
—	*Christus Redivivus*	1540	Brasenose C, Oxford/student players?/college hall?
Heywood, John	*"The Estate of Christ's Church"*	1539–45	Archbishop Cranmer/Canterbury?
Hoby, Thomas	*Free-Will*	1550	Unknown
Hunnis, Richard	(?) *Jacob and Esau*	1547–57	Chapel Royal?/boy choristers/Westminster
Ingeland, Thomas	*The Disobedient Child*	1547–60	Grammar School?/Cambridge U?/student players
Kirchmayer, Thomas	*Pammachius* (translated by Bale)	1535	Archbishop Cranmer/Cranmer's house? Christ's C, Cambridge/student players (1545)
Lupton, Thomas	*All for Money*	1559–78	Protestant nobleman?/professional troupe
Norton, Thomas and Thomas Sackville	*Gorboduc*	1562	Inns of Court/student players/Inner Temple court/student players/Westminster
Penny, Thomas	*Sapientia Solomonis* (original version by Sixt Birck)	1559–60	Trinity C, Cambridge/student players/Westminster S/boy players/at Court (1566)
Philip, John	*Patient and Meek Grissil*	1559–65	Grammar School?/boy players
Radcliffe, Ralph (or Robert?)	"The Afflictions of Job"	1546–56	Radcliffe/boy players/Hitchin S
—	"The Burning of Sodom"	1546–56	Same as above
—	"The Condemnation of John Huss"	1546–56	Same as above
—	"The Courage of Judith"	1546–56	Same as above
—	(?) "Dialogue: A governance of the Church"	1536–39	Jesus C, Cambridge/student players

AUTHOR	TITLE	DATE	AUSPICES/PLAYERS/LOCATION
——	(?) "Dialogue between Death and the Goer by the Way"	1536–39	Same as above
——	(?) "Dialogue between the Poor Man and Fortune"	1536–39	Same as above
——	"The Deliverance of Susuanna"	1546–56	Radcliffe/boy players/Hitchin S
——	"The Disobedience of Jonah"	1546–56	Same as above
——	"Lazarus and Dives"	1546–56	Same as above
Roo, John	*"Lord Governance and Lady Public Weal"	1528	Gray's Inn/student players/Inns of Court
Rudd, Anthony	(?) *Misogonus*	1566–77	Kettering Grammar S/boy players/Trinity C, Cambridge?/student players
Spencer, Rhichard	(?) *"Concerning the Sacrament	1541	Spencer's players/Salisbury
Udall, Nicholas	*De Papatu*	1537–53	Eton?/boy players/at Court 1538?
——	*Ezechias*	1537–53	Same as above, and King's C, Cambridge/student players/King's C Chapel (1564)
——	(?) *Jack Juggler*	1553–57	Westminster S?/boy players/school hall
Wager, Lewis	*The Life and Repentaunce of Mary Magdalene*	1547–53	Protestant nobleman?/professional troupe/hall setting
Wager, William	(?) *The Cruel Debtor*	1559–66	Earl of Leicester?/professional troupe
——	*Enough is as Good as a Feast*	1571	Same as above
——	*The Longer Thou Livest the More Fool Thou Art*	1559–68	Same as above/also by boy players?/ academic hall setting?
——	*The Trial of Treasure*	1559–67	Earl of Leicester?/professional troupe/hall or church setting
Wapull, George	*The Tide Tarrieth No Man*	1570–76	Protestant nobleman?/professional troupe
Watson, Thomas	*Absalom*	1546–54	St. John's C, Cambridge/student players
Wever, R.	*Lusty Juventus*	1547–53	Protestant nobleman?/nobleman's troupe
Woodes, Nathaniel	*The Conflict of Conscience*	1572–80	Norwich? Cambridge?/amateur players
Wylley Thomas	*Against the Pope's Counsellors*	1537	Cromwell/boy choristers/Yoxford; court?

Appendix B

Calvin's *Institutes of the Christian Religion*: a source of Lewis Wager's *Mary Magdalene*

Lewis Wager's *Mary Magdalene* (*c.* 1550) draws extensively upon Calvin's *Institutes*. This is evident in direct borrowings from *The Institutes*, as well as in the play's expression of basic Calvinist notions concerning man and saving grace. Three theological notions – the law, repentance, and faith – appear as personified abstractions in *Mary Magdalene*; large portions of their speeches correspond closely with passages in *The Institutes*. First of all, compare the following lines by The Lawe with what Calvin says about the function of the Law. I use Thomas Norton's English translation of *The Institution of the Christian Religion* (1561; reprint London: n.p., 1582).

In me [the law] is declared the same iustice, Which vnto God is acceptable, ... It was necessary and it dyd behoue, Considering mans pride and temeritie, Which was dronke and blynde in his owne loue, To make a lawe to shewe his imbecillitie, Except the lawe had rebuked his vanitie, So much he would haue trusted in his own strength And beleued, that through y power of his humanitie He might haue obtained salvation at length (*Mary Magdalene*, E3ᵛ–4ʳ)	The first is, that while it [the Law] sheweth to euery man the righteousnesse of God, that is, the righteousness which only is acceptable to God, it admonish, certifie, proue gilty, yea and condemne euery man of his owne vnrighteousnesse. For so is it nedefull that man blinded and dronke with loue of himselfe, be driuen both to the knowledge and the confession of his owne weakenesse and vncleannesse: for asmuch as if his vanitie be not euidently conuinced, he swelleth with madde affiance of his owne strength, and can neuer be brought to thinke of the scle(n)dernesse therof, so long as he measureth it by the proportion of his owne will. (*Institution*, II.vii. 6)

181

Wherfore as I sayd to a glasse
  compared I [the law] may be,
Wherin clerely as in the sunne
  lyght,
The weakenesse and sinne of him
  self he may se,
Yea and his owne damnation as it
  is ryght.
For the curse of God foloweth
  synne alway.

                          (*Mary Magdalene*, E4ʳ)

So the lawe is like a certaine looking
glasse wherein we beholde, first our
weakenesse, and by that our wicked-
nesse, and laste of all by them both
our accursednesse, euen as a glasse
representeth vnto vs the spottes of
our face. For when power faileth
man to follow righteousnesse then
muste he needes sticke faste in the
mire of sinnes. And after sinne by
and by followeth curse.

                          (*Institution*, II.vii. 7)

Here, in terms suggesting a direct acquaintance with *The Institutes*,
Wager states that the purpose of the Law is to declare the
righteousness or "iustice" that is only acceptable unto God, to
rebuke the vanity of man ("dronke and blynde in his owne loue"),
to expose his weakness and inability to obtain salvation by means of
his own strength. Moreover, Wager follows Calvin in comparing the
Law to a mirror in which man may see his inadequacy and sin, and his
damnation, the curse of God which inevitably follows sin. Wager also
appears to be familiar with Calvin's definition of repentance:

The vertue of Repentance I do
  represent,
Which is a true turnyng of the
  whole lyfe and state,
Unto the will of the lord God
  omnipotent,
Sorowing for the sinnes past with
  displesure & hate.

                          (*Mary Magdalene*, F4ᵛ)

Wherfore in my iudgement, repentance may thus not amisse be
defined: that it is a true turninge of
our life vnto God, proceeding from a
pure & earnest feare of God, which
consisteth in the mortifying of the
flesh and of the olde man, and in the
quickening of the spirite.

                          (*Institution*, III.iii. 5)

In addition to this view of repentance as a true turning of one's whole
life unto God, Wager, like Calvin, does not confine it to a brief period
preceding grace, but insists that the act of penitence must be
practiced throughout the believer's life: "all the life tyme in
repentyng to endure" (*Mary Magdalene*, F4ᵛ; see *Institution*, III.iii. 2).

Perhaps the clearest example in *Mary Magdalene* of direct
borrowings from *The Institutes* is evidenced in the speech of Faith.

Faith therfore is the gyft of God
  most excellent,
For it is sure knowledge and
  cognition

Nowe we shall haue a perfect
definition of faith, if we say, that it is
a stedfast and assured knowledge of
Gods kindnesse toward vs, which

Of the good will of God
   omnipotent,
Grounded in the word of Christes
   erudition,
This faith is founded on Gods
   promission,
And most clerely to the mynde of
   man reuealed,
So that of Gods will he hath an
   intuition,
Which by the holy ghost to his
   heart is sealed.
      (*Mary Magdalene*, G1^{r-v})

being grounded vpon the trueth of
the free promise in Christ, is both
reueled to our mindes, and sealed in
our heartes by the holy Ghost.
      (*Institution*, III.ii. 7)

This faith with the word hath such
   propinquitie,
That proprely the one is not
   without the other,
Faith must be tried with the word
   of veritie,
As the chyld is by the father and
   mother.
      (*Mary Magdalene*, G1^{v})

First we must be put in minde that
there is a generall relation of faith to
the worde, and that faith can no
more be severed from the worde,
than the sunnebeames from the
sunne from whom they procede.
      (*Institution*, III.ii. 6)

Yea truly, if this faith do from
   Gods word decline,
It is no faith, but a certayn
   incredulitie,
Which causeth the mynd to
   wa(n)der in strange doctrine
And so to fall at length into
   impietie.
      (*Mary Magdalene*, G1^{v})

Wherefore if faith do swerue neuer
so litle from this marke, to which it
ought to be directly leuelled, it
kepeth not her own nature, but
becometh an vncertaine lightnesse
of beliefe and wandring errour of
minde. The same Worde is the foundation wherewith faith is vpholden
and susteined, from which if it
swarue, it falleth downe. Therefore
take away the Worde, and then
there shall remaine no faith.
      (*Institution* III.ii. 6)

The word to a glasse compare we
   may,
For as it were therin, faith God
   doth behold,
Whom as in a cloude we loke vpon
   alway.
      (*Mary Magdalene*, G1^{v})

But we say that the worde it selfe,
howesoeuer it be conueied to vs, is
like a mirrour when faith may
beholde God.
      (*Institution* III.ii. 6)

The operation of Faith is not to
enquire
What God is as touchyng his
propre nature,
But how good he is to vs to know
faith doth desyre,
Which thing appereth in his holy
Scripture.

(*Mary Magdalene*, G1ᵛ)

For this is not the onely purpose in
the vnderstanding of faith, that we
knowe that there is a God, but this
also, yea this chiefly, that we vnder-
stand what will he beareth towards
vs. For it not so much behoueth vs to
knowe what he is in himselfe but
what a one he will be to vs. Nowe
therefore we are come to this point,
that faith is a knowledge of the will
of God, perceyued by his worde.

(*Institution* III.ii. 6)

It is not inough to beleue that God
is true only,
Which can neuer lie, nor deceaue,
nor do yll:
But true faith is persuaded firmly
and truely,
That in his word he hath declared
his will.

(*Mary Magdalene*, G1ᵛ)

But also it sufficeth not to beleue
that God is a true speaker, which
can neither deceiue nor lie, vnlesse
thou further holde this for vndoubt-
edly determined, that whatsoeuer
procedeth from him, is the sacred
and inuiolable truthe.

(*Institution* III.ii. 6)

Above, Wager defines faith as a "sure knowledge and cognition /
Of the good will of God," and that it is "Grounded in the word of
Christes erudition." This is a paraphrase of Calvin's assertion that
faith is a "stedfast and assured knowledge of Gods kindnesse toward
vs, which being grounded vpon the trueth of the free promise in
Christ." Wager also echoes Calvin when he says that faith is "to the
mynde of man reuealed" (Calvin: "reueled to our mindes"), and
sealed in his heart by the Holy Ghost. Moreover, both men warn that
if faith is not based on the Word, it will lead to impiety and heresy.
The mirror image re-appears, but this time it is likened to the Word,
in which man may "behold" faith. Next, Wager repeats Calvin's
statement that faith does not teach us to know the nature of God, but
simply to know his will and goodness towards man. And finally,
Wager follows Calvin in saying that it is not enough to believe that
God is true only, "Which can neuer lie, nor deceaue, nor do yll";
however, in adding that it is also necessary to believe that God "hath
declared his will" in His Word, Wager modifies Calvin's remark that
"whatsoeuer procedeth from him, is the sacred and inuiolable
truthe."

It is worth noting that while others in the Reformed tradition assumed that man must repent of sin before faith is possible, Wager, like Calvin, consistently places faith before repentance in the process of conversion. On this point of doctrine the Genevan theologian was uncompromising: "As for them that thinks that repentance doth rather go before faith than flow or spring foorth of it, as a frute out of a tree, they neuer knewe the force therof, and are moued with too weake an argument to thinke so...Yet when we referre the beginnings of repentance to faith...we meane to shewe that a man can not earnestly apply himselfe to repentance, vnlesse he know himself to be of God" (*Institution* III.iii. 1–2). In *Mary Magdalene*, Wager suggests that faith leads to forgiveness of sins, which makes contrition and repentance possible:

> And all that trust in hym with true beleue,
> That he is very God and man, into this world sent,
> God will all their synnes for his sake forgeue,
> So that they can be contrite and repent.
> (*Mary Magdalene*, F2ʳ)

And in the concluding speech of the play we are told, "By the word came faith, faith brought penitence" (*Mary Magdalene*, I3ᵛ).

Appendix C

Calvin's *Institutes*: a source of *Jacob and Esau*?

In his 1933 article, "The Date of 'The History of Jacob and Esau,'"
G. Scheurweghs refers to the number of correspondences between
lines in the Prologue and Epilogue of *Jacob and Esau* and passages in
the 1539 Latin edition of Calvin's *Institutes*.[1]

But before Jacob and Esau yet born were, Or had either done good, or ill perpetrate:	Quum nondum nati essent, nec quidpiam boni aut mali fecissent, ut secundum electionem propositum Dei maneret, non ex operibus, sed ex vocante, dictum est: maior serviet minori; sicut scriptum est: (Mal. I.2–3; Rom. IX.13)
As the prophet Malachi and Paul witness bear, Jacob was chosen, and Esau reprobate: Jacob I love (saith God) and Esau I hate.	Iacob dilexi, Esau autem odium habui. Quidnam ad haec obscuranda praetexent, qui operibus, vel praeteritis vel futuris, locum aliquen in electione assignant? Hoc enim est prorsus eludere quod contendit apostolus, non ex aliqua opeium
For it is not (saith Paul) in man's renewing or will, But in God's mercy, who chooseth whom he will. *(Jacob and Esau, Prologue)*	ratione, sed ex mera Dei vocatione pendere fratrum discrimen, quia inter nondum natos constitum fuerit. *Institutio, 248*
So on God's behalf no manner default there is; But where he chooseth, he showeth his great mercy: And where he refuseth, he doth none injury. But thus far surmounteth man's intellection, To attain or conceive, and (much more) to discuss. *(Jacob and Esau, Epilogue, Act V, Sc. X)*	Quos salutis participatione dignatur, eos gratuita eius misericordia; nullo propriae dignitatis respectu, dicimuscooptari. Quos in damnationem tradit, iis iusto quidem et irreprehensibili sed incomprehensibili ipsius iudicio, vitae aditum praecludi. *Institutio, 247*

Scheurweghs' comparison, however, does not prove that Calvin influenced the play. For while these passages contain significant parallels, Helen Thomas is certainly right in pointing out that the author of *Jacob and Esau* may have gone directly to the ninth chapter of Paul's Epistle to the Romans for the contents of his Epilogue and Prologue, rather than to *The Institutes*.[2] Yet if she exposes the weakness of Scheurwegh's hypothesis, Thomas' alternative reading of the play, discussed in her article, "*Jacob and Esau* – 'rigidly Calvinistic'?" raises some questions of its own. She argues, on the basis of certain lines in the Epilogue, that the author's opinions on predestination go directly against the teachings not only of Calvin but Luther as well, and that they are more representative of Roman Catholic doctrine. "It is very likely," she concludes, that the play "is a dramatic statement of the position of Erasmus on predestination."[3] The lines she refers to are as follows:

> Yet not all fleshe did he predestinate,
> But onely the adopted children of promise:
> For he foreknewe that many would degenerate,
> And wylfully give cause to put from that blisse.
>
> (G4ʳ)

Thomas comments, "Thus God's foreknowledge of man's future actions is given as the cause of His choice of the elect and the reprobated."[4] From the Poet's remark that foreknowledge of sin is the basis of excluding many from bliss (the meaning of the latter two lines), Thomas has deduced that election, as well as reprobation, is a consequence of God's foreknowledge of man's actions. This is, indeed, the position of Erasmus on predestination, and one which Thomas Aquinas made orthodox in Roman Catholic theology, but it is not the view expressed in *Jacob and Esau*. The Poet is saying here that while God predestined the elect to salvation, he did not actually predetermine, but only foreknew, the fate of the many others who were not elected; their degeneracy or sin is the cause of their exclusion from eternal bliss.

This "moderate" Calvinist position (that reprobation was not the object of a divine foreordinance but simply the state of those not chosen by God) was adopted by Martin Bucer and Peter Martyr,[5] two of Calvin's closest colleagues and supporters in England, and by many of their English contemporaries, notably John Bradford. Bradford was embroiled in the famous Marian debate over predestination in the King's Bench prison in 1554. Fortunately, his

contribution to the dispute has survived, and since his written
opinions upon the subject appear to have been approved by Cranmer,
Ridley, and Latimer, the three leading divines of the Edwardian
church,[6] it may be said that they generally reflect the views of most
committed English Protestants during the 1550s. Bradford writes
that it does not hurt to "affirm, teach, and preach" the doctrine that
"'Christ elected some, and not all,' since it is set forth unto man in
the Bible."[7] According to Bradford, predestination "utterly over-
throweth the wisdom, power, ableness, and choice of man, that all glory
may be given only unto God."[8] The Edwardian Reformer follows
Calvin in declaring that "election is not to be looked upon but in
Christ." "Christ's death is sufficient for all," he asserts, "but effectual
to none but to the elect only." He comes close to advocating limited
atonement in believing that Christ "prayed not" for all men, and
that "for whom he 'prayed not,' for them he died not." While
reprobation, as well as election, serve to glorify God, Bradford, like
Calvin, places the responsibility for damnation squarely on the
reprobate's shoulders. Where he significantly deviates from Calvin,
however, is in his assertion that God's rejection of the reprobate is
based not upon a positive eternal decree (as Calvin evidently
believed), but on his foreknowledge of sin: "the damned therefore
have not nor shall not have any excuse, for God, foreseeing their
condemnation through their own sin, did not draw them as he doth
his elect unto Christ."[9] Thus, when the Poet declares in the Epilogue
that God predestined "onely the adopted children of promise," and
that "he foreknewe that many [i.e. the reprobate] would degenerate,
/ And wylfully giue cause to be put from that blisse," he was
expressing this more moderate Calvinist position on predestination.

The Poet goes on to say that due to the fall, all men are subject to
damnation on account of their sins, so "Where he chooseth, he
sheweth his great mercy: / And where he refuseth, he doth none
iniury" (H1ʳ). In anticipation of those who may ask why Christ did
not offer his mercy to all of mankind, the Poet declares that the
mysteries of predestination "farre surmounteth mans intellection, /
To attaine or conceiue, and much more to discusse," and adds that
such matters must be referred to "Gods election, / And to his secret
iudgement" (H1ʳ). Here, once again, the author complies with
Calvin, who often warned against indulging in speculative thought
on predestination, for to seek knowledge of it outside of the Scriptures
is a confusing and dangerous business, and "no less madnesse than if
a man haue a will to goe by vnpassable waye, or to see in darknesse."[10]

Notes

INTRODUCTION

1 John Bale, *Three Laws*, in Happé, *Bale*, II, 99 (ll. 1181–85). I have inserted a question mark in place of Happé's period after "escape." In the lines immediately following, Infidelity adds, "But thy wolvyshness by thre crownes wyll I hyde, / Makynge the a Pope, and a captayne of all pryde," an allusion to the pope's triple crowned tiara. See Happé's comment on p. 171, and also that of Lois Potter in *Revels II*, 181.

2   Rerum interim per transennam simulachra
        Spectare haud pigeat, tantum quae praeludimus.
                ... Oculos enim sacros
        Preinde ac aures esse, qui minus decet?

See John Foxe, *Christus Triumphans*, ed. and trans. John Hazel Smith, in *Two Latin Comedies by John Foxe The Martyrologist* (Ithaca: Cornell University Press, 1973), "Prologue," p. 229.

3 The statement came just one year after *Christus Triumphans* was performed at Trinity College Cambridge in 1562, possibly with Foxe himself in attendance. See John Foxe, *Acts and Monuments*, ed. S. R. Cattley, rev. Josiah Pratt, 8 vols. (London: Religious Tract Society, 1877), VI, 31 and 57. For the record of the Cambridge production, see Alan H. Nelson, ed., *Cambridge*, 2 vols., REED (University of Toronto Press, 1989), I, 221, and II, 969 and 979. Following his return from exile, Foxe resided for a time not far away from Cambridge at the Norwich estate of his patron and former student, Thomas Howard, the Duke of Norfolk. See *Dictionary of National Biography*.

4 Patrick Collinson, *The Birthpangs of Protestant England* (London: Macmillan, 1988), ch. 4, "Protestant Culture and the Cultural Revolution," pp. 94ff.

5 Chambers, *MS*, II, ch. 25; *ES*, I, ch. 8.

6 Chambers, *ES*, I, 242.

7 See Chambers, *MS*, II, 2 and 179; *ES*, I, 237, 245. For further discussion of Chambers' views of clerical opposition to plays and his ideas about drama's gradual secularization from medieval times to Shakespeare, see O. B. Hardison, *Christian Rite and Christian Drama in the Middle Ages* (Baltimore: Johns Hopkins Press, 1965), pp. 1–34.

8 See Basil Hall, "Lutheranism in England," in *Reform and Reformation: England and the Continent: c. 1500–c. 1750*, ed. Derek Baker (Oxford: Blackwell, 1979), p. 13; A. G. Dickens, *The English Reformation* (1964; reprinted London: Fontana, 1978), p. 110.

9 For the long historiographical tradition of the Anglican vs. Puritan dichotomy and its distortions, see Paul Christianson, "Reformers and the Church of England under Elizabeth I and the Early Stuarts," *Journal of Ecclesiastical History*, 31 (1980): 463–82.

10 Patrick Collinson, "A Comment: Concerning the Name Puritan," *Journal of Ecclesiastical History*, 31 (1980): 483–88; p. 486.

11 Archbishop Whitgift applied the term reproachfully to the Presbyterians led by Thomas Cartwright, but "puritan" was also a label for many conforming Protestants such as William Perkins and William Whitaker who, while polemically anti-papist and interested in a more thoroughly reformed Church of England represented in many respects the mainstream of Protestant religious opinion of the time. Therefore, we should guard against proposing too narrow a definition of puritanism. As Collinson observes, "if we share with contemporaries a sense of Puritanism which is at once polemical and nominalistic then far from circumscribing its meaning we should regard the incidence of the term in contemporary discourse as indicative of theological, moral and social tension which should be the prime object of our investigations" ("A Comment," p. 488). See also Peter Lake, *Moderate puritans and the Elizabethan Church* (Cambridge University Press, 1982), pp. 12–14.

12 Margot Heinemann, *Puritanism and Theatre: Thomas Middleton and Opposition Drama under the Early Stuarts* (Cambridge University Press, 1980); Heinemann, "Political Drama," in *The Cambridge Companion to English Renaissance Drama*, eds. A. R. Braunmuller and Michael Hattaway (Cambridge University Press, 1990): 161–206; Martin Butler, *Theatre and Crisis 1632–1642* (Cambridge University Press, 1984); Jerzy Limon, *Dangerous Matter: English Drama and Politics in 1623/24* (Cambridge University Press, 1986).

13 Chambers, *ES*, I, 244; Norman Sanders, in *Revels II*, 21, 27–28; David Bevington also sympathizes with this view in arguing that drama shifted from doctrinal to social and economic matters during the 1560s which, as I shall show later, is not supported by evidence in the plays themselves; see *Tudor Drama and Politics* (Cambridge, MA: Harvard University Press, 1966), pp. 127–40. There does not appear to have been any Crown interference with Protestant religious drama until the later 1580s. In 1589, a licensing commission was formed by the Archbishop of Canterbury to "strike out" passages in play books dealing with matters of church and state. See chapter 6 below, pp. 165, 173–74.

14 Harold C. Gardiner's thesis in *Mysteries' End: An Investigation of the Last Days of the Medieval Religious Stage* (New Haven: Yale University Press, 1946) is challenged in Lancashire, *DTR*, xxxi, and Bing D. Bills, "The 'Suppression Theory' and the English Corpus Christi Play: A Re-

examination," *Theatre Journal*, 32 (1980): 157–68. See also Glynne Wickham, "The Staging of Saint Plays in England," in *The Medieval Drama*, ed. Sandro Sticca (Albany: State University of New York Press, 1972): 99–120; pp. 113–14.

15 See Happé, *Bale*; Wickham, *EES*, III; Lois Potter, *Revels II*, ch. 4; Murray Roston, *Biblical Drama in England* (London: Faber and Faber, 1968); Bernard Spivack, *Shakespeare and The Allegory of Evil* (New York: Columbia University Press, 1958); Bevington, *From Mankind to Marlowe* (Cambridge, MA: Harvard University Press, 1962); Bevington, *Tudor Drama and Politics*; T. W. Craik, *The Tudor Interlude* (London: Leicester University Press, 1958); Richard Southern, *The Staging of Plays Before Shakespeare* (New York: Theatre Arts Books, 1973); Alan Dessen, *Shakespeare and the Late Moral Plays* (Lincoln: University of Nebraska Press, 1986). Other studies will be cited in the chapters which follow.

16 David Bevington and Bernard Spivack view this drama primarily as a transitional phase in the English theatre's evolutionary development from primitive forms of religious expression to a complex secular art culminating in Marlowe and Shakespeare. This evolutionary view of the history of early English drama (Chambers himself had much to do with popularizing it) has faced heavy criticism particularly by medieval theatre scholars, but it is often overlooked as a problematic feature of much commentary on sixteenth-century drama. I return to this matter in chapter 3; see pp. 75–76 below. See also Hardison, *Christian Rite*, ch. 1; Wickham, *EES*, I, 314ff; William Tydeman, *The Theatre in the Middle Ages* (Cambridge University Press, 1978); Lancashire, *DTR*, "Introduction."

17 See J. J. Scarisbrick, *The Reformation and the English People* (Oxford: Basil Blackwell, 1984); Christopher Haigh, ed., *The English Reformation Revised* (Cambridge University Press, 1987); Maria Dowling, "The Gospel and the Court: Reformation under Henry VIII," *Protestantism and the National Church in Sixteenth Century England*, eds. Peter Lake and Maria Dowling (London: Croom Helm, 1987); Dowling, "Anne Boleyn and Reform," *Journal of Ecclesiastical History*, 35 (1984): 30–46; Rosemary O'Day, "The Law of Patronage in Early Modern England," *Journal of Ecclesiastical History*, 26 (1975): 247–60; Peter Clark, *English Provincial Society from the Reformation to the Revolution: Religion, Politics and Society in Kent, 1500–1640* (Rutherford, NJ: Fairleigh Dickinson University Press, 1977); Patrick Collinson, *The Elizabethan Puritan Movement* (London: Cape, 1967).

18 Jonathon Dollimore, *Radical Tragedy: Religion, Ideology and Power in the Drama of Shakespeare and His Contemporaries* (University of Chicago Press, 1984). Dollimore contends that Elizabethan writers such as Hooker and Bacon had a sophisticated understanding of ideology in both its cognitive and materialist senses and that they recognized that religion could be implemented by political authorities as a means of keeping people in a state of subjection. As we shall see in chapter 1, certainly Thomas

Cromwell entertained this view of Roman Catholicism under papal authority in the 1530s. See also Alan Sinfield, *Literature in Protestant England, 1560–1660* (New York: Barnes and Noble, 1983); and Leonard Tennenhouse's useful introduction to *The Tudor Interludes Nice Wanton and Impatient Poverty* (New York: Garland, 1984).

19 The major studies here are Eleanor Rosenberg, *Leicester: Patron of Letters* (New York: Columbia, 1955); and John N. King, *English Reformation Literature: The Tudor Origins of the Protestant Tradition* (Princeton University Press, 1982); see also Jan Van Dorsten, "Literary Patronage in Elizabethan England: The Early Phase," *Patronage in the Renaissance*, eds. Guy Fitch Lytle and Stephen Orgel (Princeton University Press, 1981): 191–206; H. S. Bennett, *English Books and Readers 1558–1603* (Cambridge University Press, 1965). Also relevant, though dealing for the most part with the period post-dating this study, are several articles in *Politics, Patronage and Literature in England 1558–1658*, 21 (1991) of *Yearbook of English Studies*, ed. Andrew Gurr, especially Margot Heinemann, "Rebel Lords, Popular Playwrights, and Political Culture: Notes on Jacobean Patronage and the Earl of Southampton," pp. 63–86.

20 See chapter 1, below. Rosenberg, *Leicester*, p. 188, suggests that Leicester and other Elizabethan patrons wisely sponsored even the more radical puritans, whose reformist agenda came close to threatening royal authority, as a means of controlling and containing their activities, which included directing their propaganda against Rome rather than their own national church. In this respect, she anticipates the work of a number of literary scholars in the past decade who maintain that subversive practices are permitted, channelled and contained by those in power. For a discussion of this theory and its problems, see Heather Dubrow and Richard Strier, "Introduction: The Historical Renaissance," in *The Historical Renaissance: Essays in Tudor and Stuart Literature and Culture* (University of Chicago Press, 1988), pp. 4–5; Dubrow's "'The Sun in Water': Donne's Somerset Epithalamium and the Poetics of Patronage," in the same book (pp. 114–15); and M. D. Jardine, "New Historicism for Old: New Conservatism for Old? The Politics of Patronage in the Renaissance," *The Yearbook of English Studies*, 21 (1991): 286–304.

21 Suzanne R. Westfall, *Patrons and Performance: Early Tudor Household Records* (Oxford: Clarendon, 1990); see also Ian Lancashire, "Introduction," *Two Tudor Interludes: Youth and Hickscorner* (Manchester University Press, 1980); Mary A. Blackstone, "Patrons and Elizabethan Acting Companies," *Elizabethan Theatre X*, ed. C. E. McGee (Port Credit, Ontario: Meany, 1988): 112–32; J. A. B. Somerset, "The Lords President, Their Activities and Companies: Evidence from Shropshire," in *Elizabethan Theatre X*: 93–111.

22 Robert Weimann, *Shakespeare and the Popular Tradition in the Theatre* (Baltimore: Johns Hopkins University Press, 1978), p. xv.

23 In a 1537 May game play "of a king how he should rule his realm," for example, the player portraying Husbandry "said many things against

gentlemen more than was in the book of the play" (*LP: Henry 8*, XII.i, 557, 585; cited in Lancashire, *DTR*, 65).

24 See Sally-Beth Maclean, "Players on Tour: New Evidence From Records of Early English Drama," in *Elizabethan Theatre X*: 55–72; Westfall, *Patrons and Performance*, ch. 3.

1 "BALE AND HIS FELOWES"

1 In the absence of a much-needed revision of J. T. Murray's *English Dramatic Companies* 1558–1642, 2 vols. (Oxford: Clarendon, 1910), my count is based chiefly on Murray but is supplemented by lists of companies in recent volumes of Records of Early English Drama and the Malone Society Collections, especially *Devon*, ed. John Wasson, REED (Toronto University Press, 1986); Lancashire, *DTR*; *Norfolk and Suffolk*, eds. David Galloway and John Wasson, MSC, IX (Oxford University Press, 1980). See also John Wasson, "Professional Actors in the Middle Ages and Early Renaissance," *Medieval and Renaissance Drama in England: Volume I*, ed. J. Leeds Barroll, III (New York: AMS, 1984): 1–11.

2 For the important critical commentary see chapter 2, note 4.

3 Leslie Fairfield, *John Bale: Mythmaker for the English Reformation* (West Lafayette, IN: Purdue University Press, 1976); King, *English Reformation Literature*; Ritchie Kendall, *The Drama of Dissent: The Radical Poetics of Nonconformity 1380–1590* (Chapel Hill: University of North Carolina Press, 1986); Paul Christianson, *Reformers and Babylon: English Apocalyptic Visions from the Reformation to the Eve of the Civil War* (Toronto University Press, 1978); Happé, *Bale*.

4 For the numerous play titles dating from the period, see appendix A. See also Sydney Anglo, *Spectacle, Pageantry, and Early Tudor Policy* (Oxford University Press, 1969), ch. 7; Chambers, *ES*, I, ch. 8; Lancashire, *DTR*, xxvii–xxviii; *Revels II*, ch. 1.

5 For the role of the Secretary and Lord Privy Seal in arranging revels in early Tudor England, see Wickham, *EES*, I, 275–76.

6 The text is in Sydney Anglo, "An Early Tudor Programme for Plays and Other Demonstrations against the Pope," *The Journal of the Warburg and Courtnay Institute*, 20 (1957): 176–79. For the proposed 1535 date, see G. R. Elton, *Policy and Police* (Cambridge University Press, 1972), p. 185.

7 For the pronouncements of Machiavelli, as well as those of John Calvin, Richard Hooker and Robert Burton to this effect, see Jonathon Dollimore's discussion of Renaissance concepts of ideology in *Radical Tragedy* (Chicago University Press, 1984), pp. 9f. To these, one might add the remarks of Thomas Cranmer, who fervently supported Cromwell's policies as Archbishop of Canterbury: "The holy decrees, as they call them, be nothing else but the laws and ordinances of the bishop of Rome: whereof the most part be made for his own advancement, glory, and lucre, and to make him and his clergy governors of the whole world, and to be exempted from all princes' laws, and to do what they list." In *Miscellaneous Writings and Letters of Thomas Cranmer*, ed. John

Edmund Cox, PS (Cambridge University Press, 1846), p. 163. For Cromwell's familiarity with Machiavelli, see Maria Dowling, *Humanism in the Age of Henry VIII* (London: Croom Helm, 1986), p. 200.

8 Anglo, "Early Tudor Programme," p. 177.

9 *Ibid.*, p. 179.

10 As early as 1533 there were public processions in the streets of London in which people went dressed and masqued as cardinals, to the great displeasure of the pope, according to one French official. By 1539, every village pastime or feast across the country seemed to include "sports and follies" debunking the Pope, reported another French diplomat. On June 17 of the same year, an elaborately conceived spectacle on the Thames depicted a mock battle in which the bishop of Rome and his cardinals on one barge were defeated and ceremoniously dumped into the river by the King and his forces on another. See Lancashire, *DTR*, 66, 199, 202; Anglo, *Spectacle*, pp. 269–70, and sources cited there.

11 For iconoclasm in this sense and many related insightful remarks, see James R. Siemon, *Shakespearean Iconoclasm* (Berkeley: University of California Press, 1985), pp. 43–75, 141–44. See also John Phillips, *The Reformation of Images: Destruction of Art in England 1535–1660* (Berkeley: University of California Press, 1973), especially chs. 3 to 5; and Earnest B. Gilman, *Iconoclasm and Poetry in the English Reformation* (Chicago University Press, 1986), ch. 2.

12 Elton, *Policy and Police*, p. 202; Anglo, *Spectacle*, p. 272.

13 John Bale, *Scriptorum Illustrium maioris Britannieae ... Catalogus*, 2 vols. (Basel, 1557–59), p. 702; see translation of relevant passage in Happé, *Bale*, I, 147 (appendix II).

14 Fairfield, *John Bale*, p. 36; Elton, *Policy and Police*, p. 233.

15 Four of his plays were "Compyled" in 1538. Around the same time, he revised *King Johan*. See list of plays in *Anglorum Heliades*; the list is given in Happé, *Bale*, I, 9; see also J. H. P. Pafford, ed., *King Johan*, MSR (Oxford University Press, 1931), p. xxii.

16 The two references are in Cromwell's financial accounts. Under September 8, 1538, an entry reads: "Balle and his ffelowes. The same day gyuen to them by my lordes comaundement at Saynt Stephens besyde Caunterbury for playing before my lorde ... xl s." The January 1539 payment: "Bale & his ffelowes. The last of January gyuen to him and his ffelowes for playing befor my lorde ... xxx s." See *LP: Henry 8*, IV, ii, 337, 339. The connection between Cromwell and St. Stephen's is noted in Clark, *English Provincial Society*, p. 51.

17 Pafford, *King Johan*, p. xviii, suggests that the remuneration to Bale's troupe by Cromwell in January 1539 might be for this showing before Cranmer, but this is highly conjectural. For the deposition of John Alforde, see *Miscellaneous Writings*, p. 388. It is worth noting that Bale translated the Latin version of Thomas Kirchmayer's *Pammachius* in 1538, which had been dedicated to Cranmer in this same year.

18 See Pafford's Introduction to *King Johan*, pp. xvii–xviii. See also Craik's account in *Revels II*, pp. 114–15; Thora Blatt, *The Plays of John Bale*

(Copenhagen: G. E. C. Gads Forlag, 1968), pp. 30–31; Honor C. McCusker, *John Bale: Dramatist and Antiquary* (1942; reprinted Freeport, NY: Books for Libraries Press, 1971), p. 75; Jesse W. Harris, *John Bale: A Study in the Minor Literature of the Reformation* (1940; reprinted Freeport, NY: Books for Libraries Press, 1970), pp. 101–3.

19 *"ob editas comedias"*; stated by Bale in *Anglorum Heliades* (BL Mss. Harley 3838), fol. 112. John De Vere, the first Protestant Earl of Oxford, was a confidant of Anne Boleyn, and as hereditary Lord Chamberlain was ranked fifth among the high offices of the royal court. He was one of the select group of noblemen who signed the articles in the House of Lords on October 1, 1529 which ousted Wolsey from power. He played an active role along with Anne Boleyn's father and brother, Wiltshire and Rochford, in the events leading up to the Submission of the Clergy in May of 1532 (see Ives, *Boleyn*, 192–93), and remained on good terms with Cromwell throughout the 1530s. He was also appointed Commissioner to depose Queen Catherine of Aragon in April, 1533, and as part of his traditional duties as hereditary Lord Chamberlain, carried Anne's crown at her coronation one month later. It is therefore not surprising to discover that one of the plays Bale composed for Oxford was entitled *On the King's Two Marriages*, which would have made a timely performance at Court around the time of Anne's coronation in 1533 and certainly no later than 1536 when both Catherine and Anne died. We know that during these same years the divorce and remarriage was a popular topic of royalist print propaganda. See Helen Miller, *Henry VIII and the English Nobility* (Oxford: Basil Blackwell, 1986), pp. 113–14, 165; Elton, *Policy and Police*, pp. 210, 174–79. It is not inconceivable that Cromwell learned of Bale's talents by way of his services to Oxford.

20 See his empassioned outcry in *The Epistel Exhortatorye* (1544), fol. 18a, quoted in chapter 2, p. 43 below. Born in 1495, Bale must have been past the age of 65 when he stirred up trouble by staging a friar-debunking play in Canterbury in the early 1560s. See Peter Clark, "Josias Nicholls and Religious Radicalism, 1553–1639," *The Journal of Ecclesiastical History*, 28 (1977): 133–35; p. 134.

21 *Calendar of State Papers, Domestic Series, of the Reigns of Edward VI, etc., Vol. I (1547–1580)*, ed. Robert Lemon (London, 1856), p. 5; Chambers, *ES*, II, 222.

22 Lancashire, *DTR*, 198.

23 *Ibid.*, 375–76.

24 *Henry VIII*, pp. 84–85.

25 Ipswich Chamberlain accounts for 1561 (after June 28): "Item, to the plaiers Peter Moone and his companie...v s"; in Murray, *English Dramatic Companies*, II, 287. For more on Moone, see Dickens, *English Reformation*, pp. 222–23.

26 Wickham, *EES*, II.i, 109.

27 Richard Beadle, "Plays and Playing at Thetford and Nearby, 1498–1540," *Theatre Notebook* 32 (1978): 4–11.

28 Lancashire, *DTR*, 393.

29 W. A. Mepham, "Municipal Drama at Maldon in the Sixteenth Century," *The Essex Review* 55 (1946): 169–75; Alan H. Nelson, *The Medieval English Stage* (Chicago University Press, 1974), pp. 215–16; see also Happé, *Bale*, I, 3.

30 John Foxe, *Acts and Monuments*, 2nd edn., 2 vols. (London: John Daye, 1570), II, 1376. See Jackson Campbell Boswell, "Seven Actors in Search of a Biographer," *Medieval and Renaissance Drama in England Volume II*, ed. J. Leeds Barroll, III (New York: AMS, 1985): 51–56; p. 52.

31 Happé, *Bale*, I, 152–56.

32 See Lancashire, *DTR*, xxv; Bevington, *From Mankind to Marlowe*, ch. 5.

33 Diarmaid MacCulloch, *Suffolk and the Tudors: Politics and Religion in an English County 1500–1600* (Oxford University Press, 1986), p. 158.

34 Happé, *Bale*, I, 154–56; Bevington, *From Mankind to Marlowe*, pp. 128–31.

35 Bevington, *From Mankind to Marlowe*, pp. 79–82.

36 Westfall, *Patrons and Performance*, pp. 111–12.

37 Murray's study (and many others which have followed it, including Lancashire, *DTR*) show also a visit to Barnstaple in 1538/39. However, John Wasson has informed me that the Lord Privy Seal's Players do not show up in the Barnstaple records until 1546/47 (when Francis Russel, the Earl of Bedford was Lord Privy Seal) and that Murray simply misread the date. See his REED edition of *Devon*, p. 40.

38 Westfall, *Patrons and Performance*, pp. 141–42.

39 See David Galloway, "The 'Game Place' and 'House' at Great Yarmouth, 1493–1595," *Theatre Notes* 31 (1977): 6–9.

40 Giles E. Dawson, ed., *Records of Plays and Players in Kent, 1450–1642*, MSC VII (Oxford University Press, 1965), pp. xv–xxii.

41 Westfall, *Patrons and Performance*, p. 141.

42 See Maclean, "Players on Tour," pp. 55–72. See also D. M. Palliser, *The Age of Elizabeth: England under the Later Tudors 1547–1603* (London: Longman, 1983), ch. 9, "Traffics and Discoveries," pp. 270f.

43 Lancashire, *DTR*, 65; Wasson, *Devon*, p. 5.

44 See Happé, "Properties and Costumes in the Plays of John Bale," *Medieval English Theatre* 2.2 (1980): 55–65.

45 The selling off of vestments and other valuables is discussed in the correspondence to Cromwell relating to the dissolutions, collected in G. Cook, ed., *Letters to Cromwell and Others on the Suppression of the Monasteries* (London: Baker, 1965), pp. 6–9, 185; see especially the letters of New College Warden, Dr. London, and of Richard Ingworth.

46 Westfall, *Patrons and Performance*, pp. 144–45.

47 Cromwell's networks in Kent and Suffolk are discussed respectively in Clark, *English Provincial Society* (see especially ch. 2); and MacCulloch, *Suffolk and the Tudors*.

48 Thomas North, *A Chronicle of the Church of St. Martin in Leicester During the Reigns of Henry VIII, Edward VI, Mary, and Elizabeth* (London: Bell and Daldy, 1866), pp. 114–15.

49 Bryan Little, *Abbeys and Priories in England and Wales* (New York: Holmes

& Meier, 1979), p. 138; J. A. B. Somerset, "Local Drama and Playing Places at Shrewsbury: New Findings from the Borough Records," *Medieval and Renaissance Drama in England Volume II* (New York: AMS, 1985): 1–32.

50 Cook, *Letters to Cromwell*, p. 9.

51 See Frederick Boas, *University Drama in the Tudor Age* (Oxford University Press, 1914), p. 27.

52 Reported to me in private correspondence.

53 Nelson, *Cambridge*, I, 112, 114, 119.

54 David Galloway and John Wasson, eds., *Records of Plays and Players in Norfolk and Suffolk, 1330–1642*, MSC XI (Oxford University Press, 1980), pp. xi–xiii.

55 Pafford, *King Johan*, p. vi and p. xiv.

56 See Happé, *Bale*, I, 12–13.

57 See *LP: Henry 8*, VIII, 373. Richard Morison suggested that a new public holiday should celebrate the English people's deliverance from "that most wicked pharao of all pharaos, the bysshop of Rome." See Anglo, "An Early Tudor Programme," p. 178. Also of interest is Archbishop Cranmer's practice of arranging iconoclastic events on feast days as part of his effort to bring the ecclesiastical calendar into line with a more gospel-oriented national church (see King, *English Reformation Literature*, pp. 151–52).

58 See Clark, *English Provincial Society*, p. 41; H. Maynard Smith, *Henry VIII and the Reformation* (1948; reprinted London: Macmillan, 1962), pp. 100–1.

59 See Blatt, *Plays of John Bale*, p. 50.

60 The King's own dislike for Becket is reflected, among other places, in a letter he wrote to the authorities at York in an effort to suppress a religious interlude of St. Thomas. The letter is quoted in full in *Revels II*, 9. Bale's play may have been designed to counter the various Catholic saint plays on St. Thomas.

61 King, *English Reformation Literature*, p. 48; Elton, *Policy and Police*, p. 206.

62 McCusker, *John Bale*, p. 78; Happé, *Bale*, I, 16.

63 Cranmer, *Miscellaneous Writings*, p. 388.

64 *Ibid.*, *Miscellaneous Writings*, p. 388.

65 For Bishopstoke and Kilkenny, see Happé, *Bale*, I, 6–7; for Canterbury, see Clark, "Josias Nicholls," p. 134.

66 Christopher Haigh, "The Recent Historiography of the English Reformation," *The English Reformation Revised*, ed. Christopher Haigh (Cambridge University Press, 1987): 19–33; pp. 24–25.

67 See J. J. Scarisbrick, *Reformation*. The evidence, much of which comes from extant wills, is discussed in Rosemary O'Day, *The Debate of the English Reformation* (London: Methuen, 1986), ch. 6; see also Haigh, "Recent Historiography."

68 Keith Thomas, *Religion and the Decline of Magic* (New York: Scribners, 1971), pp. 76–77.

69 See Richard Axton, "Folk Play in Tudor Interludes," *English Drama*:

Forms and Development, eds. Marie Axton and Raymond Williams (Cambridge University Press, 1977): 1–23; p. 22.

70 For "game" and "earnest" and other aspects of medieval dramaturgy, see Wickham, *EES*, III, 65–82. See also the discussion of Reformation dramaturgy in chapter 3 below.

71 Chambers, *MS*, II, 224.

72 Happé, *Bale*, I, 12.

73 Edmund Creeth, ed., *Tudor Plays: An Anthology of Early English Drama* (New York: Norton, 1966), pp. xxiv–xxv; Douglas W. Richards, "Preachers and Players: The Contest Between Agents of Sermon and Game in the Moral Drama from *Mankind* to *Like Will to Like*," University of Rochester Ph.D. dissertation, 1986, p. 198.

74 See Blatt, *Plays of John Bale*, p. 65.

75 *Ibid.*, pp. 63–64; Kendall, *Drama of Dissent*, p. 106.

76 *The Whole Works of Sir James Ware Concerning Ireland*, ed. Walter Harris (Dublin 1754), I, 415–17; cited in Harris, *John Bale*, p. 126.

77 See King, *English Reformation Literature*, pp. 144f.

78 Blatt, *Plays of John Bale*, pp. 132–33; see also *Revels II*, 179–80; Kendall, *Drama of Dissent*, pp. 101–31; Richards, "Preachers and Players," pp. 195–208.

79 *Exposition of the Fyrste Epistle of seynt Ihon* (Antwerp: M. de Keyser, 1531), p. ELr. Cited in Stephen Greenblatt, *Renaissance Self-Fashioning* (Chicago University Press, 1980), p. 91.

80 Udall refers to "the iuglyng sleyghtes of the Romish Babylon" and states that "Christ is no iugler neither doth he mocke or daly with our sense ... such iugling castes as the adversaries would have here in this matier of the sacrament." From Udall's translation of Peter Martyr Vermigli's *Discourse conernynge the Sacrament of the Lordes Supper* (*c.* 1550), fols. D1–D2. "The papists deck themselves like hickscorner [the Vice in the play of that title] in game-players' garments." Thomas Becon, *The Catechism of Thomas Becon with Other Pieces*, ed. John Ayre, PS (Cambridge University Press, 1844), p. 232. See also *The Works of James Pilkington*, ed. James Scholefield, PS (Cambridge University Press, 1842), p. 357. Both the above references are cited in Ian Lancashire, ed., *Two Tudor Interludes: The Interlude of Youth and Hickscorner*, Revels Plays (Manchester University Press, 1980), pp. 253–55. For Cranmer's references to priests and juggling, see Marie Axton, "Introduction," *Three Tudor Classical Interludes* (Cambridge: Brewer, 1982), p. 20. Ironically, Thomas More refers to the Protestant reformers as "these yonge iuglers hys [i.e. the devil's] scolars, Luther, Huskyn, and Tyndale" who "juggle away" the "bylief of all grace." *Confutation of Tyndale's Answer*, ed. L. A. Schuster, *The Complete Works of Sir Thomas More* (New Haven: Yale University Press, 1973) VIII (i), p. 206.

81 Quoted in Blatt, *Plays of John Bale*, p. 58.

82 *The Parable of the Wicked Mammon*, in *Doctrinal Treatises and Introductions to Different Portions of the Holy Scriptures*, ed. Henry Walter, PS (Cambridge University Press, 1848), p. 20.

83 See E. S. Miller, "The Roman Rite in Bale's *King Johan*," *Publications of the Modern Language Association* 64 (1949) : 802–22.

84 For the attack on images from 1537 through 1539, see Anglo, *Spectacle*, pp. 272–74. The attack resumed in similar fashion under Edward VI when a mechanical image of Christ was displayed, denounced in a sermon, and destroyed. See Thomas Wriothesley, *A Chronicle of England during the Reigns of the Tudors*, ed. W. D. Hamilton, 2 vols. (London: Camden Society, 1875) : I, 74–76.

85 Foxe, *Acts and Monuments*, 4th edn., V, 21; cited in Miller, "Roman Rite," p. 818.

86 *Revels II*, 181.

87 For the parody of religious ritual in Continental medieval drama, see Jarmila F. Veltrusky, "The Old Czech Apothecary as Clown and Symbol," *International Society for the Study of Medieval Theatre*, (1989) : 157–58.

88 A lengthy discussion of both these feasts is found in Chambers, *MS*, I, chs. 13 and 14.

89 Chambers, *MS*, I, 325.

90 *Ibid.*, 321–23. However, on the Continent, The Feast of Fools' popularity continued in Bale's time, and he may have witnessed it during the course of his extensive travels to Carmelite Houses in the Low Countries in 1522/23, and in France in 1527, where numerous records survive of its occurrence. See Chambers, *MS*, I, 325, and Fairfield, *John Bale*, pp. 9–10.

91 The Royal Proclamation of 1541 states in part that "children be strangelye decked and apparelid to counterfaite priestes, bysshopps, and women; ... and boyes doo singe masse, and preache in the pulpitt, with suche other unfittinge and inconvenyent usages, rather to the derision than to any true glory of God, or honour of his saints." The text is in Wickham, *EES*, III, 183.

92 Wasson, *Devon*, p. 326.

93 Chambers, *MS*, I, 325.

94 Wickham, *EES*, III, 184; Weimann, *Shakespeare*, pp. 20–22. For more on the Catholic festivals on the Continent as characterized by the "carnivalesque" spirit, and as "subversive of rationality, hierarchy and all rules imposed from above," see Veltrusky, "Old Czech Apothecary," pp. 157–58.

95 Weimann, *Shakespeare*, p. 21.

96 See John Calvin, *The Institution of the Christian Religion*, trans. Thomas Norton (1561; reprinted London: n.p., 1582), IV.xiv.4; and Calvin's commentary on Ezekiel 2:3, from *Commentaries on Ezekiel*, in Calvin, *Opera omnia quae supersunt (Corpus Reformatoren)*, ed. William Baum et al., 49 vols. (Brunswick: Schwetschke, 1863–1900), XL, 63; cited and translated in Ronald S. Wallace, *Calvin's Doctrine of the Word and Sacrament* (London: Oliver and Boyd, 1953), pp. 72–73; and Peter Happé, "The Protestant Adaptation of the Saint Play," in *The Saint Play in Medieval Europe*, ed. Clifford Davidson (Kalamazoo: Medieval Institute Publications, 1986) : 205–40; p. 228.

97 Anglo, "An Early Tudor Programme," p. 179.
98 See Happé, *Bale*, I, 116 and 118.

2 THE KING'S MEN AND OTHER TROUPES

1 See Chambers, *ES*, I, 270–71; M. C. Bradbrook, *The Rise of the Common Player* (Cambridge University Press, 1962), pp. 39–40; Craik, in *Revels II*, 111.
2 See Heinemann, *Puritanism and Theatre*; Jerzy Limon, *Dangerous Matter*. Andrew Gurr observes that Lord Howard of Effingham, the Lord Admiral, may have prompted the Lord Admiral's Men to mount the "Elect Nation" plays and other works glorifying Protestant heroes during the 1590s; see his *Playgoing in Shakespeare's London* (Cambridge University Press, 1987), p. 148. For the argument that noble patronage of drama remained powerful in late Elizabethan and Jacobean England, see David Bergeron, "The Patronage of Dramatists: The Case of Thomas Heywood," *English Literary Renaissance*, 18 (1988): 294–305.
3 Samuel Cox, writing in 1591, recalls the royal players of the past who "had other trades to live of" (Chambers, *ES*, IV, 237). In some of these trades, they may have earned a better living than that provided by full-time playing. See *Revels II*, 106; Westfall, *Patrons and Performance*, p. 127.
4 Westfall, *Patrons and Performance*, ch. 3; Lancashire, "Introduction," *Two Tudor Interludes*, pp. 24–36; Peter Greenfield, "Professional Players at Gloucester: Conditions of Provincial Performing," *Elizabethan Theatre X*, pp. 73–92.
5 *Epistel Exhortatorye of an Inglyshe Christian* (Basel, 1544), fol. 18a. Bale equates players and ministers when he refers to "godly ministers, be they writers or preachers, players or syngers" (fol. 21a). Cited in Blatt, *The Plays of John Bale*, pp. 130–31.
6 Foxe, *Acts and Monuments*, 4th edn., IV, 57.
7 John Christopherson, *Exhortation to all menne to take hede and beware of rebellion* (London, 1554), T3ᵛ. See also Boas, *University Drama*, pp. 43–44.
8 Privy Council to the Lord President of the North, April 30, 1556, in John Strype, *Ecclesiastical Memorials*, 3 vols. (Oxford University Press, 1721), III, 2, 185. See also Wickham, *EES*, II.i, 72.
9 T. E. Hartley, ed., *Proceedings in the Parliaments of Elizabeth (1558–1581)* (Leicester University Press, 1981), p. 31.
10 Thomas Dorman, *A Proufe of Certeyne Articles in Religion* (1564; reprinted London: Scholar Press, 1976), fol. 123b. The history of the minstrels remains an open field for research, but for the ballad as an instrument of Protestant propaganda in Reformation England, see Collinson, *Birthpangs of Protestant England*, pp. 106–12.
11 For the Lisles' connection with pietistic circles, see J. K. McConica, *English Humanists and Reformation Politics under Henry VIII and Edward VI*

(Oxford: Clarendon, 1968), p. 219. Nevertheless, the editor of the Lisles' correspondence remarks that Plantagenet was a career politician and that his wife leaned towards conservatism in religious matters. *The Lisle Letters*, ed. Muriel St. Clare Byrne, 6 vols. (Chicago University Press, 1981), I, 435–36.

12 *Lisle Letters*, V, 237–38.

13 See Lancashire, *DTR*, 400–1, 204. On April 10, 1543, four of the troupe's members were jailed "for playing contrary to the mayor's order." This may have been simply a case of violating a city ordinance against playing, but with the suppression of controversial religious drama in London in 1541 and nationwide in 1543, the action taken possibly stemmed from the performance of "new Scripture matter." At this point, the troupe was under the patronage of Sir Thomas Cheney who succeeded Lisle as Warden in 1542.

14 See W. R. Streitberger, "The Revels at Court from 1541 to 1559," *Research Opportunities in Renaissance Drama*, 29 (1986–87): 25–45; pp. 33–34. See also Chambers, *ES*, II, 82.

15 Streitberger, "Financing Court Entertainments 1509–1558," *Research Opportunities in Renaissance Drama*, 27 (1984): 21–45; pp. 27–29.

16 Lancashire, *DTR*, 382–83.

17 Chambers, *ES*, II, 82.

18 *Ibid.*, 83: "The eight posts figure on the fee-lists long after there were no holders left."

19 Feuillerat, *DRR (E&M)*, p. 57.

20 For Cawarden's career and his duties as Master of the Revels, see Streitberger, "Revels at Court," pp. 26–27. That Cawarden had the authority to select interludes for court performance is indicated in a letter addressed to him by William Baldwin in 1556. Baldwin reminds Cawarden of "thre yeres passed" when Cawarden offered to stage his plays at Edward VI's court, and then requests his opinion of a new play Baldwin devised for court production. The letter is in Feuillerat, *DRR (E&M)*, 215–17; see also chapter 3 below, p. 68. When Cawarden was put in charge of staging revels for Edward VI's Coronation, 46 different tailors received payment for work. This of course was not typical for most court pastimes, but it gives some indication of how many people were involved in making costumes, alone. See Feuillerat, *DRR (E&M)*, 3.

21 Streitberger, "Revels at Court," pp. 26–27.

22 Feuillerat, *DRR (E&M)*, xii–xiv; Chambers, *ES*, II, 83; *Revels II*, 109.

23 Bale, for example, identifies the seven-headed beast with the popish Anti-Christ throughout his *Image of Both Churches*, as well as in his 1550 commentary on Revelation. There, he implores the godly to pray for King Edward, who "hath so sore wounded the beast, that he may throw all his superstition into the bottomless lake again (from whence they have come) to the comfort of his people..." See *Select Works of John Bale*, ed. Henry Christmas, PS (Cambridge University Press, 1849), p. 640. Alluding to the same passage in Revelation, Richard Morison

refers to "that wicked dragon the bisshop of Rome, who devoured us before as he now hath a great parte of all christendom." See Anglo, "An Early Tudor Programme," p. 178. For the association of the Revelation beast with the papacy in the apocalyptic writings of Luther, Tyndale, Bale, and beyond, see Christianson, *Reformers and Babylon*.

24 Feuillerat, *DRR (E&M)*, 39. King suggests that the required albs, surplices, and head gear for the priests in the play refer to changes in official clerical attire planned for the new Prayer Book introduced three months later on Whitsunday 1549. See his *English Reformation Literature*, p. 180.

25 Hermits, who in early Tudor pageantry were images of goodness (see examples cited in Lancashire, *DTR*, 183, 189, 207), now became objects of anti-Catholic satire, along with monks, friars, and bishops. This is evident, as will be seen below, in the Edwardian court interlude of "The Seven Deadly Sins," where one of the vices, Sloth, appears as a hermit. In Bale's *Temptation of Our Lord*, the traditional convention of presenting Satan as a hermit in the *mystères* is cleverly exploited to exemplify Catholic hypocrisy. Half a century later, Spenser would make the same identification of the eremitical life with hypocrisy in his depiction of Archimago.

26 William Baldwin, *A Marvelous Hystory Intitulede, Beware the Cat* (London, 1570), A4^{r-v}.

27 As reported by the Venetian ambassador Il Schifanoya. See *SP: Venice*, VII (10), p. 11. Also Chambers, *ES*, I, 155–56; II, 83–84.

28 Lily B. Campbell, "The Lost Play of *Aesop's Crow*," *Modern Language Notes*, 29 (1934): 454–57. In 1540, a group of parishioners at St. Giles Cripplegate described the Mass as a thing of "pieces and patches." Cited in Susan Brigden, *London and the Reformation* (Oxford: Clarendon, 1989), p. 406.

29 See Bradbrook, *Rise of the Common Player*, p. 300, note 5. For the Hinchenbrook performance, see Boas, *University Drama*, pp. 382–85, and p. 107 below.

30 See Kenneth Varty, *Reynard the Fox: A Study of the Fox in Medieval English Art* (Leicester University Press, 1967), pp. 51–67.

31 Feuillerat, *DRR (E&M)*, 245.

32 Compare the casting chart above with Bale's costume rubric on "The aparellynge of the six vyces" in *Three Laws*: "Lete Idolatry be decked lyke an olde wytche, Sodomy lyke a monke of all sectes, Ambycyon lyke a byshop, Covetousnesse lyke a Pharyse or spyrituall lawer, False Doctryne lyke a popysh doctour, and Hypocresy lyke a graye fryre." See Happé, *Bale*, II, 121.

33 See Harris, *John Bale*, p. 68; Happé, *Bale*, I, 8–9.

34 Streitberger, "Financing," p. 37.

35 Feuillerat, *DRR (E&M)*, 3–8.

36 Streitberger, "Revels at Court," p. 33.

37 Feuillerat, *DRR (E&M)*, 26, 266, 269–70.

38 Streitberger, "Revels at Court," p. 30; Lancashire, *DTR*, 149.

39 See figure 7. Bale assigns this play to King Edward in *Scriptorum Illustrium*, vol. I, p. 674. The attribution is plausible. The King was writing a *Discourse on the Reform of Abuses in Church and State* prior to 1551, and sometime between 1551 and 1552 was presented with a copy of Calvin's essays and *Commentarii in Epistolas Canonicas*, printed in Geneva in 1551. For citations see Streitberger, "Financing," p. 37 and p. 40, note 18.

40 Luther popularized the theme early on in his *Babylonish Captivity of the Church* (1520), which attacks the bondage of the church due to the doctrine of transubstantiation and the Sacrifice of the Mass. It was quickly picked up by English reformers such as Tyndale and Frith before receiving detailed attention in Bale's *Image of Two Churches*. It would seem that the devisers of the "The Tower of Babylon" recognized the tremendous theatrical possibilities of the piece with its powerful biblical images – the Tower of Babel from Genesis, the beasts of Daniel 7 and of Revelation, the whore of Babylon portrayed in Revelation, and Anti-Christ. It is indeed the powerful outward display of the Roman rituals and vestments which "seduce" the world, as the gloss to Revelation 17.1 in the Genevan Bible reveals: "Antichrist is compared to an harlot because he seduceth the world with vain words, doctrines of lies, and outward appearance." This is in line with both Bullinger's and Bale's commentary on the whore of Babylon in Revelation. The masques and plays at Edward's court depicted Cardinals, Popes, Bishops, etc. to make this point about the outward glory and inward spiritual corruption of popery. See Christianson, *Reformers and Babylon*, pp. 9, 38; King, *English Reformation Literature*, pp. 371f.

41 For these events, see Chambers, *MS*, I, 405–7.

42 See King, *English Reformation Literature*, p. 391.

43 See Albert Feuillerat, "An Unknown Protestant Morality," *Modern Language Review*, 9 (1914): 94–96; C. R. Baskervill, "On Two Old Plays," *Modern Philology*, 14 (1916): 16.

44 Lancashire, *DTR*, 381.

45 Feuillerat, *DRR (E&M)*, 86.

46 One such dragon with hoops and canvas was included in a Hertfordshire parish play of the late fifteenth century, as noted by Peter Greenfield in "Entertainers on the Road in Hertfordshire" (seminar paper, 1991 SAA Conference, Vancouver, BC).

47 Chambers, *ES*, II, 84.

48 W. C. Hazlitt, ed., *The English Drama and Stage under the Tudor and Stuart Princes 1543–1664* (1869; reprinted New York: Franklin, n.d.), pp. 3–5; Chambers, *MS*, II, 222.

49 As late as 1551, the Venetian Ambassador refers to the "demonstrations of contempt for [the Pope] in paintings, comedies and in all their amusements." See *SP: Venice*, V, 347. A Marian exile would later recall of Edward VI's reign that "God's word in that time had the prize

and bore the bell away throughout the whole land ... With God's word was every man's mouth occupied; of that were all songs, interludes and plays made." From *A confutation of unwritten verities, made by Thomas Cranmer*; cited in J. Strype, *Memorials of Thomas Cranmer*, 2 vols. (Oxford University Press, 1840), I, 228–29; and Harold Gardiner, *Mysteries' End*, p. 57. The eighteen Protestant or anti-Catholic plays out of a total of twenty-nine known to have been written or performed during the reign is almost certainly a small representation of what once existed. See "a calendar of plays" in *Revels II*, 54–56, and *Annals of English Drama 975–1700*, ed. Alfred Harbage, rev. Samuel Schoenbaum (Philadelphia: University of Pennsylvania Press, 1964), pp. 30–32.

50 Paul L. Hughes and James F. Larkin, eds., *Tudor Proclamations*, 3 vols. (New Haven: Yale University Press, 1964), I, 478; Wickham, *EES*, II.i, 65–68; Gardiner, *Mysteries' End*, 59–62.

51 *Proclamations*, I, 517; Chambers, *ES*, III, 160.

52 Wickham, *EES*, II.i, 329–31.

53 King, *English Reformation Literature*, pp. 109–11.

54 Chambers, *ES*, I, 274.

55 King, *English Reformation Literature*, pp. 274–75, suggests that the Lord Protector's Men performed popular Reformation drama, and notes the troupe's violation of Henrician controls when they performed in London in 1545 as the Earl of Hertford's players.

56 See Lancashire, *DTR*, xxviii–xxix. No fewer than six members of Edward VI's privy council known to have supported the Protestant cause were patrons of acting companies: Edward Seymour, Duke of Somerset and Lord Protector, Sir John Russell, Keeper of the Privy Seal, William Parr, Earl of Essex, John Dudley, Duke of Northumberland, Lord Admiral and later Lord Protector, Henry Grey, Marquis of Dorset, Lord Thomas Wentworth, Lord Chamberlain. For their companies, see Murray, *English Dramatic Companies*. For Radcliffe's link with the Dorset household, see Maria Dowling, *Humanism*, p. 127.

57 *SP: Venice*, VII (18), p. 27; *SP: Simancas*, I, 62.

58 For anti-Catholic plays at Canterbury, see Clark, "Josias Nicholls," pp. 134–35; and Leslie P. Fairfield, *John Bale*, pp. 145–47. For Ipswich, see discussion of Bale's *King Johan*. For Shrewsbury, see Somerset, "Local Drama and Playing Places at Shrewsbury," pp. 1–31.

59 *SP: Simancas*, I, 62. Near the end of his career, Cecil could still think of ways of using the stage to influence public morality. In June of 1596, a broker named Howe and a solicitor named Easte were found guilty in the Star Chamber of "cozening of a young gentlemen," and were subsequently fined, whipped and pilloried at Westminster. During the trial, Cecil, as Lord Treasurer, stated that he "would haue those [tha]t make playes to make a comedie hereof, & to acte it with these names." Chambers (*ES*, I, 268) notes that Cecil received a letter dated June 25, 1597 from Sir John Hollis apparently protesting the Lord Treasurer's remarks on the last Star Chamber day in which he castigated Hollis'

great-grandfather as "an abominable usurer, a merchant of broken paper, so hateful and contemptible a creature that the players acted him before the King [Henry VII or VIII] with great applause." Both the above statements by Cecil reveal his recognition of drama as a powerful public medium. It is worth noting that the spate of Calvinist "money plays" which follow in the wake of the stage propaganda offensive at the outset of Elizabeth's reign deal with economic vice committed by profiteering brokers, merchants, and landlords who victimize naive young gentlemen as well as the poor. Since, as I will argue below, these interludes were performed by the troupes of noblemen loyal to the royal court, Cecil might have encouraged their composition and performance. For the 1596 case reported above, see *ES*, I, 267–68, and Conyers Reade, "William Cecil and Elizabethan Public Relations," in *Elizabethan Government and Society* (London: Athlone, 1961): 27–28.

60 For the Cambridge performances, see Nelson, *Cambridge*, I, 227–42. See also Boas, *University Drama*, pp. 90, 382–85. See also below, p. 107, and pp. 142–46.

61 The Queen's writing of the April 7 Proclamation is mentioned in Holinshed, *The Chronicle of England, Scotland, and Ireland* (London, 1586–87), III, 1184; cited in Harold C. Gardiner, *Mysteries' End*, p. 66; Chambers, *ES*, IV, 262–63.

62 *SP: Simancas*, I, 247.

63 Gardiner, *Mysteries' End*, p. 66.

64 For the network of Protestant officials in these cities, see Clark, *English Provincial Society*; MacCulloch, *Suffolk and the Tudors*; and Paul S. Seaver, *The Puritan Lectureships: The Politics of Religious Dissent 1560–1662* (Stanford University Press, 1970).

65 *Revels II*, 21–22.

66 It is possible, of course, that some plays were printed several years after their composition. However, such plays as *New Custom* and *The Tide Tarrieth No Man* treat matters that were highly topical around the time they were printed. See discussion of *New Custom* below.

67 Chambers, *ES*, I, 242.

68 "Calvinist and Puritan Attitudes Towards the Renaissance Stage: A History of Conflict and Controversy," *Explorations in Renaissance Culture* 14 (1988): 41–56.

69 Chambers, *ES*, I, 245.

70 Bevington, *From Mankind to Marlowe*, pp. 54–56. See also Dessen's discussion of the dramatic vitality of these plays in *Shakespeare and the Late Moral Plays*.

71 Bevington, *From Mankind to Marlowe*, p. 66. The following exclude the many other plays with earlier composition dates printed during this period: *Mary Magdalene, King Darius, Like Will to Like, Enough is as Good as a Feast, New Custom, The Tide Tarrieth No Man, The Trial of Treasure, The Longer Thou Livest the More Fool Thou Art, Horestes*, and *All for Money*. See also appendix A.

72 For Moone's troupe in Ipswich, see Vincent Redstone, ed., *Players of Ipswich*, in MSC II.iii (Oxford University Press, 1931), p. 261. Susan Brigden observes that during Henry VIII's reactionary period of the early 1540s London players sponsored and protected by citizens' groups performed Protestant plays of a virulently anti-Catholic nature. Among London civic and ecclesiastical figures who staged such plays in their homes were Thomas Hancock, George Tadlowe, and William Clycheman. On Sunday, April 8, 1543, a group of twenty artisans took part in an "unlawful disguising." See Brigden, *London and the Reformation*, pp. 344–45. For more on Hancock, see chapter 5 below. Among London civic organizations sponsoring players were the carpenters, blacksmiths, cutlers, brewers, and pewterers. See Anne Lancashire, "Players for the London Cutlers' Company," *REED Notes*, 1981.2: 10–11; and "Plays for the London Blacksmiths' Company," *REED Notes*, 1981.1: 12–14.

73 Westfall, *Patrons and Performance*, pp. 113–14.

74 King, *English Reformation Literature*, p. 274.

75 R. Willis, *Mount Tabor, or Private Exercises of a Penitent Sinner* (London, 1639), pp. 110–14. For the Willis text and its dramatic context, see Audrey Douglas and Peter Greenfield, eds., *Cumberland, Westmorland, Gloucester*, REED (Toronto University Press, 1986), pp. 362–64.

76 See Collinson, *Elizabethan Puritan Movement*, ch. 3. For the extensive lists of advanced Protestant works dedicated to these patrons, see Franklin B. Williams, *Index of Dedications and Commendatory Verses in English Books before 1641* (London: Bibliographical Society, 1962). The Duchess of Suffolk's patronage of the reformers is discussed in King, *English Reformation Literature*, pp. 105–6; Evelyn Read, *Catherine, Duchess of Suffolk: A Portrait* (London: Cape, 1962), pp. 50–78.

77 For the players sponsored by Catherine Willoughby, Duchess of Suffolk (widowed to Charles Brandon, Duke of Suffolk in 1545), see Murray, *English Dramatic Companies*, II, 71–74. Catherine of Suffolk entertained travelling players throughout the year at her estate at Grimsthorpe and received them in her London residence, Willoughby House, at Barbican (see figure 15); see also Read, *Catherine*, pp. 154–57. For the troupe of Leicester's older brother, Ambrose Dudley, Earl of Warwick, see Murray, *English Dramatic Companies*, I, 285–90.

78 For Leicester's appointment as Constable-Marshal of the Christmas entertainments at the Middle Temple in 1561, see *Revels II*, 34; and Derek Wilson, *Sweet Robin: A Biography of Robert Dudley, Earl of Leicester 1533–1588* (London: Hamilton, 1981), pp. 131–32. For his sharing the responsibilities with the Earl of Sussex in organizing revels at the royal court in June, 1572, see *The Revels History of Drama in English (1576–1613): Volume III*, ed. J. Leeds Barroll III, et al., (London: Methuen, 1975), pp. 10–11.

79 Wilson, *Sweet Robin*, p. 155.

80 Bevington, *From Mankind to Marlowe*, p. 60, suggests that Leicester's Men performed "huff-suff-and-ruff" at court in 1560, and that this play is

really *Cambises* (which includes three comic characters with those names), but the claim is tenuous at best, as pointed out by Craik in *Revels II*, 112.

81 See Leeds Barroll's discussion in *Revels III*, 10–11. The plays, none of which survive, are *Predor and Lucia* (1573), *Mamillia* (1573), *Philomen and Philecia* (1574), *Panecia* (1574), *The Collier* (1576), *A Greek Maid* (1579), *Delight* (1580), and *Talomo* (1583). See Chambers, *ES*, IV, appendix, and *ES*, II, 88–89.

82 The imaginary "Lord Cardinalls players" in *The Book of Sir Thomas More* (c. 1590) carried a repertoire of seven moral interludes. Westfall, *Patrons and Performance*, pp. 111–12, suggests that a Tudor company needed three to seven plays to operate efficiently and profitably.

83 Bevington, *Tudor Drama and Politics*, pp. 138–40.

84 Rosenberg, *Leicester*, ch. 6; Collinson, *Elizabethan Puritan Movement*, ch. 3.

85 Thomas Rogers, *A General Discovrse Against the damnable sect of Vsurers* (1578); cited in Rosenberg, *Leicester*, p. 146, note 54.

3 REFORMATION PLAYWRIGHTS AND PLAYS

1 The term "unattached plays" derives from T. W. Craik's discussion in *Revels II*, 133–39.

2 See G. E. Bentley, *The Professions of Dramatist and Player in Shakespeare's Time 1590–1642* (1971; reprinted Princeton University Press, 1984), ch. 2; and G. K. Hunter, "The Beginnings of Elizabethan Drama: Revolution and Continuity," *Renaissance Drama*, 17 (1986): 29–52.

3 By my count, of the forty-one known dramatists writing between 1531 and 1575, eighteen were clerics, eleven were schoolmasters, four were lawyers or courtiers, two were Cambridge dons, one was a clerk of the Stationers' Company, and five were of unknown profession. There was of course some overlapping between professions, but I have not placed a playwright in more than one of the above professions. For a list of Reformation playwrights and plays, see appendix A.

4 See Westfall, *Patrons and Performance*, p. 115. See also Lancashire, "Introduction," *Two Tudor Interludes*, pp. 24–36; Alan Nelson, *The Plays of Henry Medwell* (Cambridge: Brewer, 1980); Milton McC. Gatch, "Mysticism and Satire in the Morality of *Wisdom*," *Philological Quarterly*, 53 (1974): 342–62; Ian Lancashire, "The Auspices of *The World and the Child*," *Renaissance and Reformation*, 12 (1976): 96–105.

5 *The Autobiography of Thomas Whythorne*, ed. James M. Osborn (Oxford: Clarendon, 1961), pp. 243–45.

6 Feuillerat, *DRR (E&M)*, 215.

7 *LP: Henry 8*, XII.i, 244.

8 See King, *English Reformation Literature*, pp. 111–13, for Bale's use of the patronage system. Bale's chief connection at court was John Philpot, a Calvinist preacher and member of Edward's privy chamber (King, *English Reformation Literature*, p. 113). Philpot was at least on one occasion

dispatched to the Revels Office to collect materials for a court production (see Feuillerat, *DRR* [*E&M*], 24 and 264); it is possible through his influence that Bale's plays (eg. *On the Seven Sins*) might have received favor at court.

9 See Boas, *University Drama in the Tudor Age*, p. 34.

10 See John Hazel Smith, ed., *Two Latin Comedies by John Foxe the Martyrologist* (Ithaca: Cornell University Press, 1973), pp. 4–7.

11 See Mark Eccles, "William Wager and His Plays," *English Language Notes*, 18 (1981): 258–62. See also Seaver, *Puritan Lectureships*, pp. 209–10, 333.

12 The only concrete (though admittedly slender) piece of evidence linking him to Leicester is his governor's position at the free grammar school at Barnet, which was founded by the Queen at Leicester's suit. His associations with Crowley, author of *A Briefe discourse against the outwarde apparell* (*c.* 1566) among other radical works, and Thomas Wilcox, who co-authored *The Admonition to Parliament* with John Field in 1572, link him to the early Elizabethan puritans who favored reforms along Genevan lines. According to Wilcox, Wager "hath many tymes bin hot in wordes against the Popish Regiment and Ceremonies," by which was meant the pseudo-Catholic aspects of Anglican discipline and worship that radical Protestants desired expunged from the Prayer Book. Wager's puritan beliefs, however, took a more moderate turn in the early seventies. When Edwin Sandys, Bishop of London, was ordered by the Privy Council to suspend all London incumbents who refused to subscribe to the Act of Uniformity in late 1573, Wager conformed, which in turn prompted Wilcox's angry response that no one had "more deceived the godlie, then one Wager," who "now by his Subscription hath allowed all." See Eccles, "William Wager," p. 259; Cambridge University Library Ms. Mm 1,43, p. 441; H. Gareth Owen, "The London Parish Clergy in the Reign of Elizabeth I," Ph.D. thesis, London University, 1957, p. 535.

13 For Leicester's involvement in the early Elizabethan anti-usury campaign, scc above, p. 63.

14 One may also recall that it is the schoolmaster Holophernes, in *Love's Labour's Lost*, who arranges the production of "The Nine Worthies" before the Princess with himself as Judas Maccabaeus and the old curate, Sir Nathaniel, as Alexander.

15 *MS*, II, 193; Colet complains of clerics playing in interludes, which is a good indication that several did perform (*MS*, II, 193).

16 Albert Peele, ed., *The Second Part of a Register*, 2 vols. (Cambridge University Press, 1915), II: 148; Richard L. Greaves, *Society and Religion in Elizabethan England* (Minneapolis: University of Minnesota Press, 1981), p. 447

17 Bevington, *From Mankind to Marlowe*, p. 54.

18 *Lisle Letters*, V, 437–38; *LP: Henry 8*, VII, addenda, I.ii, 462–63. Printed plays, on the other hand, were considerably cheaper. In 1535, a

playbook in the shop of Wynkyn de Worde was priced at twopence (Lancashire, *DTR*, 200). In 1558, a printed interlude cost about fourpence (based on the Bungay churchwardens' purchase noted below). By the 1590s, a thirty to forty page quarto sold for sixpence (see Bennett, *English Books*, p. 256).

19 See Bevington, *From Mankind to Marlowe*, "Appendix: Plays 'Offered for Acting'," pp. 265–73.

20 Chambers, *MS*, II, 192; Lancashire, *DTR*, 90.

21 Lancashire, *DTR*, xxvi.

22 See E. Gordon Duff, *A Century of the English Book Trade* (London: Bibliographical Society, 1948), pp. 32–33. Copland printed Calvin's *Catechism* until he sold the copyright to John Kingston in 1566. See Edward Arber, ed., *A Transcript of the Stationers' Registers* (1554–1640), 5 vols. (1875–94; reprinted New York: Smith, 1950), I, 306; and Marjorie Plant, *The English Book Trade*, (1939; reprinted London: George Allen, 1974), p. 115.

23 For these printers, see William Calderwood, "The Elizabethan Protestant Press: A Study of Printing and Publishing of Protestant Religious Literature in English 1558–1603," Ph.D. thesis, University of London (1977): Part II, "Patrons and Printers"; Bennett, *English Books*, chs. 2 and 6; Rosenberg, *Leicester*, pp. 207–9; and King, *English Reformation Literature*, pp. 94–102.

24 See Nicholas Davis, "The Meaning of the Word 'Interlude': A Discussion," *Medieval English Theatre*, 6.1 (July 1984): 5–15; Glynne Wickham, "Introduction," *English Moral Interludes* (London: Dent, 1976), pp. vi–xiv.

25 Bevington, *Tudor Drama and Politics*, pp. 136–37.

26 See Willard Farnham, *The Medieval Heritage of Elizabethan Tragedy* (Berkeley: University of California Press, 1936); Spivack, *Shakespeare and the Allegory of Evil*; Bevington, *From Mankind to Marlowe*; Martha Tuck Rozett, *The Doctrine of Election and the Emergence of Elizabethan Tragedy* (Princeton University Press, 1984).

27 Hardison, *Christian Rite*, ch. 1. Dessen, *Shakespeare and the Late Moral Plays*, pp. 56–58, 134–37; Lancashire, *DTR*, xxvi. See also Michael D. Bristol, *Carnival and Theatre: Plebeian Culture and the Structure of Authority in Renaissance England* (New York: Methuen, 1985), pp. 46–47. Bristol observes the same evolutionary assumptions in Robert Weimann's *Shakespeare and the Popular Tradition*.

28 See Richard Axton, "Folk Play in Tudor Interludes," pp. 1–23. Bevington (*From Mankind to Marlowe*, pp. 10, 196–97), following Spivack, regards the "hybrid" plays of the 1560s and 1570s as a developing phase in the drama from allegory to particularization of character. The allegorical characters in these plays, he argues, uneasily mixed with a growing number of historical characters or "specific personalities." This implies too clear-cut a distinction between abstract and historical types in the hybrid plays. As Alan Dessen points out in *Shakespeare and the Late*

see press *Moral Plays* (pp. 135–37), characters named after abstractions could be every bit as "realistic" as historical figures, and historical figures as "allegorical" as the personified abstractions. This I discovered in my own production of *Enough is as Good as a Feast* at Baylor University in 1987, in which the interaction between the boasting Covetous and Worldly Man is not unlike that between Parolles and Bertram, or even Falstaff and Prince Hal (see figure 9). The point is also supported by recent studies in medieval drama which have shown that "realism" is an important ingredient of moral play characterization and that distinctions in the mysteries between personified characters and biblical characters should not be pushed too far. See W. A. Davenport, *Fifteenth-century English Drama* (Cambridge: Brewer, 1982), ch. 1; Michael R. Kelley, *Flamboyant Drama* (Carbondale, IL: Southern Illinois University Press, 1979), ch. 1. See also my discussion of "character" below.

29 Laurence Humphrey, "On John Foxe's Apocalyptic Comedy of Christ Triumphant," trans. and ed. by John Hazel Smith, *Two Latin Comedies*, p. 215. Theodore Beza, *Abraham's Sacrifice*, trans. Arthur Golding, ed. M. W. Wallace (Toronto University Press, 1907), p. 63.

30 Dessen, *Shakespeare*, p. 57.

31 Lupton's interlude exhibits the same eclectic style and commitment to "variety" that the playwright advocates in his *Thousand Notable Things of Sundry Sorts*: "Perhaps you will marvel that I have not placed them in better order, and that things of like matter are not joined together. In my judgement, through the strangeness and variety of matter it will be more desirously and delightfully read; knowing that we are made of such a mould, that delicate daintiness delights us much; but we loathe to be fed too long with one food; and that long wandering in strange, pleasant and contrary places, will less weary us, than short travel in often trodden ground" (cited in Bradbrook, *Rise of the Common Player*, p. 189).

32 See Wickham, *EES*, III, 71–72.

33 See King, *English Reformation Literature*, pp. 156f.

34 A similar device was used in the medieval *Wisdom* where seven little boys in devils' costumes crawl out from under the skirt of Anima to show that she is "full of sin." See Southern, *Staging of Plays before Shakespeare*, p. 473; and *Revels II*, 149–50.

35 This discussion of "character" in the moral interludes is much indebted to Sarah Carpenter, "Morality-Play Characters," *Medieval English Theatre*, 5.2 (July 1983): 18–28; and Dessen, *Shakespeare and the Late Moral Plays*, pp. 134–37.

character 36 This last line suggests that Inclination, like Bale's Infidelity, might have been equipped with a phallus. See woodcut of Robin Goodfellow, figure 4, on p. 32 above.

37 Ulpian Fulwell, *Like Will to Like*, TFT (1908), D3ʳ; William Wager, *The Trial of Treasure*, TFT (1908), B1ʳ; William Wager, *Enough is as Good as a Feast*, ed. Seymour de Ricci (New York: Huntington Library, 1920), A3ʳ. All subsequent references to these plays will appear parenthetically in the text.

38 Carpenter, "Morality-Play Characters," p. 21, notes the correspondence between Brecht's techniques and those employed in the moral plays and moral interludes, especially as it concerns acting and characterization. Brecht: "the actor must remain a demonstrator; he must present the person demonstrated as a stranger." "Whenever he feels he can the demonstrator breaks off his imitation in order to give explanations." Cited from *Brecht on Theatre*, trans. and ed. John Willett (London: Methuen, 1978), pp. 125–26. One might add that Brecht's practice (e.g. in *Mother Courage*) of using placards and other properties and signs with writing on them to explicitly convey meaning is also reminiscent of the interludes. See discussion of *The Tide Tarrieth No Man* below.

39 Lewis Wager, *The Life and Repentaunce of Mary Magdalene*, TFT (1908), A2ᵛ. All subsequent references to the play will appear in the text parenthetically.

40 See Mark Eccles, "Brief Lives: Tudor and Stuart Authors," *Studies in Philology*, 79 (1982): 1–134; pp. 123–24; and Wayne H. Phelps, "The Date of Lewis Wager's Death," *Notes and Queries*, 223 (1978): 420–21.

41 William was "of the age of xlj yeres and vpwards" in 1578, according to a record of his testimony in Chancery. See Eccles, "William Wager," p. 258.

42 See chapter 4 below, pp. 111, and note 43.

43 David Knowles, *Bare Ruined Choirs: The Dissolution of the English Monasteries* (Cambridge University Press, 1976), ch. 25; Maurice Powicke, *The Reformation in England* (London: Oxford University Press, 1941), p. 25; Wickham, *EES*, II.i, 109.

44 The "ridden" here provides further evidence that the strolling players travelled with a horse and perhaps a small wagon. See chapter 1 above.

45 Happé, "Protestant Adaptation," pp. 205–40.

46 Gardiner, *Mysteries' End*, p. 56.

47 Lancashire, *DTR*, 272, 107, 244.

48 *Select Works of John Bale*, p. 59; cited in Happé, "Protestant Adaptation," p. 215.

49 *Lisle Letters*, IV, 166.

50 See Robert C. Jones, "Dangerous Sport: The Audience's Engagement with Vice in the Moral Interludes," *Renaissance Drama*, 6 (1973): 45–64. See also Richards, "Preachers and Players," ch. 1; and J. A. B. Somerset, "'Fair is Foul and Foul is Fair': Vice-Comedy's Development and Theatrical Effects," in *Elizabethan Theatre V*, ed. G. R. Hibbard (Hamden, CT: Archon, 1973), 54–73. Somerset explains: "... the vices succeed at times in detaching us from our moral attitudes and making us relax, momentarily suspending our moral judgments or making us add to our sense that they are evil the further response that they are entertaining and fun .... As the vices amuse us, we can be said to share the hero's seduction. We have believed in it, have felt the springs of sympathetic laughter, and have perhaps even been called upon to assist in seduction."

51 See D. Kendall, *Drama of Dissent*, p. 110.
52 Alan Dessen, *Elizabethan Drama and the Viewer's Eye* (Chapel Hill: University of North Carolina Press, 1977), p. 134.
53 The vices make similar remarks before departing from Mary's company; Cupidity says: "Yet from your syght at this tyme we will depart, / Assuryng you to remayn styll in our hart" (D4^r).
54 Besides Calvin himself, the leading foreign authorities were Martin Bucer (Strasbourg) and Heinrich Bullinger (Zurich). Many of the foreign divines arriving in England at this time (Bucer was among them) were not merely non-Lutheran but anti-Lutheran, as A. G. Dickens points out. For Calvinism's impact in Edwardian England and after, see Dickens, *English Reformation*, particularly ch. 9; Dewey D. Wallace, *Puritanism and Predestination* (Chapel Hill: University of North Carolina Press, 1982); C. D. Cremeans, *The Reception of Calvinistic Thought in England* (Urbana: University of Illinois Press, 1949).
55 *New Custom*, TFT (1908), A4^r. All subsequent references to the play will appear parenthetically in the text.
56 For a detailed discussion of the vestarian controversy and other efforts for church reform, see Patrick Collinson, *The Elizabethan Puritan Movement*. For the text of the "Advertisements," see Henry Gee and W. H. Hardy, eds., *Documents Illustrative of English Church History* (London: Macmillan, 1975).
57 Rosenberg, *Leicester*, p. 199f; Collinson, *Elizabethan Puritan Movement*, pp. 52–53, 74, 92–93; and Wilson, *Sweet Robin*, ch. 11. See also John Strype, *The Life and Acts of Matthew Parker*, 2 vols. (Oxford University Press, 1821), II, 393–95, 423, 529.
58 Wilson, *Sweet Robin*, p. 203; Rosenberg, *Leicester*, pp. 200–201.
59 In her study, "Dramaturgy of the Anti-Catholic Morality in the Tudor Hall with Special Attention to the Screen," (Ph.D. dissertation, University of Rhode Island, 1980), Robinson reconstructs a theorized performance of this play in the Tudor manor house, Crompton Hall, in August 1572 by the six players known to be in Leicester's Men at that time. The play, however, could be most economically cast with four actors, as the title page of the printed copy indicates. It is possible that Leicester's company only had four actors when the play was first acted, since the troupe fluctuated in size during its history. In 1572, six actors are identified in their letter addressed to Leicester, in 1574, five actors are named in the famous Patent of that year, and in 1583, there may have been as few as three when Laneham, Wilson and Johnson defected to the newly formed Queen's Men. See Chambers, *ES*, II, 85–91.
60 Murray, *English Dramatic Companies*, I, 39–42.
61 A remark made by Bishop Sandys of London to Lord Burghley, August 5, 1573; cited in Collinson, "John Field and Elizabethan Puritanism", in *Elizabethan Government and Society* (London: Athlone, 1961): 127–62; p. 138.
62 More than a few would have shared the sentiments of Anthony Gilby's soldier of Berwick who exclaimed, "my heart ariseth in my body when

I see thee and thy fellows clothed like [the Pope's] chaplains, that burned the blessed Bible, and our faithful Fathers and dear brethren in our eyes" (Collinson, *ibid.*, p. 95).

63 The only solid information about George Wapull is that he was the Clerk of the Stationers' Company in 1571 (the first known clerk) and apparently remained in that post until 1575 when a successor was named. See Eccles, "Brief Lives," pp. 124–25.

64 George Wapull, *The Tide Tarrieth No Man*, TFT (1910) F2ᵛ. All subsequent references to the play will appear parenthetically in the text.

65 Peele, *The Second Parte of a Register*, I, 140–41. By "policy," Gilby and Calvinist dramatists such as George Wapull and William Wager mean "worldly wisdom."

66 See *Enough is as Good as a Feast*, D3ʳ⁻ᵛ. At the start of Elizabeth's reign, John Parkhurst, the future Bishop of Norwich, predicted that "the bishops are in future to have no palaces, estates or country seats," but the leading administrators of the Elizabethan church, like their immediate predecessors under Queen Mary, continued to enjoy incomes and privileges on a par with the wealthy aristocracy. See *Zurich Letters*, ed. Hastings Robinson, PS, 2 vols. (Cambridge University Press, 1915), I, 19; Dickens, *English Reformation*, p. 420.

67 See Brian Crow, "The Development of the Representation of Human Actions in Medieval and Renaissance Drama," Ph.D. thesis, University of Bristol, 1980, pp. 316–17.

68 See Bevington, *Tudor Drama and Politics*, pp. 133–37. The following discussion of the economic realities of early Elizabethan England is indebted to C. G. A. Clay, *Economic Expansion and Social Change: England 1500–1700*, 2 vols. (Cambridge University Press, 1984), I, chs. 2, 5, and 6; Palliser, *Age of Elizabeth*, ch. 7; Michael Foss, "Sir Thomas Gresham," *Tudor Portraits: Success and Failure of an Age* (London: Harrap, 1973): 90–109.

69 Rosenberg, *Leicester*, pp. 145–46.

70 Palliser, *Age of Elizabeth*, pp. 213–14.

71 John Stow, *A Survey of London*, ed. C. L. Kingsford, 2 vols. (Oxford: Clarendon, 1908), I, 126, 161, 163; II, 71f, 79f; see Palliser, *Age of Elizabeth*, p. 214.

72 The Elizabethan preacher William Perkins, whose *Treatise of Vocations, or Callings of Men* (1599) is the culmination of English Calvinist ideas on the calling, distinguishes between worldly and spiritual callings but concludes: "if thou wouldst haue signes and tokens of thy election and saluation, thou must fetch them from the constant practise of thy two cal[l]ings ioyntly together." See his *Workes*, 3 vols. (London: John Legate, 1608), I, 734. See also Calvin, *Institution*, III.x.6.

73 *Ibid.*; Perkins, *Workes*, I, 732.

74 See *Enough*, B1ᵛ; *Trial*, D2ʳ.

75 Henry Smith, "The Benefit of Contentation," *Three Sermons made by Maister Henry Smith* (London: Nicholas Ling, 1599), A2ʳ and A3ʳ.

76 The meaning of this title is expounded in Smith's sermon noted above:

"The godly man hath found that which all the world doth seeke, that is *enough*. Every word may be defined, and euery thing may be measured, but *enough* cannot be measured nor defined, it changeth euery yere: whe[n] we had nothing we thought it *enough* if we might obtain lesse then we haue: when we came to more, we thought of an other *enough*, so *enough* is alwaies to come, though too much be there already." Moreover, "couetousness may gaine riches, but it cannot gaine rest," which is reserved for the godly who are content with what divine providence has given them (B4^v and C1^r).

77 See also Perkins, *Workes*, I, 745; Smith, *Three Sermons*, C1^r.

78 Charles and Katherine George, *The Protestant Mind of the English Reformation* (Princeton University Press, 1962), p. 58.

4 REFORMATION DRAMA AND EDUCATION

1 And an estimated twenty-five percent of the nation's youth were under the age of ten in 1546. See E. A. Wrigley and R. S. Schofield, *The Population History of England 1541–1871* (Cambridge, MA: Harvard University Press, 1981), pp. 563–66; D. V. Glass and D. E. C. Eversley, eds., *Population in History: Essays in Historical Demography* (London: Edward Arnold, 1965), pp. 207, 212. The relevance of these statistics to the Reformation is treated in Susan Brigden, "Youth and the English Reformation," *Past and Present*, 95 (1982): 37–67; p. 37.

2 On May 27, 1549, the London Court of Aldermen tried to prohibit all youths and servants from attending interludes by ordering them to be kept at home between the hours of 10 p.m. and 4 a.m until Michaelmas. Youths were not "to resort to any such unlawful assemblies and gatherings of people together at any interludes or other unlawful games upon the holy day." Corporation of London Record Office, Repertory 12 (1), fol. 91v; also fols. 99, 162v. See also Brigden, "Youth and the English Reformation," p. 61 and references cited there; Barrett L. Beer, *Rebellion and Riot: Popular Disorder in England during the Reign of Edward VI* (Kent State University Press, 1982), p. 162. In a letter to Secretary Cecil in 1564, the Bishop of London, Edmund Grindal, called for the suppression of plays due to the "histriones, common playours; who now daylye, butt speciallye on holydayes, sett vp bylles, whernto the youthe resorteth excessively." The letter is reprinted in Chambers, *ES*, IV, 266–67.

3 See Joan Simon, *Education and Society in Tudor England* (Cambridge University Press, 1967) pp. 170 and 247.

4 *Ibid.*, p. 180.

5 This is stressed, among other places, in a statement of the dramatic policy of Eton College in 1560–63 by William Malin, Headmaster. See T. H. Vail Motter, *The School Drama in England* (1929; reprinted Port Washington, NY: Kennikat Press, 1968), pp. 50–51. Acting taught "good behaviour and audacitye," according to an old player-pupil of

Richard Mulcaster, schoolmaster and play director at the Merchant
Taylors' School in the 1570s and 1580s. Cited in F. P. Wilson, *The
English Drama 1485–1585*, 2nd edn., rev. G. K. Hunter (Oxford University Press, 1969), p. 154.

6 For Protestant school drama on the Continent, see Joseph E. Gillet,
"The German Dramatist of the Sixteenth Century and His Bible," in
Publications of the Modern Language Association, 34 (1919): 465–93;
Chambers, *ES*, I, 245–49.

7 See the translation of "De Honestis Ludis" in Wickham, *EES*, II.i,
appendix C, 329–31: p. 329.

8 Wickham, *EES*, II.i, 330.

9 *Ibid.*, 330.

10 *LP: Henry 8*, XII.i, 529. The item, "Mr. Hopton's priest, for playing
before my Lord with his children, 22s. 6d," is for April 2, 1537 (*LP:
Henry 8*, XIV.ii, 328). The prominent family in east Suffolk where
Wylley's vicarage was located was the Hoptons, led by Arthur Hopton,
Knight of the Body since 1516, who was a relative and member of the
Duke of Suffolk's circle based in Suffolk during the 1530s and active in
court diplomacy. See MacCulloch, *Suffolk and the Tudors*, p. 72 and p. 58.
Wylley may have served as Hopton's chaplain or perhaps mastered the
school under Hopton's patronage. One should perhaps mention that
John Bale may have taught schoolboys as part of his duties as Bishop at
Kilkenny, Ireland, in 1553, where "The yonge men" performed his
mystery plays, *God's Promises, Johan Baptystes preachinge*, and *The
Temptation of Our Lord*. See *The Vocacyon of Johan Bale to the bishoprick of
Ossorie in Irelande* (Wesel: Dirik van der Straten, 1553), fols. 23r-v.

11 Song schools were "the most numerous and important kind of
elementary schools" in the later Middle Ages. For these schools and the
role of the local priest in teaching children their ABCs, see Craig R.
Thompson, *Schools in Tudor England* (Ithaca: Cornell University Press,
1958), pp. 2–3.

12 The date usually given for the school's foundation is 1538, but Motter,
School Drama, p. 225, shows that this is an error. For Bale's report and
listing of plays (which he urged Radcliffe to publish but apparently to no
avail), see *Scriptorum Illustrium*, I, 700. On Radcliffe's tutoring of Dorset's
children see Dowling, *Humanism*, p. 127.

13 MS Brogyntyn 24 at the University of Wales contains three dialogues by
Radcliffe dedicated to and evidently composed for presentation before
Henry VIII: "A Governance of the Church," "Between the Poor Man
and Fortune," and "Between Death and the Goer by the Way" (dated
between 1536–39). These are translations of dialogues by Ravisius
Textor, popular grammar school texts of the period and suitable for
Radcliffe's pupils. Ralph is assumed to be Robert Radcliffe, the
grammar master of Jesus College during the 1530s who is mentioned in
correspondence to Cromwell. See Roston, *Biblical Drama*, pp. 57–58;
and Lancashire, *DTR*, 96.

14 *Revels II*, 128.
15 Simon, *Education and Society*, p. 181.
16 See Somerset, "Local Drama and Playing Places," p. 27.
17 See Chambers, *ES*, IV, 211. In 1579, five boys from Shrewsbury performed in Richard Legge's *Richardus Tertius* at Ashton's old College of St. John's, Cambridge (noted in Wilson, *English Drama 1485–1585*, p. 154).
18 Roger Ascham, *The Scholemaster*, ed. R. J. Schoeck (Don Mills, Ontario: Dent, 1966), p. 47.
19 Somerset, "Local Drama and Playing Places," pp. 27–29.
20 Chambers, *ES*, IV, 211.
21 Simon, *Education and Society*, pp. 315–17.
22 See W. K. Jordan, *Edward VI and the Threshold of Power* (Cambridge, MA: Harvard University Press, 1970), p. 232; Thompson, *Schools*, p. 8.
23 See Motter, *School Drama*, pp. 226f, and Lancashire, *DTR* (see index).
24 Ascham, who admired the classical authors for their eloquent Latin style but was skeptical of their moral value, indicates that Terence and Plautus were frequently performed in grammar schools: "And euen now in our dayes *Getae* and *Daui*, *Gnatos*, and manie bold bawdie *Phormios* to, be preasing in, to pratle on euerie stage, to medle in euerie matter, when honest *Parmenos* shall not be hard, but beare small swing with their masters" (Chambers, *ES*, IV, 191; Ascham, *The Scholemaster*, p. 45). Alexander Nowell, future Dean of St. Paul's, instituted the practice of performing plays by Terence and Plautus during Christmas while headmaster of Westminster School between 1544–47 (Lancashire, *DTR*, 204).
25 Most of the titles of plays mentioned in the financial records for performances by schoolboys at court between 1558 and 1576 indicate secular and apparently noncontroversial subject-matter (Chambers, *ES*, II, 4–7; Motter, *School Drama*, p. 15). However, accompanied by Cecilia of Sweden, the Queen was present for the Westminster School's production of *Sapientia Solomonis* in January 1566. See *Sapientia Solomonis, Acted before the Queen by the Boys of Westminster School*, ed. Elizabeth R. Payne, Yale Studies in English, 89 (New Haven: Yale University Press, 1938); and Wilson, *English Drama 1485–1585*, p. 92.
26 See A. R. Moon, "Nicholas Udall's Lost Tragedy 'Ezechias'," *Times Literary Supplement*, 19 (April 1928): p. 289; Lancashire, *DTR*, 132, and sources cited there.
27 See C. C. Stopes, *William Hunnis and the Revels of the Chapel Royal* (Louvain: A. Uystpruyst, 1910).
28 As, for example, when a performance of Aristophanes' *Plutus* was used to exemplify the new pronunciation of Greek developed at St. John's, Cambridge, in 1536; see Lancashire, *DTR*, 95–102, 244–49. For a detailed discussion of these plays, see Frederick Boas' still unsurpassed *University Drama*, chs. 2 to 5.
29 See chapter 3 above, p. 81, and Lancashire, *DTR*, 97.

30 See *The Correspondence of Matthew Parker, D.D. Archbishop of Canterbury 1535–1575*, ed. J. Bruce and T. T. Perowne, PS (Cambridge University Press, 1853), pp. 20–30; *Revels II*, 17.

31 John Foxe, *Christus Triumphans*, "Dedicatory Epistle," p. 209. In the same year, Laurence Humphrey, President of Magdalen College, Oxford, requested Foxe's permission to produce his play at Magdalen, but there is no record of it actually taking place (see John Hazel Smith's introduction to the play, p. 34).

32 The relevant correspondence is found in Nelson, *Cambridge*, I, 231–44. See also Boas, *University Drama*, p. 90.

33 Translated by M. A. S. Hume in *SP: Simancas*, I, 375. See also Boas, *University Drama*, pp. 382–85.

34 *Revels II*, 34.

35 Edward Halle, *The Union of the Two Noble and Illustrate Families* (London, 1548), fol. 154v. Wolsey had Roo briefly imprisoned. For Fish's role, see Boswell, "Seven Actors," p. 51.

36 John Foxe, *Acts and Monuments*, 2nd edn. (London: John Daye, 1570), II, 1152–53. Cited in Boswell, "Seven Actors," pp. 51–52.

37 See Samuel Tannenbaum, "A Note on *Misogonus*," *Modern Language Notes*, 45 (1930): 308–10; David Bevington, "*Misogonus* and Laurentius Bariona," *English Language Notes*, 2 (1965): 9–10; Lester E. Barber, ed., *Misogonus* (New York: Garland, 1979), pp. 11–25.

38 *Nice Wanton*, TFT (1909), A2^r. Despite the widespread assumption that girls did not attend grammar schools, it is not unusual to find them mentioned attending them, especially in those of Cathedral foundations. However, it was often frowned upon in the injunctions of some major schools. Thomas Becon attacked this attitude, stressing the need for girls to engage in study and commending the founding of schools to teach them godliness and virtue (Becon, *Catechism of Thomas Becon*, p. 377). See Simon, *Education and Society*, p. 189; and Norman Wood, *The Reformation and English Education* (London: Routledge & Kegan Paul, 1931), pp. 77–78.

39 Among other works, these sentiments are expressed in Sir Thomas Eliot, *The Boke named the Governour* and Thomas Starkey, *A Dialogue between Reginald Pole and Thomas Lupset*. See Simon, *Education and Society*, pp. 156–57 and 366–67.

40 Craik, *Tudor Interlude*, p. 34.

41 See Eccles, "William Wager," pp. 258–62; and Seaver, *Puritan Lectureships*, pp. 80, 162, 209–11, 333; Chambers, *ES*, II, 73.

42 See Simon, *Education and Society*, pp. 344–47. For More's plays, see Wilson, *English Drama 1485–1585*, p. 90. Wolsey's great household, and that of Abbot Richard Whiting (some 300 sons of nobility were brought up in the latter's), were major centers of learning for youths seeking preferment and advancement within the church (see Simon, *Education and Society*, p. 99). Some plays were almost certainly composed by noblemen's tutors, who were much in demand in the great households

(Simon, *ibid.*, p. 101). One such example is the almoner in the Earl of Northumberland's household during the early years of the century. See Westfall, *Patrons and Performance*, pp. 119–20. We should not overlook Skelton who was Henry VIII's tutor for a time. Radcliffe, noted earlier, tutored the children of the Marquess of Dorset (Dowling, *Humanism*, p. 127).

43 Cited in Simon, *Education and Society*, p. 340. That clergymen were hired by wealthy households to teach children during Elizabeth's reign is evident from some remarks by Stephen Gosson in *Plays Confuted in Five Acts* (1582) that after writing his first polemical pamphlet against the stage *The School of Abuse*, "I departed from the City of London, and bestowed my time in teaching yong Gentlemen in the Countrie, where I continue with a very worshipfull Gentleman, and reade to his sonnes in his owne house" (See Chambers, *ES*, IV, appendix C, 214). Gosson himself of course was a former playwright. Had he been appointed to teach by a troupe-sponsoring nobleman during his playwrighting years prior to the rise of anti-stage sentiment, would he not have been disposed to devise interludes for that nobleman's troupe?

44 The title page announces that the comedy is especially necessary for "such as are like to come to dignitie and promotion," and Wager seems to have had a noble audience particularly in mind when the play's Prologue states that a good education is profitable "for them chiefly / Which by birth are like to have gubernation / In public weals, that they may rule ever justly." However, if commissioned for a noble household, the play is equally relevant to a popular audience of youths and their elders. The most convincing evidence that the play was actually performed and that its printed version was intended primarily for acting troupes rather than readers is provided by the play text itself, which appears to be based on a prompt-book or actor's copy with stage directions such as "read as fondly as you can devise." "Laugh all three at his reading." William Wager, *The Longer Thou Livest the More Fool Thou Art*, TFT (1910), A2^{r-v}.

45 See Brigden, "Youth and the English Reformation," pp. 43–51.

46 One Richard Wever studied at Oxford in 1524, served as a fellow of St. Chad's College, Shrewsbury in 1546, and became prebend of Bubbenhall in the diocese of Lichfield in 1549, where he remained until 1554. In 1556 he was, according to John Foxe, examined by the Marian authorities at Lichfield, but resumed his clerical duties as the prebend of Hansacre until 1559. See Helen S. Thomas, ed., "Introduction," *An Enterlude Called Lusty Iuuentus*, The Renaissance Imagination (New York: Garland, 1982), pp. xi–lxvii; pp. xii–xiii.

47 Wilson, *English Drama*, pp. 96–101.

48 For example, the preacher Good Counsel rebukes Youth for neglecting his divinely appointed calling when he meets him passing away the time in idle pleasure; see Richard Wever, *Lusty Juventus*, TFT (1907), A2^v. Royal injunctions from 1536 to 1547 enjoin parents, masters and

governors to set children and servants "even from their childhood" to learning or to some honest exercise, occupation or husbandry. Parish priests should exhort and use every means to instruct children to prevent idleness, begging, stealing "or some other unthriftiness." See *Visitation Articles and Injunctions of the Period of the Reformation*, eds. W. H. Frere and W. M. Kennedy (London: Longmans, 1910), II, 3–8; and Simon, *Education and Society*, p. 173.

49 The religious mandate of a Protestant education is anticipated by John Colet who in framing the statutes of St. Paul's Grammar School stated that its primary aim is "by this school specially to increase knowledge and worshipping of God and Our Lord Christ Jesu and good Christian life and manners in the children" (Simon, *ibid.*, p. 80).

50 See also *Nice Wanton*, A1ᵛ; *Jacob and Esau*, TFT (1909), A4ʳ⁻ᵛ; *The Longer Thou Livest the More Fool Thou Art*, A2ᵛ. Becon declares that "our will is alway evil, or at the least prone unto evil, even from our cradles upward." *Catechism of Thomas Becon*, p. 154. Here he is following Calvin who, in referring to infants, says that "Their whole nature is a seed of sin; hence it can be only hateful and abhorrent to God" (Calvin, *Institution*, II.i.8).

51 Martin Bucer stresses this point: "Unless the minds of children are... made accustomed to the obedience of Christ as soon as they have the capacity for understanding, there grow from a root of evil origin briars and thorns of the kind of evils which drive away the seed of the word from their hearts so as to prevent it from being received,... so that later they can only be helped toward amendment by laws in the way that medicine helps a body wasted by disease, when that body would reject or even render the medicine harmful to itself." *De Regno Christi*, ed. and trans. Wilhelm Pauck, in *Melanchthon and Bucer*, Library of Christian Classics, XIX (London: Westminster, 1969), p. 185.

52 *Nice Wanton*, C2ʳ:

> A yonge plant ye may pla[n]tte & bowe as ye wyll:
> Where it groweth strong, there wyll it abyde styll.
> Euen so by chyldren; in theyr tender age,
> Ye may worke them like waxe, to your own entent;
> But if ye suffer them longe to liue in outrage,
> They wil be sturdy and stiffe, and will not relent.

See also *The Disobedient Child*, TFT (1908), G4ᵛ. Philip Stubbes in *The Anatomie of Abuses* (London: Richard Jones, 1583), p. 185, writes: "So long as a sprigge, twist, or braunche, is yong, it is flexible and bowable to any thing a man can desire; but if we tarie till it be a great tree, it is inflexible and unbowable... So, correct children in their tender yeres, and you may bow them to what good lore you will your selfe; but tarie till they be old, than is it to late, as experience teacheth daylie."

53 *Nice Wanton*, A2ʳ; *Jacob and Esau*, H1ʳ; *Lusty Juventus*, F1ʳ.
54 *Nice Wanton*, A1ᵛ; *Lusty Juventus*, A2ᵛ. Becon writes, "idleness is the chief

'mistress of vices,' as a certain ballad hath. Nothing doth so open both windows and doors to the tempter as sluggish idleness " (Becon, *Catechism of Thomas Becon*, p. 101).

55 If *Lusty Juventus* blames the Catholicism of the older generation for the lamentable state of the nation's youth, it also reflects the common perception of the time that youth are at the vanguard of the Reformation. As Hypocrisy laments:

> The worlde was neuer mery
> Since children were so bolde:
> Now euery boy wil be a teacher,
> The father a foole, and the childe a preacher
>
> (C4ᵛ).

56 Nicholas Sheterden, soon to be martyred under Mary I, wrote to his mother imploring her to "consider your own soul's health is offered you; do not cast it off: we have not long time here." Roger Holland and Robert Plumpton were among the others who, like Barnabus, were successful in converting their parents. See Brigden, "Youth and the English Reformation," p. 58, and works cited there.

57 Calvin, *Institution*, II.v.5.

58 Becon, *Catechism*, p. 353.

59 Edmund S. Morgan, in his study, *The Puritan Family* (Boston, MA: Trustees of the Public Library, 1944), offers some valuable insights into the Calvinist relation between grace and education: "Good habits did not themselves bring saving grace, but they furnished one of the main channels through which grace could flow. God alone would determine whether the channel should be filled, but when He saved a man, He often used this means. It was important to teach a child good habits, not because they would save him, but because it was unlikely that he would be saved without them. If his education was neglected, his chances of salvation were small, but if education had provided a means of grace, there was every hope that God would use the means" (p. 52).

60 George Gascoigne, *The Glasse of Gouernment*, TFT (1914), K2ʳ⁻ᵛ.

61 Pilkington, *Works*, pp. 219–20. For Pilkington's founding of grammar schools, see Simon, *Education and Society*, pp. 307, 309.

62 Wylley by no means started the trend of controversial school drama at Yoxford in 1537. Ten years earlier when Henry VIII was still regarded by the Pope as *Defender of the Faith* the choirboys of St. Paul's staged an anti-Lutheran interlude in which the King and Cardinal Wolsey were depicted as heroes. And the tradition extended to the end of the century when the Chapel boys were involved in the *Isle of Gulls*' controversy.

63 The case for William Hunnis as author has been forwarded by C. C. Stopes, in *William Hunnis*, and more recently by N. S. Pasachoff, in *Playwrights, Preachers and Politicians: A Study of Four Tudor Old Testament Dramas* (University of Salzburg Press, 1975), pp. 16–55. Hunnis was appointed chapelmaster in 1568, the year of *Jacob and Esau*'s second printing. The same year that the play was licensed (1557/58), Hunnis

was imprisoned in the Tower for his involvement in a plot to dethrone Mary I, "his property, books, and papers, at the mercy of friend and foe, censor or publisher." A no less fervent claim has been made for Udall's authorship by Leicester Bradner, "A Test for Udall's Authorship," *Modern Language Notes*, 42 (1927): 378, primarily on the basis of metrical similarities between the play and *Ralph Roister Doister*.

64 For the music of the Chapel Royal, see Peter Le Huray, *Music and Reformation in England 1549–1660* (1967; reprinted Cambridge University Press, 1978), pp. 57–89, 172–226; and Stopes, *William Hunnis*, pp. 266–67; for the recruiting, number, and acting abilities of the Edwardian Chapel boys, see Stopes, *William Hunnis*, pp. 12–15; *Revels II*, 121, 211–12; Craik, *Tudor Interlude*, pp. 28, 42–45; for doubling see Bevington, *From Mankind to Marlowe*, p. 30.

65 The importance of the word "history" is indicated by its appearance in title, head-title, and running-title, as Wilson, *English Drama 1485–1585*, p. 94, has observed.

66 This of course does not mean that it was the first play to do so. See Southern, *Staging of Plays before Shakespeare*, p. 363; and Bevington, *From Mankind to Marlowe*, p. 30.

67 "Hunting dogs" were used in two productions at Cambridge, the first at King's College in 1552/53 for *Hyppolytus*; the second at Peterhouse in 1572/73 for an unidentified play. See Nelson, *Cambridge*, II, 1127 and 1145.

68 That at least one tent is represented in the acting place is evident from the numerous references in the dialogue and the stage directions to the characters going into or emerging from "the tente." Chambers (*ES*, III, 24–25) suggests three tents are needed, one for each of Isaac, Esau and Jacob. Craik, however, has shown that only one tent might be represented, while Southern's more recent detailed analysis proposes a simple curtained traverse on front of a hall screen, with at least two openings, the main one leading into the tent proper ("Isaacs Tente"), the other into Esau's "parte of the tent." Other entrances and exits, (e.g. when characters arrive from the hunt or from the neighboring "Tentes"), were facilitated by the screen doors. Southern also suggests that the author might have been familiar with classical stage conventions for entrances and exits: "the one on the actor's right for characters coming from the near neighborhood, and that on the left from characters coming from a distance." See Southern, *Staging of Plays before Shakespeare*, pp. 361–74. For Craik, see *Tudor Interlude*, pp. 122–23.

69 This is clearly illustrated in Bale's *King Johan* where the English monarch is envisaged as "a faythfull Moyses," who "withstode proude Pharao, for hys poore Israel / Myndynge to brynge it out of the la[n]de of Darkenesse."

70 Esau exemplifies the addiction of young men of birth to hunting, hawking and idle pleasures (see Simon, *Education and Society*, p. 366). Some gentlemen believed that learning was for peasants' sons and that their sons should learn only to hawk and hunt skillfully, which received

the satirical response from Richard Pace who said that on attending a foreign ambassador, such a gentleman's son could only blow his horn while the learned peasant sons would offer advice (Simon, *ibid.*, p. 100).

71 See Pasachoff, *Playwrights*, p. 24, and references to the Church fathers cited there.

72 Bevington, *Tudor Drama and Politics*, p. 112. See also Pasachoff, *Playwrights*, pp. 16–55, and Wickham, *EES*, III, 232.

73 John Knox, *The First Blast of the Trumpet Against the Monstrvovs Regiment of Women* (Geneva, 1558; reprinted Amsterdam: Theatrvm Orbis Terrarvm, 1972), p. 50. See also John Ponet, *A Shorte Treatise of politike power* (Strasbourg, 1556; reprinted Amsterdam: Theatrvm Orbis Terrarvm, 1972), D6^r; and Christopher Goodman, *How Svperior Powers oght to be obeyd of their svbiects* (Geneva: John Crispen, 1558; reprinted Amsterdam: Theatrvm Orbis Terrarvm, 1972), p. 50.

74 See Wickham, *EES*, III, 232–33. That later English Protestants compared Marian Catholicism to Esau and Elizabethan Protestantism to Jacob is evident in John Prime's *The consolations of David Breefly Applied to Queene Elizabeth*: "When a Spanish Prince and an Italian Priest ruled England, when superstition, humane diuices, will-worshippinges, and grosse idolatrie in a strange toung ouerruled al, then were our good spoiled, our flesh martyred, our bodies burnt, and our ashes scattered, and our very soules sterued ... Well, for this time hether to (God bee thanked) Iacobs hand hath beene strong enought to hold Esau by the heel, and if some midwives helpe out blooddy Esaus forces once again, Got that hath preserued us so long, will not we hope, forsake us now." Cited in Pasachoff, *Playwrights*, p. 48.

75 Chambers, *ES*, I, 275.

76 John Christopherson, *Exhortation to all menne to take hede and beware of rebellion* (1554); cited in Boas, *University Drama*, p. 44. Among the taverns and inns Christopherson refers to might have been the Saracen's Head in Islington where the Protestant preacher, John Stot, a Scot, was arrested (and subsequently executed) just prior to the performance of a play scheduled to take place there on December 12, 1557. Players performing *A Sacke fulle of Newes* were also briefly arrested at the Boar's Head without Aldgate the following September 5 (Lancashire, *DTR*, 158, 216). Other seditious plays were reported and prohibited in the heavily Protestant counties of Kent and Essex (at Canterbury and Hatfield Broad Oak) in 1557. All this evidence points to drama's continued use, however sporadic that may have been, as an instrument of Protestant propaganda during the Marian years.

77 "Houses" were often constructed on the stage floor in Tudor court performances. Nelson (*Cambridge*, II, 717) observes that "houses" were required for all Latin comedy staged at Tudor Cambridge and a regular feature of other plays. There is also mention of a gate before Boungrace's residence, as well as two entrances. For more on the staging see Craik, *Tudor Interlude*, p. 13; Southern, *Staging of Plays before Shakespeare*,

pp. 423–24. The play was apparently performed in the evening during the Christmas season, perhaps on St. Stephen's Day or Innocents Day, the annual feast day devoted to children. The Prologue addresses the audience "Good evine" and "this night," and references appropriate to St. Stephen's Day (December 26) and Innocents' Day (December 28). See Marie Axton, *Three Tudor Classical Interludes*, p. 20.

78 See Axton, *Three Tudor Classical Interludes*, pp. 15–16.

79 Juggler and Vice are equated in Elizabethan writing ("mimus: a vice in a plaie, a jester, a juggler, or merrie conceited fellow"); Axton, *ibid.*, p. 18.

80 See Gayley, *Representative English Comedies*; and Farmer, ed., *Anonymous Plays*, *3rd Series* (1906; reprinted New York: Barnes & Noble, 1966), pp. 278–79.

81 Bevington, *Tudor Drama and Politics*, p. 126.

82 Chambers distinguishes between "the jugglers in the narrower sense, the *jouers des costeaux* who tossed and caught knives and balls, and the practitioners of sleight of hand, who generally claimed to proceed by *nigremance* or sorcery." See *MS*, I, 71. For the other meanings, see Axton, *Three Tudor Classical Interludes*, pp. 18–20.

83 *The Ressurreccion of the Masse*, B4^v. Cited in Blatt, *Plays of John Bale*, p. 132.

84 Axton, *Three Tudor Classical Interludes*, p. 19.

85 *Ibid.*, p. 20. Thomas Cranmer, *Archbishop Cranmer on the Sacrament of the Lord's Supper*, ed. John Edmund Cox, PS (Cambridge University Press, 1844), p. 262. For Cranmer's other references to transubstantiation as juggling see pp. 243, 256, and 260.

86 Calvin, *Institution*, IV.xvii.28. The whole argument against transubstantiation among the more extreme Edwardian Protestants is summed up by Bucer: "They now assume, that it cannot with reason be supposed of Christ, that he is in heaven without being circumscribed by physical space; ... that it cannot be understood that the same body of Christ is in heaven and in the Supper ... Reason does not comprehend what you teach respecting the exhibition and presence of Christ in the Supper: therefore these teachings are not true." *Original Letters Relative to the English Reformation*, ed. Hastings Robinson, 2 vols., PS (Cambridge University Press, 1846–47), II, 544–45; see also H. C. Porter, *Reformation and Reaction in Tudor Cambridge* (Cambridge University Press, 1957), p. 66.

87 Dickens, *The English Reformation*, pp. 257–58. See also Wickham's suggestion that the play is "a satire specifically directed against the spearhead of the Counter-Reformation, the newly founded Jesuit order and the casuistry in argument for which its members became a byword in Elizabethan and Jacobean England," in *EES*, III, 76–78.

88 The latter inveighs against popery as "a foule stynking puddle of idolatrie and supersticyon to endeless damnation." This is in line with Udall's anti-Romanist introduction to Erasmus' *Paraphrase*. See Axton,

Three Tudor Classical Interludes, pp. 2–3; and Wilson, *English Drama 1485–1585*, p. 104.

5 CHURCHES AND OTHER PLAYING PLACES

1 See Southern, *Staging of Plays before Shakespeare*; Wickham, *EES*, I; Craik, *Tudor Interlude*; *Revels II*.
2 For a reconstruction of the medieval *Mankind* on a booth stage within the inn-yard setting, see William Tydeman, *English Medieval Theatre 1400–1500* (London: Routledge & Kegan Paul, 1986), pp. 31–52.
3 See Wickham, *EES*, II.i, 184–96; and Wasson, "Professional Actors," p. 5; ch. 4, note 76 above.
4 These above-noted inns were perhaps among the "Taverns, inns and victualling houses" referred to in November 1565 as venues where "money is paid or demanded for hearing plays." About 1660, Richard Flecknoe states that the players "about the beginning of Queen Elizabeths reign" began to "set up Theaters, first in the City (as in the Inn-yards of the Cross-Keyes, and Bull in Grace and Bishops-Gate Street at this day is to be seen)." *A Discourse of the English Stage*, in *The English Drama and Stage under the Tudor and Stuart Princes*, ed. W. C. Hazlitt (1869; reprinted New York: Franklin, n.d.): 275–81; p. 276. Chambers, *ES*, II, 357. See also Chambers, *ES*, II, 379ff; and Bradbrook, *Rise of the Common Player*, p. 54. As we noted in chapter 4, Protestant plays were suspected of being performed in taverns during Queen Mary's reign.
5 For performances in the halls of the London livery companies, see Jean Robinson and D. J. Gordon, eds., *A Calendar of Dramatic Records in the Books of the Livery Companies of London, 1485–1640*, MSC III (Oxford University Press, 1954); and Wickham, *EES*, II.i, 185–86.
6 See G. E. Bentley, "New Actors of the Elizabethan Period," in *Modern Language Notes*, 44 (1929): 368–72; p. 370.
7 See Wickham, "Staging of Saint Plays," pp. 114–15 (and figure 4), and p. 119. For Shrewsbury, see Somerset, "Local Drama and Playing Places," pp. 1–31. Lindsay's production is also examined in John MacQueen, "Ani Satyre of the Thrie Estaitis," *Studies in Scottish Literature*, 3 (1966): 139–43; and Joanne Spencer Kantrowitz's *Dramatic Allegory: Lindsay's "Ani Satyre of the Thrie Estaitis"* (Lincoln: University of Nebraska Press, 1975).
8 For open-air staging and its financing, see Tydeman, *Theatre in the Middle Ages* (Cambridge University Press, 1978), chs. 5 and 8 respectively; and his *English Medieval Theatre*, pp. 189–98. For Lincoln, Norwich, and Coventry, see Nelson, *Medieval English Stage*, chs. 6, 7, and 8.
9 See Tydeman, *Theatre in the Middle Ages*, ch. 3. See also Richard Leacroft, *The Development of the English Playhouse* (Ithaca: Cornell University Press, 1973), pp. 1–4; Bevington, "The Staging of Twelfth-Century Liturgical Drama in the Fleury *Playbook*," in *The Fleury Playbook: Essays and Studies*, eds. Thomas P. Campbell and Clifford Davidson (Kalamazoo: Medi-

eval Institute, 1985): 62–81; and Fletcher Collins, Jr., *The Production of Medieval Church Music-Drama* (Charlottesville: University Press of Virginia, 1972), pp. 24–34. All of these studies draw on Karl Young, *The Drama of the Medieval Church*, 2 vols. (Oxford: Clarendon, 1933); see especially II, 507–13.

10 The play in question is *The Pardoner and the Friar* (Southern, *Staging of Plays before Shakespeare*, pp. 250–53, 340).

11 Chambers, *MS*, II, 191; and *ES*, I, 336.

12 Bevington, *From Mankind to Marlowe*, p. 12.

13 Wasson, "Professional Actors," p. 7.

14 Anthony Munday, *A Second and Third Blast of Retrait from Plaies and Theaters* (London, 1580; reprinted New York, Garland, 1973), p. 128; cited in Chambers, *ES*, IV, appendix C, 210. The printing of the City's coat of arms in the work indicates the London corporation's patronage.

15 Bradbrook, *Rise of the Common Player*, p. 218; Bradbrook cites William Langham, *A History of the Three Cathedral Churches of St. Paul* (1873), 55–56.

16 See J. H. Bettey, *Church and Community: The Parish Church in English Life* (Bradford-on-Avon, England: Moonraker Press, 1979), pp. 50–53.

17 Happé, *Bale*, II, 103 (ll. 1329–31). For early Protestant attitudes towards church consecration, see Thomas, *Religion and the Decline of Magic*, pp. 57–59.

18 Somerset, "Local Drama and Playing Places," p. 6; Galloway and Wasson, eds., *Records of Plays and Players*, p. 5.

19 Playing "in the church" (with some variation in spelling) appears in ecclesiastical and civic accounts for churches in Hadleigh (1547/48), Leicester (1551), Plymouth (1549/50; 1565/66; 1573/74), Plymstock (1568), Ashburton (1533/34; 1534; 1535/36), Barnstaple (1552/53); Sherbrooke (1543), Louth (1556/57), Long Sutton (1547/48; 1562/63; 1572/73), Witham-on-the-Hill (1554), Braintree (1523; 1525), Halstead (1529), Swaffham (1512/13), West Ham (1576/77, Norwich (1590: "in christechurch" – the Cathedral), Marlow (1608: "in the churche lofte"), and Doncaster (1574). To these we might add "in the chapel" at Norwich (1564/65; 1616), Great Burstead (1579), and King's College, Cambridge (1564). It should be noted that for many counties (e.g. densely populated Kent), the churchwardens' accounts where such references are likely to be found have not been examined; the above list, therefore, is far from complete and serves only to show how widespread churchplaying was. There are of course many other instances in the collected records where the evidence indicates fairly clearly that playing took place in the church. The above references are based on the various recent record collections by Records of Early English Drama and The Malone Society, and also on Lancashire's *Dramatic Texts and Records of Britain*.

20 Mepham, "Medieval Plays in the 16th Century at Heybridge and Braintree," *Essex Review*, 55 (1946): 8–18.

21 Lancashire, *DTR*, xxiv, 196, 198.
22 *LP: Henry 8*, XVII, no. 282, pp. 156–57.
23 Recorded in William Turner's *The Rescvynge of the Romishe Fox* (1545), G2ʳ. Cited in Lancashire, *DTR*, 205. About 1535, Morison advised the Crown to suppress lewd and ribald "playes of Robyn hoode, mayde Marian, freer Tuck," in favor of anti-papal religious drama. See the text in Anglo, "An Early Tudor Programme," pp. 176–79. For more on Morison and Cromwell's propagandist campaign, see chapter 1 above.
24 See Charles T. Prouty, "An Early Elizabethan Playhouse," in *Shakespeare Survey* 6 (1953): 64–74. Prouty offers a very useful description of the interior of this building for playing purposes during the 1560s.
25 See Bradbrook, *Rise of the Common Player*, pp. 217 and 227, who cites Gosson's *Play's Confuted in Five Acts* (1582), D3ᵛ.
26 Wasson, "Professional Actors," pp. 7–8.
27 Samuel Harsnet, *Declaration of Egregious Popish Impostures* (London, 1603), pp. 114–15. In 1591, Samuel Cox also recalls that earlier in the century amateur players "used to play either in their town-halls, or some time in churches, to make the people merry." See his letter to an unknown correspondent in Chambers, *ES*, IV, 237.
28 Murray, *English Dramatic Companies*, II, 402; cited in Wasson, "Professional Actors," p. 7.
29 This is borne out by Mepham's "Medieval Plays" and by the important research undertaken by John Coldewey in Kent. See his "Early Essex Drama: A History of its Rise and Fall, and a Theory Concerning the Digby Plays," Ph.D. dissertation, University of Colorado, published in 1972. For a different view – that there is a gap in the performances of religious plays between 1525/26 and 1561 – see Somerset, "Local Drama and Playing Places," p. 2.
30 See Gardiner, *Mysteries' End*. For the Norwich play, see *The Norwich Grocer's Play*, in *Non-Cycle Plays and Fragments*, ed. Norman Davis (Oxford University Press, 1970), pp. 11–18.
31 Cited in MacCulloch, *Suffolk and the Tudors*, p. 163.
32 See Galloway and Wasson, *Records of Plays and Players*, p. 162.
33 See Lancashire, *DTR*, 251; and Victor J. Adams, "When the Players Came to Poole," *Dorset Year Book* (1978): 129.
34 For accounts of Hancock's preaching at Poole, see Clair Cross, *Church and People 1450–1660* (Atlantic Highlands, NJ: Humanities Press, 1976), pp. 92–93; 110–11.
35 See Brigden, *London and the Reformation*, p. 345.
36 See Galloway, *Norwich*, p. 31; Lancashire, *DTR*, 239, 386.
37 See Seaver, *The Puritan Lectureships*, p. 80.
38 Dickens, *The English Reformation*, p. 276.
39 North, *Chronicle of the Church of St. Martin*, p. 114.
40 *Ibid.*, pp. 150–51.
41 See Coldewey, "The Last Rise and Final Demise of Essex Town Drama," *Modern Language Quarterly*, 36 (1975): 239–60; pp. 253f; see

also Prouty, "An Early Elizabethan Playhouse," p. 66, for sale of "all tholde peynted clothes 12s" at Trinity Chapel.

42 See "Cromwell's Accounts," in *LP: Henry 8*, IV.ii, 337, 339.

43 N. A. Pegden, *Leicester Guildhall: A Short History and Guide* (Leicester: De Vayle Litho, 1981), p. 7.

44 Nelson, *Cambridge*, I, 234.

45 In addition to Stokys' report, the eyewitness accounts were by Abraham Hartwell of King's College, Nicholas Robinson of Queen's, and an anonymous writer. The documents and plays are discussed in Boas, *University Drama in the Tudor Age*, pp. 89–98. For a reconstruction of the ground plan of the stage and seating arrangements and further discussion of staging (to which my summary is indebted), see Wickham, *EES*, I, 247–50, and figure 17. A cut-open scale reconstruction of the stage in King's College Chapel appears in Leacroft, *Development of the English Playhouse*, p. 13 (figure 10).

46 Nelson's translation, *Cambridge*, II, 1141; noted by Boas, *University Drama*, p. 96.

47 See R. Willis and J. W. Clark, *Architectural History of the University of Cambridge*, 4 vols. (Cambridge University Press, 1886), II, 38–39, 141, 206–7, and 561. Porter, *Reformation and Reaction*, pp. 67–69. See also G. W. O. Addleshaw and Frederick Etchells, *The Architectural Setting of Anglican Worship* (London: Faber and Faber, 1948), pp. 25f; Phillips, *The Reformation of Images*, chs. 4 and 6.

48 See A. D. Mills and G. R. Proudfoot, eds., *A Corpus Christi Play and Other Dramatic Activities in Sixteenth-Century Sherborne, Dorset*, in MSC IX (Oxford University Press, 1971–77), pp. 1–15; Lancashire, *DTR*, 262.

49 Galloway and Wasson, *Records of Plays and Players*, p. 162.

50 Suggested by Wasson, *Devon*, p. xxvi.

51 For example in his injunctions of 1551/52 for the dioceses of Gloucester and Worcester, Bishop Hooper ordered that screens, along with other partitions which separated the minister from the people, be taken down (Addleshaw and Etchells, *Architectural Setting*, p. 25). However, the Elizabethan authorities, by way of the Royal Order of 1561, restored the use of screens, though minus ornamentation such as the upper section displaying rood, parapet, and images (*ibid.*, pp. 30–31).

52 Stanley Kahrl and Richard Proudfoot, eds., *Records of Plays and Players in Lincolnshire 1300–1585*, MSC VIII (Oxford University Press, 1969), p. 5.

53 North, *Chronicle of the Church*, p. 162; G. H. Cook, *The English Mediaeval Parish Church* (London: Phoenix House, 1954), pp. 185–87; Bettey, *Church and Community*, pp. 44–46. As late as 1644, the "large spacious Church" at Cartmel, Lancashire, had "scarce any seats in it." Reported in Douglas and Greenfield, *Cumberland, Westmorland, and Gloucester*, p. 219.

54 The citation, along with a discussion of the case, is found in Coldewey, "The Last Rise and Final Demise," p. 247.

55 Galloway, *Norwich*, p. 52.
56 Nelson, *Cambridge*, I, 234.
57 See Suzanne R. Westfall, "The Chapel: Theatrical Performance in Early Tudor Great Households," *English Literary Renaissance*, 19 (1989): 171–93; pp. 176–78.
58 Chambers, *ES*, III, 27–28.
59 Bevington, *From Mankind to Marlowe*, pp. 30–31. Thomas Wharton's *History of English Poetry* (1774–81) quotes passages from a supposedly lost pamphlet of 1569 entitled *The Children of the Chapel Stript and Whipt* which claims that the boys of the Chapel Royal performed in the chapel on the sabbath: "Even in her maiesties chappel do these pretty vpstart youthes profane the Lordes Day by the lascivious writhing of their tender limbs, and gorgeous decking of their apparell, in feigning bawdie fables gathered from the idolatrous heathen poets" (quoted in *ES*, II, 34–35). Although there is reason to believe that these quotations are spurious and indeed Wharton's inventions, the other evidence presented above suggests that there is a ring of truth to the sentiments expressed and that Wharton may have based the passages on no longer extant documents. See Bradbrook, *Rise of the Common Player*, p. 294, note 2; and *Revels II*, 123, note 1.
60 King, *English Reformation Literature*, pp. 290–94. Support for the configuration of two half-choirs for Becon's play is found in Hillebrand's summary of the staging of a "dialogue with songs" performed by the Chapel Royal choristers on May 6, 1527. For the summary, see *Revels II*, 120.
61 Bevington, *From Mankind to Marlowe*, p. 56.
62 "I toke Christes testament in my hande and went to the market crosse, the people in great nombre folowinge … The younge men in the forenone played a Tragedye of Gods promises in the olde lawe at the market crosse with organe plainges and songes very aptely. In the afternone agayne they played a Commedie of Sanct Johan Baptistes preachinges of Christes baptisynge and of his temptacion in the wildernesse to the small contentacion of the prestes and other papistes there." Excerpted from *The Vocacyon of Johan Bale to the bishoprick of Ossorie in Irelande*, fols. 24^{r-v}; quoted in Happé, *Bale*, I, 6–7.
63 Craik, *Tudor Interlude*, p. 9.
64 Harbage and Schoenbaum, *Annals of English Drama*, pp. 22–23. See also the Chronological Table in Braunmuller and Hattaway, *Cambridge Companion to English Renaissance Drama*, p. 420.
65 Stage direction, line 178. All translations are those of Happé, *Bale*.
66 See McCusker, *John Bale*, pp. 76–86; Blatt, *Plays of John Bale*, pp. 149–52.
67 Thirty singers and upwards was not uncommon. See John Stevens, *Music and Poetry in the Early Tudor Court* (London: Methuen, 1961), p. 297; and *Key Words in Church Music*, ed. Carl Schalk (St. Louis: Concordia, 1978), p. 66.

68 See *Studies in the Performance of Late Medieval Music*, trans., ed. Stanley Boorman (Cambridge University Press, 1983), pp. 121 and 184. Howard Mayer Brown, "Musicians in the *Mystères* and *Miracles*," *Medieval English Drama: Essays Critical and Contextual*, eds. Jerome Taylor and Alan H. Nelson (University of Chicago Press, 1972): 81–97, pp. 84–85.

69 Brown, *Musicians*, p. 91; Tydeman, *Theatre in the Middle Ages*, p. 182.

70 MacCulloch, *Suffolk and the Tudors*, p. 158, observes that Suffolk maintained his own itinerant choir. After his marriage to Catherine Willoughby, Brandon became a strong supporter of religious reform.

71 See A. R. Myers, *The Household Book of Edward IV: The Black Book and the Ordinances of 1478* (Manchester University Press, 1959), p. 135; Westfall, "Chapel," p. 175, note 13.

72 Happé, *Bale*, II, 128, note to G178.

73 Francis W. Galpin, *Old English Instruments of Music*, 4th edn., rev. Thurston Dart (New York: Barnes and Noble, 1965), pp. 166–67; and Edward F. Rimbault's still authoritative *The History of the Organ* (London: Robert Cocks, 1877), pp. 43f.

74 *Ibid.*, p. 42.

75 *Ibid.*, p. 52. In some instances laborers were paid for moving the organ from one part of the church to another. For example, at Holy Trinity Church, Coventry, a churchwarden's account for 1559 records "Item payd for carriying in [th]e organes in to Iesus chapell ... iiij d." See Ingram, *Coventry*, p. 494.

76 Lancashire, *DTR*, 272.

77 Rimbault, *History of the Organ*, pp. 79–83.

78 See Kenneth H. Jones, "St. Stephen's Church, Hackington, and Its Possible Connection with Archbishop Baldwin," *Archaeologia Cantiana* 44 (1932): 253–68. The following discussion of the church's history and interior is also indebted to the Rev. Michael Chandler, Rector of St. Stephen's, who generously supplied me with information and documentation pertaining to the church during my visit there in August 1989, and to James Gibson who has researched the churchwardens' accounts of St. Stephen's and other Kentish churches for a forthcoming study with REED.

79 Vallance's account and the indenture are in Jones, *ibid.*, pp. 264–68.

80 Cook, *The English Mediaeval Parish Church*, pp. 156f; see also Westfall, "Chapel," pp. 176–77.

81 Bettey, *Church and Community*, p. 43.

82 Surprisingly, Richard Southern has not considered Bale's works in *The Staging of Plays before Shakespeare*. He states that they "have already received much study" (p. 304), although apart from *King Johan* the performance dimension of the plays has not been treated in any depth. Happé and Blatt offer brief but insightful suggestions for staging, for which I am indebted below.

83 See Craik, *Tudor Interlude*, p. 50 and plate 1; see also Happé, "Properties and Costumes," p. 57.

84 See Craik, *Tudor Interlude*, pp. 54–55 for details.
85 See Blatt, *Plays of John Bale*, p. 149.
86 See Southern's full discussion of this matter, in *Staging of Plays before Shakespeare*, pp. 95–98.
87 Blatt, *Plays of John Bale*, p. 149, refers to the illustration of David in *The Cologne Bible* (1478), which influenced illustrations of numerous Protestant Bibles, including the Great Bible of 1539. For the illustration of David, see James Strachan, ed., *Pictures from a Mediaeval Bible* (Boston: Beacon, 1959), p. 73.
88 For this parallel configuration, see Happé, *Bale*, II, 127.
89 E. S. Miller, "The Antiphons in Bale's Cycle of Christ," *Studies in Philology*, 48 (1951): 629–38; p. 633.
90 Happé, *Bale*, II, 127, note to G70.
91 Happé, "Properties and Costumes," p. 56.
92 As "double" antiphons, the Advent antiphons both preceded and followed the Magnificat at Vespers. See Miller, "Antiphons," p. 637.
93 From *The Image of Both Churches* (c. 1545), in Bale, *Select Works*, p. 536.
94 Happé, in *Bale*, I, 23; Stevens, *Music and Poetry*, pp. 283–85.
95 See Schalk, *Key Words in Church Music*, p. 112; Happé, *Bale*, I, 24.
96 The order is 1, 5, 6, 7, 2, 3, 4. Miller explains: "In liturgical position, 2 would have made Noah refer to the burning bush and Ten Commandments, 3 made Abraham refer to Jesse's descendants, and 4 made David refer to himself; but, at the end, they made David refer to the prophet before him and Isaiah say his own prophecy" ("Antiphons," p. 636).
97 *Ibid.*, pp. 630–31.
98 Bale may have revived or continued an early medieval tradition of staging a prophet play during Advent in the church setting. *Ordo Repraesentationis Adae*, *Ludus Danielis*, and the St. Nicholas plays have all been considered as Advent season productions. See Wickham, *EES*, III, 258–59, and David Bevington, ed., *Medieval Drama* (Boston: Houghton Mifflin, 1975), p. 78.
99 Harbage and Schoenbaum, *Annals*, p. 26.
100 Rosemary Woolf, *The English Mystery Plays* (Berkeley: University of California Press, 1972), p. 218.
101 Happé, *Bale*, I, 13.
102 See G. W. Bromiley, *Baptism and the Anglican Reformers* (London: Lutterworth, 1953), pp. 20 and 91f.
103 As suggested by McCusker, *John Bale*, p. 84.
104 See Woolf, *English Mystery Plays*, p. 219.
105 Anglo, *Spectacle*, p. 258. Blatt, *Plays of John Bale*, p. 151, and Happé (*Bale*, II, 148), point to the use of a mechanical dove in the Chester *Noah*, line 275 s.d. In *The Conversion of St. Paul*, the conversion sequence requires staging. After Saul says "His mercy to me is right welcome: / I am right glad that it is thus" (ll. 290–91), the stage direction reads: "Hic aparebit Spiritus Sanctus super eum" ("Here, the Holy Spirit [in the form of a dove] appears above him"). A second direction follows

shortly after (1. 292): "Discendet super te Spiritus Sanctus" ("The Holy Spirit descends upon you"). Textual references and quotes above taken from Wickham, *English Moral Interludes*, p. 116.

106 Audience singing may also be implied in *God's Promises* where Esaias Propheta, alone before the spectators, leads into the singing of the antiphon at the conclusion of act 6 by saying: "Helpe me in thys songe to knowledge hys great goodness" (1. 798).

107 *The Temptation*, ll. 92, 187, 268.

108 Craik, *Tudor Interlude*, p. 9.

109 See Woolf, *English Mystery Plays*, p. 221; Happé, *Bale*, II, 153, note to T203.

6 CHANGING REFORMATION ATTITUDES TOWARDS THEATRE

1 For example, one thinks of objections to playing in the city of London by Bishop Edmund Grindal in 1564 and Bishop William Alley the following year (see Chambers, *ES*, IV, 192, 266–67). It is not as well known that both these clerics sponsored and hosted actors during this same period and therefore must have approved of plays under certain conditions. Alley patronized "the Bishop's players" who performed within and beyond his Exeter diocese between 1559 and 1561, and even wrote a play entitled *Aegio*, while Grindal hosted and paid for a performance by the boys of Westminster at Putney in 1567. See Wasson, *Devon*, p. 466; Chambers, *ES*, II, 73.

2 Challenging the traditional view that censorship was the overriding factor in the decline of these productions, Ian Lancashire writes: "One wonders whether ecclesiastical authorities would have had the success they did in suppressing scriptural plays at York, Coventry, Chester, and Wakefield if these towns had not been facing financial collapse and if their civic officials had not been vulnerable to local pressure to cut, drastically, public expenditure" (Lancashire, *DTR*, xxxi). See also Bills, "The 'Suppression Theory,'" pp. 157–68; and Coldewey, "Last Rise and Final Demise," pp. 239–60.

3 Contemporary estimates of the capacity of the amphitheatres is about 3000. See Gurr, *Playgoing in Shakespeare's London*, p. 22; see also Richard Hosley, "The Theatre and the Tradition of Playhouse Design," in *The First Public Playhouse: The Theatre in Shoreditch 1576–1598*, ed. Herbert Berry (Montreal: McGill-Queen's University Press, 1979): 47–80; pp. 76–77.

4 *An Acte for the Punishement of Vacabondes and for Relief of the Poore & Impotent*, June 29, 1572, section 5. The extract is in Chambers, *ES*, IV, 269–71.

5 John Stockwood, *A Sermon Preached at Paules Crosse* (London, 1578); excerpts reprinted in Chambers, *ES*, IV, appendix C, 200. Muriel Bradbrook suggests that due to his backing by the City and prominent noblemen, perhaps these figures were supplied by his masters; *Rise of the*

Common Player, p. 70. It seems likely that economic considerations were an underlying motive for Leicester's securing an exclusive patent for his acting company to perform in London in May 1574.

6 On December 3, 1581, the players petitioned the Privy Council to override the ban on playing by the City Corporation and grant permission to resume "their common exercise of playing within and aboute the Cittie of London," "having noe other meanes to sustayne them, their wyves and children but their exercise of playing." Extract from the Minute of the Privy Council, December 3, 1581, in "The Remembrancia," in *Dramatic Records of the City of London*, ed. E. K. Chambers, MSC I (Oxford University Press, 1907): 295; and *ES*, IV, appendix D, 283.

7 For the importance of noble patronage to late Elizabethan and Jacobean drama, see Bergeron, "Patronage of Dramatists," pp. 294–305.

8 The same conclusion is reached by Gardiner, *Mysteries' End*, p. 67, note 12. There was, of course, a concerted effort underway in the North, led by Archbishop Grindal (during his tenure at York) and his deputies to censor, if not abolish, civic drama containing Catholic elements.

9 William Ringler, *Stephen Gosson: A Biographical and Critical Study* (Princeton University Press, 1942), p. 80; Heinemann, *Puritanism and Theatre*, p. 29.

10 Field's letter is in Chambers, *ES*, IV, appendix D, 284. For Walsingham's letter to the Lord Mayor of London in 1583, ordering the resumption of weekday playing, see Chambers, "The Remembrancia," MSC, I, 553.

11 For this power struggle, see Wickham, *EES*, II.i, ch. 3; and *ES*, I, ch. 9.

12 For Gosson's hiring by the City, see Ringler, *Stephen Gosson*, pp. 26–28. Arthur F. Kinney, in *Markets of Bawdrie: The Dramatic Criticism of Stephen Gosson*, Salzburg Studies in English Literature (University of Salzburg, 1974), p. 151, refutes some of Ringler's evidence but, according to Jonas Barish, not the remarks of a "careful compiler" who later stated that Gosson was "engaged" to challenge abuses by "the Judges, the Templars, and the Puritans of all professions and conditions." *The Antitheatrical Prejudice* (Berkeley: California University Press, 1981), p. 89. For Munday the evidence is more concrete. He was employed by the City to devise their pageants, and his *Second and Third Blast of Retrait from Plaies and Theatres*, presumably the sequel to Gosson's first blast in *The School of Abuse*, is decorated with the cross and dagger of the City arms. For Munday and also for John Stockman and City patronage, see Bradbrook, *Rise of the Common Player*, pp. 70 and 75.

13 However, they would have insisted, with Calvin, that "true aquaintance with God is made more by the ears than by the eyes," and that "if signs only are presented to our eyes, they will be, as it were, dead images"; see pp. 39–40, above. The Morison quote is from *A discourse touching the reformation of the lawes of England* (*c.* 1536); reprinted in Anglo, "An Early Tudor Programme," pp. 176–79; see p. 179. For the above quotes from

Calvin's *Commentaries on Exodus* and *Commentaries on Ezekiel*, see Wallace, *Calvin's Doctrine*, pp. 72–73.

14 Patrick Collinson, *From Iconoclasm to Iconophobia* (University of Reading Press, 1986), pp. 8f. See also his *Birthpangs of Protestant England*, p. 98.

15 See M. Sellers, "The City of York in the Sixteenth Century," *English Historical Review*, 9 (1894): 299; and Coldewey, "The Last Rise and Final Demise," pp. 258–59. See also Seaver, *Puritan Lectureships*.

16 Anthony Munday, *A Second and Third Blast*, p. 103.

17 John N. King, with reference to Bale, casts some light on this matter: "Reformation mingling of sacred and profane diction contradicts later notions of piety and decorum. Bale himself divorces blasphemy from the obscene in *A Christen Exhortacion unto Customable Swearers* (c. 1543), a text that contrasts impiety with the proper 'maner of sayinge grace.' ... The reformers lived in an age that could still intermingle piety with earthiness, sharing Luther's fondness of invective, jokes, puns, and proverbs." See *English Reformation Literature*, p. 93. See also the comments of Collinson, *Birthpangs of Protestant England*, p. 105.

18 See Roston, *Biblical Drama*, pp. 118–19.

19 Gosson, *Playes Confuted in Five Acts* (1582; reprinted New York: Johnson, 1972), G7^v.

20 See Stubbes, *Anatomie of Abuses*, pp. 144–46. This was the complaint of the Lord Mayor to the Privy Council in July, 1597; players, he writes, "maintaine idleness in such persons as haue no vocation & draw apprentices and other seruantes from their ordinary workes." See Chambers, "Remembrancia," p. 171.

21 See Bradbrook, *Rise of the Common Player*, p. 74; Steven Mullaney, *The Place of the Stage* (Chicago University Press, 1988), p. 47.

22 Gosson, *Playes Confuted*, E5^r.

23 For mimicry in this sense, I follow Barish, *Antitheatrical Prejudice*, p. 96.

24 *Exposition of the Fyrste Epistle of seynt Ihon* (Antwerp: M. de Keyser, 1531), E1^r. See also chapter 1 above, p. 36.

25 The best discussion of this matter with relation to Bale's Vices is in Kendall, *The Drama of Dissent*, pp. 101–22.

26 Translated from Farel's letter to Calvin, June 16, 1546, in Calvin, *Opera*, XII, 315. Farel also warns: "Isti qui tam delectantur ludis, utinam non serio dolore torqueantur!" Like Farel, Tyndale also exhorts the people to "counterfeit Christ." See his *Doctrinal Treatises*, p. 20.

27 Munday, *A Second and Third Blast*; cited in Barish, *Antitheatrical Prejudice*, p. 104.

28 Calvin quotes the biblical injunction: "A woman shal not weare the apparel of a man: neither shall a man put on the garments of a woman. For whosoeuer doth so, is an abhomination to the Lord thy God" (Deuteronomy 22:6). He then comments: "In these maskings & mummings, when men put them-selues into womens apparel, and women put the(m)-selues into me(n)s as ye know: what comes of it? Although no euil ensued thereof, yet the verie thing it self displeseth God.

We heare what is said of it in this place. *Whosoeuer doth it, is an abhominatio(n)*. Ought not this saying to make the haire of our heades stand vp, rather than wee would prouoke Gods wrath vpon vs wilfully? But besides this, we are sure [that] the suffring hereof is the opening of a gap to all whoredome. At a word, such disguisings are but inticements of baudry, as experience prooueth." See Calvin, *The Sermons of M. John Calvin vpon the Fifth Booke of Moses Called Deuteronomie*, trans. Arthur Golding (London: George Bishop, 1583), pp. 773–74.

29 For example, in *The English Gentleman*, Richard Braithwait refers to a dispute which took place between Genevan ministers over a young boy's impersonation of a woman in a play celebrating the league concluded between the cantons of Berne and Tiguris. "In the end," Braithwait informs us, "it was agreed of all parts, that they should submit the determination of this difference, with generall suffrage and consent, to the authenticke and approved judgement of their *Beza*, holden for the very Oracle both of Vniversitie and Citie. This controversie being unto him referred, he constantly affirmed, that it was not only lawfull for them to set forth and act those *Playes*, but for Boyes to put on womens apparell for the time. Neither did he only affirm this, but brought such *Divines* as opposed themselves against it, to be of his opinion, with the whole assent and consent of all the Ecclesiasticall Synod in Geneva." See Richard Braithwait, *The English Gentleman* (London: John Haviland, 1630), p. 184

30 Bale, *Three Lawes*, in Happé, *Bale*, II, ll. 425–26, ll. 475–90.

31 Richard Crashaw, *Sermon preached at the Crosse, Feb. xiiij.*, 1607; extract reprinted in Chambers, *ES*, IV, 249; William Prynne, *Histriomastix* (London: Michael Sparke, 1633), p. 529.

32 Edmund S. Morgan, "Puritan Hostility to the Theatre," *Proceedings of the American Philosophical Society*, 110 (1966): 340–47; Michael O'Connell, "The Idolatrous Eye: Iconoclasm, Anti-Theatricalism and the Image of the Elizabethan Theatre," *English Literary History*, 52 (1985): 279–310.

33 See Mullaney, *Place of the Stage*, ch. 2; Stephen Orgel, *The Illusion of Power* (Berkeley: University of California Press, 1975), p. 2.

34 John Stockwood, "A Sermon Preached at Paules Crosse" (1578), cited in Chambers, *ES*, IV, 200.

35 See John Field, *A godly exhortation* (1583; reprinted New York: Johnson, 1972), A2^r and C6^v; and John Northbrooke, *A Treatise wherein Dicing, Dauncing, Vaine playes, or Enterludes ... are reproued* (London, 1577), p. 82; cited in Chambers, *ES*, IV, 198.

36 Field, A5^r. The "elect nation" theory was popularized by, among other writers, John Foxe in *Acts and Monuments*.

37 *An Apology for Actors* (1612; reprinted New York: Johnson, 1972), B4^r.

38 Heywood, "An Apology," G2^v.

39 Gosson, *Playes Confuted*, C5^r–6^v; Munday, *A Second and Third Blast*, p. 104; Stubbes, *Anatomie of Abuses*, p. 145.

40 Gosson, *Playes Confuted*, C7^r and D1^r.

41 See Bevington, *Tudor Drama and Politics*; Heinemann, *Puritanism and Theatre*; Butler, *Theatre and Crisis*.
42 See H. H. Adams' much overlooked *English Domestic, or Homiletic Tragedy: 1575 to 1642* (New York: Columbia University Press, 1943).
43 In addition to Heinemann's *Puritanism and Theatre*, book-length studies include Butler, *Theatre and Crisis*; Rozett, *The Doctrine of Election*; Limon, *Dangerous Matter*; Robert G. Hunter, *Shakespeare and the Mystery of God's Judgements* (Athens, GA: University of Georgia Press, 1976).

NOTES: APPENDIX C

1 See G. Scheurweghs, "The Date of 'The History of Jacob and Esau'," *English Studies*, 15 (1933): 218–19.
2 Helen Thomas, "Jacob and Esau – 'rigidly Calvinistic'?" *Studies in English Literature*, 9 (1969): 199–213; p. 203.
3 *Ibid.*, p. 213. Thomas believes that the play was written by Nicholas Udall who had translated works by Erasmus into English. For the authorship question, see p. 220, note 63 above.
4 *Ibid.*, p. 202.
5 Peter Martyr, who served as Doctor of Divinity at Oxford in 1550, argued that "predestination refers to saints only while the reprobate are not predestinate, since sin is the only cause of reprobation." Cited in R. T. Kendall, *Calvin and English Calvinism* (Oxford University Press, 1979), p. 30. For Bucer's views, see *Melanchthon and Bucer*, ed. Wilhelm Pauck (London: Westminster, 1969); and Francois Wendel, *Calvin: The Origins and Development of His Religious Thought*, trans. Philip Mairet (Glasgow: Collins, 1965), pp. 280–82.
6 John Strype, the late seventeenth-century historian who had access to many no longer extant documents related to the controversy, writes the following: "Bradford was apprehensive that they [the free-willers] might now do great harm in the church, and therefore out of prison wrote a letter to Cranmer, Ridley, and Latimer, the three chief heads of the reformed (though oppressed) church in England, to take some cognizance of this matter, and to consult with them in remedying it. And with him joined Bishop Ferrar, Rowland Taylor, and John Philpot... Upon this occasion, Ridley wrote a treatise of *God's Election and Predestination*. And Bradford wrote another upon the same subject; and sent it to those three fathers in Oxford for their approbation: and, theirs being obtained, the rest of the eminent divines, in and about London, were ready to sign it also" (Strype, *Memorials of Thomas Cranmer*, I, 502–3).
7 *The Writings of John Bradford*, ed. E. A. Townsend, 2 vols. (Cambridge University Press, 1848), p. 311.
8 *Ibid.*, I, 315.
9 *Ibid.*, I, 219–20; see also Calvin, *Institution*, III.xxiv.5.
10 Calvin, *Institution*, III.xxi.2.

Bibliography

PRIMARY SOURCES

Abbreviations

MSR   Malone Society Reprints. Oxford University Press, 1907–
TFT   Tudor Facsimile Texts. Ed. J. S. Farmer. London: Jack, 1907–14

PLAYS

Appius and Virginia. TFT, 1908.
Bale, John. *The Complete Plays of John Bale*. 2 vols. Ed. Peter Happé.
   Cambridge: Brewer, 1985–6.
God's Promises. TFT, 1908.
King Johan. Ed. J. H. P. Pafford. MSR, 1931.
Three Laws. TFT, 1908.
Bassanese, Francesco Negir. *A Certayne Tragedie wrytten fyrst in Italian, by
   F. N.B. entituled, Freewyl*. Trans. Henry Cheeke. London: J. Charle-
   wood, 1959.
Beza, Theodore. *Abraham's Sacrifice*. Trans. Arthur Golding. Ed. M. W.
   Wallace. University of Toronto Press, 1907.
The Book of Sir Thomas More. MSR, 1911.
Foxe, John. *Christus Triumphans*. In *Two Latin Comedies by John Foxe the
   Martyrologist*: *Titus et Gesippus and Christus Triumphans*. Ed., trans., intro.
   by John Hazel Smith. Ithaca: Cornell University Press, 1973.
Fulwell, Ulpian. *Like Will to Like*. TFT, 1909.
Gascoigne, George. *The Glasse of Gouernment*. TFT, 1914.
Hickscorner. TFT, 1908.
Horestes. TFT, 1910.
Impatient Poverty. TFT, 1907.
Ingeland, Thomas. *The Disobedient Child*. TFT, 1908.
Jack Juggler. In *Three Tudor Classical Interludes*. Ed. Marie Axton. Cambridge:
   Brewer, 1982.
Jack Juggler. TFT, 1912.
Jacob and Esau. Eds. John Crow and F. P. Wilson. MSR, 1956.
Jacob and Esau. TFT, 1908.
July and Julian. Eds. Giles Dawson and Arthur Brown. MSR, 1955.
King Darius. TFT, 1907.

236

Lupton, Thomas. *All for Money*. TFT, 1910.
Mankind. In *English Moral Interludes*. Ed. Glynne Wickham. London: Dent, 1976.
Misogonus. Ed. Lester E. Barber. New York: Garland, 1979.
New Custom. TFT, 1908.
Nice Wanton. TFT, 1909.
Nice Wanton. In *English Moral Interludes*. Ed. Glynne Wickham. London: Dent, 1976.
Norton, Thomas, and Thomas Sackville. *Gorboduc: or Ferrex and Porrex*. TFT, 1910.
The Norwich Grocer's Play. In *Non-Cycle Plays and Fragments*. Ed. N. Davis. Early English Text Society. Oxford University Press, 1970.
The Pedlar's Prophecy. TFT, 1911.
Phillip, John. *Patient and Meek Grisell*. Eds. W. W. Greg and R. B. McKerrow. MSR, 1909.
Preston, Thomas. *Cambises*. TFT, 1910.
Respublica. TFT, 1905.
Sapientia Solomonis, Acted before the Queen by the Boys of Westminster School. Ed. Elizabeth R. Payne. Yale Studies in English No. 89. New Haven: Yale University Press, 1938.
The Trial of Treasure. TFT, 1908.
Wager, Lewis. *The Life and Repentaunce of Mary Magdalene*. Ed. F. I. Carpenter. University of Chicago Press, 1904.
The Life and Repentaunce of Mary Magdalene. Ed. J. S. Farmer. TFT, 1908; reprinted New York: AMS Press, 1970.
Wager, William. *Enough is as Good as a Feast*. Ed. Mark Benbow. Regents Renaissance Series. Lincoln: University of Nebraska Press, 1967.
Enough is as Good as a Feast. Ed. Seymour de Ricci. Huntington Facsimile Reprints. New York: Huntington Library, 1920.
The Longer Thou Livest the More Fool Thou Art. TFT, 1910.
Wapull, George. *The Tide Tarrieth No Man*. TFT, 1910.
Wever, Richard. *Lusty Juventus*. TFT, 1907.
Lusty Juventus. Ed. Helen Thomas. The Renaissance Imagination. New York: Garland, 1982.
Woodes, Nathaniel. *The Conflict of Conscience*. TFT, 1911.

NONDRAMATIC WORKS

Ascham, Roger. *The Scholemaster*. Ed. R. J. Schoeck. Don Mills Ontario: Dent, 1966.
Baldwin, William. *A Marvelous Hystory Intitulede, Beware the Cat*. London, 1570.
Bale, John. *Scriptorum Illustrium maioris Britannieae ... Catalogus*. 2 vols. Basel, 1557–59.
The Select Works. Ed. Henry Christmas. PS. Cambridge University Press, 1849.

The Vocacyon of Johan Bale to the bishoprick of Ossorie in Irelande. Wesel: Dirik van der Straten, 1553.

Becon, Thomas. *The Catechism of Thomas Becon with Other Pieces.* Ed. John Ayre. PS. Cambridge University Press, 1844.

Bevington, David, ed. *Medieval Drama.* Boston: Houghton Mifflin, 1975.

Bradford, John. *The Writings of John Bradford.* Ed. E. A. Townsend. 2 vols. PS. Cambridge University Press, 1848.

Braithwait, Richard. *The English Gentleman.* London: John Haviland, 1630.

Bruce, Jay. and Perowne, T. T., eds. *The Correspondence of Matthew Parker, D.D. Archbishop of Canterbury 1535–1575.* PS. Cambridge University Press, 1853.

Bucer, Martin. *De Regno Christi.* In *Melanchthon and Bucer.* Library of Christian Classics XIX. London: Westminster, 1969.

Calendar of State Papers, Domestic Series, of the Reigns of Edward VI, etc. Ed. Robert Lemon. London: 1856.

Calvin, John. *The Institution of the Christian Religion.* Trans. Thomas Norton. 1561; reprinted London: n.p., 1582.

Opera omnia quae supersunt (Corpus Reformatoren). Ed. William Baum, *et al.* 49 vols. Brunswick: Schwetschke, 1863–1900.

The Sermons of M. John Calvin vpon the Fifth Booke of Moses Called Deuteronomie. Trans. Arthur Golding. London: George Bishop, 1583.

Chambers, E. K., ed. *"The Remembrancia." Dramatic Records of the City of London.* MSC I. Oxford University Press, 1907.

Christopherson, John. *Exhortation to all menne to take hede and beware of rebellion.* London, 1554.

Cook, G. H., ed. *Letters to Cromwell and Others on the Suppression of the Monasteries.* London: Baker, 1965.

Cranmer, Thomas. *Archbishop Cranmer on the Sacrament of the Lord's Supper.* Ed. John Edmund Cox. PS. Cambridge University Press, 1844.

Creeth, Edmund, ed. *Tudor Plays: An Anthology of Early English Drama.* New York: Norton, 1966.

Dawson, Giles, ed. *Records of Plays and Players in Kent 1450–1642.* MSC VII. Oxford University Press, 1965.

Dorman, Thomas. *A Provfe of Certeyne Articles in Religion.* Antwerp, 1564; reprinted London: Scholar Press, 1976.

Douglas, Audrey, and Peter Greenfield, eds. *Cumberland, Westmorland, and Gloucester.* REED. University of Toronto Press, 1986.

Feuillerat, Albert. *Documents Relating to the Revels at Court in the Time of King Edward VI and Queen Mary.* Louvain: A. Uystpruyst, 1914.

Documents Relating to the Revels at Court in the Time of Queen Elizabeth. Louvain, A. Uystpruyst,1908.

Foxe, John. *Acts and Monuments.* Ed. S. R. Cattley. 4th edn., rev. Josiah Pratt. 8 vols. London: Religious Tract Society, 1877.

Acts and Monuments. 1st edn. London: John Daye, 1963.

Galloway, David, ed. *Norwich.* REED. University of Toronto Press, 1984.

and John Wasson, eds. *Records of Plays and Players in Norfolk and Suffolk, 1330–1642.* MSC XI. Oxford University Press, 1981.

Gee, Henry, and W. H. Hardy, eds. *Documents Illustrative of English Church History*. London: Macmillan, 1975.

Goodman, Christopher. *How Svperior Powers oght to be obeyd of their subiects*. Geneva: John Crispen, 1558; reprinted Amsterdam: Theatrvm Orbis Terrarvm, 1972.

Gosson, Stephen. *Playes Confuted in Five Acts*. London, 1582; reprinted New York: Johnson, 1972.

Greg, W. W., and G. C. Moore Smith, eds. *The Academic Drama at Cambridge: Extracts from College Records*. MSC II. Oxford University Press, 1923.

Hartley, T. E., ed. *Proceedings in the Parliaments of Elizabeth I*. Leicester University Press, 1981.

Hazlitt, W. C., ed. *The English Drama and Stage under the Tudor and Stuart Princes 1543–1664*. 1869; reprinted New York: Franklin, n.d.

Holinshed, Raphael. *The Chronicles of England, Scotland, and Ireland*. London, 1586–87.

Hughes, Paul L. and James F. Larkin, eds. *Tudor Proclamations*. 3 vols. New Haven: Yale University Press, 1964.

Hume, M. A. S., ed. *Calendar of Letters and State Papers Relating to English Affairs, Preserved Principally in the Archives of Simancas*. 4 vols. London, 1892–99.

Ingram, R. W., ed. *Coventry*. REED. University of Toronto Press, 1981.

Kahrl, Stanley J., and Richard Proudfoot, eds. *Records of Plays and Players in Lincolnshire*, 1300–1585. MSC VIII. Oxford University Press, 1972.

Knox, John. *The First Blast of the Trumpet Against the Monstrvovs Regiment of Women*. Geneva, 1558; reprinted Amsterdam: Theatrvm Orbis Terrarvm, 1972.

Letters and Papers, Foreign and Domestic, of the Reign of Henry VIII, eds. J. S. Brewer, J. Gairdner, and R. H. Brodie. 21 vols. London: Longman, Green, Longman, & Roberts, 1862–1932.

The Lisle Letters. Ed. Muriel St Clare Byrne. 6 vols. University of Chicago Press, 1981.

Mills, A. D, and G. R. Proudfoot, eds. *A Corpus Christi Play and Other Dramatic Activities in Sixteenth-Century Sherborne, Dorset*. MSC IX. Oxford University Press, 1971–77.

More, Thomas. *The Complete Works of Sir Thomas More*. Ed. L. A. Schuster. New Haven: Yale University Press, 1973.

Munday, Anthony. *A Second and Third Blast of Retrait from Plaies and Theatres*. London, 1580; reprinted New York: Garland, 1973.

Myers, A. R., ed. *The Household Book of Edward IV: The Black Book and the Ordinances of 1478*. Manchester University Press, 1959.

Nelson, Alan, ed. *Cambridge*. REED. 2 vols. University of Toronto Press, 1989.

Original Letters Relative to the English Reformation. Ed. Hastings Robinson. 2 vols. PS. Cambridge University Press, 1846–47.

Perkins, William. *Workes*. 3 vols. London: John Legate, 1608.

Philpot, John. *The Examinations and Writings of John Philpot*. Ed. R. Eden. PS. Cambridge University Press, 1842.

Pilkington, James. *The Works of James Pilkington.* Ed. J. Scholefield. PS. Cambridge University Press, 1842.

Ponet, John. *A Shorte Treatise of politike power.* Strasbourg, 1556; reprinted Amsterdam: Theatrvm Orbis Terrarvm, 1972.

Prynne, William. *Histriomastix.* London: Michael Sparke, 1633.

Redstone, Vincent, ed. *Players of Ipswich.* MSC II.iii. Oxford University Press, 1931.

Robertson, Jean, and D. J. Gordon, eds. *A Calendar of Dramatic Records in the Books of the Livery Companies of London 1485–1640.* MSC III. Oxford University Press, 1954.

Robinson, Hastings, ed. *Zurich Letters.* 2 vols. PS. Cambridge University Press, 1915.

Smith, Henry. *Three Sermons made by Maister Henry Smith.* London: Nicholas Ling, 1599.

State Papers and Manuscripts Relating to English Affairs, Existing in the Archives and Collections of Venice, and in Other Libraries of Northern Italy. Eds. Rawdon Brown and G. Cavendish-Bentinck. 7 vols. London, 1864–90.

State Papers Relating to English Affairs, Preserved Principally in the Archives of Simancas. Ed. M. A. S. Hume. 4 vols. London,1892–99.

Stow, John. *A Survey of London.* Ed. C. L. Kingsford. 2 vols. Oxford: Clarendon, 1908.

Strachan, James, ed. *Pictures from a Mediaeval Bible.* Boston: Beacon, 1959.

Stubbes, Philip. *The Anatomie of Abuses.* London: Richard Jones, 1583.

Tyndale, *Doctrinal Treatises and Introductions to Different Portions of the Holy Scriptures.* Ed. Henry Walter. PS. Cambridge University Press, 1848.

Veltrusky, Jarmila F. "The Old Czech Apothecary as Clown and Symbol." *International Society for the Study of Medieval Theatre,* (1989): 157–58.

Visitation Articles and Injunctions of the Period of the Reformation. Eds. W. H. Frere and W. M. Kennedy. London: Longmans, 1910.

Wasson, John M., ed. *Devon.* REED. University of Toronto Press, 1986.

Whythorne, Thomas. *The Autobiography of Thomas Whythorne.* Ed. James M. Osborn. Oxford: Clarendon, 1961.

Wriothesley, Thomas. *A Chronicle of England During the Reigns of the Tudors.* Ed. W. D. Hamilton. 2 vols. London: Camden Society, 1875.

SECONDARY SOURCES

Adams, Henry Hitch. *English Domestic, or Homiletic Tragedy: 1575 to 1642.* New York: Columbia University Press, 1943.

Adams, Victor J. "When the Players Came to Poole." *Dorset Year Book,* (1978): 129.

Addleshaw, G. W. O., and Frederick Etchells. *The Architectural Setting of Anglican Worship.* London: Faber and Faber, 1948.

Anglo, Sydney, "An Early Tudor Programme for Plays and Other Demonstrations against the Pope." In *Journal of the Warburg and Courtnay Institute,* 20 (1957): 176–79.

Spectacle, Pageantry, and Early Tudor Policy. Oxford University Press, 1969.

Axton, Marie, ed. "Introduction." *Three Tudor Classical Interludes.* Cambridge: Brewer, 1982.

Axton, Richard. *European Drama of the Early Middle Ages.* University of Pittsburgh Press, 1975.

"Folk Play in Tudor Interludes." *English Drama: Forms and Development.* Eds. Marie Axton and Raymond Williams. Cambridge University Press, 1977: 1–23.

Barber, Lester E., ed. *Misogonus.* New York: Garland, 1979.

Barish, Jonas. *The Antitheatrical Prejudice.* Berkeley: University of California Press, 1981.

Baskervill, C. R. "On Two Old Plays." *Modern Philology,* 14 (1916): 16.

Beadle, Richard. "Plays and Playing at Thetford and Nearby, 1498–1540." *Theatre Notebook,* 32 (1978): 4–11.

Beer, Barrett L. *Rebellion and Riot: Popular Disorder in England during the Reign of Edward VI.* Kent State University Press, 1982.

Bennett, H. S. *English Books and Readers 1558 to 1603.* Cambridge University Press, 1965.

Bentley, G. E. "New Actors of the Elizabethan Period." *Modern Language Notes,* 44 (1929): 368–72.

The Professions of Dramatist and Player in Shakespeare's Time 1590–1642. 1971; reprinted Princeton University Press, 1984.

Bergeron, David. "The Patronage of Dramatists: The Case of Thomas Heywood." *English Literary Renaissance,* 18 (1988): 294–305.

Bettey, J. H. *Church and Community: The Parish Church in English Life.* Bradford-on-Avon, England: Moonraker Press, 1979.

Bevington, David. *From Mankind to Marlowe.* Cambridge, MA: Harvard University Press, 1962.

"*Misogonus* and Laurentius Bariona." *English Language Notes,* 2 (1965): 9–10.

"The Staging of Twelfth-Century Liturgical Drama in the *Fleury Playbook.*" *The Fleury Playbook: Essays and Studies.* Eds. Thomas P. Campbell and Clifford Davidson. Kalamazoo: Medieval Institute, 1985.

Tudor Drama and Politics. Cambridge, MA: Harvard University Press, 1966.

Bills, Bing D. "The 'Suppression Theory' and the English Corpus Christi Play: A Re-Examination." *Theatre Journal,* 32 (1980): 157–68.

Blackstone, Mary A. "Notes Towards a Patrons Calendar." *REED Notes* (1981): 1–11.

"Patrons and Elizabethan Acting Companies." *Elizabethan Theatre X.* Ed. C. E. McGee. Port Credit, Ontario: Meany, 1988: 112–32.

Blatt, Thora B. *The Plays of John Bale.* Copenhagen: G. E. C. Gads Forlag, 1968.

Boas, Frederick. *University Drama in the Tudor Age.* Oxford University Press, 1914.

Bolwell, Robert W. *The Life and Works of John Heywood.* New York: Columbia University Press, 1921.

Boorman, Stanley, ed. *Studies in the Performance of Late Medieval Music.* Cambridge University Press, 1983.

Boswell, Jackson Campbell. "Seven Actors in Search of a Biographer." *Medieval and Renaissance Drama in England Volume II.* Ed. J. Leeds Barroll, III. New York: AMS, 1985: 51–56.

Bradbrook, M. C. *The Rise of the Common Player.* Cambridge University Press, 1962.

Bradner, Leicester. "A Test for Udall's Authorship." *Modern Language Notes,* 42 (1927): 378–80.

Braunmuller, A. R., and Michael Hattaway, eds. *The Cambridge Companion to English Renaissance Drama.* Cambridge University Press, 1990.

Brecht, Bertolt. *Brecht on Theatre.* Trans. and ed. John Willett. London: Methuen, 1978.

Brigden, Susan. *London and the Reformation.* Oxford: Clarendon, 1989.
"Youth and the English Reformation." *Past and Present,* 95 (May 1982): 37–67.

Bristol, Michael D. *Carnival and Theatre: Plebeian Culture and the Structure of Authority in Renaissance England.* New York: Methuen, 1985.

Bromiley, G. W. *Baptism and the Anglican Reformers.* London: Lutterworth, 1953.

Brown, Howard Mayer. "Musicians in the *Mystères* and *Miracles.*" *Medieval English Drama: Essays Critical and Contextual.* Eds. Jerome Taylor and Alan H. Nelson. University of Chicago Press, 1972: 81–97.

Brownstein, O. L. "The Saracen's Head, Islington: A Pre-Elizabethan Inn Playhouse." *Theatre Notes,* 25 (1972): 68–72.

Burke, Peter. *Popular Culture in Early Modern Europe.* Aldershot, Hants: Wildwood House, 1988.

Butler, Martin. *Theatre and Crisis 1632–1642.* Cambridge University Press, 1984.

Calderhead, Iris G. "Morality Fragments from Norfolk." *Modern Philology,* 14 (1916–17): 1–9.

Calderwood, William. "The Elizabethan Protestant Press: A Study of Printing and Publishing of Protestant Religious Literature in English 1558–1603." Ph.D. thesis, University of London, 1977.

Campbell, Lily B. "The Lost Play of *Aesop's Crow.*" *Modern Language Notes,* 29 (1934): 454–57.

Cantor, Leonard, ed. *The English Medieval Landscape.* Philadelphia: University of Pennsylvania Press, 1982.

Carpenter, Sarah. "Morality-Play Characters." *Medieval English Theatre,* 5.2 (July 1983): 18–28.

Chambers, E. K. *The Elizabethan Stage.* 4 vols. Oxford: Clarendon, 1923.
The Medieval Stage. 2 vols. Oxford: Clarendon, 1903.
Notes on the History of the Revels Office Under the Tudors. New York: Burt Franklin, 1967.

Christianson, Paul. *Reformers and Babylon: English Apocalyptic Visions from the Reformation to the Eve of the Civil War.* University of Toronto Press, 1978.
"Reformers and the Church of England Under Elizabeth I and the Early Stuarts." *Journal of Ecclesiastical History*, 31 (1980): 463–82.

Clark, Andrew. "Maldon Records and the Drama." *Notes and Queries*, 10th series, 7 (1907): 181–83, 422–23.

Clark, J. W. *Architectural History of the University of Cambridge.* 4 vols. Cambridge University Press, 1886.

Clark, Peter. *English Provincial Society from the Reformation to the Revolution: Religion, Politics and Society in Kent, 1500–1640.* Rutherford, NJ: Fairleigh Dickinson University Press, 1977.
"Josias Nicholls and Religious Radicalism, 1553–1639." *Journal of Ecclesiastical History*, 28 (1977): 134–35.

Clay, C. G. A. *Economic Expansion and Social Change: England 1500–1700.* 2 vols. Cambridge University Press, 1984.

Coldewey, John C. "Early Essex Drama: A History of its Rise and Fall, and a Theory Concerning the Digby Plays." Ph.D. dissertation, University of Colorado, 1972.
"That Enterprising Property Player: Semi-Professional Drama in Sixteenth-century England." *Theatre Notes*, 31 (1977): 5–12.
"The Last Rise and Final Demise of Essex Town Drama." *Modern Language Quarterly*, 36 (1975): 239–60.

Collins, Fletcher. *The Production of Medieval Church Music-Drama.* Charlottesville: University Press of Virginia, 1972.

Collinson, Patrick. *The Birthpangs of Protestantism.* London: Macmillan, 1988.
"A Comment: Concerning the Name Puritan." *Journal of Ecclesiastical History*, 31 (1980): 483–88.
The Elizabethan Puritan Movement. London, Cape, 1967.
From Iconoclasm to Iconophobia. University of Reading Press, 1986.
"John Field and Elizabethan Puritanism." *Elizabethan Government and Society.* London: Athlone, 1961: 127–62.
The Religion of Protestants. Oxford: Clarendon, 1982.

Cook, G. H. *The English Mediaeval Parish Church.* London: Phoenix House, 1954.

Craik, T. W. *The Tudor Interlude.* Leicester University Press, 1958.

Cranmer, Thomas. *Miscellaneous Writings and Letters of Thomas Cranmer.* Ed. John Edmund Cox. 2 vols. PS. Cambridge University Press, 1846.

Cremeans, C. D. *The Reception of Calvinistic Thought in England.* Urbana: University of Illinois Press, 1949.

Cressy, David. *Education in Tudor and Stuart England.* London: Edward Arnold, 1975.
Literacy and the Social Order: Reading and Writing in Tudor and Stuart England. Cambridge University Press, 1980.

Cross, Claire. *Church and People 1450–1660.* Atlantic Highlands, NJ: Humanities Press, 1976.

Crow, Brian. "The Development of the Representation of Human Actions in Medieval and Renaissance Drama." Ph.D. thesis, University of Bristol, 1980.

Davenport, W. A. *Fifteenth-century English Drama*. Cambridge: Brewer, 1982.

Davidson, Clifford, ed. *The Saint Play in Medieval Europe*. Kalamazoo, MI: Western Michigan University Press, 1986.

Davies, Catherine. "'Poor Persecuted Little Flock' or 'Commonwealth of Christians': Edwardian Protestant Concepts of the Church." In *Protestantism and the National Church in Sixteenth-Century England*. Eds. Peter Lake and Maria Dowling. London: Croom Helm, 1987.

Davies, C. S. L. *Peace, Print and Protestantism 1450–1558*. London: Hart-Davis MacGibbon, 1977.

Davis, Nicholas. "The Meaning of the Word 'Interlude': A Discussion," *Medieval English Theatre*, 6.1 (July 1984): 5–15.

Dessen, Alan. *Elizabethan Drama and the Viewer's Eye*. Chapel Hill: University of North Carolina Press, 1977.

　Shakespeare and the Late Moral Plays. Lincoln: University of Nebraska Press, 1986.

Dickens, A. G. *The English Reformation*. 1964; reprinted London: Fontana, 1978.

　"Peter Moon: The Ipswich Gospeller and Poet." *Notes and Queries*, New Series, (1954): 513–14.

Dickinson, J. C. *Monastic Life in Medieval England*. New York: Barnes and Noble, 1962.

Dixon, R. W. *The History of the Church of England from the Abolition of the Roman Jurisdiction*. 6 vols. 3rd edn. London, 1895–1902.

Dollimore, Jonathon. *Radical Tragedy: Religion, Ideology and Power in the Drama of Shakespeare and His Contemporaries*. University of Chicago Press, 1984.

Dowling, Maria. "Anne Boleyn and Reform." *Journal of Ecclesiastical History*, 35 (1984): 30–46.

　"The Gospel and the Court: Reformation under Henry VIII." *Protestantism and the National Church in Sixteenth-century England*. Eds. Peter Lake and Maria Dowling. London: Croom Helm, 1987.

　Humanism in the Age of Henry VIII. London: Croom Helm, 1986.

Dubrow, Heather. "'The Sun in Water': Donne's Somerset Epithalamium and the Poetics of Patronage." In *The Historical Renaissance: Essays in Tudor and Stuart Literature and Culture*. Eds. Heather Dubrow and Richard Strier. University of Chicago Press, 1988: 114–15.

　and Richard Strier. "Introduction: The Historical Renaissance." In *The Historical Renaissance: Essays in Tudor and Stuart Literature and Culture*. Eds. Heather Dubrow and Richard Strier. University of Chicago Press, 1988: 1–12.

Duff, E. Gordon. *A Century of the English Book Trade*. London: Bibliographical Society, 1948.

　English Provincial Printers, Stationers and Bookbinders to 1557. Cambridge University Press, 1912.

Eccles, Mark. "Brief Lives: Tudor and Stuart Authors." *Studies in Philology*, 79 (1982): 1–134.

"William Wager and His Plays." *English Language Notes*, 18 (1981): 258–62.

Elton, G. R. *Policy and Police.* Cambridge University Press, 1972.

Reform & Reformation: England, 1509–1558. Cambridge, MA: Harvard University Press, 1977.

Fairfield, Leslie P. *John Bale: Mythmaker for the English Reformation.* West Lafayette, IN: Purdue University Press, 1976.

Farnham, Willard. *The Medieval Heritage of Elizabethan Tragedy.* Berkeley: University of California Press, 1936.

Feuillerat, Albert. "An Unknown Protestant Morality." *Modern Language Review*, 9 (1914): 94–96.

Foss, Michael. "Sir Thomas Gresham." *Tudor Portraits: Success and Failure of an Age.* London: Harrap, 1973: 90–109.

Galloway, David. "The 'Game Place' and 'House' at Great Yarmouth, 1493–1595." *Theatre Notes*, 31 (1977): 6–9.

Galpin, Francis W. *Old English Instruments of Music.* 4th edn. rev. Thurston Dart. New York: Barnes and Noble, 1965.

Gardiner, Harold C. *Mysteries' End: An Investigation of the Last Days of the Medieval Religious State.* New Haven: Yale University Press, 1946.

Gatch, Milton McC. "Mysticism and Satire in the Morality of *Wisdom.*" *Philological Quarterly*, 53 (1974): 342–62.

George, Charles and Katherine George. *The Protestant Mind of the English Reformation.* Princeton University Press, 1962.

Gildersleeve, V. C. *Government Regulation of the Elizabethan Drama.* New York, 1908; reprinted 1961.

Gillet, Joseph E. "The German Dramatist of the Sixteenth Century and His Bible." *Publications of the Modern Language Association*, 34 (1919): 465–93.

Gilman, Earnest B. *Iconoclasm and Poetry in the English Reformation.* University of Chicago Press, 1986.

Glass, D. V., and D. E. C. Eversley, eds. *Population in History: Essays in Historical Demography.* London: Edward Arnold, 1965.

Greaves, Richard L. *Society and Religion in Elizabethan England.* Minneapolis: University of Minnesota Press, 1981.

Greenblatt, Stephen. *The Power of Forms in the English Renaissance.* Norman, OK: University of Oklahoma Press, 1984.

Renaissance Self-Fashioning. University of Chicago Press, 1980.

Greg, W. W. *London Publishing between 1550 and 1650.* Oxford University Press, 1956.

Gurr, Andrew. *Playgoing in Shakespeare's London.* Cambridge University Press, 1987.

Haigh, Christopher, ed. *The English Reformation Revised.* Cambridge University Press, 1987.

Hall, Basil. "Lutheranism in England." In *Reform and Reformation: England and the Continent: c. 1500–c. 1750.* Ed. Derek Baker. Oxford: Blackwell, 1979.

Happé, Peter. "Properties and Costumes in the Plays of John Bale."
   Medieval English Theatre, 2.2 (1980): 55–65.
"The Protestant Adaptation of the Saint Play." *The Saint Play in Medieval
   Europe*. Ed. Clifford Davidson. Kalamazoo: Medieval Institute Publi-
   cations, 1986: 205–40.
Harbage, Alfred, ed., and Samuel Schoenbaum, rev. *Annals of English Drama
   975–1700*. Philadelphia: University of Pennsylvania Press, 1964.
Hardison, O. B., Jr. *Christian Rite and Christian Drama in the Middle Ages*.
   Baltimore: Johns Hopkins University Press, 1965.
Harris, Jesse W. *John Bale: A Study in the Minor Literature of the Reformation*.
   1940; Freeport, NY: Books for Libraries Press, 1970.
Harrison, William. *The Description of England*. Ed. Georges Edelen. Ithaca:
   Cornell University Press, 1968.
Hattaway, Michael. *Elizabethan Popular Theatre*. London: Routledge &
   Kegan Paul, 1982.
Heinemann, Margot. "Political Drama." In *The Cambridge Companion to
   English Renaissance Drama*. Eds. A. R. Braunmuller and Michael
   Hattaway. Cambridge University Press, 1990: 161–205.
*Puritanism and Theatre: Thomas Middleton and Opposition Drama under the
   Early Stuarts*. Cambridge University Press, 1980.
"Rebel Lords, Popular Playwrights, and Political Culture: Notes on
   Jacobean Patronage and the Earl of Southampton." *Yearbook of
   English Studies*, 21 (1991): 63–86.
Hoskins, W. G. *Devon*. Newton Abbot: David and Charles, 1972.
Old Devon. Newton Abbot: David and Charles, 1966.
Hoseley, Richard. "The Theatre and the Tradition of Playhouse Design."
   In *The First Public Playhouse: The Theatre in Shoreditch 1576–1598*. Ed.
   Herbert Berry. Montreal: McGill-Queen's University Press, 1979:
   47–80.
Hunter, G. K. "The Beginnings of Elizabethan Drama: Revolution and
   Continuity." *Renaissance Drama*, 17 (1986): 29–52.
Hunter, Robert G. *Shakespeare and the Mystery of God's Judgements*. Athens,
   GA: University of Georgia Press, 1976.
Jardine, M. D. "New Historicism for Old: New Conservatism for Old? The
   Politics of Patronage in the Renaissance." *Yearbook of English Studies*, 21
   (1991): 286–304.
Jones, Kenneth H. "St. Stephen's Church, Hackington, and its Possible
   Connection with Archbishop Baldwin." *Archaeologia Cantiana*, 44
   (1932): 253–68.
Jones, Robert C. "Dangerous Sport: The Audience's Engagement with
   Vice in the Moral Interludes." *Renaissance Drama*, 6 (1973): 45–64.
Jordan, W. K. *Edward VI and the Threshold of Power*. Cambridge, MA:
   Harvard University Press, 1970.
Edward VI: The Young King. Cambridge, MA: Harvard University Press,
   1968.
Kantrowitz, Joanne Spencer. *Dramatic Allegory: Lindsay's "Ane Satyre of the
   Thrie Estaitis."* Lincoln: University of Nebraska Press, 1975.

"Dramatic Allegory; or, Exploring the Moral Play." *Comparative Drama*, 7 (1973): 71–73.

Kelley, Michael R. *Flamboyant Drama: A Study of " The Castle of Perseverance," "Mankind," and "Wisdom."* Carbondale, IL: Southern Illinois University Press, 1979.

Kendall, R. T. *Calvin and English Calvinism*. Oxford University Press, 1979.

Kendall, Ritchie. *The Drama of Dissent: The Radical Poetics of Nonconformity 1380–1590*. Chapel Hill: University of North Carolina Press, 1986.

King, John N. *English Reformation Literature: The Tudor Origins of the Protestant Tradition*. Princeton University Press, 1982.

Kinney, Arthur F. *Markets of Bawdrie: The Dramatic Criticism of Stephen Gosson*. Salzburg Studies in English Literature. University of Salzburg Press, 1974.

Knowles, David. *Bare Ruined Choirs: The Dissolution of the English Monasteries*. Cambridge University Press, 1976.

The Religious Orders in England. Cambridge University Press, 1959.

Lake, Peter. *Moderate Puritans and the Elizabethan Church*. Cambridge University Press, 1982.

Lancashire, Anne. "Players for the London Cutlers' Company," *REED Notes*, 1981.2: 10–11.

"Plays for the London Blacksmiths' Company," *REED Notes*, 1981.1: 12–14.

Lancashire, Ian. "The Auspices of *The World and the Child*." *Renaissance and Reformation*, 12 (1976): 96–105.

Dramatic Texts and Records of Britain: A Chronological Topography to 1558. University of Toronto Press, 1984.

"Introduction." *Two Tudor Interludes: Youth and Hickscorner*. Manchester University Press, 1980.

Leacroft, Richard. *The Development of the English Playhouse*. Ithaca: Cornell University Press, 1973.

Le Huray, Peter. *Music and Reformation in England 1549–1660*. 1967; reprinted Cambridge University Press, 1978.

Lewalski, Barbara. *Protestant Poetics and the Seventeenth-century Religious Lyric*. Princeton University Press, 1979.

Limon, Jerzy. *Dangerous Matter: English Drama and Politics in 1623/24*. Cambridge University Press, 1986.

Little, Bryan. *Abbeys and Priories in England and Wales*. New York: Holmes and Meier, 1979.

Loach, Jennifer, and Robert Tittler. *Mid-Tudor Polity, c. 1540–1560*. London: Macmillan, 1980.

MacCaffrey, Wallace T. *Exeter, 1540–1640*. Cambridge, MA: Harvard University Press, 1958.

MacCulloch, Diarmaid. *Suffolk and the Tudors: Politics and Religion in an English County 1500–1600*. Oxford University Press, 1986.

Maclean, Sally-Beth. "Players on Tour: New Evidence From Records of Early English Drama." *Elizabethan Theatre X*. Ed. C. E. McGee. Port Credit, Ontario: Meany, 1988.

MacQueen, John. "Ane Satyre of the Thrie Estaitis." *Studies in Scottish Literature*, 3 (1966): 139–43.

Manning, R. B. *Religion and Society in Elizabethan Sussex*. Leicester University Press, 1969.

McConica, J. K. *English Humanists and Reformation Politics under Henry VIII and Edward VI*. Oxford: Clarendon, 1968.

McCusker, Honor C. *John Bale: Dramatist and Antiquary*. 1942; reprinted Freeport, NY: Books for Libraries, 1971.

McLuskie, Kathleen E. "The Poets' Royal Exchange: Patronage and Commerce in Early Modern Drama." *Yearbook of English Studies*, 21 (1991): 53–62.

McPherson, David. "The Attack on the Stage in Shakespeare's Time: An International Affair." *Comparative Literature Studies*, 20.2 (Summer 1983): 168–82.

Mepham, W. A. "Medieval Plays in the 16th Century at Heybridge and Braintree." *Essex Review*, 55 (1946): 8–18.

"Municipal Drama at Maldon in the Sixteenth Century." *Essex Review*, 55 (1946): 169–75.

Miller, E. S. "The Antiphons in Bale's Cycle of Christ." *Studies in Philology*, 48 (1951): 629–38.

"The Roman Rite in Bale's *King Johan*." *Publications of the Modern Language Association*, 64 (1949): 802–22.

Miller, Helen. *Henry VIII and the English Nobility*. Oxford: Basil Blackwell, 1986.

Moon, A. R. "Nicholas Udall's Lost Tragedy 'Ezechias.'" *Times Literary Supplement*, 19 (April 1928): 289.

Morgan, Edmund S. *The Puritan Family*. Boston, MA: Trustees of the Public Library, 1944.

"Puritan Hostility to the Theatre." *Proceedings of the American Philosophical Society*, 110 (1966): 340–47.

Morgan, Paul. *English Provincial Printing*. Birmingham: College of Commerce, 1959.

Motter, T. H. Vail. *The School Drama in England*. 1929; reprinted Port Washington, NY: Kennikat Press, 1968.

Mullaney, Steven. *The Place of the Stage*. University of Chicago Press, 1988.

Murray, J. T. *The English Dramatic Companies 1558–1642*. 2 vols. 1910; reprinted New York: Russell, 1963.

Nelson, Alan H. *The Medieval English Stage*. University of Chicago Press, 1974.

The Plays of Henry Medwell. Cambridge: Brewer, 1980.

North, Thomas. *A Chronicle of the Church of St. Martin in Leicester During the Reigns of Henry VIII, Edward VI, Mary, and Elizabeth*. London: Bell and Daldy, 1866.

O'Connell, Michael. "The Idolatrous Eye: Iconoclasm, Anti-Theatricalism and the Image of the Elizabethan Theatre." *English Literary History*, 52 (1985): 279–310.

O'Day. Rosemary. *The Debate of the English Reformation*. London: Methuen, 1986.

"The Law of Patronage in Early Modern England." *Journal of Ecclesiastical History*, 26 (1975): 247–60.

Oliver, L. M. "John Foxe and the Drama *New Custom*." *Huntington Library Quarterly*, 10 (1947): 407–10.

Orgel, Stephen. *The Illusion of Power*. Berkeley: University of California Press, 1975.

Owen, H. Gareth. "The London Parish Clergy in the Reign of Elizabeth I." Ph.D. thesis, London University, 1957.

Oxley, J. E. *The Reformation in Essex*. Manchester University Press, 1965.

Palliser, D. M. *The Age of Elizabeth: England under the Later Tudors 1547–1603*. London: Longman, 1983.

Pasachoff, N. S. *Playwrights, Preachers and Politicians: A Study of Four Tudor Old Testament Dramas*. Salzburg Studies in English Literature. University of Salzburg Press, 1975.

Peele, Albert, ed. *The Seconde Parte of a Register*. 2 vols. Cambridge University Press, 1915.

Pegden, N. A. *Leicester Guildhall: A Short History and Guide*. Leicester: De Vayle Litho, 1981.

Pevsner, Nikolaus. *South Devon*. Harmondsworth, England: Penguin, 1952.

Phelps, Wayne H. "The Date of Lewis Wager's Death." *Notes and Queries*, 223 (1978): 420–21.

Phillips, John. *The Reformation of Images: Destruction of Art in England, 1535–1660*. Berkeley: University of California Press, 1973.

Plant, Marjorie. *The English Book Trade*. 1939; reprinted London: George Allen, 1974.

Porter, H. C. *Reformation and Reaction in Tudor Cambridge*. Cambridge University Press, 1957.

Powicke, Maurice. *The Reformation in England*. Oxford University Press, 1941.

Prouty, Charles T. "An Early Elizabethan Playhouse." *Shakespeare Survey*, 6 (1953): 64–74.

Read, Evelyn. *Catherine, Duchess of Suffolk: A Portrait*. London: Cape, 1962.

Reade, Conyers. "William Cecil and Elizabethan Public Relations." *Elizabethan Government and Society*. London: Athlone, 1961: 21–55.

Redgrave, G. R., ed. *The Short Title Catalogue of Books Printed in England, Scotland, and Ireland, and of English Books Printed Abroad 1475–1640*. London: Bibliographical Society, 1926.

The Revels History of Drama in English (1500–1576): Volume II. Eds. Norman Sanders, Richard Southern, T. W. Craik and Lois Potter. New York: Methuen, 1980.

The Revels History of Drama in English (1576–1613): Volume III. Eds. J. Leeds Barroll, III, Richard Hoseley, Alvin Kernan, and Alexander Leggat. London: Methuen, 1975.

Ribner, Irving. "Ulpian Fulwell and his Family." *Notes and Queries*, 195 (1950): 444–48.

"Ulpian Fulwell and the Court of High Commission." *Notes and Queries*, 196 (1951): 268–70.

Richards, Douglas W. "Preachers and Players: The Contest Between Agents of Sermon and Game in the Moral Drama from *Mankind* to *Like Will to Like*." Ph.D. dissertation, University of Rochester, 1986.

Rimbault, Edward F. *The History of the Organ*. London: Robert Cocks, 1877.

Ringler, William. *Stephen Gosson: A Biographical and Critical Study*. Princeton University Press, 1942.

Robinson, Madeleine. "Dramaturgy of the Anti-Catholic Morality in the Tudor Hall with Special Attention to the Screen." Ph.D. dissertation, University of Rhode Island, 1980.

Rose, Elliot. *Cases of Conscience*. Cambridge University Press, 1975.

Rosenberg, Eleanor. *Leicester: Patron of Letters*. New York: Columbia, 1955.

Roston, Murray. *Biblical Drama in England*. London: Faber and Faber, 1968.

Rozett, Martha Tuck. *The Doctrine of Election and the Emergence of Elizabethan Tragedy*. Princeton: Princeton University Press, 1984.

Scarisbrick, J. J. *The Reformation and the English People*. Oxford: Basil Blackwell, 1984.

Schalk, Carl, ed. *Key Words in Church Music*. St. Louis: Concordia, 1978.

Scheurweghs, G. "The Date of 'The History of Jacob and Esau.'" *English Studies*, 15 (1933), 218–19.

Seaver, Paul S. *The Puritan Lectureships: The Politics of Religious Dissent 1560–1662*. Stanford University Press, 1970.

Sellers, M. "The City of York in the Sixteenth Century." *English Historical Review*, 9 (1894): 299.

Shapiro, Michael. *Children of the Revels: The Boy Companies of Shakespeare's Time*. New York: Columbia, 1974.

Siemon, James R. *Shakespearean Iconoclasm*. Berkeley: University of California Press, 1985.

Simon, Joan. *Education and Society in Tudor England*. Cambridge University Press, 1967.

Sinfield, Alan. *Literature in Protestant England 1560–1660*. New York: Barnes and Noble, 1983.

Smith, H. Maynard. *Henry VIII and the Reformation*. 1948; reprinted London: Macmillan, 1962.

Somerset, J. A. B., "'Fair is Foul and Foul is Fair': Vice-Comedy's Development and Theatrical Effects." *Elizabethan Theatre V*. Ed. G. R. Hibbard. Hamden, CT: Archon, 1973: 54–73.

ed. "Introduction." *Four Tudor Interludes*. London: Athlone, 1974.

"Local Drama and Playing Places at Shrewsbury: New Findings from the Borough Records." *Medieval and Renaissance Drama in England Volume II*. Ed. J. Leeds Barroll. New York, AMS: 1985: 1–31.

"The Lords President, Their Activities and Companies: Evidence from Shropshire." *Elizabethan Theatre X*. Port Credit, Ontario: Meany, 1988: 93–111.

Southern, Richard. *The Staging of Plays before Shakespeare.* New York: Theatre Arts Books, 1973.

Spivack, Bernard. *Shakespeare and the Allegory of Evil.* New York: Columbia University Press, 1958.

Stevens, John. *Music and Poetry in the Early Tudor Court.* London: Methuen, 1961.

Stopes, C. C. *William Hunnis and the Revels of the Chapel Royal.* Louvain: A. Uystpruyst, 1910.

Streitberger, W. R. "Financing Court Entertainments, 1509–1558." *Research Opportunities in Renaissance Drama,* 27 (1984): 21–45.

"The Revels at Court from 1541 to 1559." *Research Opportunities in Renaissance Drama,* 29 (1986–87): 25–45

Strype, John. *Ecclesiastical Memorials.* 3 vols. Oxford University Press, 1721.

The Life and Acts of Matthew Parker. 2 vols. Oxford University Press, 1821.

Memorials of Thomas Cranmer. 2 vols. Oxford University Press, 1840.

Tannenbaum, Samuel. "A Note on *Misogonus.*" *Modern Language Notes,* 45 (1930): 308–10.

Tennenhouse, Leonard, ed. "Introduction." *The Tudor Interludes Nice Wanton and Impatient Poverty.* The Renaissance Imagination. New York: Garland, 1984.

Thomas, Helen S. "Jacob and Esau – 'rigidly Calvinistic'?" *Studies in English Literature,* 9 (1969): 199–213.

ed., "Introduction." R. Wever. *An Enterlude Called Lusty Iuuentus.* The Renaissance Imagination. New York: Garland, 1982.

Thomas, Keith. *Religion and the Decline of Magic.* New York: Scribners, 1971.

Thompson, Craig R. *Schools in Tudor England.* Ithaca: Cornell University Press, 1958.

Tydeman, William. *English Medieval Theatre 1400–1500.* London: Routledge & Kegan Paul, 1986.

The Theatre in the Middle Ages. Cambridge University Press, 1978.

Van Dorsten, Jan. "Literary Patronage in Elizabethan England: The Early Phase." *Patronage in the Renaissance.* Eds. Guy Fitch Lytle and Stephen Orgel. Princeton University Press, 1981: 191–206

Wallace, Dewey E. *Puritanism and Predestination.* Chapel Hill: University of North Carolina Press, 1982.

Wallace, Ronald S. *Calvin's Doctrine of the Word and Sacrament.* London: Oliver and Boyd, 1953.

Wasson, John. "Professional Actors in the Middle Ages and Early Renaissance." *Medieval and Renaissance Drama in England: Volume I.* Ed. J. Leeds Barroll, III. New York, AMS, 1984: 1–11.

Weimann, Robert. *Shakespeare and the Popular Tradition in the Theatre.* Baltimore: Johns Hopkins University Press, 1978.

Wendel, Francois. *Calvin: The Origins and Development of His Religious Thought.* Trans. Philip Mairet. Glasgow: Collins, 1965.

Westfall, Suzanne R. "The Chapel: Theatrical Performance in Early Tudor Great Households." *English Literary Renaissance,* 19 (1989): 171–93.

Patrons and Performance: *Early Tudor Household Revels*. Oxford: Clarendon, 1990.

White, Paul Whitfield. "Calvinist and Puritan Attitudes Towards the Renaissance Stage: A History of Conflict and Controversy." *Explorations in Renaissance Culture*, 14 (1988): 41–56.

"Lewis Wager's *The Life and Repentaunce of Mary Magdalane* and John Calvin." *Notes and Queries*, 226 (1981): 508–12.

Wickham, Glynne. *Early English Stages*. 3 vols. London: Routledge & Kegan Paul, 1959–80.

"The Staging of Saint Plays in England." *The Medieval Drama*. Ed. Sandro Sticca. Albany: State University of New York Press, 1972: 99–120.

ed., "Introduction." *English Moral Interludes*. London: Dent, 1976.

Williams, Franklin B. *Index of Dedications and Commendatory Verses in English Books before 1641*. London: Bibliographical Society, 1962.

Willis, R., and J. W. Clark. *Architectural History of the University of Cambridge*. 4 vols. Cambridge University Press, 1886.

Wilson, Derek. *Sweet Robin: A Biography of Robert Dudley, Earl of Leicester 1533–1588*. London: Hamilton, 1981.

Wilson, F. P. *The English Drama 1485–1585*. 2nd edn. rev. G. K. Hunter. Oxford University Press, 1969.

Wilson, Jean. *Entertainments for Elizabeth I*. Cambridge: Brewer, 1980.

Wood, Norman. *The Reformation and English Education*. London: Routledge & Kegan Paul, 1931.

Woolf, Rosemary. *The English Mystery Plays*. Berkeley: University of California Press, 1972.

Worth, Richard Nichols. *History of Plymouth from the Earliest Period to the Present Time*. Plymouth: Brendlen, 1871.

Wrigley, E. A. and R. S. Schofield. *The Population History of England 1541–1871*. Cambridge, MA: Harvard University Press, 1981.

Young, Karl. *The Drama of the Medieval Church*. 2 vols. Oxford: Clarendon, 1933.

Index

Southern, Richard, 5, 8, 61, 77, 130, 133, 147, 221n. 68, 229n. 82
Southey, Thomas, player, 46
Southwark, 19, 133
"special grace," 116–17
spectacles, anti-papal, 14, 58, 107, 194n. 10
Spencer, Richard, priest, player, 20, 71
Spenser, Edmund, 202n. 25
Spivack, Bernard, 5, 85, 191n. 16, 209n. 28
staging: with animals, 120, 221n. 67; on booth stage, 130, 224n. 2; with chair, 77, 210n. 34; with choirs, 149, 156, 228n. 60; in the church, 142–62; in the hall, 130, 142, 148; with "houses," 120, 124, 221n. 68, 222n. 77; in King's College Chapel, 143–46; lighting, 107, 143, 148; with mechanical dove, 160, 230n. 105; open-air, 131, 149, 151, 224n. 8; *platea*, 147, 150, 156; on raised stage, 146; with rood loft, 146–47, 227n. 51; in St. Stephen's Church, 149–62; on scaffold stage, 146; with tents, 120, 221n. 68; with traverses, 120, 148–49, 221n. 68
Stamford, Linc., 27
Stanley, Henry, Lord Strange, 54
Staple Inn (Calais), 45–46
Star Chamber, the, 204n. 59
Stationers' Company, the, 73, 118, 207n. 3, 213n. 63
Statute of Articifers (1563), the, 95
Stockwood, John, schoolmaster, preacher, 165, 232n. 12
Stokesley, John, Bishop of London, 15
Stokys, Matthew, Cambridge University registrar, 143
Stopes, C. C., 220n. 63
Stot, John, Scottish preacher, 222n. 76
Stow, John, chronicler, 96
Strange, Lord, *see* Stanley, Henry
Strasbourg, 57, 65, 88, 101
Streitberger, W. R., 54
Strype, John, 235n. 6
Stubbes, Philip, 166, 173; *Anatomie of Abuses*, 166, 219n. 52
Sturm, John, Strasbourg educator, 101
Submission of the Clergy (1532), the, 195n. 19
Suffolk (county), 69, 139, 215n. 10
Suffolk, Duchess of, *see* Catherine Willoughby
Suffolk, Duke of, *see* Charles Brandon
Suffolk's Men, Duchess of, 63, 206n. 77; Duke of, 21, 53
Sunday playing, 148, 172
Supposes, The (G. Gascoigne), 107

Sussex, Earl of, *see* Radcliffe, Thomas
Sweden, 216n. 25
Switzerland, 4
Swaffham, Cambs., 225n. 19
Syston, Leics., 137

Tadlowe, George, London citizen, 206n. 72
Talbot, Francis, Earl of Shrewsbury, President of the North, 63
Talomo, 207n. 81
Taunton, Somerset (parish church of), 82
Taylor, John, choirmaster, 111
Taylor, Rowland, rector, 139, 235n. 6
Temptation of Our Lord, The (J. Bale), 28, 34, 34, 215n. 10; casting of, 20; date, 158; "gresynges" in, 161; performance conditions at St. Stephen's, 160–62
Tennenhouse, Leonard, 6
Terence, 105
Textor, Ravisius, Humanist educator, 215n. 13
Thame, Oxfordshire, churchwardens of, 152
Theatre playhouse, the, 164, 171, 172, 174
Thersites, 113
Thetford Priory, 19, 20, 22, 23, 25, 26
Thomas, Helen, 122, 187, 235n. 3
Thomas, Keith, 30
Thorndon, Suffolk, 15–16, 158
Three Laws (J. Bale), Bale's acting in, 2, 21; casting of, 20–21; on Catholic clergy (corruption of), 27, 34, 35; on Catholic images, 1–2, 40, 56, 83, 135; on the "church universal," 135; costumes, 23, 56, 154–55; dramaturgy, 30–32, 35, 83; rehearsal at Bishopstoke, 29–30; transvestism in, 171
Three Ladies of London, The (R. Wilson), 64
Tide Tarrieth No Man, The (G. Wapull), audience, 205n. 71; and Elizabethan puritans, 60, 93–94; on ecclesiastical reform, 89, 93–94, 165; on economic reform, 76, 94–98
Titus et Gesippus (J. Foxe), 70
Totehill, Henry, shipman, 29
Tower of Babylon, The, 54, 203n. 40
Tracie, William, martyr, 82
transubstantiation, *see* Catholic
transvestism: and anti-theatricalism, 170–71; in *The Life and Repentaunce of Mary Magdalene*, 85; in *Three Laws*, 171
Trial of Treasure, The (W. Wager), 73, 78, 95–97
Trinity Chapel, St. Botolph's without Aldersgate, 136–37, *138*, 147